# ANGLER

# ANGLER

## THE
## LUCKIEST
## FISHERMAN
## IN THE UNIVERSE

KEITH KIRTS

FLOCK OF
GREEN
PARROTS

FLOCK OF GREEN PARROTS
Imnaha, OR, 97842
(310) 829-2752 / (541) 577-3203

Copyright ©1985, 2017 by Keith Kirts
All rights reserved.

Cover Art:
James Mathers
(see list of Mathers' books at end)

Book Design:
Pablo Capra

ISBN: 978-1-882639-29-8

# CONTENTS

# DEDICATION

This book is for my grandfather, Ed Snyder, who taught me how to fish for crappies with live minnows on a cane pole at Indian Lake, Ohio.

And for my grandmother, Lucy Mae Snyder, who fried those fish. Finger licking good, but watch out for the bones.

And for my fishing club, The South Bay Fly Fishers, in Los Angeles. Thanks for all the good times in the Eastern Sierras.

# CHAPTER ONE

## BEGINNER'S LUCK

The people, industries and military of Earth had polluted the land and oceans of that planet until very little grew, and nothing worth catching swam in the waters. Most of the people and all of the fishermen then migrated upwards.

Rita Bardona Resnick, Ph.D.
from *History of the Tournament*

"When we first came out here, winning wasn't everything, like it is now. We were all friends, weren't we? You were probably too young to remember, but that's how it was— friendly competition. It was fun to beat your dad and that blowhard, Carthy, into a pudding. Now, I don't know... it's becoming serious.

Ira Fairborne
quoted in *History of the Tournament*

A T twenty-three years old, Rich Rodney Tourbo was the eighty-fifth richest man in the galaxy. His mother was the fifth richest. When he someday inherited her vast real estate holdings, he would still only be the fifth richest person. Billions of Confederation dollars separated the Tourbos from Baron Farouk Bardona, the shipping magnate, who was currently the fourth richest. But no matter how rich he became, R.R. would still be a walking danger zone.

Rich Rodney Tourbo had just gotten his first passion other than sex. It was fishing. Last autumn, Rita Bardona, his ex-college room-mate, had invited him aboard her father's para-yacht, and had shown him how to hold a rod and reel. She wasn't his girlfriend *exactly*, but she *was* his best friend, and someday he intended to marry her. But fishing...! Glorious! He was good at it...! He was masterful. Skill oozed from of his fingertips as he held the rod, reeling up fish after fish. Big ones, too. One was over five pounds. Of course, he'd slipped once or twice on the wet deck, but he hadn't been badly injured. The scabs had healed nicely. Then there was that little accident when he was steering the boat. Embarrassing, but he had offered to pay for the damage. It didn't look very serious. The boat didn't sink, or anything.

Buying into the Galactic Star Fishing Tournament had been relatively easy, given his social position; but keeping it from his mother was a little dicey. A career as a fisherman wouldn't please her too much. Mom hated sports and sportsmen, unless the sport or sportsman was making a real estate deal with her. She didn't like non-sportsmen either. The only things she liked were possessions, gorgeous young women and Pomeranians, in that order. And she did not care for other people's yipping Pomeranians. Young women and possessions were always warmly regarded, no matter whose they were. Women and possessions could often be enticed into changing hands.

And she doted on Rich Rodney, since the day she had been unable to break her deceased husband's will, which left control of half the corporation to their only child in the event of Larue's death. That day, Mom Tourbo made up her mind to love the boy dearly. She suddenly regarded him as a precious possession.

Mom Tourbo did not believe strongly in education. She would have happily purchased a mail order doctorate for the boy at any university, but a stipulation in the will stated that he should earn a degree in Comparative Humanities from The University of Tesla, Reich and Hayden on Diston Prime before he inherited sixty-six million in Confederation dollars outright, and several dozen small planets. TR&H was a very tough school. After his mother endowed a new research library in memory of dear deceased Larue, Richie had done splendidly at college. In matters of scholarship, he credited himself with being quite gifted, whereas in point of fact, he was lucky. What Rich Rodney attributed to genius level intelligence inherited from his father was really the result of computer generated testing where yes and no answers, or even multiple choice questions, had supplanted written examinations at the undergraduate level. Rich Rodney was very skilled at guessing. His luck consistently gave him something like ninety-one percent correct answers, and sometimes higher. Had he gone on to post-graduate work, the shock of his ineptitude would have been brutal; but luckily, he hadn't.

At twenty-three years of age, Rich Rodney had completed his bachelor's degree, and now had the money and planets to start life with. He knew virtually nothing about Comparative Humanities, but was blithely unaware of it. He smiled a lot when he wasn't tripping over something.

His mother, who had always been the brains behind the real estate empire, suggested that his first act as a wealthy adult should be to fire his father's attorney, Clive McAndrews. Old McAndrews had somehow inserted that clause about earning a degree into the will, and had fought her through three courts, winning in each. She had behaved as if the will's corporation inheritance clause was incidental. Her well-mounted law suits were aimed at proving that her late husband was insane. Why would any sane man require a bewilderingly rich kid to *earn* a degree? After losing at the Inter-Confederation High Court of Appeals, she grudgingly paid the court cost and the tuition for Richard to study Comparative Humanities at TR&H, and bought a new champagne colored Pomeranian puppy for herself.

Mom Tourbo, as she was affectionately known, loathed every living thing about Clive McAndrews. She had intense daydreams of siccing a hunting pack of Pomeranians on the lawyer. While she ate peach ice cream, the tiny dogs would yip unceasingly and tear him to bits in a blood frenzy. She invited him frequently to her estate on Talmage Heights, but he was always regretfully too busy.

But R.R. had a mind of his own, and so still retained his father's swashbuckling friend. At Rich Rodney's insistence, McAndrews had used his considerable old boy influence to obtain young Tourbo a membership invitation to the Star Anglers Tournament on the QT. McAndrews found it amusing to think that simply by taking the kid fishing, he would probably ensure his job as watchman to the billions.

Accompanying young Tourbo to the G&G Boatworks, Clive made sure that he didn't get schtupped on his para-yacht. The good Baron was rumored to allow glitches to be built into an opponent's boat. After satisfying himself that the warranty clause was fully binding on Thaddeus Golan, the boatwright, he and the boy adjourned to a nearby bistro, where R.R. knocked over the champagne caddy, then a small vase of flowers on the table. Clive once again marveled at how little like his father young Tourbo was. Nor like his mother, for that matter. McAndrews was convinced that there'd been a mix-up in the maternity ward.

While the boat was being built, McAndrews advertised for a captain and crew. He organized several fishing trips for himself and the boy with the best guides that money could buy—virtually every famous fisherman except Pike Resnick, who had wanted to take the money, God knows, but was committed to a trade show circuit. "Next year...?" Pike offered, standing on his dock at Gallatin Bay. McAndrews had left that option open. He liked Resnick in spite of the fact that the poor jerk was about the worst money manager in the galaxy. And Richie turned out to be a pretty damn good fisherman, even without Resnick. At least, he always caught fish. Whether it was skill or not is every fisherman's secret. Clive McAndrews was content with that.

Rich Rodney had been sexually precocious since the age of three. His early nannies thought it was so cute when he made a fool of himself over pretty little girls in the park or at various other outings. But Richie knew even then that he also lusted after the little girls' exotic mothers, and after each one of the nannies in turn as they rotated through the seasons. Like a never sated bee buzzing around an eternal supply of flower blossoms, he was drawn to gawk in adoration at shop girls, Tri V actresses, dancers of any variety, art tutors, his mother's friends and clients—in short, any female with a pretty face. He couldn't help it. He loved alluring females. Long hair of any color, curling limply, gave him goose bumps. The strange, wonderful curve of a female flank tore his soul. And the bulge of a soft breast ripped his heart open. He adored pretty women and was simply powerless not to stare at them. Having no young males to compare himself to, R.R. thought that this rather normal behavior was aberrant and probably sinful.

Tragically, he was much too shy to follow through on his heart-felt staring. Occasionally one of his targets became self-conscious under his outrageous gaping. "Why are you staring at me like that, Rich Rodney," a young mother might snap with annoyance. This direct confrontation plunged Richie into paroxysms of embarrassment. Exposed...! His disgusting lust for women burning his face red, he would cast his eyes down and creep away. Blessedly, he was too short and nerdy to be noticed very often.

Short people are often very well coordinated. Richie remembered running and skipping happily through his nursery as a child, normal in every way. Then in a surprise back-stabbing surge, his feet began a period of rapid growth, while his body staunchly refused to follow suit. A decade of stumbling over throw rugs and other assorted carnival tricks followed. His astounding clumsiness made him the butt of innumerable jokes at prep school and through four years of college, and gained him the unwanted reputation of a clown. In point of fact, Richie was mortally chagrined at the antics of his big feet. To save his fragile ego, he had learned to put a fool's smiling face on his frequent episodes in free-fall. Before he began studying Ken Pao Ri, his self-image was a mass of scar tissue, an uneasy companion to his bloody knees and elbows.

But the clumsiness was yet another aspect of his astounding luck. Even discounting the vast luck of his birth into financial super-abundance as accidental, his day-to-day luck was astronomical. Never once, for instance, in any of his heart-chilling falls had he broken even one tiny bone, whereas a normal person would have been dead many times over from multiple neck fractures. Unaware of his good luck, Richie assumed that his battle-scarred shins were the laughing stock of the universe, and a terrible retribution for his sexual deviation.

And to make matters worse, Rich Rodney had fallen madly in love with Rita Bardona the first instant he had seen her in the dorm room at the U of TR&H. But, so far, nearly five years later, he hadn't found the courage to mention it to a living soul.

*

Rich Rodney Tourbo made his entrance to the Star Anglers Tournament at the Tidetable Chart House on Wexley Common on the foggy dawn of June 1ˢᵗ, and promptly fell down the three steps into the dark taproom. Tripping into a room was typical, so Richie was grateful that a bulky fisherman named Mordachi Skinner caught him by the new fishing vest collar before he made a total buffoon of himself.

The captain and crew that McAndrews had hired waited nervously aboard his boat, The Comparative Humanity. Captain James "Big Jim" Whalen was a skilled fisherman, who had previously captained four seasons with Jean Santos. He wanted his own boat in the worst way. When Clive McAndrews offered him double the salary and double the points in any prize purse, Whalen jumped for it.

McAndrews had also arranged for a local guide to be hired on every planet. And he had taken out a large insurance policy on Rich Rodney and all the members of his crew, listing himself as beneficiary.

*

By nightfall, Big Jim Whalen's head was spinning. He had been the captain of The Comparative Humanity for one day, and that was already one day too long. The Tourbo kid was the single clumsiest person he had ever witnessed. He wanted to have a drink and laugh it off, but he had a sinking feeling that he and his crew were in real danger. Naturally, a novice fisherman can be risky until he learns the ropes, but this kid, his boss, was amazing. On the virtually empty boat, he had sunk a treble hook into Brownie Samson, the deck hand. Just like a snake, the kid had whipped out a cast without looking behind, and had impaled Brownie's shoulder—it could easily have been an eye or an ear. Brownie had howled with pain.

Before Big Jim could get down from the bridge to help, stupid Tourbo had embedded another barb of the treble hook into his own thumb while trying to extract the one from Brownie. Big Jim had never seen anything like it. Both of them hopping around the deck stuck to each other, bleeding and yowling. Grabbing his diagonal cutters, Big Jim snipped the hook free of the boss and silently apologized to Brownie. After a stern lecture on safety, he had flown immediately back to the harbor. While both men were at the hospital for serum tetanus shots and hook removal, he had gone in search of a big supply of barbless hooks. Better to miss an occasional fish than to have a repeat of that madness. Without a barb, hook removal is rather simple.

On the other hand, Tourbo was lucky as sin. No doubt about it. He'd caught a keeper blue in the Marina. While Big Jim was explaining how to cast the star drag reel, the kid had snagged a nice little blue, fifty inches long, and horsed him up to the gaff. The Comparative Humanity was in the running before they'd even baited a hook—but at what cost, Big Jim wondered with an uncharacteristic shiver. An ugly premonition kept forcing itself into his mind, and he kept pushing it back.

Now on the fourth day, they were leading the Tournament with a three hundred and sixty-seven pound blue delilah, and Big Jim had a new deck hand. Brownie had recovered from the fish hook, but being tripped overboard by Tourbo's foot during the fight for the big delilah was too much for him. He climbed up an emergency ladder dripping wet and quit with no notice, vowing he'd rather be poor and alive than dead or maimed for life. Big Jim felt the same way, but he needed the prize money for his boat. He started hanging out on the flying bridge after that, simply shouting instructions down to Rich Rodney and the new deck hand.

The new guy, Silas Weathertal, was swarthy like a New Phoenician, where his sea papers said he hailed from, but Big Jim had a hunch that the guy was lying. Something about him didn't seem quite human. Well, he could dump Silas after Amora. But maybe he should keep him on. The guy really was an excellent deck hand. He was giving the boss all kinds of fishing tips, and he seemed able to stay out of harm's way. And Silas hadn't seen Wiggins, the local guide, take that crack on the jaw with the butt of Tourbo's rod. Wiggins couldn't tell him the tale now, because he couldn't talk. His jaw was wired shut and he was recovering on the beach—paid off to keep quiet. Sport fishing can be a hazardous business.

Well, three more days here. Then they could get on to safer waters. He chuckled to himself at the insanity of that statement. But at least, they might win this leg. That would be a plum. Winning any category provided a nice supplemental purse, like lap winners got in motor racing. Big Jim Whalen needed that plum.

*

Fishing was harder work than Rich Rodney had realized. Sun up to sundown they were out on the crystal water. So far he'd caught forty-two keeper blue delilahs, not to mention the small ones and the hundreds of other species that they weren't looking for. Truthfully, Richie had been a little dismayed when Captain Whalen kept ordering the fish released. Only the first one and the huge prize fish had been kept. Richie had wanted to show off those other fish in the Marina, too. It seemed a pity to toss them back so somebody else could catch them.

And by golly, he was leading the Tournament! That seemed like an incredible long shot with all the great fishermen here. But he felt like he really was getting the hang of fishing. There was nothing particularly difficult about it. So really, why shouldn't he be leading? Between Captain Whalen's skill and his own, they were a match for anyone.

That's why Richie had nixed the idea of staying in port, even if it was protocol to stay in when you had the biggest fish. Captain Whalen was just being considerate. He's always worried that I'm going to get hurt. Well, I guess it is his job to see that I'm safe. He seemed to understand when I told him that bruised ribs might keep a cry baby at home, but they certainly wouldn't stop me.

R.R. rocked gently in his fishing chair. Ouch...! The ribs definitely *were* tender. He still didn't quite see how the rod butt could have slipped out of the socket like that. And poor Wiggins was so brave. I knew right away that his jaw was broken from the way it cracked when the rod hit it. I know I shouldn't blame myself. Okay, so it wasn't my fault. Like Silas said, there's no way a rod can slip out of the cup. And Wiggins could have been any other place on the boat, instead of standing right there waiting to get smashed. It wasn't even a very big fish, nothing like my big blue beauty. Richie eased his ribs against the back of the padded fishing chair. Maybe I should ask Rita about the various fisherman protocols, he thought.

# STAR ANGLERS TOURNAMENT
## *PRIZE LIST*
### AND OTHER EXPENDITURES

FIRST PLACE                40% of purse
SECOND PLACE               20% of purse
THIRD PLACE                12% of purse
FOURTH PLACE               8% of purse
FIFTH PLACE                5% of purse

1st Place Moon Halibut             Entry fee returned
1st Place All Other Fish           $10,000
35 Judges' Wages (174 man weeks)   $174,000 Confederation
Burial Fund                        As needed
Contingency                        As needed
Interest on capital 10 weeks       to Johann Miller,
                                   Tournament Judge


**ENTRY FEE:**        $200,000 CD
                             x 25
                      $5,000,000
                      - 85% prizes
                        $750,000
                      - $200,000
                        $550,000
                       - $90,000
                        $460,000
                      - $174,000

                      **$286,000**

# ◆ RULES of the GALACTIC ANGLERS TOURNAMENT ◆

One keeper length fish must be caught in each
category in order to proceed to the next planet.

There is a maximum time span of one week in each category—Dawn of the first
day to Midnight of the last. But after having caught a species fish and properly
registering it with an official judge, the contestant fisherman is free to pursue
other events in his/her life; but may not land on the subsequent planets of the
Tournament for any reason without permission of the Tournament Head Judge.

Category fish must be taken in proper sequence—
during the 7 days assigned to that species.

All fish will be caught on hook and line, and will be played only by the
Tournament fisherman. Gaffing or netting may be accomplished by an assistant.

All local fish and game laws will be rigorously adhered to.

Points are awarded in each category:
5 points—1st Place; 4 points—2nd; 3 points—3rd;
2 points—4th and 1 point—5th Place.

Chicanery of any form will result in ejection from the current
Tournament and prizes—and probable elimination from
further Star Anglers Tournament competition.

## ◆◆ SCHEDULE OF FISHING ◆◆

| DATES | FISH SPECIES | PLANET |
|---|---|---|
| JUNE 1 - JUNE 7 | BLUE NOSED DELILAH | AMORA |
| JUNE 8 - JUNE 14 | HOWLER | BETA TORGA XII |
| JUNE 15 - JUNE 21 | TIGER MUSKY | ASHENDON A.R. |
| JUNE 22 - JUNE 28 | DEEP WATER SCUT | GIEDON |
| JUNE 28 - JULY 4 | PHANTOM TROUT | STREAMSIDE |
| JULY 5 - JULY 11 | LARCHMONT 'CUDA | NEW COLUMBUS |
| JULY 12 - JULY 18 | GLANS SALMON | DELTA 5 TANGO |
| JULY 19 - JULY 25 | RAZORFIN | BLIZWAK-HOJMER |
| JULY 26 - AUG 1 | SWAMPFISH | SEGUMI 6 |
| AUG 2 - AUG 8 | MOON HALIBUT | WATER MOON SOLERI |
| AUG 9 | TALLY DUE 0900 HRS | TIDETABLE - WEXLEY |

◆ ◆ ◆

# CHAPTER TWO

## RED SNAPPER

"Actually, among us boys, winning is pretty much the thing—
otherwise you'd just go fishing by yourself. I would."
Mordachi Skinner
quoted in *History of the Tournament*

THE hot, sunny afternoon found Pike Resnick in the marina boat-
yard, scraping barnacles underneath the hull of his boat, the Jumper, which was up on a dry dock cradle after a losing bout with a very
pissed-off blue-nosed delilah on the first morning of the Tournament.
Four days ago, to be specific. The huge fish had bitten off part of the
fantail, which included the ends of two pre-formed ribs.

This morning, he had caught a much smaller delilah in a rented
skiff and was qualified for this leg. If the Jumper got fixed in time to go
to Beta Torga XII for the howler fishing, everything would be normal.
The nagging premonition that all was not well could probably be attributed to heartburn.

Besides being hot, the day was very humid. Sweat dripped off him
as he worked, sticking his sodden blue work shirt to his back. Up above,
a crew of boat wrights swarmed over the boat, sawing and sanding the
hole in the stern into proper shape for a laminated patch. The repair job
would be as strong as new, Pike wasn't worried about that. He wasn't
worried about rewiring the grid either, it was just a question of paying
attention. What he *was* worried about was the little pink rubber dinghy
which had just tied up to the nearest dock. Seeing it made his pulse rate
climb steeply.

The dinghy belonged to Rita Bardona, and she didn't seem to be
wearing any clothes. Her long dark hair hung to her shoulders, and her

erogenous zones were spectacularly visible, even at fifty yards. What the heck was she up to? Pike had known Rita since she was a little girl. She clearly was not little anymore.

A pleasant surge of blood tingled through Pike's lower extremity at the sight of her. She really *was* naked. Far fucking out! Her father did not deserve a daughter like Rita, that much was clear. Pike speculated that perhaps the Baron was not Rita's real father, even though there was a strong family resemblance.

The peculiar fact that he and the Baron were business partners in the Resnick Thruster patent complicated his natural tendency to bed the girl, and had for several years. Pike had been naive enough to permit an option clause in the original development contract which allowed Bardona first refusal on all stock sales. To date, Bardona had only let one small block of shares get away from him, the ten percent that Pike had been forced to sell after the divorce. A bidding war between the Baron and Sid Ulmann, Pike's patent attorney, had gotten out of hand. Sid had paid about twice too much for the stock. Farouk had scoffed at the attorney's stubbornness as he failed to raise the winning bid.

But having years ago gained control of the patent, the Baron was able to force his point of view on the boat buying public. The asinine viewpoint was this: he wanted para-yacht ownership to remain an exclusive club, reserved for Tournament members. No fleets of commercial fishing boats. No fleets of fancy pleasure yachts. Just fishing boats for Tournament members. He only allowed two new para-yachts to be built in any year, unless a previous owner wanted a new model and agreed to convert the old one into a regular power launch upon delivery of the new one. This absolutely firm and fly-brained stance kept Pike in virtual penury unless he won some portion of the Tournament. Winning this year seemed like a thin reed on which to pin his hopes when he looked at the boat up in dry dock.

So Pike turned his attention to Rita instead. She was walking up the boat ramp, heading straight for him. The sawing stopped on her side of the boat. Pike heard several workers moan in anguish, not even able to summon a wolf whistle. He smiled, watching her hips swaying. Utterly enchanting. And what a bold move. Pike loved boldness in women. His heart—already very tilted toward Rita—tilted even farther.

"Hi, Pike," Rita called, waving from twenty feet out. She walked into the shade of the boat and stood a few feet away, doing nothing to protect her nakedness from his eyes. "I heard you stayed in today," she said, breathlessly. "So I thought you might want to go swimming. Sure is hot, isn't it…"

Pike wiped his forehead with the back of his hand and placed the barnacle scrapper carefully on a sawhorse. Strangely, his hands were steady; but he could see Rita's heart pounding inside her tanned rib cage. She had put herself way out on the limb for this superb little exhibition. And she *was* wearing a bathing suit, after all. A thoroughly transparent bikini made of some kind of soft, invisible plastic. What a fantastic invention! The suit hid absolutely nothing, and yet made him discontent that she was wearing so much. He felt compelled to find a way to get her alone so he could take the damned suit off. Then he would be able to see exactly what he could see now. He decided to buy a piece of stock in the plastic company with the next money he got. Fortunes would turn on this.

"Pretty revealing suit," he observed. "I didn't realize how well you had developed."

"I wanted to be sure I attracted your attention away from this interesting barnacle scraping," she purred, feeling her knees go limp as she watched him smile. He was so handsome. She wanted to crawl right inside his sweaty shirt and feel his slippery skin against hers.

Being so exposed was deliciously erotic, and made her feel unexpectedly shy—both feelings at the same time. Amazing sensations stretched her to the limit south and north, not a place she could live in very long. What had she been thinking to try this stunt? She had never put herself this far over the edge before. But since Pike didn't grab her immediately in a passionate embrace, the shyness won out.

"Do you have a shirt I can borrow?" she asked, looking at his work shirt. "I only did this for you, so you wouldn't feel so bad about your boat. I can't really be seen this way."

Pike grinned down at her. It had been obvious that eventually something like this was going to happen between them. Whenever they had met during the last few years, it was there—waiting to begin. A mutual attraction hanging in the air, waiting.

"So you took pity on me and decided this was the day to make my life worthwhile?" he asked, with a grin.

"I played you the best ace I have. Don't look for me to be so completely forward in the future. I don't know what came over me?"

"I accept," he said, simply.

"The shirt, please," she answered, holding out her hand. "And I want a tour of your boat. You've never managed to invite me aboard before."

"Haven't I...? Well, that part of my poor manners can be remedied." He took his shirt off, draped it over her shoulders and led her to the boat yard's step ladder, which was the only current way to climb aboard. "I only wish I had a transparent shirt to give you. But I don't." He held the ladder while she climbed up and hopped lightly over the rail. Well, there she was. Rita on the boat. Home at last. Life does begin at thirty-nine. He climbed up the ladder to join her.

Rita had been at the Tournament with her father every year since it began, so a fishing yacht was no big news to her. She wanted to satisfy her curiosity about how he lived. Was he a ship-shape sailor or messy—things like that.

"That's the bait well," he said, pointing out the first thing that came to view, the circulating tank on the fantail.

"Lovely," she said, smiling at him. "So round." She was ninety-seven percent certain that he liked her a lot, and today she intended to make sure of the other three percent. "I'm shy, and these nice carpenters are staring at me," she said, pulling the shirt closed.

"Think how uncomfortable you might be if Dec and Lester were here. I doubt if either of them would be tongue-tied." Dec Madrigul, a Segumi Indian, was First Mate and Lester Wunderman was the cook. The three men were very tolerant of each other after eleven seasons together—they had to be, The Jumper wasn't that roomy.

"I waited until they left," she assured him. "Isn't that why binoculars were invented. Hopefully, they'll be gone for a few hours."

"Hopefully," Pike agreed. "They went fishing."

"And this must be your lovely galley," Rita said, pulling him through an open doorway. Galley is a nautical term meaning general eating space, knock around room and kitchen. The Jumper's galley took up the whole deck level of the boat, except for the wide fishing deck encircling it. A hatch led down to the sleeping quarters, and stairs led up to the flying bridge. He watched her eyes taking in the bachelor galley. Amazing violet eyes flecked with green, wide-spaced in the tanned face, sparkling with secrets. Pike had a weakness for light colored eyes, and hers were the kind to get lost in. Until today, he had carefully avoided looking at Rita's eyes except in moving glimpses, feeling it was wrong somehow. Her eyelashes were long, the tips sun bleached. The eyebrows were dark and natural, or perhaps artfully crafted so as to appear unaltered. Her nose was long and straight, perfectly balanced with her face. And her lips were generous, with no hint of meanness. Luscious really. Yielding. Her chin was regular, square but soft. From long experience with her father, Pike knew that the square chin was capable of setting like a bulldog's and never giving up. Her long neck lead down to the superb depressions under her clavicles and the lovely shoulders, and beyond that....

"Nice galley," Rita chided. "Most people have curtains on windows."

"Most people who live here like to see out their windows," he said. He didn't want The Jumper feminized. "The guest room can have curtains, if you want."

A para-yacht is a beautiful thing. It is equally at home in the air or in the water, a condition that few other man-made machines can claim, except perhaps Timex watches. All classifications from the three-passenger fishing smack to the twelve berth pleasure craft are made to order for their original owners. Therefore, the sport fishing fleet fitted each member like a true mirror, reflecting whims and sensibilities, and the condition of the wallet. A fishing boat is by nature a working vessel, so it places a premium on stability in rough water, and must have enough open deck space to play and land a big fish. A Tournament fisherman must have a helmsman and one deck hand, at a minimum. Few fish over fifty pounds can be landed without help. And a guide in unknown waters is certainly useful. During the Tournament a judge is always on board, so most yachts sleep at least five. The crews become as addicted as the fishermen, in many cases staying on from year to year with whoever will hire them. Some even have partnership arrangements.

The problem of how to get a lumbering, deep-ballasted water craft airborne, so that the leap to hyper-space could be made, had plagued boat designers since the first hydrofoils were able to flit here and there through the galaxy. From their position above the water's surface, hydrofoils had been leaping into space for several generations, and in spite of their restricted payload, were the backbone of the intergalactic shipping industry for water mining. But hydrofoils were not really fully suitable for fishing.

Then one day sixteen years ago, a young marine biologist working on his dissertation, came across an odd property of water. It can become a solid launching platform for a split instant, if at that instant a magnetic mega-force is thrust downward. The force bonds the positive hydrogen molecules to form a grid for a nano-second. In that fraction of time, a boat (or any floating object) can squirt past the bonded surface like a cork held under water and be freed. As part of the reaction, a quantity of pure oxygen is released.

In the next instant, the hydrogen is rejoined with new oxygen molecules in that loose bond that is the magic of water—but during that grid locked micro-second, the young man reasoned, the leap to para-space and then hyper-space should be possible.

That biology student was Pike Resnick, of course. At one time, fourteen years ago, Pike owned four/fifths of the universal patent on the Resnick Thruster. One tenth of original stock was sold to his patent attorney, Sidney Ulmann, for services rendered. Another original tenth was sold to Farouk Bardona in exchange for a development deal for the Thruster. This was before Bardona had taken the honorific Baronet, which he felt was somewhat modest considering his holdings. He could have been King Bardona of the Starfleck System if he had chosen. A small but significant portion of the Baron's possessions now consisted of seven/tenths of the Thruster patent, which he sat on—not allowing the Thruster to be used, except in boats for the Star Anglers' Tournament. Sid Ulmann had bought an additional tenth at auction to make one/fifth currently in his portfolio. And Pike had managed to retain a tenth. Like many inventors and fishermen before him, Pike was not much of a businessman. Luckily, he had won prize money nine out of the thirteen years of the Tournament. He really was a heck of a fisherman. Most of his debts were paid off. He had no trouble sleeping, these days.

*

The Jumper was the first para-yacht ever made, and for that reason was full of unexpected idiosyncrasies. Pike had designed her stem to stern with the help of Thaddeus Golan, the master boat wright on Galatin Bay, and Aaron Galatin, a local kid who had become an aeronautics engineer. G&G Boatworks still made all the para-yachts—and still crafted them by hand for specific owners. Some days Pike was happy about that, and some days he gritted his teeth.

Being the prototype version, the Jumper was somewhat over-engineered. She was heavier than the current models and maybe not quite as spatially functional inside, and certainly not so luxurious as some of the fancier boats. She had miles of extra wiring circuits, and the power plant was more than twice what he had ever needed. But Pike was fond of the old tub. He treated her like an artist treats his early works, the ones that made him famous. She was casual and lived in, but he didn't allow kids and tourists to spill soda pop on her. Children and tourists rarely came aboard. After fourteen years, he could detect few signs of decay, and if the truth were known, he felt more secure on her than he did on her sleeker sisters. The extra weight was a positive factor as far as he was concerned. He had designed her to be able to ride out the worst storm. If he had wanted a cork, he would have built her that way.

*

"I don't want to live in your lovely guest room," Rita said, with an impatient shake of her head. "If I wanted a room of my own, I could just stay on the Lady Slipper, where I have scads more space." The Baron, who doted on Rita, had allowed her to name his traveling house yacht. She'd chosen Lady Slipper, being a romantic little girl at the time. Left to his own devices, the Baron would probably have chosen a name like The Ravaging Demon or some such; but the Lady Slipper it had always been. "And I could do my research from afar," she added.

"Research?"

"I'm thinking of getting my Ph.D."

"Staying at home would probably keep your folks a lot happier, if that's a concern."

"Would it keep you happier?" she asked, digging the question into his awareness. "Think carefully." She uncrossed her arms and shook her hair off of her shoulders. "Hot, isn't it?" she said.

"Well, I have a well-known weakness for transparent bathing suits hanging over my shower stall."

"Then I'm not staying in a guest room."

"Okay, but you'll find my room a little cozy. I didn't build a master suite. I didn't really count on you showing up when I designed her."

"No prize for short-sightedness." She poked his shoulder with a hard brown finger. "Aren't you a little eager to show me *our* bedroom?" she asked, with a mischievous grin.

"Down there." This was turning into a very fine afternoon in spite of everything. "After you," he said, gallantly.

She slid sailor-style down the hatch ladder to the sleeping quarters. It was much smaller than the Lady Slipper. Quaint. Nice. "I saw you looking at me every chance you got these last few years." She stepped away from the ladder.

"I tried not to stare," Pike said, sliding down to join her below deck.

*

When they finished making love, he was still able to smile. That was about all he could do—lay there and smile, and be utterly at peace. He had just experienced a titanic event. No other words seemed able to cover the experience. His heart was finally slowing down, bumping against his chest wall. Or maybe it was her heart. He couldn't tell. Had they really become one person?

"Is that your heart or mine?" he murmured in her ear. Rita's face was turned slightly away from him on the pillow.

"Yours," she said, speaking slowly from far away. "You were very excited. I was calm throughout, except when I made those strange yelping sounds. Maybe we'll become addicted."

"That's a thought," he agreed. The sound of the saw and laser generator came back to his ears. He remembered that his boat was injured. Strange how he'd forgotten that for over an hour.

"I'll need to take several sex breaks during my working day. Writing a doctoral thesis takes a lot of concentrated brain work, which is not necessarily healthy for people unless they exercise."

"Being a doctor is fine," he answered sleepily. "In case somebody gets hurt."

"Ha ha. In anthropology. I'm writing about the Tournament."

"Hmmm." Closing his eyes seemed like an exceptionally pleasant notion, so he did.

"Sweet dreams," she whispered, pulling the sheet up over them. A blanket was tacked up over two of the portholes. His shirt covered the third. She sighed and snuggled her flank against his. "Oh, by the way, do you know Richie Tourbo?"

"We've met a few times," he said, already heading toward unconsciousness.

"He's a friend of mine from college."

"You told me." Was this really the time to start talking about other guys, he wondered.

"I think he's going to be needing a new captain. Some sort of strange accident happened to the one he had."

"What's that got to do with me?"

"Well, nothing; but your boat is rather damaged, isn't it?"

"They're fixing it."

"That's not what I heard. Anyway, I'll introduce you to Richie. He's a nice guy. He'll make you a good deal."

"I don't want a good deal."

"He's in First Place."

"I know."

"I just want you to stay with the Tournament, now that we're finally together," she murmured, kissing his deltoid muscle.

"I will," he whispered. "If you insist on having curtains try to pick out simple ones, without flowers and lace." His eyes closed again.

Rita smiled to herself. "Even if you end up captaining Richie's boat, I promise I'll keep sleeping with you," she said.

Pike didn't answer, which Rita thought was a very curious response. Was he asleep already?

*

On Friday evening, Pike was sitting in the Amora House dining room waiting for Rita and the Tourbo kid. His heart skipped a couple of beats when he saw her come through the double doors on Rich

Rodney's arm. She looked ravishing with her dark hair framing the shoulders of a pale mint colored safari jacket. A thin scarf of dark green silk accentuated the long line of her neck. Her face was serene and her violet eyes were laughing. Pike hadn't seen her for two longish days. She had set this meeting up on the computer phone from her father's boat. The shock of seeing her now was intense. He took a sip of water and smiled at them.

"You know Rich Tourbo, don't you, Pike?" Rita asked, maneuvering Richie a step ahead of her so she could blow a kiss at Pike.

"Nice to see you again, Rich," Pike said, standing up. "Quite a thrill to be in 1st Place, isn't it?"

"It's a new experience for me," Richie said, shyly. "I think I could learn to like it." He grinned, boyishly.

"I've been throwing myself at this man since I was a little girl," Rita confided to Rich Rodney, before sliding into a chair. "But he's in business with Daddy, and until recently, he hasn't looked twice at me." She smiled sweetly. "This is so much fun having dinner with both of you. Doing this thesis is the smartest thing I ever did, isn't it, Richie..?"

"Sure seems like it," Richie agreed. His heartiness was a little strained. "Boy, I'm starved," he said, rubbing his hands together. "I can't tell you what an honor it is to have dinner with you, Captain Resnick. It's my treat. I insist."

"Oh, good," Rita bubbled. "Let's start with some caviar and champagne. And call him Pike." She signaled a waiter, and patted Rich Rodney's hand. "You certainly seem different, RR. I've never seen you with a sunburn, have I?"

"I don't think so," Richie said. He seemed quite distracted.

Where have you been for two days? Pike wanted to ask her, but he didn't. Are you with me or not? Instead he flagged the waiter.

Rita raised her water glass in a toast. "Here's to Champion fishermen. Daddy will have a kitten if you win someday, R.R."

Richie tilted his head to one side so he could briefly contemplate Rita, then he turned his attention fully on Pike.

"They say you're not going to be able to fix your boat in time to continue," he stammered.

Pike squeezed his lips together, but nodded for the kid to continue. The bad news had arrived earlier that afternoon. The fabricated ribs wouldn't anchor correctly and had to be re-done. Pike was fit to be tied, but what could he do about it? Nothing.

"I really feel strange about your boat. I wasn't even thinking about offering to hire you since you're so high above me, and you probably have things you want to do; but Rita insisted that you'd prefer to stay with the Tournament if possible, and it seems that I need a new captain.

Rita says she wants to go with us and write about you and the Tournament, so that gave me the nerve to ask, sort of. As far as financially, I can certainly make it worth your while if you'd consider bringing your crew and yourself to guide me through the Tournament." He stopped talking and waited nervously.

Pike added up the pluses and minuses. "I might be smart to take out a large insurance policy," he said with a grin.

There didn't seem to be room for Rich Rodney to stand on dignity, so he smiled back. "I know I'm somewhat accident prone; but if I had someone with your expertise to help, I could relax to some extent."

"You're accident prone to a monumental degree," Rita corrected, with a giggle. Richie blushed and cocked his head to one side.

"What happened to Big Jim?" Pike asked. "He got you off to a beautiful start."

Richie looked confused. He glanced at Rita. She nodded for him to tell it. "Well," he began. "Captain Whalen had to be taken to a back specialist on Alpha Alba. He said himself that he was thinking about wearing muckerball pads, and if he had, he probably would have just gotten a few bruises instead of a broken coccyx."

Pike momentarily lost his bearings in the green/violet irises of Rita's eyes. They seemed to change color minute by minute. Impossible to describe. How old was she now...twenty-one, twenty-two?

"R.R. wanted a lesson in how to gaff a fish, for some reason," Rita stated.

"So I would know how," Richie explained for the manyieth time. "That's no mystery. To be proficient, you need to know all about your craft."

"Captain Whalen was fishing so that Richie could learn to gaff," Rita said. "He caught a little fish and Richie gaffed it expertly, but instead of dumping it on the deck, he dumped it right on Captain Whalen, who staggered backwards and landed on the seat of his pants when he lost his footing after the gaff handle caught him in an unmentionable place. That about sums it up. He'll be in a float cast for a month or so, and after that he should be able to walk again."

"You weren't there," Richie sniveled.

"No, but that's the skinny, attributed to Big Jim himself after the morphine loosened his tongue."

"Well, yes," Rich said, miserably. "That's pretty much how it went; but the darned fish flapped just at the wrong time. And he was too heavy. We should have had two gaffs."

"Possibly true," Rita said, giving the kid very little mercy. "But you are amazingly accident prone. Remember that time with the vacuum cleaner?"

"Oh sure, bring up ancient history."

"You should hear about some of the manic things Richie used to do in school before you decide," Rita said, punching Richie on the arm.

Rich Rodney took the champagne bottle from the caddy and refilled their glasses. "Pike doesn't want to hear stuff like that," he said, loosening the collar of his shirt. "Tell us a little about glans salmon and phantom trout, sir. The guide books don't go into enough detail on the fresh water species."

Rita stared at Pike's jugular vein, pleased to note that it was pulsing rather rapidly. Other than that, his countenance was placid—Pike to the core. She winked at him, then took a sip of champagne and winked again.

"You should ask Rita's father about phantom trout," Pike said, pulling his eyes away from Rita toward Rich Rodney. "He's the expert on them."

"I doubt if the Baron would have too many helpful hints for me," R.R. said, uncomfortably.

Rita graced the younger man with a flashing smile. "I might help you," she teased. "Maybe we should shoot straight over to Streamside from here. Maybe Pike could go with us?"

"I can't," Rich Rodney replied, sourly. His mouth turned down for the first time all evening. "It's against the rules, and besides I have to encounter my mother sometime soon. She isn't quite sure when she'll have a spare few minutes to correct my frivolous direction."

"You poor thing," Rita said, with suppressed delight. "Let's order dinner. You need lots of good nutrients to withstand your dear mother."

Pike watched them share an unspoken joke at Rich Rodney's mother's expense. It was obvious that the two of them were close friends, just how close he couldn't tell. Hell of a mess coming up, he told himself again, if you continue to chase young women. Especially this one. What if she gets deep in your heart? She's practically there already.

"You may not believe this," Rita began in story mode, tripping on her suppressed laughter, "but one time R.R. was cleaning our dorm apartment and he got wrapped up in the vacuum cleaner cord, and it pitched him out through the open window." She started laughing for real.

"That wasn't my fault!" Richie interjected, firmly.

"I wish I could have seen the whole thing, but when I came home from class, there he was dangling out the third story window. About a hundred firemen were crawling all over the dorm. They had a net set up down below and ladders. But they couldn't pull him up because he had the cord wrapped around his neck!" Rita was laughing so hard that she could barely continue with the story. "Kids were leaning out the windows all around him, throwing ropes and yelling at the firemen to be careful! I couldn't even get upstairs because R.R. had somehow shorted out the electricity in the whole building!! The elevators didn't work!"

"You could have walked up," Rich Rodney commented, dryly. "Besides that, it was entirely the fault of that vacuum. If you had gotten the one without robot arms, none of it would have happened. That thing never liked me."

"Well, what about the time you got your foot caught in the mall escalator?" Her laugher cascaded over the table. "I suppose it didn't like you either?!"

Rich Rodney grinning, patiently. "I'm trying to be more careful, now," he said, knocking over the sugar bowl with the cuff of his sports jacket. That sent Rita into gales of laughter. Mercifully, dinner came. The waiter was funny, but not funny enough to laugh at.

"Do you use live bait for glans salmon?" R.R. asked, carefully cutting a bite of his calamari appetizer. "Or are artificials more effective?"

What Pike thought of glans salmon was better suited to a male smoker than to polite dinner conversation. He had never known why the fish was on the circuit, except that it had been the first year and had remained on, one of the Big Six. Disgusting, smelly fish, not even a true salmon, but a bastardized shad. "The only thing going for them," he said to Richie, "is they fight like devils. I don't like the smelly things, but they give you lots of action. The rules specify a fly rod and feather lure. I usually tie on a white streamer."

"Dick fish," Rita said, quite clearly. At that precise instant, the Amora House experienced one of those quiet moments that occur occasionally amid the clatter of a busy dining room. Several customers looked over at the pretty girl mouthing profanities. The Amora House was as polite as polite society got in Port Arthur. The upper crust, such as it was, didn't really care to hear about dick fish. The quiet spot intensified until one could hear the kitchen help clattering dishes.

"Whoops, a faux pas," Rita grinned impishly, unable to contain her high spirits and not even trying to. Being slightly offensive to Amora notables was not something that embarrassed her.

"Excuse me," she said audibly, to the large room. "I meant glans salmon." That sent her and Pike into quiet, but sustained laughter. Rich Rodney laughed as loudly as they did, but it was unclear if he was laughing at them or something else, since he probably hadn't gotten the joke.

"There's one other thing you should know, Richie," Rita continued, sweetly. "I'll be bunking in Pike's room while I'm doing my research." She let her statement fall with a thud, to see how it would be received. Rita hated chicanery. If honesty would get her what she wanted, she seldom resorted to sleight of hand.

"Uh," Richie answered, trying to place that fact into his internal revolving credit apparatus, but only managing to get it into a slot machine. It came up two cherries and a lemon. He pulled the handle again—two lemons and a gold bar. "Uh, you could have my room," he offered. "I usually sleep on shore."

"I know that, and thank you," she said, virginally—which she wasn't, as R.R. knew perfectly well. She'd had a good bit of experience in college and he'd been included in discussions about sexuality with their other dorm mates. "Pike and I talked it over," she said. "We may not have sex every night, of course; but if you were a woman trying to write the best paper she could on the Tournament, wouldn't you want to get as close as possible to the person who knows more about it than anyone else?"

It sounded reasonable to Pike, even though it was play acting for Tourbo's benefit. Or maybe it wasn't. Maybe her entire ploy with him, the transparent bathing suit and everything was aimed at getting her paper written. Catch the ring. Round and round we go. "Don't make the kid nervous," he growled. "He wants his mind clear to catch fish."

"He knows where I'm coming from," Rita said.

"Of course, I do," Richie replied, knowing he rarely knew much of anything about her motivations, but that didn't stop him from loving her. He fiddled with his fork. "I would always want you to stay on my boat for whatever reason. And feel free to use my room. Honest, I'm usually not in it, and I know you need your space sometimes."

"Thank you," she said, touched and happy. She had won with hardly a ruffle. "I will use your room, if I need to. I'm going to help Lester with the cooking and cleaning to earn my keep."

"Fine," Richie answered. He flicked his eyes to Pike for any coherent feedback that might be available.

"Worry about fishing," Pike advised. "The rest of it will work out. She'll probably be staying in your room most of the time."

Richie smiled, gratefully.

"I won't be," Rita said. "But it's nice to know it's available."

"Fine," Pike said, taking a sip of champagne.

*

When dinner was over, the threesome walked down to the wharf to look at Richie's boat. Pike had agreed to captain the Tourbo kid for enough money, win or lose, to fix The Jumper and pay the entry fee for next year. If Richie happened to do well, the rewards would increase.

On the down side, he wasn't his own man for the first time in ages.

Rita had suggested that having her waiting in bed in the larger Captain's quarters of Richie's boat would make up for any wounded pride; but he wasn't so sure. Being a hired hand was going to be a very different experience than he was used to.

"Hello, Captain Resnick," a mellow, disembodied voice said when he stepped onto the deck. "My name is George, the ship's computer. A pleasure to meet you."

"Hello," Pike answered. He looked over at Richie.

"Latest model," Richie said, proudly.

"I understand you are still fishing with the original computer model, Captain. Don't worry, I'm not much improved over the early ones. I just have a bit larger vocabulary."

"Sounds good," Pike said. He'd been meaning to upgrade, but hadn't gotten around to it. This would be a good test run.

*

Sunday at dusk, a half hour before they were going to shove off for the Beta Torgas, Rita came aboard with her overnight bag. She took it downstairs, stopped briefly to brush her hair, then came back on deck. Pike was still up on the bridge, so she climbed the outside ladder. Something was wrong. She was eager to see him, but he wasn't returning her eagerness.

Pike watched her climbing the ladder. He had been checking out the new fish finder and thinking of all the reasons not to get involved. One: Richie could easily turn into a jealous monster—or worse, *he* would be jealous if Rita flirted with Richie. Either situation would be very unpleasant. Two: Rita was too young—which was fine for now, but practically guaranteed heartbreak down the road. Three: Women were known to be bad luck on a boat. But Rita wasn't bad luck for him—she had already fixed him up with a ticket for next year. So figure that one out.

Rita smiled at him through the window. He smiled back. She was such a knockout! He must be totally insane to have second thoughts.

She slipped into his arms and raised her lips. They kissed hello. She had only been away on the Lady Slipper for an hour, but it was a family rupturing event for her to bring a suitcase to Pike's boat, even a small one. She wanted to be kissed like he loved her and understood her commitment.

"Not getting cold feet, are we?" she asked sweetly, studying his face.

"Of course not," he lied, clearing his throat. Rita was a mind-reader, evidently. That was kind of unnerving. "Is your stuff all moved in?"

"I brought some nylons to hang over the shower stall." She paused. "I know that you're nervous about lots of stuff, which is understandable. I also know that you *are* having second thoughts, *Captain* Resnick, but forget it." She smiled tightly at him. "It's perfectly true that if I kept living on Daddy's boat, it might be easier on everybody. I could even sleep over, and everybody could look the other way." Pike nodded. "That *would* make fewer waves, but I'm not going to," she stated with happy finality. "I already did the hard work for us. I threw myself at you, didn't I?"

"Somewhat," Pike agreed.

"You would never have found a way, so I was bold for both of us. Now it's your turn to make a gesture. I know we're a good match, and I know you want me more than you can almost conceive of. I can tell—but you're acting a bit clammed up. It's not life threatening, you know." She smiled. Pike smiled back. "We'll live together until it goes sour—if it ever does. It'll be fun, don't you think?" Pike nodded. "Lester and Richie don't seem blown out," she added.

"I know. They think we're a foursome."

She looked at him squarely. "I know I can't replace Dec, but it was his decision to leave, not mine."

"I know."

"I know you know. I'm going to write my thesis—you're going to fish with Richie. And we'll fool around whenever we need to get exhausted. Pretty simple, really."

"I guess you're right." He smiled. "We're meant for each other." Pike glanced over at The Jumper riding so calmly on the dry-dock cradle.

"Hey, Lester...!" she yelled down at the fantail. "The Captain's decided I'm okay!" The battered cook looked up at them, grinning.

\* \* \*

# CHAPTER THREE

## KID LUCKY

"Winning? Well, Rita, off the top of my head, I'd say that
winning is like a place to go to. A zone of contentment. All
the cogs slide into place magically, and suddenly everything
you do is smooth and successful. And your name is all over
the leader board."

Dresden Carthy
quoted in *History of the Tournament*

"I'm not sure my views will help you get a Ph.D.; but to me
winning is a sunrise on a world you've never been to. Straining your tits to land a big fish is the payment for the sights.
No strain, no gain. Something like that."

Ethyl Bierly
quoted in *History of the Tournament*

THE week of howler fishing was half over on Beta Torga XII. After
a First Place victory with Blue-nosed Delilah on Amora, incredibly,
Rich Rodney was leading on this leg, too. And Pike had to admit that
there was a very likable side to the kid—Rita had been right about
that. For one thing, Richie was generous to a fault. He took the crew to
dinner every night, instead of having Lester cook as he normally would
have. With Dec gone until the Tournament visited Segumi, most of the
fishing deck work fell to Lester. Richie would have been delighted to
carry Dec, of course, and there was plenty of room on The Comparative Humanity, but Dec insisted that this was a good opportunity to
spend a whole cycle of seasons with his tribe, and his wife and family.
He needed to make some decisions for the future. The inherited job of
head chief of the Piets would be offered to him soon. It was not going

to be an easy choice, whichever way he went. Once you've tasted the outside Universe, a swamp culture can seem pretty rustic, even if you're the king.

So Richie's new crew settled into the job of helping him catch fish. The kid hadn't committed to a favorite brand of rod or lures yet, so nearly every day, foam crates arrived on the high-liner from mail order outfitters and manufacturers—new stuff that Richie bought to test out. It was fun and there were always classy gifts for everybody, like realwool shirts that cost a fortune. A Newell micro reel for panfish and a split datura wood fly rod, hand made by Red Alcott on Sankor for Pike. A copper bottom sauce pan for Lester. Deck shoes and animal skin bikinis for Rita—which Pike thought was a bit too personal, although he didn't say so. The kid was so offhand about spending money that it was hard to turn him down. The only really irksome thing about old Rich Rodney, aside from his being a clumsy meathead, was his abnormal luck.

There weren't many howlers around this year. Friction storms during the last two breeding seasons had taken a toll. Storms on the Beta Torgas could be real doozies with waterspouts that suck up fish and even coral reefs. But R.R. was catching scads of fish. There were some damn good fishermen here, but Richie had already boated sixty-three fish, while the total howlers caught by the other twenty-three entrants was only sixty. Maybe it was just a lucky run. Probably was. But the kid had beginner's luck in spades. It was uncanny.

Howlers are an ugly, cabazon-type fish that lurk in the reefs and aren't particularly dangerous if you don't let them bite you. A poison sack inside their lower jaw holds exotic neo-curare poison that shoots up through two hollow hypodermic fangs, anesthetizing a victim fish in seconds and a man in minutes. Death comes from respiratory shutdown in about twelve minutes, unless anti-venom serum is administered. Not too many people go swimming on Beta Torga XII, although some suicidal natives do. They say a howler doesn't necessarily release the poison if he's just cruising by for a quick bite of thigh for lunch.

Pike thought Richie would be safe if he didn't get within five feet of a fish once it was boated. So that was the deal they made. Richie could catch them. Lester or Pike would unhook every single fish and show it to the judge. They shook hands on the deal. So far no one had been bitten.

Howlers don't grow very big, sixty pounds is a giant. There is no legal size restrictions at all and no bag limit, because the Beta Torga XII government would love to see them all caught. With their miles of white sand beaches, the tourist trade would thrive, except for the howlers. However, they're motherlessly hard to catch. They don't start biting until twilight and by the time the moon comes up, they're done feeding. Of course, the fishermen fish for them all day, and all night if they haven't caught one, but any time except twilight is a waste of energy.

Besides the poison, howlers have another eerie trait that no doubt keeps a few tourists away. In spite of being a true fish, they crawl out on the white sandy beaches at night to eat their catch and howl at the twin moons. One of these moons is always visible at feeding time, sometimes both of them. Their orbits are worked out perfectly for the howler.

It's not really howling, actually—they should really be called screechers—the sound they make is a little worse than fingernails on a chalk board. It sets most people's teeth right on edge and keeps them there all night. Daytime is for sleeping on Beta Torga XII. Ear plugs are routinely donned at dusk. Fishermen who can't change their sleeping schedule get a little weary by the end of the week, and they don't catch many fish either.

Another disgusting direct consequence of the nightly howler concert is the carcasses of dead, partially eaten fish and ducks filled with howler poison which litter the beaches every morning. Instead of being eaten by a well-organized fauna, most of this refuse lays there in the sun, rotting, because only two species of scavenger had developed a resistance to howler venom. One is a huge, evil smelling buzzard, which is capable of carrying a human baby away to feed the chicks. Every year several native babies go that route, so the buzzards are not loved by the population in spite of the fact that they clean up the beaches. The other scavenger is a hubcap-sized armored land crab, which is inedible because of the howler toxin they consume. Besides nipping unwary people, they have the annoying habit of tunneling under the foundations of beach houses in their spare time.

The government would be pleased to poison all the howlers, but no known poison will kill them without decimating everything else in the oceans. Consequently, the tourist trade on Beta Torga XII flourishes briefly once a year—when the Tournament fleet visits. Crazy space fishermen think that the harder a fish is to catch, the more prized it is. Normal tourists shy from the planet, which makes the fishermen happy. They love unspoiled worlds.

Oddly, Rich Rodney didn't seem to mind the nightly howler serenade. He claimed he thought the screeching was musically interesting. Maybe that accounted for why he was leading all comers with a thirty-two inch specimen, which weighed just over sixteen pounds. He'd caught it yesterday evening on a simple dropline baited with half of the hard-boiled egg he'd been eating. At the tavern last night, several of the veteran fishermen were suddenly eager for his viewpoint on bait fishing, and on any other topic. That's the way fishermen are. They think if a guy can catch fish, his views on brain surgery and interplanetary politics become relevant—or maybe they think his luck will rub off. Even Pike found himself more open-minded to Richie's odd ideas. After all, Rich Rodney had a degree in Comparative Humanities from U of TR&H, which was a very good school.

On the other hand, it was difficult to think of Rich Rodney in terms other than "the kid." He was so short, and besides he had that boyish face and the grin that never went away. His arms had muscled out a few pounds worth, Pike observed from the bridge, watching him fishing off the stern. And after the massive sunburn had peeled away, he was finally getting a tan. Yep, he was starting to look almost human. How strong was his desire is to be a Champion Fisherman? Maybe he'd be content to just tag along as one of the boys. It was too early to tell.

Pike noticed himself taking inventory of Rich Rodney, and decided that was perfectly normal given the circumstances. Next year the kid would join the ranks of his competition. Pike had the gnawing inkling that Rich Rodney might possibly give him, and everybody else, a real run for the money. Cost would be no object. He'd get the finest equipment without thinking about it. And the best guides, and he'd be nice to the guides and generous, and they'd work hard for him.

Damn, he's got another hook up! Pike watched the rod arc as Rich Rodney braced his feet on the deck. That damned luck is going to cause me a lot of trouble, Pike groused to himself. The kid was going to be a formidable opponent, and a likable one, which was even worse.

Rich Rodney took a step backwards. In doing so, he put his foot on a dead anchovy, which was lying on the deck. The anchovy was slippery. The foot skidded out from under him and he did the splits, smashing against the side of the live bait well. His reel screeched as line shot off. Dazed, he got to his feet and continued playing the fish.

Yep, I got a real first class competitor here, Pike laughed to himself, backing the engine to keep the slack out of Richie's line. He was getting used to The Comparative Humanity's skittish response. The blockier design of The Jumper gave her a better traction. Actually, losing The Jumper may have a silver lining. I'll be able to talk to Thaddeus Golen with authority. I knew these new boats were too sleek, but he kept insisting they were fine. Luckily nobody else knows how well The Jumper handles or they'd be up in arms.

"Nice acrobatics," Pike yelled down from the bridge. "Let's see you do that again. I'd like to learn that one."

Rich Rodney grinned and kept reeling.

Lester Wunderman limped cautiously around the live bait well holding the gaff hook, but staying well out of the kid's way. Richie may be a clown, Pike thought, but he's got a damned fish magnet, and that isn't for sale just anyplace.

*

Richie Tourbo woke up from a short nap in the Torga Excellency Hotel, which was a far cry from the luxury hotels he was used to. The bed was lumpy, but at least it was clean. Oh, well, fishermen have to take their comfort where they can. It was better than staying on the boat. For some reason, he didn't love sleeping aboard; but, of course, he didn't have to love it. That's what hotels were for.

Someday soon he was going to take a day off to visit his mother and try to explain where he'd been this last month—and also try to defend the spending of half a million Confederation dollars on a fishing boat and crew fees.

The money was his own, of course; but the checks cleared through the corporation bookkeepers, so his mother would hear about them. He'd never seen any reason to hide his transactions before, and didn't hide them now, actually; but she would demand to know why he ducked away from his bodyguards. He was going to tell her that he was grown up now and had his own pursuit of happiness to look after. Mom wasn't going to like that.

On the other hand, she never consulted him on what she did with her life—never asked his opinion on anything, for that matter. Maybe he had as much disdain for sharp real estate deals as she did for sports. He'd just had the very best two weeks of his whole existence, and he wasn't going to allow a flock of dull-brained bodyguards to clutter up his boat just to make her happy.

And why exactly was he programmed to always please his mother? Even if he won the Tournament someday, she was sure to sniff down her cosmetically enhanced nose at him. Wow…! That's an absolute first, Rich Rodney marveled. I actually considered *winning* the Tournament! That's the first time I ever, *ever*, felt like I could excel at anything athletic! But why couldn't I win it? I'm ahead right now. A plan started to formulate in the damp recesses of his brain, the same brain that had won high academic honors for him. The alarm clock on the night stand clattered.

Rich Rodney jumped off the bed and almost fell down as his legs tried to compensate for the rocking motion of the boat. There was no boat in his hotel room. That was a rather revolting aspect of ocean fishing. His body continued to roll for hours after he was ashore. There must be a way to allow the semi-circular canals to adjust more quickly, but he hadn't found it yet. No matter, he had to get ready. He was having dinner with Pike and Lester and Rita, and he still had about a million questions to ask so he'd be ready for the next fish category, Tiger Muskies on Ashendon A.R. He would be going to Ashendon immediately after seeing his mother.

Rita was going with him on the visit, in her brother's boat, actually. She was always doing unexpected things like that for him. Things that made his life a heck of a lot easier. In spite of his fondness for her, Rich Rodney had a sneaky feeling that she might have coerced him into asking Pike to captain the boat just so she could have a romance. It was quite evident that she was attracted to Pike.

Rich Rodney had to smile at that. He stepped into the shower and slipped on a bar of soap. He leaped up quickly with no broken bones and adjusted the shower jet. Yes, Rita was a sly one. So sly she was transparent. And Pike seemed fond of her, in a fatherly way. But everything was fine. So what if Rita slept in Pike's room—or even in his bed? That was a well-known way of doing in-depth research—especially for a woman. Research? Oh, sure! R.R. might be a nice guy, but he wasn't totally born yesterday. Fortunately, he wasn't the jealous type.

*

But there were a few little problems in the lovers' bedroom. A compromise had been made that was driving them both a little crazy. Against nature and any sensible way to proceed, they had agreed not to screw. The agreement had happened the first night on Beta Torga XII, when Rita decided it was time to teach Pike a lesson. He wasn't acting sufficiently grateful for her favors, in fact, he was acting confused. How dare he!

There's a limit to how much a girl will tolerate. Besides, Beta Torga's twin moons made her arousal feel different here than it had on Amora. Unfortunately, she didn't take note of that fact. One moon was almost full while the other had waned to a sliver. Very confusing emotionally, but very subtle. The moons, or something, made her feel like she needed to have the upper hand.

Pike and Rita were both a little tipsy after Monday night's dinner at Richie's hotel on Beta Torga XII. They returned alone to the boat, where they collapsed, fully clothed, on the bed, but his lips seemed to hold back when they kissed. So she decided to teach him the lesson— if he wanted to get screwed, he was supposed to act happy about it. "Don't get the wrong idea about this, Champ," she said. "I've been thinking that maybe we shouldn't make love again until we get to know each other much better. After the Tournament is over might be about the right time. We can be close friends, like we have been, until it seems like we should be lovers again. How does that sound?" She expected an argument—which she was willing to lose and blame on drunkenness. Passion, naturally, brooks no delay.

But much to Rita's surprise and irritation, Pike was relieved at the news. The pressure he'd been feeling evaporated and he smiled at her for the first time all day.

"Really?" he asked, relaxing luxuriantly. "That's great. You really are perceptive. That's exactly what I've been feeling, but I was afraid to mention it, in case you'd get angry." He kissed her eyelids, then kicked off his deck shoes. Cuddling her to him, he buried his face in her dark hair and fell asleep floating on the aroma of mild balsam.

Well, that served her right, she fumed. Trickery had never worked for her—why did she keep trying it? But it had been sweet of him to kiss her eyes. She lay beside him, feeling his strength. Sleep was nowhere in sight. She would have liked to get up and unpack her suitcase, but she didn't. This was certainly an unusual way to bind anyone to her. But Pike *was* an unusual man. A warrior, wasn't he? She knew from the hours spent in somewhat colorless sociology classes that warriors were supposed to hold their women in high regard.

Some sociologists believe that all people are divided into three classes: warriors, intellectuals and businessmen. But Pike is also an intellectual with his inventions. Intellectuals live in an ivory tower by themselves. But one thing she did know, Pike was no businessman. Businessmen thought of women as possessions to be bought and sold. Oh, hell, she didn't know what she knew. That was always the problem with Pike and his damned green eyes. But he smelled good. Kind of like sea wind. She had no idea in the world if this ploy would work out, but at least she was here now in his bed. That was something no other woman could say. She practiced a petulant frown, then changed her mind and practiced a smile. She had to pee, but Pike's arms still encircled her, so she kissed his chin and let herself drift.

* * *

# CHAPTER FOUR

## TIGER MUSKIES

"I try to win every single day of the Tournament. Each time
I make a cast, I'm ready to catch a record fish. But do I think
winning is important? What I really think sounds kind of
stuffy; but what's important is being a half-way decent person. If winning doesn't interfere with that, then winning is
fine."

Harry Dolan
quoted in *History of the Tournament*

ASHENDON A.R. is a water planet in a foggy swirl of other water
worlds around a dying giant red sun. Nowhere else in the galaxy
is there a situation quite like this, as far as anyone knows. Seen from
far away, the twenty-seven misty water worlds look similar to the rings
around the planet Saturn in the Sol System, but up close the whole system whirls stoically and ecstatically around its sun in a vast rainbow of
tiny water droplets.

The A.R. System had been discovered by one Augustine Radamacher, who named each planet for a lady friend. It was a pick-up line that
seldom failed. "Want'a have a planet named after your adorable self?"
Augie crooned this invitation to the waitress or dance hall girl of his
choice, soon followed by a pre-honeymoon trip to visit the A.R. System. All's fair in love and planet naming. On the official planet naming
form, he coupled the lady's name with his own initials—similar to a
teenage boy carving initials on a smooth tree. Radamacher had long
since drowned, but his love affairs live on. The fourth planet from the
red sun is named after Ashendon, a bar room beauty from Sempies Solis
in the Contini System.

Water worlds are peculiar places. To be classified as one, the land mass must be less than five percent. Some water worlds have great stands of underwater forests or aquatic plants that occasionally cut loose to form floating islands. Others are complete deserts. Some have evolved intelligent species similar to mermaids, with gills for breathing. The Star Anglers don't care if they are on a water world or not—as long as the fishing is good.

On Ashendon there are no mermaids and no land at all. Well, to be accurate, there is a lot of land, but it's all underwater. The water is fresh water, a phenomenon of the incessant rain and peculiar soil minerals that balance the tendency of salinity through evaporation. The third week of the Tournament is always on Ashendon, and there was plenty of grumbling this year about the Tourbo kid winning both of the early categories. The guys and girls were itchy. A couple more wins and the kid might have an uncatchable lead.

Pike Resnick, conversely, was starting to feel an edge of confidence. Blues and howlers had never been his strength, and the kid had managed to stumble through them without him. Now they were moving into Pike's prime zones. His past fishing success was quite simply due to Pike's having a thing for the later categories. With a drop of luck, he'd be able to nudge Richie into the history books. So Pike was feeling pretty chipper when The Comparative Humanity splashed down near the floating marina on Ashendon without its fisherman.

Rita had taken R.R. to Talmage Heights to see his mother. Pike and Lester had nothing to do until the boss showed up, except rendezvous with their new judge and bullshit with the guys, none of whom were around since they were all out fishing.

Ashendon was enjoyable in spite of the mugginess. It was certainly no place for a water colour painter, the air being hung with hovering moisture. When the humidity reached a hundred percent, it rained big soft drops. The rest of the time it was misty. Blue skies never broke the dew layer, but enough light rays filtered through it to furnish the verdant underwater vegetation with the components needed for a cloud forest type growth cycle. That's where the big striped muskies lurked, swimming in and out of the subaqueous growth like shadow tigers. They were the largest fish on the planet. Adult specimens had no natural predator, so they feared nothing. They fed when they were hungry. which was often, and lazed in the jungle when they weren't. But the muskies had a psychological weakness that Pike counted on. They could be made angry, angry enough to smash at the source of the irritation. Making a thousand pound tiger angry had its down side; but hey, that was the name of the game.

There was no resident human population on Ashendon, but entrepreneurs from the nearest inhabited planet, Caroline A.R., maintained the marina and provisioned the fleet. They also enforced the strict bag limit of one muskie per week over sixty inches and no smaller fish of any kind. They obviously didn't want their prime resource overfished, nor their food concessions diminished by fresh fish on the table. Usually the fishermen weren't interested in keeping muskies anyway, so the restrictive regulation didn't bother them much—but catch and release of a large muskie, with its underslung scissors jaw, called for a deft touch. A technique had evolved over the years of leading a non-keeper fish into a submerged cargo net, then craning it out of the water for a quick weigh-in, photographing and certification by the judge. Then, simply snipping the line off near the hook to release the fish. The uncoated steel hook was left to rust out, as it would in the fresh water.

It was during a snipping operation nine years ago, that Lester Wunderman had developed his limp. An angry twelve foot tiger had somehow tail walked out of the net and leaped aboard in the few seconds that the grid was off. He scissored off a gory bite of Lester's upper thigh, before flopping over the rail back into the watery forest. First aid and reconstructive surgery saved Lester's life and livelihood, but left him with a gimp. But the next year, he had wanted his job back. Braver men than Lester Wunderman may exist somewhere, but Pike didn't know any.

The floating marina was empty, except for Bardona's Lady Slipper—tied up in a nearby slip. The Baron always brought his house yacht along, as well as two full-sized fishing boats. Rita had borrowed one boat and one brother to fly her and Richie to visit the Mater. Some of the members bitched about Bardona's multitude of boats, since he wouldn't sell them an extra para-yacht to live on, but they never bothered to change the Rules to prohibit him. Why anger the petulant goose who might have glitches built into their next boat?

Pike was eager to start looking for muskies; but the kid was the fisherman. If he wanted to neglect prime fishing hours, it was up to him. Pike made a few entries in the Captain's log, then stretched out for a mid-morning siesta. There was no telling how long Rich and Rita would be away. The trip had been put off day after day on Beta Torga, when Richie could have easily gone. Now, that he should be fishing, he goes. Well, Pike couldn't help any of it. By all accounts, Mom Tourbo was a real fire breather. Maybe Richie would hurry back with his tail feathers singed.

*

Talmadge Heights was a garden planet, now owned almost entirely by Mom Tourbo. The whole shebang was her private estate and she regarded the subservient population, complete with an appointed government, police department and Coast Guard as her serfs, which in essence they were. She liked things that way—owned and controlled, and therefore well-mannered.

Mom tried to keep her perspective, if not her real estate dealings, scrupulously honest. In other words, she didn't mind fooling others, but she didn't like fooling herself. And it seemed that she had perhaps deluded herself about her loving son.

Lord knows she had always tried to love him—well, how could you really *love* somebody who was constantly breaking things; but she had gotten him the best nannies and tutors, if that wasn't a sign of her love she didn't know what was. It was hardly her fault if these women always liked her better than they did the boy. Yes, Rodney's childhood had made many sweet memories for Mom—the conquest of each new nanny had been delicious.

Now little Rodney had changed from the sweet, obedient child who always tried to curry her favor into an obnoxious, willful demon bent on destruction, just like his father. Larue J. Tourbo had been a ghastly mistake for her. He was a filthy brute, always wanting to paw and fondle her at the little real estate office, begging her to marry him—saying that her business skills would be a great asset to him.

Just a brute. The pain and humiliation of that one tipsy night—the supposedly wonderful wedding night—had never left her. His hairy, disgusting body crushing her until finally she had let him have his way. Truly disgusting. That was certainly not part of the wedding contract. She had let Mr. Larue Tourbo know of her disgust the next morning, after lying awake all night listening to his contented snorking. At breakfast, she had demurely suggested that she would have a bedroom of her own. No more snoring. He had laughed at her in his brutish way and had gone out to carouse with his hateful friend, Clive McAss.

Seeing that she would have to take matters into her own hands, demure Lillith simply removed all of her new husband's things from the bedroom, piling them in the hallway, and ordered a servant to install a substantial hasp on the inside and outside of the door. She snapped a padlock through the outside lock, thereby wiping her hands of further brutishness.

Then with her sleeping arrangements on a firmer footing, she had herself driven down to her tiny office, where Larue had had the good sense to meet her when he was looking for some commercial property to purchase. She called a painter to repaint the sign out in front, and ordered new letterheads and business cards from the stationer. When Larue came to retrieve her late that evening, she took time out from the interesting deal she was working on to proudly point out the new shingle to him, even though her lout of a husband was drunk and fawningly in heat. The sign said: L&L TOURBO LTD. His name and his sixty-five million credit nest egg would turn into billions under her calculating watchfulness. Sadly, Larue wouldn't be around to see what good management could do.

Several days of whining and barking about sleeping alone convinced the wounded bridegroom that he should visit his holdings in the Ainendrenhen System, where a manly sporting event would be attracting sporting ladies. Lillith barely listened as he tried to entice her to come along. She informed him sweetly that she loathed sporting opportunities and that perhaps he should find a traveling companion—she had plenty to occupy her at the office. The demure way she offered the new arrangement caused Larue's eyebrows to arch all the way up to his hairline. She always remembered that touching moment with a smile.

Sadly, The Eye called her within the week to report the tragic news that Larue had been atomized by a meteor after purchasing a few hundred uninhabited planets on his way back from Ainendrenhen. To a large extent, she had forgotten he was gone. The pre-nuptial agreement left everything to her, naturally, unless there was a child. Not wishing to offend any of Larue's friends, Lillith arranged for a memorial service at which she wore simple black. That afternoon, she found time to drop into the office to complete a pending deal on an apartment complex, which she rechristened The Larue Towers. She thought it was a fitting memorial. And it was for eight years, until progress demanded that a new spaceport be built on that section of land. Mega bucks changed hands.

*

A few months after Larue's death, Lillith was as surprised as everyone else to see that she was starting to plump around the middle. But she took it stoically. Marital duty was attempting to overpower her again. No way that was going to happen. She hoped fervently that the baby would be a girl, and plowed back into her work. As a concession to impending motherhood, she encouraged everyone to call her Mom and hired a sweet young thing named Sandra to help with the paperwork at the office.

But Richard Rodney had been born as a little boy instead of a girl. And now he was starting to act as brutishly as he father had—foolishly endangering his life and her future granddaughters by going fishing. And he had made out a last will and testament that she had never seen. What was a mother to do?

"Lovely to see you again, dear," Mom said to Rita. "How is your charming father?"

"He's not doing very well," Rita laughed. She had come along to Talmadge Heights mainly to bolster R.R.'s moral courage. He claimed he could handle the chore himself, but support of friends was high on Rita's list of things to do. And besides she wanted to see how deftly Richie's mother operated on him, since Rita herself had pushed him into this antagonistic position of being a fisherman. "Daddy's tied for sixth place, way behind Richie."

"Oh, you're in fifth place, darling?" Mom said distastefully, turning her gaze back to the uncomfortable boy.

R.R. nodded feebly, hoping the subject would change. He had wanted to inform his mother about his new life in a more circumspect manner. Trust Rita to confront everything head-on.

"He's in sole possession of 1st place," Rita gloated. "Pike and I are so proud of him that we could burst."

"Pike...?" Mom asked, arching her eyebrows disapprovingly.

"Pike Resnick," Rita answered, liking the matter of fact way the name slid off her tongue. "He's captaining Richie's boat. We were lucky to get him."

"I see," Mom said, dripping scorn on the fusion-glass coffee table where three cups of peppermint tea sat cooling. In her opinion, Pike Resnick was a profligate wastrel, who should have been wealthy but had squandered his chance. Certainly a dangerous influence on her impressionable son.

"How have you been, Mother?" R.R. asked, conversationally. "Any interesting deals in the works?"

"Thank you for asking, dear boy, but why should you be concerned that I'm headed for an early grave. Go have your fun, while I spend my days worrying about you, and my nights listening to the wailing of my unborn granddaughters. Since I learned that you dismissed your loyal security friends, I haven't had a moment's rest. That's why I look so peaked, as I'm sure you have noticed."

R.R. risked a glance from his lap up to the crocodile's face. She looked radiant with health and meanness, like always. "There's no room on the boat for security people," he mumbled.

"Nonsense. Just because I'm an old lady, doesn't mean I'm senile."

"And they're not my friends," he said, finding a little courage. "You always call them my security friends, but they're intrusive bodyguards. You never even consulted me about whether they were needed or not. Truthfully, Mother, there's no job for security guards just now. Fishing isn't dangerous."

"Oh, I hadn't realized that. In fact, I'd always heard the opposite. Don't they make a lot of man-crowing hype about how dangerous and exciting it's supposed to be?" She turned her reptilian eyes back onto Rita. At least the boy had excellent taste in women, Mom noted with satisfaction. Lovely and so well-heeled. She felt a sudden lust to get her hands on a few of the Baron's assets, or Rita's. "Is that true, Rita?" she inquired. "Fishing on all those outlandish places is completely safe for a frail boy like Richard?"

"Well, I wouldn't say completely safe," Rita vacillated.

"I knew it!" Mom yelped. "Why would you fabricate a brutish lie like that, Richard? You worry a body to death! You always have, one thing after another."

"That's not true, Mother. You've never worried about me, and there's no need to be so theatrical."

"Theatrical...?! How would you know what a mother goes through with an ungrateful son like you? I'm calling some security friends right now, and you *will* take them back to your stupid boat! And don't go damaging them like the one I sent to Amora."

R.R. digested that news. Silas must have been the one. No wonder he was so helpful all the time. "I'm not taking any security friends, Mother. Please don't make an issue of this. I came for a pleasant visit with you. I'm an adult now, and I'm hoping you'll accept that fact." He reached for the tea cup, but inexplicably it slipped from his fingers, smashing the priceless matching saucer. R.R. scowled, retrieved the cup and drank the remaining swallow of tea. A servant scurried in to mop up the coffee table.

"I knew I should have served Richard in his plastic tea service, but I was so hoping he'd gotten over his clumsiness now that he's an adult," Mom explained to Rita. "How is your father's new boat, dear?" she asked. A pitying expression graced her well-preserved face. "I heard from our insurance people that it's much better than the old one."

"It's quite nice," Rita responded. "Daddy is fishing with it on Ashendon. He can be so petty sometimes."

Rich Rodney squirmed.

"Not at all," Mom said, sweetly. "That's how the game is played. You children are getting old enough to be interested in the rules, don't you think? And speaking of rules, the next thing I would like to discuss, darling boy, is the enormous amount of investment capital you seem to be frittering away on dangerous foolishness."

"I think it's time for us to be running along, Rita," Richie said. In the process of standing up, his knee rapped solidly on the sharp corner of the coffee table. Groaning, but undaunted, he limped toward the door.

"Let me ring for breakfast, dear," Mom said, sedately. "You can't go out without your breakfast."

*

An hour before sunset, as fog started to whisper, Farouk Bardona's second fishing boat splashed down in the marina on Ashendon. It docked next to the Lady Slipper. Four people stepped onto the floating wharf: Rita, Richie and his two large bodyguards, who appropriately flanked R.R. until he demanded that they walk ten paces behind him and Rita. In this configuration, they made their way around the floating docks of the marina until they came to the Comparative Humanity.

Pike stepped out on deck as the foursome approached.

"Ready for fishing, Captain, sir," Rich Rodney announced to Pike, with a smart salute.

"Too foggy now. We'll hit it hard in the morning. Where were you all day? They were biting like crazy." Pike smiled at the kid, and felt his member hardening at the sight of Rita. It was kind of ridiculous to get all hot and bothered every time he saw her, but really, this was the most alive he'd felt for a long time—maybe ever. That's interesting. This may be the sexiest and the most alive I've ever felt. As each day passed he was under more sexual strain—living with her, but not having her. But hey, no strain, no gain. He caught her eye as the two bodybuilders walked up and stopped a pace behind the pair.

"Why can't we go out now? Isn't sunset the best time?" R.R. asked, jumping aboard. His sudden movement startled his guards.

"Dusk is best for howlers, I imagine that's what you're thinking of," said reasonable Pike Resnick, fishing instructor to the rich and famous. "To land a muskie, you have to be able to see. That's impossible in this pea soup, as you will notice."

"Shoot," said Rich Rodney, using his strongest oath. He tripped over a well-protected cleat inside the starboard rail that was virtually impossible to trip over. Stumbling profoundly, his feet somehow caught together, pitching him nose first into the scuppers. Both security men swarmed onto the deck. One moved into a defensive position to block any attack that Pike might decide to make, the other leapt to help Rich Rodney up.

"Hands off!" Richie yelped, jumping up. "And get off this boat. Neither I nor Captain Resnick invited you on board." The guard's faces got that out of kilter look .

Pike watched Rita laughing delightedly from the dock.

"What's going on here?!" Lester Wunderman thundered, coming out of the galley with a fully charged harpoon gun. "You heard him! Off the boat." Lester looked hastily to Pike for confirmation. Pike shrugged. He saw the frightened face of Edmund Messier, their judge this week, appear at the galley window.

The security friends looked at the harpoon, then at each other. Finally they looked tightly at Rich Rodney. "I think I missed something here, Mr. Tourbo, sir," the largest one said.

"Yes. I meant to explain earlier. Your services aren't needed on the boat. My mother will pay you and you will remain on the dock at all times, staying as far away from me as possible. Is that clear?"

"Why would you pay us, unless we were guarding you?"

"I'm not paying you, my mother is. I just said that. If she wants to pay you to relax on Ashendon, that's her business, isn't it."

"Yes, sir. I guess it is. Won't we have to tell her that you're uncooperative?"

"Tell her whatever you want to. But first get off this boat. Lester, shoot the big one first, if he's not dockside in seven seconds."

"Yes, sir," Lester answered, crouching slightly and pointing the harpoon at the man's muscular belly.

Both bodyguards were on the dock by the time Richie had counted to four. "Very good," he said. "Stop simpering, Rita, and come aboard. All you've done all day is simper at me."

"I never simper," Rita corrected. "I was laughing at you." Nevertheless, she stepped gracefully aboard.

"Where should we bunk down, sir?" the smaller man asked, deferring the essentials of his personal comfort to his employer as he always did.

"That's not my problem," R.R. said. "Call my mother and ask her. I told her there wasn't room for you here. But if you do call her, there's a faint chance that she'll stop paying you for doing nothing. She hates to waste investment capital."

The bodyguards looked at each other again. Working for rich crazies was such a drag. Here they were, stranded on a foreign world.

"Go have dinner at that pub up the dock," Pike said. "I'll come and get you straightened out in a little while."

"Thank you, Captain," they both said in unison, and marched toward the pub.

"Put the harpoon away, Lester," Pike said. "And get out the gallon of mercurochrome for Richie's hands. I think he skinned them."

Lester grinned. "Are you staying for dinner?" he asked Rita and Rich Rodney.

Rita flicked a look at Pike and nodded yes.

"Do you think it would be all right for me to fish off the fantail for awhile, just so I get a feel for the water?" Rodney asked.

"You're the boss, boss," Pike said. "Why ask me?"

"Of course, I have to ask you. I just want to fish for awhile, if it's not breaking any rules."

"There are no rules about when to fish. Just don't catch any. It would interrupt dinner in the worst way." He grinned at the kid. "Harry Dolan caught an 800 pounder this morning. We'll have to go some to top that. You should get to know Harry. He's a fine fisherman."

*

Night had fallen by the time Rita, Pike and Messier had cracked open the first bottle of wine and started on the appetizers. Lester was puttering over his sauce pans, making some kind of special dish for dinner. Pike knew Edmund Messier had started nibbling at his private bottle around four o'clock, when it became evident that there would be no fishing today. The scholarly little man had been with the Tournament for several years and was a competent judge. It wasn't an easy job to readjust to a new boat and crew every week. If he liked to drink on his off days, that was his business. The Tournament got progressively more dangerous from this point forward. Taking a drink relieved the pressure; but alcohol sluggishness increased the danger, so Pike himself seldom indulged.

"Pleasant trip to Talmadge?" Pike inquired of Rita.

"Yes, very. The Tourbo's are very interesting together. Do you know Mom?"

"I know of her, but we've never met." In spite of the deal that he had made with Rita, abstinence was making him a little crazy. She was always around—supposedly working on her famous thesis at the terminal in Pike's room—their room. It didn't seem like he should push himself on her, or insist on anything just now. It was a question of getting adjusted, she said, when he had asked about the situation. It had only been a week, she said—which was almost true. It had been ten days.

She didn't act unavailable in public. Probably everyone who saw them together assumed they were an item. Well, they were an item! The way they looked at each other was intense. Sparks flew, didn't they? Or was that only his perception? She usually sat beside him at meals—was always attentive and often snugly—in public. He was friendly, but restrained. In private, she wasn't ready yet. And he didn't see any winning moves except to wait—and that, of course, was not a guaranteed winning move.

"Well, Mom Tourbo doesn't think too highly of you," Rita laughed.

"I guess that proves she's as shrewd as they say."

"Yes, I guess it does," she answered, winking at Mr. Messier. Rita shifted her gaze to the side window, watching the white fog drifting lazy as a cloud billow. Why did *she* always have to be the one to initiate intimacy? That's not the way it was supposed to work. Why didn't he drag her into the bedroom or something? But he wasn't going to, was he? Maybe Mom Tourbo was right. Pike was too indecisive to protect his own interests. Maybe he was that way in everything. No, he was a brilliant inventor and a really brilliant fisherman, and that's what he wanted to be. He had to be judged on that criterion, didn't he? Her father might take advantage of Pike financially, but never at fishing. But did she want to marry a fisherman? Yes, her heart screamed. He's good. He's fine! I'm happy when I'm here with him. Throw yourself at him. Who cares what I said before?

Instead of a proposal from Pike, her impasse was broken by the shrieking of a 4.0 reel. "Holy shit!" Rich Rodney yelped from outside. "I've got one! Cripes, help me!!"

Rita and Pike scrambled up from the table. Lester took a second to turn off the burners before he hobbled after them.

Outside, Pike ran to the bridge with the reel screaming in his ear. "Loosen up on the drag, kid! Les, get him in the chair!!" Pike started the engine, toggled up the running lights to full brightness and lit the defense grid. The boat had twin spotlights mounted above the bridge. He hit the switch and pointed them at the fog bank where the heavy line was diving downwards.

"Got him!" Lester shouted. He wrapped his arms around Richie and dragged him backwards toward the fighting chair. "Don't hurt me with your cussed clumsiness, or I'll kill you," he hissed in R.R.'s ear. "Hold onto the rod until I get you strapped in. Relax damnit! Not that relaxed! Act right!!" Lester snapped the harness rings into their keepers, then made sure the rod was seated properly and the safety line was secured.

"It's a big one, Pike!" Rich Rodney yelped. "Can we keep him!"

"Keep him?" Lester griped. "He's gonna take all the line, then snap you off and laugh about it. I ought to cut him off, now."

"Can't we try for him, Pike..?" the kid pleaded

"He's using the big outfit," Lester said. "But he'll snap off sure, if we stay in the slip."

"How big is he, Lester?" Pike yelled. "Damn this fog!"

"Pretty big. He's ripping the line off, but we can't take him without room to maneuver."

"I heard you! Okay, let's try it," Pike said, feeling very unsure that this was the right move. On the other hand, a fisherman does not scoff at luck. The kid might never get another bite, if he didn't try for this one.

"What should I do?" Rita yelled.

"Jump down and cast us off," Pike yelled back. "Then run up to the pub and get those two goons to help set up some spotlights. As many as you can find."

Rita hopped neatly over the rail, landing with bent knees. "Those guys won't have credit to rent anything with," she yelled up at Pike. She unwrapped the stern line from a big cleat on the dock.

"Use yours," Pike said. "Hurry up with the lines."

"Daddy will kill me," she laughed, untying the bow line from its cleat.

"Well, use mine or Richie's! Just get the fucking lights going! I can't see a thing."

"Shove off! You're clear," she called, casting the bow line onto the deck. "Floodlights would be better. Spots just reflect in this soup."

Pike feathered the engine and gently backed out of the slip. "Lights. Lots of them. Spots or floods or flashlights. Anything!" He smiled tightly as Rita ran up the dock into the fog.

Edmund Messier stumbled out on deck. "Are you serious about fighting a fish?" he inquired of Pike.

"Looks that way," Pike replied. The boat was clear of the slip and headed into a fog bank. "Slow him down as much as you can, Lester! I want to stay within sight of this stupid wharf!"

"Brace your feet, kid, and lean on that rod," Lester said. "You have to play him all yourself. I can't help."

"I know that," R.R. said.

"I know you know, but I'll be right here to back you up. Keep thinking about not hurting me and yourself. That should be primary in your mind."

"Thank you," Rodney said. "I know. I admire you and Pike too much to hurt you. I was careful during the howlers, wasn't I?"

"Howlers ain't muskies," Lester reminded himself, with a shudder.

"How big do you think this one is?"

"Pretty big. You got ahold of him, so you're the expert. How big is he?"

"Gosh, he feels as big as a house."

"Well, that's how big he is then," Lester said. "House size."

Edmund Messier peered out into the white/black nothingness. "I better get my camera ready," he slurred, and went down to his stateroom.

"Lean on him, Richie!" Pike called. "But don't try to turn him! I don't want him snagging an anchor cable!" The marina platform was deep anchored with two inch cables at each corner, fastened to long pitons driven into core rock. If the fish wrapped around a cable, he was home free.

"Let the strain go down to your legs if you can," Lester advised. "You won't be able to fight him with your arms, you're not strong enough. Nobody is."

"I'm pushing as hard as I can," Rich Rodney growled. He shoved his feet harder against the foot rest, and looked around for Rita, who was nowhere in sight. Didn't she care that he was fighting a monster?

"Concentrate on what you're doing."

"I am. Where's Rita?"

"Pike sent her off."

"Oh," he said, looking at the line again. If Pike sent her off, then naturally she wouldn't be watching.

"Half empty!" Lester called out to Pike, meaning the reel was half empty.

"Give him a full turn of drag," Pike answered. "I'll go to idle. Let Mr. Tiger pull the boat awhile. That ought to get him jumping."

"Give your drag a full turn," Lester said, relaying the message. "The other way, kid. Twist it the other way. Righty, tighty. That's better."

Rich Rodney turned the drag a full turn, then grabbed back onto the rod with both hands.

"Should I hook up the cable helpers?" Lester called.

"Yes," Rich Rodney gasped.

"Not yet," Pike answered. They were fully in the fog bank. It was eerily quiet inside. Pike could barely make out the shapes of Lester and the kid. He turned the spotlight on them. "I thought I told you not to catch any fish, Richie!" he taunted. "Now, look at the mess we're in..!"

"I didn't try to. I never thought anything big would bite, just those little shiny purple ones I was saving for bait."

"What shiny purple ones?" Pike said, uneasily. "Where are they?"

"In the bait tank. Where else would bait be? Who'd ever think anything would bite on a hunk of old tinfoil? Cripes, I just stuck it on so I could see where I was casting."

Pike took a quick fix on the dim lights of the wharf, and hurried down the ladder. Good old Lester was already dipping the bait net into the live well. "Hurry up," Pike urged, under his breath. "Before Edmund gets back."

"Go fix him a drink," Lester said, dipping a wiggling bait fish over the side. "How many of these did you catch, Richie?"

"I don't know. A few."

"How many?!" Pike exploded, in a whisper. "Didn't you read the rules?"

"Of course, I did."

"How many have you got out?" Pike asked Lester.

"Six. It's too dark in there to see. Shine the light in the tank."

"That's how many I caught," Rich Rodney said. "Six."

"What's this one, then," Lester asked with high irony, flinging a seventh over the rail like it was poison.

"It must have been in there already. What's the big deal? This fish is getting extremely heavy, by the way."

"Explain it to him after you're sure the tank is clean. I'll let the water out and put the spot directly on it." Pike leaped back up the ladder, focused the spotlight directly on Lester. After flicking a switch that emptied the bait well, he left the bridge and went down below.

Pike found the judge in his tiny forward stateroom screwing a precision camera onto a suction base tripod. "Got a flashlight in your kit?" he asked Messier.

"I believe I have," he answered, distractedly.

"Bring it. And you're bringing your strobe pack, too, aren't you? We're going to need all the light we can get."

Pike disappeared into his cabin, then reappeared with a six cell flashlight and a storm lantern, which he had unscrewed from the wall.

"Oh, and I'd jump into some long johns, if I were you," he suggested. "It's going to be wet and chilly waiting on the kid. He doesn't have much experience. Lord knows how long we'll be standing around. Sorry about this, Edmund."

"That's why they're paying me," Messier said, pleasantly. "I'll put on some coffee if Lester's too busy."

"Thanks," Pike said, climbing back up the ladder. "You're a good man."

Back on deck, he made a bee-line for the bait tank and shined the bright flashlight into the shallow water. A nine inch shiner skittered madly around the inside of the tank. "Get this one, Lester. That makes eight."

"Nine," Lester replied.

"Lester explained the rule about catching only one fish," R.R grunted, leaning against the heavy fighting rod. "I didn't think that applied to bait fish. I'll be more careful and ask about anything that's not totally clear next time."

"No sweat," Pike said lazily, now that the danger of disqualification had passed. "How you holding up?"

"Fine," the kid lied. "This is really fun."

Lester netted the offending shiner and flipped it overboard.

"They were all alive," Pike commented to Richie, "so technically we're okay with the law, now. Oh, incidentally, that ratty piece of tinfoil you found is my top secret primo bait for tiger muskies."

"It is..?"

"Yep. Don't know why, but it drives them nuts. That's my secret. Don't be telling *anyone* about it."

"I won't."

"I mean it."

"Fine! I won't tell anyone. You think I'm a blabber mouth?"

"Lester will knock if off with the gaff as soon as the fish is netted. If anybody asks, you were baiting with a strip of dead mullet."

"I'll remember."

The line slackened suddenly. "Crank it like mad, kid! He coming up for some jumping. Watch him, Les!" As Pike ran for the bridge, the fog bank exploded into dazzling brightness. White light ricocheted off of each fog droplet. Rita had found some lights. Good girl. Maybe we'll survive the night.

"That's better," Lester called. "Still can't see anything, but at least it's daylight."

R.R. played the fish he couldn't see through a series of jumps. Pike jockeyed the boat to keep the line taut. It was an odd experience in the fog bank, one that most people would never know.

Messier climbed onto the bridge lugging his camera and strobe outfit. "Plenty of light now," he observed. "Coffee's ready. I'll bring it out."

"Good," Pike said, never taking his eye off the line.

"I'll be sober in time for the netting," Messier said.

"Good," Pike repeated. "You were perfectly right to think it was a day off. It's my fault for getting us into this."

Messier smiled lopsidedly. "The boy has unusual luck," he said. "Everyone's talking about it."

"It takes all kinds," Pike said. "You ever been involved in a netting in this kind of fog?"

"No," Messier answered. "Maybe he'll break off." He started back down the ladder. "Black or cream?" he asked.

"Black," Pike answered.

The marine radio crackled to life. "Breaker, breaker," Rita's voice invaded the bridge. "Hello, Comparative Humanity..?"

Pike pressed the speak button. "Thanks for the lights, Rita. Much better. All fine here, but busy."

"You still have the fish?"

"Still do. The kid's doing fine."

"If you land him, I'll have a very special surprise for you, Pike. Can't tell you what it is over the airwaves. Over and out."

"That sounds pretty much A-okay. Out here." A little surprise would finish this evening off just right. He stuck his head out the window. "How's the kid doing, Lester?!"

"Fine," Lester's muffled voice carried up to the bridge.

"My arms are starting to get really exhausted," R.R. grunted, feeling like he should convey that fact to somebody. He had just fought something huge out in the fog through three jumps which almost tore his shoulders from their sockets. Mercifully, the fish was diving now.

"Course they're tired," Lester said. "But you're fine. Can't overheat in this soup."

"I should do more weight lifting. I never knew how tiring this could be. That delilah I caught was easy compared to this."

"You're fine. Save your breath. Rest one arm at a time until you feel the strength ooze back in her. Unless you feel the fish rushing to the surface again. You know what that feels like now, don't you?"

"Yes, I do." He gratefully let go of the pole with one hand, breathing a big sigh of relief.

"Coffee's coming. That'll warm you up."

"I don't like coffee."

Lester's mouth bent in a frown. "What *do* you like?" he asked. He'd been serving the kid coffee for a week. Had he been pouring it out? "I wouldn't recommend much alcohol while we're fighting him. It don't do to be tipsy or too brave for the netting."

"Orange juice," the kid said.

"Okay, I'll get you some."

"Hurry, he might jump again. I'm not sure I can hold him alone."

"Get the net and crane ready, Lester!" Pike's voice boomed from overhead. "It's been almost an hour! We'll try to take him after the next series of jumps!"

"Maybe we should play him all night and take him in the morning," Lester suggested.

"That's too long for Richie!"

"I could put the helpers on."

"No. They'd flip the fish off, if he jumps. We'll get him soon. He's tired now. He's just laying out there."

"I know," Lester agreed.

"I'll go back easy. Make up some line. Then we'll annoy him into jumping again."

"Standing by to make up line," Lester said. Edmund Messier appeared out of nowhere with two mugs of steaming coffee. "Thanks, Judge," Lester said. "Could you bring a glass of orange juice, no ice, no booze, for the fighting chair. I'd get her myself, but we're going to make up some line."

"I heard," Messier said, going back to the galley.

Forty-five minutes later, the half-inch thick yellow polyethylene cargo net was sinking on the port side of the boat. All four corners of the net were cabled to the electric hoist, which was sticking out over the side. And the fog was still thick. The fish could get away easily at this point simply by making a run to port and snarling in the net. But the fish didn't know that, and it was up to Pike to maneuver the boat, so that this fact remained a secret from the muskie. The task was to bring the supposedly tired fish alongside and swim him over the net without tangling the line, then quickly hoist him into the air. While he was being weighed automatically, Messier would snap a full body shot, then switch to a telephoto lens and snap a close-up showing a hook in the fish's mouth. With that done, Lester would break the line and they'd lower the net. The fish would swim away to fight another day. And everybody would be happy. Sounds simple on paper.

Rich Rodney's arms ached unbearably. He was sure the shoulder sockets were permanently sprung. They were in a state of rigid lock. He used the one arm relaxation technique that Lester had suggested without much relief. Back and forth from pain to excruciating pain. The minute he gripped the rod, pain rictorized the forearm, then quickly jumped to his triceps and deltoid. His back muscles were locked up, too, but he could ease that pain by scooching around in the rock hard fighting chair. All he really wanted to do was hand the rod over to Lester, or even throw the damned thing overboard. What did he care if the fish beat him? It was only a stupid fish! Nobody should have to take this kind of punishment. The rules were so stupid! Why couldn't the deck hand fight part of the stupid fish? Oh, God, his arms ached so much! If I just lift the rod butt a little, it will spring out of the cup and I can live again.

"How you doing, kid?" Pike asked, from behind his ear. He put his big hands on R.R.'s thin shoulders and massaged the knotted muscles.

"Fine," Rich Rodney replied. "Hanging in there." What was Pike doing, sneaking up like that?

"We're going to try for him now. You're doing great. Much better than I thought you would. A lot of people quit on a fish this size."

"I'm not quitting," R.R. rasped.

"Course not. We've got him now."

"Right," the kid said, pumping himself up with false bravado. Naturally, he was going to land the bastard fish. There was never a thought of chickening out.

"Okay," Pike said. "While I'm standing here, I want you to hold the rod one handed, and shake your other arm out. Shake it good and hard to let the life back in."

R.R jumped at the suggestion, shaking his right arm jerkily. Oh, God, it felt heavenly! Nothing has ever felt this good! He switched to the left arm.

"Do it some more," Pike said, watching the kid flail. "We know you don't have much experience, but the only way to get experience with a big fish is to hook one. Kind of like the school of hard knocks, huh, kid?"

"It's fun. I'm learning a lot. He sure is heavy."

"Yep, nobody knows that until they hook up to one. Anyway, that part is almost over. The next part can be very lively, and sometimes dicey; so I'm going to talk you through it. If he gets off under these conditions, it's nothing to be ashamed of. You fought him splendidly."

R.R. felt his chest swelling with the praise as Pike explained the netting procedure. He thought he might cry. It was so damned wonderful to be accepted by men like Pike and Lester. Finally Pike was done with the explanation. Rodney realized in a panic that he might not have been paying attention. He couldn't remember any of it.

"I don't know if I got that," he grunted. "After he comes toward the net, then what?"

So Pike went over it again while Lester rechecked the crane and went below for a pit stop.

"The main thing is not to freeze up or come unglued. Just keep firm pressure on his mouth. That will keep his head up. Lester and I will do the rest of it. Lester will be counting on you to hold him steady. I don't have to tell you that what Lester will be doing is almost superhuman. I'm counting on you to help him every way you can. And that means to stay icy calm."

"Why?"

"Why what...? Calm is the best. What else could that mean?"

"Why is it superhuman?"

"Well, partly because it's dangerous under good conditions, but in fog like this it's very nerve wracking. And partly because a big tiger took his leg."

"Jeese, I didn't know that."

"Anyway, don't worry about Lester. He's got balls of steel. He'll do his job, if it can be done. Just don't fuck him up when you see how big the fish is."

"I won't," R.R. vowed.

"You're famous for fuck-ups. Just stay in the chair and hold the rod steady, unless Lester tells you something different. If he says anything, do it. As far as safety goes, the grid is on full power. If the fish is in the water, he can't come at you. But when we haul him high in the net, the grid won't keep him out. As soon as the net comes up, you unbuckle, but stay put. Keep the tension on, so that the line stays up and out of the way. If the fish comes loose, you run—and I mean run, for the galley. Don't try to help Lester, you'll only fuck him up. Got that?"

"Yes, sir."

"But it will probably go smoothly. Let's hope it will."

"Yes, sir. How long until we start?"

"Two minutes. Shake your arms out again."

*

The muskie glided to the surface. R.R.'s eyes bulged at the size of him. The great underslung jaw snapped once, showing millions of pointed teeth.

"He's hooked good," Lester shouted from the fantail. He held the long-handled gaff in both hands like a quarter staff. "Back easy, Pike!"

"Backing easy," Pike called. "How big?"

"Big enough. Stand by the crane button."

"Standing by the crane," Pike answered. From the bridge nothing was visible, just fog. "You'll have to set up on the deck for the photos," he said to Messier. "I want him in the air for ten seconds maximum. The instant I see the second flash, I'm letting him go."

"What about the weigh in?" Messier asked.

"Shit," Pike swore. The read-out scale was on the side of the crane boom. He'd have to wait until Messier verified the weight.

As an alternative, they could kill the fish, Pike thought, naming him their one keeper. Then there would be much less risk; but if bigger fish were taken by the other guys, they wouldn't do well in this leg. "Is he big enough for a keeper?!" Pike shouted.

"Can't tell," Lester called. "Harry's already got eight hundred. This one might go six or seven. Maybe more."

Pike weighed all the elements in a micro-second. "We'll take this one for our counter!" he barked.

"Good plan," Lester concurred, now that the plan was made. "Stand by to crane."

"I can't see to shoot from up here! Get a zap!"

"Going for it!" Lester answered, quickly limping toward the galley.

"What's happening?!" R.R. yelled.

"Hold tight, kid. Change of plan. We're taking this one. Everything's the same for you. Keep a fair pressure on him. It's almost over now!"

"Fine. I can see him, Pike! He's huge! He's looking right at me!"

"Hold tight! You're hooked up good. The fish can't do a thing down there with the grid on! I told you that, didn't I?"

Lester gimped back to the fantail.

"Standing by with the zap!" he called. "Ready to crane?"

"Standing by to crane!" Pike answered. He looked over at Edmund Messier. "You any good with a las cannon?" he asked.

"Yes. Adequate."

"Stand by the cannon then. Don't shoot unless you can see."

"Roger, Captain," Messier said. Climbing up the ladder, he strapped into the laser cannon harness. He would have enjoyed being friends with these men, but his personality didn't make friends easily. He snapped on the power and adjusted the beam to fine. "I'm ready," he called, "but I can't see a thing."

"Back slow!" Lester shouted from down below. "He's coming in."

"Back slow," Pike answered, fingering the throttle.

"Crane...!!" Lester yelled.

Pike hit the crane button. The gears meshed and the net started up.

"Hit him, kid!!" Lester yelped. "He's going through!"

"What...?!" R.R. yelped back.

"Yank on him!! Now...!!"

R.R. rared back on the rod. He watched in awe as the huge striped fish thrashed up until he was almost standing on his tail. Jaws snapped on one of the net cables, severing it like it was nothing. Rodney's fishing line snapped with a crack like a rifle shot, slamming R.R. sideways in the fighting chair. After a startled moment, Rodney threw the rod aside and started fumbling with the harness.

The fish crashed back into the water. The weakened net, working only with three of its four cables, collected him, hauling his huge muscular tail out of the water. He twisted and bucked in the net, his head completely free of any confinement. "Keep him coming!!" Lester squalled. The crane groaned, but kept hauling its cargo of thrashing fish up. Green water cascaded off the monster. Waiting for a brain shot, Lester angled along the rail with the stun gun, a yard away from the twisting bulk.

Rich Rodney scuttled for the galley, dripping a trail of blood from a bloody nose, which the whip-lashing rod had inflicted. He stood in the galley door, bleeding.

"Still craning!" Pike yelled. "How are we looking?!"

The fish made a mighty effort to get free. His gigantic head cleared the water, twisting to snap at the net. Lester fired. The high-voltage blast ripped into the forehead plate. The tail convulsed, slapping the gunwale a terrible blow where Lester had stood a second before. Rich Rodney's hair stood on end, but Lester continued shooting, pinpointing a line of shots down the backbone, trying to quiet the fish by breaking his spine. Finally he hit the right spot. The fish quivered, then lay still in the net.

"That's it!" Lester called. "Haul him up! Weigh him!"

Rich Rodney stepped timidly out of the galley and stood beside Lester, feeling terribly proud of the bravery he had witnessed. The huge fish hung in the air beside the boat. It was as long as the whole fantail, and they had caught it. "He's so big," R.R. said, almost reverently.

Lester Wunderman grinned voraciously. "You got yourself a fine muskie, Mr. Rich. You done a very fine job of fighting him."

"I was afraid when he got close. Thank you for shooting him. That was extremely brave what you did."

"Well, Pike couldn't see him from the bridge," Lester said, glad the kid had complimented him, but disregarding it. He did feel good about the fish. "It would have been worse trying to release him in this slop. We were damn lucky Pike decided her this way."

"Seven hundred twenty-nine pounds!" Pike called out of the fog.

"729," Lester glowed. "See, that's a perfect fish. You're in $2^{nd}$ place, Rich. Couldn't be better."

Pike walked over from the crane. He shook R.R.'s hand and looked the fish over. "I was scared shitless the whole time," he laughed. "But you got a nice fish. We'll photograph it in the slip. And you got yourself a real fish story to tell. Not too many people will be topping this one."

R.R. grinned.

"Yes, sir," Lester grinned, happily. "We can all tell this one for years to come. And we would have a whole shitload of witnesses except that nobody could see their own weenie through this pea soup."

"What happened to your nose," Pike asked, handing the kid a handkerchief.

R.R. dabbed at his nose and saw the blood for the first time. "I thought I was catching a cold," he said. "Boy, that's lucky. I hate being all stuffed up."

Pike flicked a look of disbelief at Lester. "We'll use the rest of this week to try out some different techniques, Richie, so you won't be caught so flatfooted next time."

"Fine," Rich Rodney answered. "Let's go show this beauty to Rita."

"Let's do that," Pike agreed.

"Did you guys already eat dinner?" the kid inquired.

"I think maybe I can rustle up a little something for you, Mr. Richie," Lester said, seriously. "Or it might be we'll get somebody to buy at the pub dockside."

"I'll be happy to buy," R.R. said deliriously.

"You just hold tight, Mister. You let somebody offer first when we get back. All of these people have plenty of money."

Richie nodded.

Pike climbed up to the bridge and threw the boat into slow forward, pointing her at the lights. Edmund Messier was standing near the cannon drinking a beer.

"I couldn't see one thing down there through the fog, Captain Resnick. If something had gone wrong, it would have been shit city. My knees won't stop shaking."

"Nothing went wrong," Pike said. "Your knees are shaking because you're cold. I told you to put long johns on."

"I did," Messier said.

Pike laughed, "Did you bring a beer for me?" he asked.

* * *

# LEADERS

| | DELILAH | TORGA HOWLER | TIGER MUSKY | D.W. SCUT | PHANTOM TROUT | LAR BARRACUDA | GLANS SALMON | RAZORFIN | SWAMPFISH | MOON HALIBUT | TOTAL |
|---|---|---|---|---|---|---|---|---|---|---|---|
| Farouk Bardona | | | 2 | | | | | | | | 5TH 2 |
| Ethyl Bierly | 2 | | | | | | | | | | 5TH 2 |
| Angmar Blirt | | | | | | | | | | | |
| Bill Bolen | | | 3 | | | | | | | | 4TH 3 |
| Dresden Carthy | 4 | | | | | | | | | | 3RD 4 |
| JB Dillingham | | OUT | | | | | | | | | |
| Harry Dolan | 3 | 2 | 5 | | | | | | | | 2ND 10 |
| Macky Duff | | | | | | | | | | | |
| Ira Fairborne | | | 4 | | | | | | | | 3RD 4 |
| Buddy Jay | | | | | | | | | | | |
| Sandy Kind | | | | | | | | | | | |
| Hank Knofsinger | | | | | | | | | | | |
| Peter Marcuso | | | | | | | | | | | |
| Trini Morales | | | | | | | | | | | |
| Pike Resnick | | OUT | | | | | | | | | |
| Erwin Sandor | | 3 | | | | | | | | | 4TH 3 |
| Jean Santos | | 1 | | | | | | | | | 1 |
| Mordachi Skinner | | | 4 | | | | | | | | 3RD 4 |
| Tyrone Stickle | | | | | | | | | | | |
| Chip Takahachi | | | | | | | | | | | |
| RR Tourbo | 5 | 5 | 1 | | | | | | | | 1ST 11 |
| Mike Tucker | 1 | | | | | | | | | | 1 |
| Nacho Tutupo | | | | | | | | | | | |
| Ed Wood | | | | | | | | | | | |
| Big John Zales | | | | | | | | | | | |

| | | |
|---|---|---|
| 1ST | = | 5 points |
| 2ND | = | 4 points |
| 3RD | = | 3 points |
| 4TH | = | 2 points |
| 5TH | = | 1 points |

# CHAPTER FIVE

## PINK SNAPPER SURPRISE

"Winning, hell yes. I could tell you more about winning and losing, girlie, than most people would want to know about. I been fishing this thing for a long time and never came close to winning, and I ain't the only one. But let victory reign, I say."
Macky Duff
quoted in *History of the Tournament*

R ITA'S surprise was extraordinary. It came later in the evening.

First, Pike had the muskie photographed, and reweighed on the dockside scale to make sure the scale on the kid's boat was calibrated properly. It was. They were in 2nd place, but Pike doubted that they'd stay there. 729 pounds is whale-sized most places, but not on Ashendon. A tiger muskie of just over 1900 pounds, had been caught here several years ago by Ethyl Bierly, the burly, fiercely competitive red head. Pike suspected that Ethyl had stretched the rules a tiny bit, but there was no doubt that somebody on her boat had caught the giant muskie. Big ones do live here. Thousand pounders are fairly common. The Tournament winner was usually in that weight range. Pike told Richie not to get his hopes up that they would do much more than qualify in this round. It was true that nobody had taken a muskie in a fogbank before, so the kid got to relish that particular glory. Fishing stories of that crazy magnitude are hard to come by.

Richie posed for a few photographs to send to his mother, with the two security guys prominently placed in the background. Then Harry Dolan insisted on taking them all to dinner. He was leading this leg and there was no chance now that Tourbo could knock him out of 1st, not with Pike as his captain. Pike would never advise the kid to risk killing another fish by accident. Not this early in the Tournament. Hardluck Harry was in good spirits at dinner. So was Richie, who tried to replenish all of his burned up carbohydrates at one meal.

Toward the end of an excellent dinner, Rita announced to the gathered fishermen, including her father and mother at another table, that she had gotten permission from her advisory committee to do her doctoral thesis on *The Economic And Bio-Cultural Benefits Resulting To Distant Planetary Systems From Hosting the Star Tournament.* Everyone applauded lustily, since they were all half potted. Pike applauded, but he had known about the thesis for several days, and hoped this wasn't the surprise she had promised. After the conversation had swept back to fishing, Rita's laughing eyes met his and she leaned over to whisper in his ear.

"I'm willing to renegotiate our agreement, or take a time out," she whispered, touching his ear lobe with her lips. "I think you need a reward."

"Maybe we should discuss this in private," he suggested. "Rather soon." He meant immediately.

"You think somebody might overhear our whispering and tell us not to renegotiate?" She nudged his shoulder with the tip of her left breast.

"No, I guess not," Pike replied.

What a stupid year for his boat to be broken. Pike was still unsure about the kid's reaction to a full-blown affair between Rita and his captain. Simple human nature dictated that trouble was ahead, but so far everything was okay—maybe because of the no sex agreement.

Pike knew the kid liked Rita more than he let on. His eyes were always trailing her. A real dumb situation. On the other hand, Rita was no fool. She and Richie must have worked something out regarding that, after all they had been roommates.

Pike relished the feeling of his ego swelling. Rita, obviously, had a flaw in her operating system; but if she found him irresistible, why should he miss out on the fun? "Why don't we fly over to Galatin and I'll show you my cottage. We can have a little privacy for the rest of the week since we can't fish here anymore." As an afterthought, he smiled at Farouk's wife, Maggie, who seemed to be watching them.

"Galatin would be fun," Rita said, suddenly remembering something. "Isn't Galatin where you invented the Thruster?"

Pike nodded. It's nice to be remembered.

"Sure," she said, enthusiastically. "Let's go. I can get some extremely critical research done. Why didn't I think of that?"

*

The rules didn't allow them to visit the next planets on the schedule, so Galatin Bay seemed like the perfect place to teach the kid some ocean tactics and the basics of fly fishing in relative safety and comfort. Another reason for visiting Galatin was his workshop. A couple of ideas that he wanted to tinker with had been nudging him. One was an accelerator, the other was a tide clock that would revolutionize time keeping, if it worked. Having Rita along should make it into a perfect vacation week. Richie could stay on the boat with Lester or at a hotel, and the lovebirds would have the cottage alone.

*

R.R. had been so exhausted from fighting the muskie that he headed for his bunk immediately after telling the story fourteen times to fourteen different people. Strange how they had all wanted to hear every little detail in spite of his yawning. Once he hit the bunk, he was untroubled by the gentle swelling of the tide, and fell asleep instantly. Any unexplained sounds of love, didn't intrude into his fish dreams.

All night long Richie replayed the giant fish, hour after slogging hour, and woke up still aching, but exhilarated. It was rather a jolt to step out on deck and find the bright sunshine of Galatin Bay blinding him. He quickly slid back down the ladder to retrieve his dark glasses. On deck once more, he was relieved to find that the boat was indeed moored securely to Pike's wharf. Yes, there was Pike's house, with the dog on the front porch and the quaint little village scattered along the bay—just like it had been when he and Clive visited Galatin Bay looking for Pike. For a minute there, Richie had thought he was losing his mind. Pike hadn't mentioned coming to Galatin.

Perhaps you're wondering where all the sexual precocity that Rich Rodney grew up with (the nannies, ogling his mother's friends, etc.) went to? He wasn't displaying much of it at the Tournament. The answer is, it hadn't gone anywhere. He hadn't even submerged it in the interest of sportsmanship. Except for his darling Rita, who he was much too in love with to ogle every minute, there had been scarcely any females around for two weeks. What a blessing that was. His subconscious mind knew that he'd been given a break to get on with this business of being a man. And he was doing it, wasn't he? Heck, yes. He was showing all these gnarly salts that Tourbo blood had what it took to rise to the top like rich cream. He tripped over the end of a tie-down line and hurtled head first toward the railing, breaking his fall at the last split second with a Ken Pao Ri elbow stroke. The fall jarred his elbow substantially, but not his dignity. He jumped up, delighted that no one had seen him, and since his fall had knocked the gangway gate open, Richie decided that the gang plank leading to quay side was an omen to go exploring. Strange that Pike hadn't told him they were coming here; but hey, Pike was the captain. When you're traveling with a legend, one place was as good as another. Sometimes better.

After doing a few shoulder rolls to get his arm working again, Richie hurried back to his room to dress for exploring by donning his hip boots and cinching the straps up to his belt. He drank a glass of juice in the empty galley, then hopped neatly onto the quay. According to the guide book, three of the upcoming categories of fish required wading. This seemed like a good time to get used to wearing boots.

The deceptively innocent harbor water lapped quietly against the quayside. Maybe it would be a good idea to install a small historical marker somewhere on this dock, he thought. Nothing fancy, just a bronze plaque set in the cracked cement. Something like: *On this spot Clive McAndrews brought the young R.R. Tourbo to meet Pike Resnick.* That seemed appropriate. He would hire an artist to design it. Maybe a foot square. Or what the heck, two feet square with some pictures of tournament fish in bas relief. Darn good idea. Where do these astounding ideas come from? Simply amazing.

Several weather-beaten old geezer fishermen sat on the wharf mending their nets. They smiled up at him, so he smiled back, charitably. The old codgers had probably heard about his growing reputation. Pike probably told everybody.

"Nice morning," he said, stepping nimbly around the nets. No tangling feet for the 1st Place Fisherman. No thanks, not today. He felt positively ebullient.

"Real nice hip boots," cackled one of the sinewy old men.

"Those sure are some fine deck boots, sonny," another old fart grinned. His face creased in a thousand wrinkles. "I been looking for a pair like that myself, to keep my old knees dry. Where'd you get 'em?"

R.R. felt his face reddening. They were making fun of him, but so subtly that he couldn't figure out what to say back to complete the joke sequence. Of course it was a good idea to keep your feet and knees dry. The old coot probably had arthritic knees. R.R. just smiled and walked on past; but unfortunately, his attention had been distracted from his feet and the nets. His toe caught on a knotted corner and the darned net seemed to come alive.

A few minutes of inspired thrashing left Richie hopelessly snarled, like a bottle fly in a spider's web. A cacophony of hilarious cackling assaulted his ears as a crowd gathered to watch.

Pike hadn't said much after finding Rich Rodney trussed up on the quay. Obviously, the kid would pay for the nets, so Pike simply cut him free with a minimum of fuss. Richie was strangely quiet during the whole episode. Later on, he offered the excuse that he'd slipped and let it go at that.

"So I thought what we'd do this week is teach you the rudiments of fly fishing," Pike offered between bites of cold pasta salad. The three of them, Rita, the kid and he were having lunch on the porch. Pike's sheep dog, a huge Banta Terror, was carefully staked in the side yard on a short tether out of harm's way. Richie had very nearly choked the two hundred pound dog to death by tangling up in his leash while trying to pet him. The dog was now safely way out there in the shade of a lemon tree. Lester was somewhere in town doing Lester-type stuff. "Casting, roll casting, knot tying and reading the water," Pike said, listing the elements of fly fishing.

"Great," R.R. replied, enthusiastically. "We're on the same wavelength. That's why I was wearing my hip boots. Fly fishing looks so graceful—just like Ken Pao Ri."

"Have you got a fly rod?"

"Yes, sir. I bought a beauty. Clive took me to get it. Same place I ordered that one for you."

"Good," Pike said. "Let's go try it out."

Rita smiled, thinking she should bring along the first aid kit, but said nothing.

*

From the start, R.R. was a genius at flycasting. His eight foot hand-built, two weight Alcott rod was perfectly balanced to a hand-tooled single action reel filled with the double taper floating line that Red Alcott had recommended for phantom trout. The reason for using double taper being that soft casts were preferable, so as not to spook the cautious fish.

For the practice session, Pike had taken him to a long, flat pond at a country club golf course. Champion Fishermen and very rich kids are often allowed to practice fly casting wherever they want to. Pike chose the site partly because there were no monster fish in the pond to leap on R.R.'s hook and distract him from the lesson, but mainly because there was nothing to snag the back cast except the pin on Hole 12, twenty-six yards behind. So far the kid had snagged the pin every single time. Pike had demonstrated how to tie the surgeon's knot six times after the ultra-light tippet broke when Richie tried to jerk it free. R.R. was getting that knot down pretty well. Pike thought he might not have to demo it the next time. Rita was in stitches. She volunteered to run up on the green and replace the flag both times that the kid had jerked it out. It's not so easy to rip a pin out of the cup from the disadvantage of a low angle at twenty-six yards. The very thin tippet used for phantom trout is not exactly suitable for pin pulling.

"Come on, Rich, quit screwing around," Pike urged, genially. The kid was ossifying Pike's brain synapses. Eight times in a row. "You realize there's going to be trees in the way of the back cast when we get on a river. Make a shorter cast. The fly simply has to get in the water."

R.R. noticed that his ears were burning. Somebody was probably talking about him, somewhere.

"You've got a natural flair," Pike said. "I can tell. Just shorten up and get it in the water. Then I'll teach you to roll cast, which is why we're out here. Next time we'll leave Rita at home, if she makes you nervous."

"Why would Rita make me nervous?" Richie inquired. As instructed, he reeled ten yards of flyline back into the reel. Then he picked up the remaining line neat as you please, kept it aloft for one false cast and sent the tiny fly arching toward the pond water. "I thought you wanted me to make long casts. Everybody says you have to for phantoms trout."

"Yeah, that's for trout," Pike agreed. "This is golf course fishing where you use shorter casts because of all the overhanging pins. Okay, let's try a roll cast."

But before he had time to explain the maneuver, the pond water dimpled under the kid's dry fly, then with a swoosh and a belly flop, a three pound phantom trout pounced on the fly. Line zipped out of the reel. R.R. had no idea how to play a fish on the willowy rod, so he held on with two hands and let the fish rip. To compensate for his lack of skill, his feet slipped out from under him on the inch high bluegrass and he skidded artfully down the sandy bank on his ass. The water he landed in was only knee deep; but sitting down, it was ass deep.

"Hold him, kid...!" Pike yelled encouragement.

Rita hugged Pike around the waist. "Isn't he just incredible?" she simpered.

"Incredible," Pike agreed.

"What should I do...?!" R.R. bellowed.

"Just hold the rod. It's an ornamental pond, where can he run to? Look out he doesn't jump in your pocket and fillet himself on your knife."

"What kind is he? Boy, he sure is fighting!" The sweet little rod was bent in a high arch, because Richie had clamped one hand over the fleeing line.

"Let him take some line, boy!"

Richie let loose of the line and almost lost the rod in the resultant lurch that followed. "What kind of fish is it?"

"A phantom trout, what else. That's what you're fishing for, isn't it?"

"That's really strange," Rita marveled. "I thought phantoms could only live in fast flowing water. Somebody must have put some in this pond and they survived like alligators in sewers. Very strange."

"If you think that's strange," Pike said, dead-pan, "I snipped the hook off that fly, so Richie wouldn't catch himself or us while he was practicing. The fucking fish is holding it in his pouty little mouth and won't let go."

"Maybe it's caught in his gill or something," Rita suggested.

"Don't bet on it," Pike said.

Meanwhile the fishermen toiled and moiled on Ashendon A.R. raising muskies from the weed beds, keeping them or tossing them back, depending on how they felt about their fishing luck. Because of the keeper rule, muskies were a tough class. Different crews had various kinds of luck with the netting process. All that mucking around with cranes bounced many fish off before they could be properly weighed. Occasionally, somebody failed to hook another. The Baron, Farouk Bardona, found himself in that tricky position.

Earlier this morning he had lost a fifty pound fish that he wanted to weigh, so he'd be qualified, but not keep. The clumsy deck hand who misjudged the net was on his way to unemployment, and didn't even know it yet. Working a crane wasn't that difficult.

At any rate, the Baron was still plying the waters in search of a big fish. There was plenty of time, and just qualifying wouldn't do much good given his lousy showing in the preceding categories, not when he had his sights set on winning the Tournament.

It had filled his black heart with euphoria to see Resnick's boat irreparably damaged on the first day of the Tourney, leaving the field wide open for a real fisherman. Half of the other bozos didn't really give a shit about winning, they were in it for the sport. Farouk had never understood that kind of addle-brained thinking. He was dying to win the Tournament, why else pay the entry fee? His crew and his local guides were always top flight, costing a small fortune. To get the best, he spared no expense, cinching up the people he wanted long in advance, paying twice the going rate to get the best. Since he was so generous, it seemed fair to withhold the last payment if a guide failed to deliver; and naturally, if a deck hand fumbled a landing, he was looking for a job the next day. Winning was serious business, there was no room on his yacht for a fuck-up.

While everyone else referred to their craft as fishing boats, Farouk's was always a yacht. That was the name, para-yachts, why not call a thing by its name? He seldom fished from the Lady Slipper. That was his home. Was there a reason to discommode himself or his family in order to go fishing? He thought not. Two secretaries and an accountant lived permanently aboard the house yacht, and his computer system was up-graded whenever an upgrade was available. All this kept the Baron plugged into the intergalactic business deals that fueled his far flung empire and allowed him to root out misfits. Incompetence at any level of the empire was dealt with swiftly. Why put off firing a sluggard long enough to let him make another mistake? His fortune had not been built on bleeding heart policies. But he had never won the Tournament and that rankled. Grated his nerve endings. He was a much better fisherman than any of these assholes, and the biggest lucky asshole of them all, Resnick, was out of the water. Beautiful. No last minute runs of luck to ace Farouk out this year. But we should have landed that runty muskie. Christ, what if they suddenly stopped biting? His good categories were still ahead.

And Rita. That girl was determined to turn his hair pure white—she wasn't satisfied with grey streaks. Going off with Resnick and that lucky, brainless kid. Well, the kid was rich, so partly okay; but he wasn't doing a damned thing to increase his net worth, and that was creepy. Creepy and clumsy. Rita could get hurt at any second around him. How she survived three years at school with Mr. Clumsy was a miracle. What was a father to do, forbid her to socialize with a geek she'd lived with at that freaky liberal moron college? Tourbo's money might one day be useful. But probably not. As a father, Farouk was too soft where Rita was concerned, and he knew it. But what could he do? His little girl liked to have fun, and he couldn't deny her that. But why was that lucky jerk-off Tourbo hanging around with Resnick? Maybe old Resnick was inventing something else, and was wooing Tourbo to invest. The kid was shrewd, in spite of being brainless—had to be with a mother like that. What was that sleazy bastard Pike up to, besides trying to seduce Rita, just to get my goat. He was a disgusting, poverty stricken lecher. What could she ever see in him? Easy, Farouk old boy, don't get worked up. He tried to remember if he'd taken his blood pressure pill with breakfast, but couldn't recall. In fact, there was no memory of breakfast at all.

"Joseph...!" he called out to his black Creolite chef. "Fix me a breakfast special!"

"Yes, sir, Baron," the chef answered, sticking his head out the galley door. "Did you want that the same as the first one?"

"Exactly the same," Farouk replied, stifling a yawn.

"Right away, Baron. Will you eat in the galley or should I bring the folding table?"

"The table. I have to keep thrashing," he chuckled, baronially. How had that miserable, bumbling Chet messed up the net work on that perfect fifty pound fish? Didn't he know I always have a tough time with muskies? And it was rotten luck to draw shit-head Barrow for the judge on this leg. The fucker was unbribable.

* * *

# CHAPTER SIX

## DEEP WATER SCUT

"What is winning? Winning is one thing for a woman and
something else for a man. Unfortunately, no woman has ever
won the Tournament; but as far as we know, no man has ever
gotten pregnant. Kind of a trade off."

Jean Santos
quoted in *History of the Tournament*

ON Sunday morning, Pike and Rita were still at the Galatin Bay
cottage, getting to know each other. Richie had rented a room for
the week at the Galatin House Bed & Breakfast, after Rita made it clear
that he was not invited to stay at Pike's cottage. He could visit, after
calling first. The house and workshop were full of breakable inventions
and family heirlooms that Rita quickly became protective of. Rich accepted her visiting arrangements without a murmur, evidently used to
Rita setting the rules, or aware that his mere presence seemed to shatter
stainless steel lawn furniture. But all week they had eaten lunch and
dinner as a group, discussing strategy—and R.R. had even learned fly
casting after a fashion.

Leaving the golf course, Pike moved the lessons to a deserted beach
where trout wouldn't be a distraction. True, several flying fish had
zipped out of the nearby breakers to commit suicide by nabbing his
fly over the white sand, but Richie could make a pretty good cast after
twenty hours of practice.

*

Having endured eleven days of abstinence, the lovers were both very ready to be affectionate. The affection lasted all week and by Sunday a lot of tension had evaporated. Pike knew how to manage quite well on his home territory—a fact that Rita was delighted to have confirmed. On Richie's boat he was tentative with her, here he was fine. Even Pike recognized the difference after she commented on it several times. He even laughed about it. When you're the king of your own cottage and the dove you've fetched is feeding you wild grapes and doing other pleasantries, it's easy to laugh.

Pike had even managed to spend some hours on several new inventions while Rita was writing. Tinkering had been fun until about midweek, when it became apparent that the tide clock wouldn't work universally. Too much moon discrepancy. So he had put it away with the other breakable putterings to be looked at later, and started the drawings for a new leverage system that had just occurred to him.

Lester was back on the boat, sporting a purple shiner around his left eye, gained Pike had heard while defending R.R.'s reputation to a large drunk. Otherwise he was in good spirits. Lester enjoyed his shore time. A few good fights cleanse the poisons, he was fond of saying.

When Pike called to report his flight plan to Giedon, he found that the kid's muskie was locked pretty solidly in 4th place. Three luckless boats were still fishing, among them Farouk Bardona's. Pike chuckled to himself. Farouk always ate shit with muskies. He had probably missed half a dozen little ones and now his boat was in panic. The guide had no doubt been fired without his final paycheck. Farouk was a character all right. The guides and deck hands all laughed at him behind his back, but they couldn't afford not to sign on at double fee. But 4th Place was good. Very good. If it held up.

Late Sunday afternoon, the Comparative Humanity left Galatin Bay and after a brief visit to hyperspace splashed down in the deep water harbor on Giedon's main island. Most of the fishing boats were already berthed in the swanky marina, and since fishing couldn't start until midnight, the traditional non-stop party was blasting on the Yacht Club dock, which glowed greenly under a huge neon sign: Scut Capitol of the Universe.

Giedon was the most industrialized of all the worlds in the Tournament. Every year it looked more prosperous than the last. This was due to the Baron.

Except for some sea birds, the large islands were mostly barren when the Tournament first started coming. The Baron took a liking to the place, probably because he had a thing going with scut. He seemingly owned this leg. More fondness developed with each victory. Finally, he moved a large part of his manufacturing empire up to Giedon and the other planets of the Starfleck System. Except for para-yachts. He would have moved the para-yacht factory, too, but Thaddeus Golan wouldn't budge.

Why could the Baron catch scut when he had such a terrible time with muskies? Impossible to say. Although scut are true fish and not mammals, they are exceedingly like small whales. They eat nothing but plankton, and thus are almost impossible to entice to a lure or bait. Actually, Pike never understood where the sport was in scut fishing, and he voted against the category whenever the question was raised. True, they are delicious to eat, and none of the flesh went to waste, since it was canned for export, but that was hardly reason enough to hound and kill the lugubrious hogs. Farouk thought hooking up to a wallowing sea hog and being towed all over the ocean was the greatest of fun. Finally exhausted, the monster floats to the surface, rupturing its swim bladder in the process.

Well, screw it, the party was always swinging on Giedon. The Yacht Club was composed mainly of executives from Bardona Wingless, so putting on a yearly fete for the boss and his friends made good business sense. Having a photo snapped beside a smiling Farouk with his prize fish was considered a prime road to advancement. The Lady Slipper and Farouk's two fishing smacks still weren't at their traditional tie up beside the fake lighthouse. Pike was delighted. That meant the Baron was still slugging it out on Ashendon. Or maybe a pirate got him. Fat chance of that. All three yachts always traveled together. Between them they carried enough armament to stop an invasion armada.

Rita and Richie joined Pike on the bridge as he maneuvered along the marina channel past hundreds of fancy sailing sloops and power cutters. As always a big sailing regatta in honor of the Tournament would begin with a fireworks display the instant Bardona showed up. Since he was invariably late, the good toadies sailed up and down the channels all day flying their nautical flags and getting potched. It was an awesome display of asskissery.

"Welcome to Giedon, party planet of the stars," Pike said to the two kids.

"Gosh," R.R. said. "It's pretty crowded."

"Don't worry, all these good folks will be slaving away at the sweat shops tomorrow and the rest of the week to impress the boss. We'll have the ocean strictly to ourselves. Not even a rowboat will get in the way."

Rita smiled. "What Pike means," she said to R.R., "is that Daddy's factories are here. Most of these people work for him."

"Oh, that's right," Richie replied. He dimly remembered knowing that Giedon was where many of the Baron's factories were. So this was the same Giedon. There were so many planets, it was hard to keep them all straight.

"Nose to the grindstone is what Farouk likes best," Pike said, motoring the boat into its assigned slip.

Rita wrinkled her pretty nose. "These factories make a lot of really useful things," she said, in defense of her father.

"Truer words were never spoken," Pike agreed.

Richie smiled a big lop-sided grin. Rita had always had a hard time saying nice things about her father. Too bad the Baron didn't give her a little more to work with.

So it looked like the kid's 4th place muskie would hold up, giving him another two points for a total of twelve. With any kind of normal distribution of luck on the remaining planets, that might be enough to win the Oscar. Pike had once come in second on fourteen points, without winning any category.

Aah, but it was a teensy nerve-wracking. The kid was such a klutz that he might swamp the boat at any minute. Maybe he'd trip over the toilet bowl on one of his trips to the head, knock the sea caulks loose and not tell anybody until it was too late. Pike held a strategy conference with Lester, while Rita and Richie reconnoitered the Yacht Club party. Having agreed to keep an extra eye open, Pike and Lester went ashore to chat up the local fishermen about recent catches.

Around ten o'clock Pike found Rita and the kid sitting at a table with Dresden Carthy, Jean Santos and a few other fishermen. A bevy of celebrity hounds were buying champagne. The discussion centered around the complete ease of catching scut. The only trick being to catch a bigger one than the Baron's. Empty magnums of champagne were being constantly replaced with full ones by uniformed waiters.

When Pike sat down, Jean Santos was pretty much in her cups. "That awful Baron!" she slurred, theatrically. "Everybody knows he has a huge one penned up. Frogmen swim down and put his hook in it. There's no other explanation for him winning every year, but nobody can prove it." She simpered in Rita's direction.

Rita smiled back, somewhat amused. People were always attacking her father. He seemed to relish the notoriety.

"This year will be different" Jean yapped, sipping her champagne. "I plan to fish right off his bow all week long. My third mate happens to be Lanny Davits, the photographer from Sports Aloft." She glanced around the table expectantly. Several sycophants nodded knowledgeably. "Lanny's job will be to stay on deck with his camera and his sunscreen, and photograph anything at all that looks suspicious. This year we're going to catch the old fox!"

Snorts of laughter greeted her pronouncement. Even Dresden Carthy thought Jean's scheme was wonderful. He rocked with alcoholic mirth and applause. He must be trying to line himself up to screw Jean, Pike supposed. Trying that hard wasn't necessary, but Dresden apparently didn't want to risk rejection.

Jean Santos was a woman who liked sex almost any way it was presented. She reportedly screwed everybody on her boat. Part of her crew's shipping papers was an agreement not to make jealous scenes. She was not a one man woman. Pussy or purse was the way she described the arrangement, when she got drunk and loud. Jean never finished very high in the Tournament, since her crew was chosen more for good looks and dong size than fishing ability, but she seemed to enjoy herself afloat. An heiress can spend her money fishing, if she wants to.

After a few minutes of listening to drunken chit-chat, Pike said he was going back to the boat and advised Richie and Rita not to drink much. Scut were fished in deep water far from shore, where the wave conditions could turn ugly with storm or wind. A belly full of champagne could make life ungallant.

"Loosen up a little," Jean Santos demanded. "You've always so serious, Pike. How often do we get to a nice party like this? Young people like to have fun."

Pike smiled stiffly in reply and stood up to leave. Rita rose too and came around the table. "I'm worried about Daddy," she said. "Everybody else is already here."

"We can call Ashendon if you want," he said, strolling along the brightly lighted quay, nodding to people he knew. She slipped her arm around his waist. Their hip bones fit together nicely, without bumping. "He can fish for muskies until midnight, so I wouldn't start worrying until then."

"I know. I worry about him unless I'm with him, then I don't worry at all. Isn't that stupid? You don't like him very much, do you?"

"He hasn't given me much reason to."

"I know. That's really stupid, too. I know he admires you, but he's so controlling. I hate it when he's like that. I don't let him do it to me, and seriously, Pike, you shouldn't either."

"It's a little late for that."

"I mean on your new things."

"Oh, sure. My new fabulous inventions, like the tide clock," he said, with more of an edge of sarcasm than he had intended. The envisioned leverage system for encouraging big recalcitrant fish to come up and jump, thereby tiring themselves out, hadn't panned out particularly well either. He hadn't been able to solve the crux of the project, so it was still in limbo. And the reports he'd heard the last few hours weren't very encouraging about scut. There had been a bumper crop of plankton earlier in the year and scut were plentiful, but some shift in the warm water current where both scut and plankton flourish had caused no scut to be caught closer inshore than the Flat Bank for over a month—and the Flat Bank was a hundred miles out to sea. Joy of living. It was a very big ocean. He'd have to chart girds and hunt his butt off to find the current. Stupid ocean. Fish finders and temperature gauges were only allowed on the water. No fly-over scanning. Airborne technology existed, of course. Commercial fishermen used it; but for Tournament fishing it was considered unsporting. Oh, well, somebody would find the current, then they could all start fishing. The Baron, of course, would decoy for a few days, then putter out to his fish cage where his frogman would make the hook up. Or something like that.

Speaking of the devil! Rita squealed delightedly as the Lady Slipper popped into view over the marina, followed closely by Farouk's two fishing yachts. The boats splashed down near their empty moorings, and deck hands scurried to hoist a day-glo orange Big Fish flag. The flag was normally used to alert judges and dock hands that a big fish was coming in. They were also good for a captain's ego. Since Bardona obviously hadn't caught a scut yet, it could only mean that Farouk had caught a prize tiger and wanted to brag about it here. Shit, Pike thought.

A loudspeaker on the Lady Slipper coughed to life. Bardona's grating voice blasted the yacht club and surrounding counties. "Hey, Resnick...!" the augmented voice gloated. "Read 'em and weep! You and the klutz just got dropped to 5th place! The plot thickens!"

"Shit," Pike said, aloud. A murmur started among the crowd, and turned to scattered applause as the toadies realized who was speaking and what the bantering words meant. Within seconds the evening was rent by a roar of approval. A skyrocket burst over the fake lighthouse. The fireworks show had begun. The beloved Baron had arrived victorious and the party could begin. Pike left Rita to greet her father and mother without him, and went aboard The Comparative Humanity to compare notes with Lester and start working on the scut finding charts.

*

At 6:00 AM, Pike and Lester along with Curtis Plotkin, the judge for this leg, were in the galley, breakfasting on tea and dry toast. Old time sailors have a healthy regard for their stomachs when unknown sea conditions are in the offing. Inshore fishing, where a land mass is constantly on the horizon, has nothing to do with deep water scut. Last night, Pike and Lester had decided on a scouting plan for the day. Since there was nothing to discuss now, they ate in silence. Both were aware that neither Rita nor the kid were aboard and hadn't been last night.

Due to the Baron's big muskie, Richie had lost a point, and now had only eleven, which probably wouldn't be enough to win. Hardluck Harry already had ten. Well, maybe this would be Harry's year. He was certainly due. A good man can't be held down forever.

The other boats were puttering out of the marina trying to be deceptive about where they were going. The kid should be ready to fish, too, but he wasn't. Not a whole lot to discuss about that either, so the crew munched toast in silence. Richie was supposed to be a fisherman. Pike wasn't about to go chasing around Giedon looking for him. Anyway, he had spotted the bodyguards last night, staying unobtrusively out of the way, but on duty nevertheless. It was a good bet that the kid wasn't kidnapped. More probably Jean and Carthy had gotten him plastered and he was sleeping it off in his hotel room. So...? So the kid was an adult. If he didn't want to fish, there was no law requiring it. Rita was also an adult. Not a particularly courteous one it seemed, when it came to informing her bunk mate as to a change in sleeping arrangements. But hey, Pike wasn't in the mood to chase her either. She was with Richie or on the Lady Slipper or somewhere else.

After breakfast was finished, Lester went about his business of re-lubricating the big reels. Pike gave Plotkin a tentative day off, advising him to stay aboard and be available until noon, in case the boss showed, then he crawled into the engine room for some routine maintenance, which didn't need to be done since the boat was brand new. He felt like a chump, a feeling he detested, but one that kept showing up year after year—part of the Resnick emotional repertory.

About 8:30, Rich Rodney came waltzing down the dock, grinning ear to ear. His bodyguards stopped at the end of the quay and stood there with their thumbs up their asses.

"Morning!" R.R. beamed. "Well, I'm all chowed down and ready to go." The grin abated somewhat as he noticed that all the other boats were gone. "Where is everybody?" he asked, hopping lightly through the open gangway. His ankle twisted slightly when he landed, but he shook it off.

"Oh, they went to test their engines, I guess," Pike said, employing high irony. He could feel the heat rising under his tan shirt collar, but absolutely vowed he wouldn't let the kid's stupidity get to him. It was R.R.'s problem, not his. Pike had thought about telling him last night, but decided that the best way to cure the kid's gullibility was to let him get burned over and over. Pike couldn't hold his hand through all of life's difficulties. Richie was either going to be a fisherman or he wasn't.

"I guess we should test ours too, huh?" Richie suggested, cheerfully.

"Gosh, I feel like fishing. Too bad scut never bite until late afternoon." He stroked a deep sea reel affectionately. "Well, should we fire her up?"

"Lester and I already tested her. She's fine." He wished he had a 2x4 to brain the goofball with. Gentle sarcasm never seemed to work. Maybe a more direct method would. "Out of curiosity, which one of your new drinking buddies let you in on the habits of scut?"

"Oh, everybody knows about that," he said, airily. "That's why they like to come to Giedon. It's a change of pace."

"Kind of like with howlers," Pike replied, dryly.

"I never thought of that, but it is. Say, you guys weren't waiting on me to have breakfast, were you?" Pike nodded his head in the negative. "Oh, good, because I just had a mammoth breakfast on the Lady Slipper. Do you suppose the Baron eats like that every day? Unbelievable. They just kept bringing stuff. Pancakes, bacon and eggs, sausage, fruit compote, fresh biscuits and gravy. It must cost him a fortune to feed all that crew."

"The Baron was there?" Pike asked, knowing Farouk had gone to sea hours ago.

"No, actually, just Rita and her mom and the secretarial staff. He had to see about some trouble at the factory. I guess it's lucky for him scut are so easy to catch. He doesn't have much time for fishing while he's here."

"That's where Rita is, on the Lady Slipper?"

"Yeah, she's going shopping with her mother today. Kind of an obligatory shopping spree, they're part owner of all the shops. I guess she'll be here before we go out, but maybe she won't."

"Let me suggest something gently to you, Richie. You're so full of shit, you're eyeballs are floating."

That knocked the idiot's grin askew.

And Pike went on. "All your great new friends and advisors are fucking with you because you're ahead of them, and even more so because you're a tenderfoot. Everything you did since you went ashore last night was wrong. And believe me, they're all laughing at the good one they pulled."

"Yeah...?"

"Yes. Tournament fishermen are kind of shitty about having their fun with greenhorns."

"Yeah, like what for instance?"

"I could write a book. You're a perfect target, apparently."

"Like what...?" R.R. was getting a little hot. He didn't know what this was about, but he could tell that Pike was angry. Maybe he was mad about the Baron inviting him and Rita to spend the night, and not asking Pike. Well, that was too darned bad. Old man Pike wasn't around. He'd already turned in. "Come on, tell me how full of shit I am?" he demanded.

Pike leaned on the smooth gunwale and began his list. "First of all Dres Carthy and Jean the Wonder Girl got you sloshed on champagne, so you'd be hung over and sick today. Then they filled your head full of bull about how easy scut are to catch. Right?"

"I drank very little champagne. I don't like it."

"But you now think scut are a snap to catch, right?"

"Everyone says so. It must be true, a conspiracy can't be that big."

"It's true, all right. After you hook them, they're easy to catch. But hooking them is almost impossible. Get it!" Pike exploded. "You were had, and then lulled to sleep by half truths. They don't want you to be sharp. And now you've missed a whole day of fishing, which you'll probably need since the scut are very scarce this year. But nobody mentioned that, I'll bet. Did they...?"

R.R. started to look a little unsure of himself. "Scarce? Isn't this the scut capitol of the Universe?"

"Yes and no. It is the *only* place that scut live, but not this week. And not even this month. The currents changed and the scut are out to sea. Which is where all your competitors are. Looking for the vanished scut!"

"Oh." Richie glanced around the marina again. Sure enough, the fishing boats were gone. That they were fishing seemed a far better explanation than testing their engines. After all, they *were* here to fish. "Well, let's go then," he said, rubbing his hands together. "We've only lost a few hours."

"Another part of the joke. The good Farouk stuffed your belly with greasy food. If I put you on those big seas, you'll be sick as a dog and unable to fish. I can't fish for you, so today is out. Maybe we can fly over and see what's going on."

"I insist we go," R.R. chirped. "I will instruct my mind not to be sick. I haven't been sick in weeks."

"Great. You make up your mind, and I'll lay bets. There's more than one way to get rich around here. Hey, Lester! You want to bet me the kid won't get sick with his belly loaded down with pancakes?"

Lester limped out of the galley. "Hi, Rich," he said. "What's this bet?"

"Nah," Pike shrugged. "I couldn't give you long enough odds. Go back to what you were doing."

"Making hard biscuits for the week?"

"Fine."

Lester didn't question Pike, who apparently needed him for a moment and now didn't need him. He went back to the galley.

Richie appeared deep in troubled thought. "I can't believe Rita would let me do something that was dangerous to winning. She wants us to win."

"Well, giving her the benefit of the doubt, let's say her father fooled her, too. Rita, whatever she might be, is not a fisherman. If she wanted to, she could have a boat of her own; but obviously, she isn't interested in that. This time of year the Tournament is her home, because of a foible of her father's. She might even have a tendency to believe what her father says."

"I see," Rodney said.

"I sincerely doubt if you do," replied Pike. "I've got you sized up as a fairly nice kid who likes to live on the positive side of things. However, your good buddy, Baron Bardona, is a heartless prick, who would do anything to win this show. Tricking his daughter into tricking you is completely within his range of prickdom. And lest you forget, he didn't want you in the Tournament from the first."

"He apologized for that last night," R.R. murmured.

"Swell," Pike said. "And you shook his slimy hand."

Rich nodded.

"I guess that pretty well covers it. For future reference, my friends on this cruise are Mordachi Skinner and old Ira Fairborne. I'm not as chummy with Harry Dolan, but he's an honest man, and won't win by knavery. If you don't love getting reamed, confide your dockside chats to those three. And to be on the safe side, check what they, or anybody else, tells you with me or Lester."

Richie nodded again, feeling chastened. The Baron had warned him not to trust those three, specifically. This manhood stuff had a lot of angles. "Can't we try it, at least?" he implored. "I feel fine. If it turns out I'm not up to it, we can come back, can't we?"

"Sure, kid. That's the spirit. No hooks in the water, no fish. Right?

"Right."

Richie was never so sick in his entire life. Dying would have been pleasurable compared to dying this way. He had held on as long as he could, but the waves kept coming like bilious sick green mountains. Finally, he unstrapped himself from the chair and flopped onto the deck with his head next to a cleat hole in the gunwale and let fly. Lester tied a life line around his ankle.

After what seemed like a lifetime, Pike relented and hauled him into the galley, then flew back to the marina. The whole experience had lasted slightly more than an hour. Pike had made one mark on his carefully worked out grid.

Back on solid ground, sitting at a table under an awning at the yacht club, R.R. was fine. The bodyguards had been surprised to see him, but they now stood watchfully and not very inconspicuously in the shade of the clubhouse ten yards away.

"Don't let this sour you on fishing," Pike warned, ordering a shore-side breakfast for himself. "Be in the galley before dawn tomorrow and Lester will make sure you're a happy fisherman."

"I will," R.R. promised. "I think I'll go find Rita and her mother and do some shopping instead of watching you eat, if that's all right."

"Good plan. Buy something nice for Lester, since he cleaned up after you."

R.R. nodded miserably and tottered away, not even bothering to trip over his feet.

*

By that night, things were back to normal. Rita had resumed sleeping in Pike's bed, saying that for the time being she was feeling amorous. She then insisted on a complete description of how much he had missed her last night.

And on Wednesday the warm current was discovered by Ira Fairborne and Mordachi Skinner searching in tandem, 175 miles NNW of the marina. How it had shifted way out there was anybody's guess, but there it was and so were the scut. Not that Ira and Mordachi had a notion of telling anyone where the current was. On Wednesday evening, when they landed in the marina each with big scut hausered to his aft deck, they took the precaution of flying in from the wrong direction. Breasting up to the yacht club bar with a cooked up story about where the current was, they had a great time adding elaborate details to the lie. In fact, they had no thought of returning to the current the rest of the week, unless someone else found it and caught a bigger scut. But technology foiled them.

Everybody had been fishing sections, drawing detailed charts and keeping a close eye on the other boats with long range radar. Giedon had millions of hectares of open water, but the radar had been developed to pin point boats in trouble, and it also pinpointed boats in fat city as easily. So on Thursday, fishing had returned to normal. But R.R.s luck hadn't.

Pike explained the technique patiently. Find the plankton concentration, chart the fish's direction on the fish finder and drift the hook into his mouth as he seines up the plankton. Fine. Richie understood everything, but he couldn't do it. He said it was alien to fishing. It wigged out his fish catching apparatus. Wigged out? So they tried all day Thursday and into the night, and while everyone else was flying fresh catch flags, they weren't. Pike fumed. The perfect end to a per-fect tournament. Shut out in the easiest category of all. And scut were plentiful in the current. There was hardly a time all day that one or two weren't on the Loran screen.

Again on Friday, Pike maneuvered the boat perfectly over forty or fifty fish. After thirty misses, he sent Rita down to the fishing deck to distract the kid. Maybe if his brain was disengaged from scut, he could hook one. But he didn't.

By Saturday, Richie had completely lost faith in his ability. He laughed condescendingly at himself every time a drift failed. Pike was beside himself. How could the kid's luck get fucked up for no reason? He was still a beginner, wasn't he? Shouldn't beginner's luck still apply? Just one scut! What was so impossible about that? Not even a big one. Any size. Where was the clumsy shithead of yore? Even Curtis Plotkin took a turn at coaching him. Why not? If Richie aced himself out of the tourney, one judge would be out of a job.

Sunday dawned stormy and very windy. Small craft warnings were up; but if they didn't fish, they'd be going back home broke. Pike insist-ed, however, that Rita stay ashore for safety. The stormy seas would be very hairy today. He relayed the news to her, while she was still snug-gled in the warm bunk. He had to admit that sleeping with her already felt normal—even permanent. She always smelled so damned good, and she never twisted up the covers or pushed him to the edge of the bed.

"You think I'm unlucky, don't you?!" she murmured, stretching la-zily.

Warning flags came out. "I never said that," he said

"You didn't have to. You've been acting like it all week It's bullshit! Women are no more unlucky than eating bananas."

Pike blanched. Eating bananas on board a fishing boat, or even having them, is thought by most skippers to be unlucky beyond words. How that superstition came into being nobody knows, but it's a major no-no. "Have you been eating bananas?" he asked.

"No, I have not! Do you think I'm stupid?"

"Has Richie?"

"How would I know? Why don't you ask him?" She grabbed her clothes and stomped out of their room. Crossing the tight hallway, she slammed into Richie's suite. The door banged closed and Pike heard the deadbolt snick into place. "I'm not getting off the boat, so just take your bad luck and shove it!" she shouted through the teak door.

Pike sucked at his front teeth and pulled his foul weather gear out of the gear closet. Maybe Richie ought to wear his hip boots. That might get his luck going.

"Hey…!!" Rita yelled through the door. "There's bananas in here!"

She opened the door and stepped out holding a hand of blackening bananas.

Pike stared at the overripe fruit, shaking his head in disbelief.

"They were sitting on the top shelf of his closet," Rita laughed. "God knows how long they've been there."

"Since last Sunday while you were shopping," Pike said, grimly. He was glad the bananas had been found, but it was still a lousy day for fishing. And he'd always believed that bananas were just an old wife's tale.

But when Richie came aboard, he questioned him about the rotting fruit. Abashed, he admitted they were a spur of the moment gift from Dresden Carthy. Dresden said he always kept bananas in his room for emergency snacks, since they're so rich in potassium. Potassium gives you stamina. It had seemed like a good idea to R.R. That way he wouldn't have to bother Lester for a snack every time he got hungry.

So the Comparative Humanity steamed out of the marina for a day of scut fishing in hell. But before leaving, Pike steered close by Carthy's boat. Dresden waved gaily at them. He would not be going out today—nobody would who had a fish. Pike watched with satisfaction as Lester heaved the rotting mess right at Dres, who ducked. Bananas splattered against the sparkling clean galley wall.

"Have some bananas!" Lester yelled in outrage.

Carthy stood up, laughing good-naturedly. "Happy fishing," he called back.

Nobody on the Comparative Humanity believed that bananas could be bad luck. Really, it was preposterous. How could a fruit, part of nature's bounty, be bad luck unless somehow a person choked on it? But by eight AM, under impossible sea conditions, R.R. had managed to hook a good-sized scut, even though none had shown up on the fish finder. A strange kid, Pike thought for the thousandth time.

On his own, Richie had decided to cast out to get a feel for the new reel he had purchased last night. And the scut had hit the wiggly lure he had tied on the line, apparently charging full blast from somewhere out of range of the finder. The force of the hit pulled R.R. half overboard; but Lester had been standing right there admiring the new reel. Lester grabbed the safety line that the kid wore against the treacherous weather, and got him to put the reel in free spool. In a few minutes all was calm except the sea. They were being towed over the white caps by the fish. The line wasn't as heavy as Pike would have liked, but then the scut wasn't gigantic. Three hours of fighting the sea and the fish, put the scut aboard, and they qualified to keep fishing. It was kind of a mixed blessing, but Pike accepted his fate and got off an EJmail to Dec Madrigal, confirming that they still wanted him to guide them through the Segumi Swamps, if they got that far.

*  *  *

# LEADERS

| | DELILAH | TORGA HOWLER | TIGER MUSKY | D.W. SCUT | PHANTOM TROUT | LAR BARRACUDA | GLANS SALMON | RAZORFIN | SWAMPFISH | MOON HALIBUT | TOTAL | |
|---|---|---|---|---|---|---|---|---|---|---|---|---|
| Farouk Bardona | | | 2 | 5 | | | | | | | 4TH | 7 |
| Ethyl Bierly | 2 | | | | | | | | | | | 2 |
| Angmar Blirt | | | | | | | | | | | | |
| Bill Bolen | | | 3 | | | | | | | | | 3 |
| Dresden Carthy | 4 | | | | | | | | | | 5TH | 4 |
| JB Dillingham | | OUT | | | | | | | | | | |
| Harry Dolan | 3 | 2 | | 5 | | | | | | | 2ND | 10 |
| Macky Duff | | | | | | | | | | | | |
| Ira Fairborne | | | 4 | | 3 | | | | | | 4TH | 7 |
| Buddy Jay | | | | | | | | | | | | |
| Sandy Kind | | | | | | | | | | | | |
| Hank Knofsinger | | | | | 2 | | | | | | | 2 |
| Peter Marcuso | | | | | | | | | | | | |
| Trini Morales | | | | | | | | | | | | |
| Pike Resnick | | OUT | | | | | | | | | | |
| Erwin Sandor | | 3 | | | | | | | | | | 3 |
| Jean Santos | | 1 | | | | | | | | | | 1 |
| Mordachi Skinner | | | | 4 | 4 | | | | | | 3RD | 8 |
| Tyrone Stickle | | | | | 1 | | | | | | | 1 |
| Chip Takahachi | | | | | | | | | | | | |
| RR Tourbo | 5 | 5 | 1 | | | | | | | | 1ST | 11 |
| Mike Tucker | 1 | | | | | | | | | | | 1 |
| Nacho Tutupo | | | | | | | | | | | | |
| Ed Wood | | | | | | | | | | | | |
| Big John Zales | | | | | | | | | | | | |

| 1ST | = | 5 points |
|---|---|---|
| 2ND | = | 4 points |
| 3RD | = | 3 points |
| 4TH | = | 2 points |
| 5TH | = | 1 points |

# CHAPTER SEVEN

## PHANTOM TROUT

"What *is* winning…? Well, look around you. Everyone here is a winner—big time. If you've got that much dough to spend on fishing, you're doing something right.
Alaska Bill Bolen
quoted in *History of the Tournament*

THERE are many paradise worlds in the Universe. Streamside is one of them. The mountains are majestic and temperate. The skies are blue and dotted with fleecy clouds. And the streams are wild and swift flowing. Ten park rangers live year round on the planet—the only permanent human residents. No native population ever developed. Tourism is carefully monitored.

Streamside is classified as a wild planet by the Blith Nadi Planetary Society. The Tournament pays the entire yearly cost of the rangers, even supplies them with helicopters, in exchange for exclusive fishing rights and total use of the planet for one week every summer. Non-fishing tourists and photographers are semi-free to roam the wilderness for the rest of the year, funneling their cash into the rangers' and Blith Nadi's pockets. Everybody is happy, and the phantom trout, which are the main attraction, don't take much of a beating.

Phantoms are so wary, even in this practically virgin territory, that catching one requires the ultimate in fishing skill. Their tiny mouths match the plentiful hatch of minuscule midges and mosquitoes, and the almost invisible black femto gnats. An imitation of the gnat is tied on an .000 hook, and even that is too large. The usual tippet is eight ounce breaking strength, as phantoms spook at the shadow of stronger leaders. No fish under two pounds may be kept, so many keepers break off. Then too, the streams being wild and full of snags presents a further hazard to the ultra light leaders. All the deeper pools are shaded by ancient deciduous arboretums which leap out after hooks. The Tournament fall-off rate at Streamside is alarming some years, even though a quiet fisherman might see dozens of lunker phantoms splashing in the pools, chasing the nearly invisible insects.

Pike loved the wild gorges with their fast flowing brooks—it was exquisite to spend time in such unspoiled nature. This year, to be honest, it was a relief to get Richie situated on dry land for a week. The hazards to arms and legs were certainly there in spades, but at least, he probably wouldn't drown. Well, if he did drown, he'd have to work at it. Phantoms tended toward shallow water.

The kid was back to his jolly self again, tripping over guy ropes in the tent city where everybody was camped for the week, and generally making a nuisance of himself. It was a far cry from a public campgrounds, of course. Most people hired outfitters to set up their bivouac, complete with a gourmet chef—but still, a hundred yards from the campsite you were in wilderness, and the park rangers made sure it stayed that way. No trails were cleared, no chopping of firewood to leave chips around. If an ambitious cook could lug a deadfall branch into camp, fine. Otherwise, fuel for cooking was flown in.

*

The stream Richie had drawn for the first day was absolutely gorgeous—bubbling lyrically through a leafy summertime canyon. Pike said it was a good draw. Little blue and green birds were tweeting happily. As long as the birds kept tweeting, Richie knew he was moving quietly enough. They were like a noise barometer. One reason he could be so quiet was that the chest waders he'd had custom made on Giedon fit perfectly, unlike his hip boots. No binding when he walked. Sticky rubber soles for non-slip traction in the stream bed. He felt confident about his ability to walk, and also to roll cast under the trees. He'd been practicing on Giedon every night in a rented indoor swimming pool. And just to make sure that he was in a quiet frame of mind, he had jumped out of bed at 3:00 AM to sit cross-legged for a deep mantra meditation that he'd been reminded of in the Ken Pao Ri quarterly magazine. On the long hike to the stream, he kept saying the mantra over and over inside his head. When it was finally time to tie on a fly and step down to the water, he was extremely quiet, blissed out almost. The birds tweeted riotously, knocking themselves out.

Using slow motion hand signs, Pike indicated that he wanted the first cast to float past a submerged log at the edge of a riffle thirty yards away. An easy cast.

Richie crept to the water's edge and felt the cold brook water gurgling over his boots. What an idyllic spot, he thought, smiling. He adjusted the collar of his new green-checked flannel shirt which he'd worn for the occasion. Rita was filming the whole thing with a mini-cam. She thought a film would augment her thesis. Rita was so gifted at woodcraft, Richie thought proudly. Even glued to the eye-piece of the recorder, she moved through the woods like a naiad, silence in motion. He felt so klutzy near her, but he must be doing all right. The birds were still tweeting gaily, like a bird opera. Baritones, tenors and sopranos.

Taking a second cautious step into the stream, and feeling very confident, he cleared his arm for casting. The tailored fishing shirt flowed perfectly across his shoulder with no trace of tightness. The rubber sole of his boot grabbed a submerged rock like it was a sidewalk. No problem. If there was such a thing as paradise, this spot must be close to it. He pulled his forearm back to make a short false cast, and the solid rock under his foot tilted. Both boot feet slipped out from under him. Down he went with a splash. Off to the races.

Yelping, he saw Rita's laughing face turn to alarm as he zipped past. The water was so fast that he couldn't regain his footing. There was Pike's face, yelling something, but the white water roared around his ears and he couldn't hear what the words were. Then it was down the river in a dizzying ride. The strong current owned him, dunking him under until his lungs were about to burst, then bouncing him against a rock and shooting him to the surface. The stupid water wasn't even particularly deep, that was the dumb part, just incredibly powerful and it wouldn't let him get his footing because the wader legs had filled with air, and his feet were floating. Richie couldn't force them down to get a purchase on the stream bed. Then suddenly the stream deepened.

Seeing that the kid was in serious trouble, Pike sent Gil Tanner, their judge for phantom trout, rushing back to camp for a rescue helicopter. Even if Richie floated all the way to Lake Gloria, they would find him. Pike and Rita scrambled along the tangled bank, watching Richie disappear downstream.

R.R. floated along at a manic pace in the deep channel, twenty miles an hour or faster. His waders were belted around the waist. The guy he'd bought them from said this would keep him dry, even if it was raining. Richie hadn't believed him, remembering the time his hip boots had gurgled full after that slip at the golf course; but by golly, the guy was right. The belt worked. Air trapped inside the legs was acting like a pair of reverse water wings. Which might have been fine, except that his head was constantly being forced under the surface, making it difficult to breathe. He had to struggle to catch a breath.

Cripes, he couldn't get the waders off. Forget it. He'd just have to float along until he could grab a snag or something, so he could force his feet down. Richie began to look around with that in mind, and suddenly the bottom dropped out and he was plunging through space.

Freefall. Just him and tons of green/white water, falling. He screamed feebly. Well, it was frightening. He'd never been slung over a waterfall before. What an experience! Nothing to hold on to, not even water. Just falling, faster and faster. Somehow his boots, being heavier, responded to gravity and he hit the deep catch pool at the bottom of the falls feet first, sparing him the ignominy of a ruptured skull or worse.

After an eternity underwater watching some lunker phantom trout, who did nothing whatever to help him, he broke the surface gasping, with no feeling in his legs. Then the raging current had him again. This time there were big rocks to dodge, boulders that had evidently been pushed over the falls like he had. After the first hundred boulders, the joy of trying to grab one as he swept past became a chump's game, and he refused to play. His hands were too numb anyway. He simply tried to avoid the rocks, kicking off if a collision was inevitable.

Hours later, well, it couldn't have been hours, his rational mind insisted, he was swept into a quiet estuary where he was able to grab a tree root and pull himself halfway out of the water. The current still jerked strongly at his legs, and his arms lacked the strength to haul his body on up the bank. In despair, he hooked one arm around the root and wiggled the other around a stiff clump of wild grass. He lay there, exhausted, as the river yanked at his floating rubber-soled waders, wanting him back.

The birds resumed their tweeting. If they stopped, it would probably mean that Pike and Rita were on their way. Pike and Rita. Richie had had plenty of time lately to think out all the angles of that conjunction. Regarding them as a couple didn't work right, nor a coupling; so he usually thought of them as a conjunction. More like a natural phenomenon. The girl he loved had chosen to sleep with another man, thumbing her nose at convention and all the Tournament fishermen who were like uncles to her, and at her bastard of a father. And at Richie, too—her one true lover. She had to realize that he loved her, didn't she? Of course, she did. Because of that fact, she had taken the trouble to explain to R.R. exactly what she was doing before she did it. So that he wouldn't be upset. Research for her thesis. Fine. The thesis was important to her, although Lord knew she didn't need a doctorate to make her way in the galaxy. But she thought she did. Fine. But didn't she realize that it hurt him, her one true lover? Of course, she did. That was one of the things he loved about her—the ability to cut through the bull crap and get right to the heart of the matter. No emotionality for her. And, of course, she never gave him the opening he needed to tell her about his deep and unrelenting love. How could an otherwise perceptive person fail to make a small doorway for the most important thing in her life? What a mystery love was.

But this sleeping with Pike Resnick, right under his nose, that was one step too far, wasn't it? One step more than a sensitive human could bear, wasn't it? Truthfully, it was. Did she think he was made of thermo-plastic? Well, he wasn't. But he had to get farther up this bank. The river kept sucking at him. If his grip slipped it would pull him back in. Sadly, he didn't have the strength to gain an inch. He was stuck between a heavenly river bank and wet hell.

On the other hand, the conjunction of Pike and Rita was a good test of his love. Another good test. Sometimes he felt like a gnarly old tree trunk from all the good tests she'd given him. And just to think that he hadn't known her at all until three years ago when his mother had insisted he move into a co-ed dorm, so she could meet his roommates. What an experience meeting Rita had been. The first instant he saw his dark-haired beauty, he fell madly in love, and hadn't come up for air since. Of course, he *had* tripped over something to ruin that first moment. His suitcase. He had fallen over his suitcase. A trivial accident. Gashed his head open on an ouija board gizmo that was lying on the rug. The doctor had stopped the blood loss with hardly any effort. Three or four stitches. Ten at most. But still, since that incredible bit of ill luck, Rita had thought of him as a stumble bum. Just like a woman to get the wrong impression right off the bat like that.

And of course, Rita and Pike's so called relationship was mostly his fault, too. He had pestered her into restarting her long time acquaintance with Pike, so he could get to know the great man, too. It was hardly her fault that she was attracted. What woman wouldn't be? So really he had no right to complain. Correct. No right at all. And they weren't actually "sleeping" together. I mean, hell's bells, he himself had slept in the same bedroom with her every night for over two years. Shared the same bathroom and shower. And while they had never actually slept in the same bed, or "slept" together, he for one didn't consider their relationship to be brotherly and sisterly. Rita was an outrageously avant-garde girl. She didn't take kindly to being told what to do, Richie knew that much. If she wanted to sleep in the same bed with Pike, she would. If she was short-sighted about sensing his own deep, true, pure feelings; well, he could overlook that. Everybody has a weak spot. Short-sightedness was Rita's. He was certainly not going to demand that she stop work on the thesis. No, he would show true chivalry and wait until she had the doctorate before he professed the full extent of his love.

In his exhausted but blissful state, he was unable to restrain the hot tears of self pity. Watching the tears fall onto the long bladed grass under his nose, he sobbed out his misery. Poor Rich Rodney, poor little rich boy with nobody to truly understand or love him. What a miscarriage of justice. So noble, so full of selfless devotion, so battered by love and the river of life. He fell asleep, hoping his scalding tears would drown the little bugs in the grass that kept crawling onto his lips and up his nose, and into his ears. Poor little Rodney. He couldn't even let go of his handholds to protect himself from bugs. Nobody cared about him.

Pike and Rita found the twisted body laying half in, half out of the water. Running through the underbrush along the trout stream had left them both scratched and sweaty. Seeing the small broken body was a crude shock. What a stupid, senseless tragedy, Pike thought. The stream was only four feet deep at its deepest.

"Oh, my God!" Rita cried, hurdling past Pike and sliding down the stream bank. "Richie!! Richie! Say something!" She pounded his back.

R.R. opened his swollen eyes and stared at his beautiful angel of mercy. "You found me," he said. "I knew you would."

"He's alive!" Rita thrilled. "Thank God. We were so worried about you."

"Pull me out, would you. I think my legs are broken."

"Grit your teeth," said Pike. He took the kid's arms and gingerly pulled him up the bank. Richie didn't scream in pain, he just lay on the bank tiredly. "You took quite a trip there, Rich. Two, maybe three miles. Never could regain your footing, huh? Can you move your legs?"

"It feels like it's still pulling at me," R.R. said, languidly.

Rita tore a section of her blouse hem. Wetting it in the river, she started cleaning Richie's face.

If the kid's legs were broken, it was bye-bye for the Tournament, Pike speculated. Of course, he was glad to find Richie alive, but since he *was* alive, reality loomed. Oddly enough there was a tangle of fly line wrapped around the waders below the knee. And something was jerking on the line where it disappeared into the relatively quiet pool. "I'll be damned," he said, kneeling carefully so as not to touch the flyline. "How bad is he hurt?" he asked Rita.

"His head seems all right, I think. What about his legs? He said they were broken."

R.R. lay quietly listening to them talking about him. He loved it. He also loved the concerned expression on both of their faces—especially Rita's. At last, she was showing her feelings.

"I thought his legs were really screwed up when we first saw him,"

Pike said, "but now I don't. He's got a fish on. See, the line is tangled around his legs."

"Oh, for God's sake! Is that all you ever think about?"

"Well, he's in the Tournament," Pike responded, as if that explained everything. "I can't play it for him, but if he brings it in to shore, I can net it."

"You don't have a net."

Sheepishly, Pike pulled a folding net from a deep pocket of his fishing vest.

"This is too much," Rita said, peevishly. "He's half dead!"

"Hey, kid, are you up to doing a little fishing? I think you've got one on."

"Huh?" R.R. queried, raising his head.

"From the strain on the line, it looks like a good one. Don't rush yourself, but see if you can sit up. You might as well bring him in, then you'll be qualified, and you can take a rest for a few days. Get a cast for your leg, or whatever."

"Pike, this is too cruel!" Rita said. "How can you even suggest such a thing to my poor baby."

Richie looked up at her with cow eyes. Her poor baby. All right! Now he was getting somewhere. "No, Pike is right," he grunted, showing more pain than he actually felt. "It's like your thesis—fishing is important to me." He smiled selflessly, and hoisted himself to a sitting position with great difficulty. Most of the difficulty was caused by the flyline twisted tightly around his calves.

And by golly, there *was* a fish jerking on the line. Some uncanny natural fisherman's impulse must have caused him to twist the line around his feet as he was falling. After pulling a few yards of line in, hand over hand, he felt the weight of the fish. By golly, he's a hefty one. Richie wished he had the rod and reel to land him with, but he didn't. Actually, the rod must be attached to the other end of this line. That was a stroke of good fortune. R.R. had never expected to see the pretty little fly rod again.

"Should I pull the rod in first, so I can play him?" he asked Pike.

"You're doing fine this way," Pike advised. "Just keep him coming in. Don't let the pressure off him or he'll probably get off."

"But with the rod…"

"Who knows where the rod is. It's probably snagged somewhere."

"Oh, right," R.R. agreed. He hadn't thought of that.

"I'll get it for you afterwards," Pike said.

"God, I wish I had my camera!" Rita said suddenly, sounding miffed. She had tossed it on the bank when she'd taken off running downstream. "I'll go get it," she blurted, suddenly jumping up and running back the way she'd come. "Wait for me to get back," she yelled.

R.R. quit hauling the line in. Actually, he legs felt pretty good, but his hands already hurt. Being tender from the long submersion, the line was cutting into them. Well, not quite cutting the flesh, because the fly-line was soft and thick, but it was definitely making them sore. He was glad for the chance to rest. Too bad he didn't have a cleat or something to wrap the line around, even a stick.

"What are you waiting for?" Pike asked.

"Well, for Rita," he said, explaining the obvious.

"She won't be back for an hour. I saw her drop the camera almost where we started." Although he had posed for many photographs and videos, he always thought of them as a distraction from the main business at hand, catching fish. If Richie hadn't been posing for the camera, he might not have fallen in. Probably would have, knowing him, but maybe not.

"Could you find me a stick?" R.R. asked.

Pike was hovering at the water's edge with the net. He looked back at the kid. "A stick?" he asked. It was apparent that Richie would get a great pair of shiners out of his swim. His eyes were already starting to darken.

"To wrap the line around," explained the poor baby.

"You'll lose him if you dick around with a stick. Just pull him in. He's only a few yards out. I can see him. Damned nice fish. Good going."

"He's a scrapper," Rodney admitted. "He probably came from under the falls. There's some big ones there." Pike notched that bit of information for next year.

Richie recommenced bringing the line in. But why should he be doing what Pike wanted? Rita needed a film for her thesis. Wasn't he obligated to wait for the woman he loved? Of course, he was. He was the fisherman here, not Pike. And what about a judge?

"Gut it out, kid! A couple more pulls and he's ours. Yes, sir! He's a big one! See him?"

Well, so what, Rodney thought. I'll catch this one for Pike, and Rita can get a movie of me doing it right next time. This is embarrassing anyway. He tugged the line a few more feet, hand over hand, as it bit into his water-logged hands.

Pike hovered over the water like a blue heron, extending the net at a forty-five degree angle. Suddenly he swooped, then staggered into the stream, hoisting out a net full of flopping silver fish.

"Goddamn, boy! This is a damn nice fish!" he shouted, exuberantly. "Okay, hot damn, he's safe in the net. I'm gonna keep him in the water, with the line on him, still wrapped around your feet until the judge gets here. I sent Gil running back to camp to get a rescue helicopter. Shouldn't be more than another few minutes. The park rangers keep several choppers standing by for us." Pike submerged the net full of trout into a shallow pool. "You're okay for another five minutes, aren't you?"

"Five minutes? Oh, sure. I'm fine," he lied. When was he going to learn? He should have trusted his hunch and waited for Rita. Now the video was ruined, and he still couldn't crawl up the bank.

*

Baron Farouk Bardona regarded his touch with a femto fly to be unequaled. He should have been the unparalleled master of phantoms because of one simple secret—patience. With his line poised for a cast, he would sometimes stand immobile for as much as an hour until he saw the precise kind of a surface dimple he was looking for. A big dimple meant the largest fish were over being afraid of his presence in the pool and regarded him as a new rock or tree stump. Then he would make a cast to the dimple. Often his god-like patience rewarded him with a strike. Yes, his skill as a stalker was indeed superb. All of these upstarts and most of the old-timers could take a lesson from him. He got more strikes from bigger fish than anybody. All the judges said so. Unfortunately, that also made him a laughing stock. Phantoms, once they were on the hook, had his number. Even small ones could usually tangle his line and break off. Naturally, this infuriated the Baron. As did many other things.

During the long quiet hours spent ass-deep in a trout stream, he had time to reflect on all of his hatreds and on any upcoming business deals. It was a real love/hate relationship he brought to the phantoms every year. On the one hand, there was no finer thing than to kill one of the timid, treacherous fish here in this virgin setting. He took a fierce pleasure in bopping the little fucker with the leaded zap he carried for just that purpose. His feather he called it, after the old Earthside Indian custom of calling a salmon club a feather.

Yes, and the exquisite torture of standing so immobile, with only his thoughts flickering hotly—he loved the phantoms for affording him that pleasure, too. Ever chief among his hate reveries was that snipe, Pike Resnick. What a confident, loathsome individual. It gave Farouk intense gratification to bring the secure cocksucker to his knees time after time. Pike, the great scoundrel, whom everyone admired. That craven, backstabbing prick had taken the cowardly, shitsucking, fiendish route of seducing Farouk's innocent little daughter in order to get back for some imagined slight. The whoremongering cur! How could he stoop so low, even him? The hound. The bloody hound must spend all his waking hours dreaming up ways to get back at me. The thought that Pike suffered greatly in his weak attempts to wrest control of the Thruster patent away from his iron grip, gratified the Baron. He'd never get it back, the filthy mongrel. Not now! Not after he'd deflowered the fairest blossom in the nine galaxies. No way, Fido boy! I made you famous, and from now on all you do is whine and beg. Not even enough gumption to take your licking like a man, you flea-bitten excuse for a cocksure mutt.

There were others on Farouk's spleen venting list, of course. Thousands of others. Literally, everybody he'd ever met—including innocent Rita and that lucky feeb, Tourbo, and his goddamned lawyer, too. There was a cocksucker who didn't waste his life chasing fish around. No indeed. Every year without fail at Tournament time, McAndrews plotted unfriendly take-overs and other slimy tricks to get his hands on Thruster stock. The man had no shame. Why couldn't he relax and enjoy life? Clive McButthole McAndrews wasn't even particularly good at business or negotiation. Farouk had proved that time after time, but the maggot wouldn't go away. Farouk was getting pretty sick of it, actually. His blood boiled when he thought of all the money he was losing while he stood frozen, waiting for a chickenshit phantom trout to show itself. Come on, you motherfucker, he raged. Come out and fight like a man! This is my year to win!

God how he despised fish. Every year, every motherfucking year, some chickenshit bastard like Resnick humbled him, while faggots like McAndrews tried to bleed him dry. Billions! It cost him billions to waste his time standing up to his cojones in a cruddy river. If I ever win this cocksucker, he groused, you can bet your ass I'll never show up to another stinking tournament! Why should I? I'm the best fisherman that ever lived. Why should I waste my time hanging around with these lice? The Plan spun through the too tightly wound tendrils of his mind. Goddamn right. The Plan. If he ever won the pissfucking Tournament, then The Plan would lock into place. Years ago he had promised that special treat to himself. Years ago. He was going to buy every planet on the fucking schedule, especially the Big Six. Especially this one, Streamside! And nuke the fuck out of them! Beautiful! The perfect reward.

The dimple he was waiting for appeared to the far left of the pool almost under the boughs of a windfallen grazzlenut tree. Farouk drew his arm back with infinite patience and made a textbook roll-cast, placing the minute fly within an inch of the dimple. The fly settled to the surface of the brook, barely making a ripple. Water exploded! The phantom grabbed the black gnat and made a sizzling run across the pool, where it leaped in the air shaking its head—and broke the line like it was nothing. The whole fight had lasted maybe four seconds.

Farouk Bardona gritted his teeth and swore savagely under his breath. Then with a hearty grin, he turned to his guide and the judge. "These Phans are sure scrappers, aren't they?" he joked, happily.

*

In another manifestation of his incredible luck, R.R. was only superficially damaged in his river rafting trip. Twin shiners and bruised ribs do not an invalid make. What was important about the whole experience was that his darling Rita had declared her love for him. It was true that she acted very annoyed that he hadn't waited for her to get back with the camera before landing the fish. He told her straightforwardly that he had seen her point and considered waiting, but had decided to land the fish before the helicopter came to spook it.

The helicopter, with the judge, arrived eighteen minutes after Rita got back with the mini-cam. And she refused to speak to him for the next two days.

Richie, who was becoming knowledgeable about women's ways, interpreted that as a healthy sign. A stormy relationship, he called it. While turning over the raw steak on his eye, he even went as far as to suggest to Lester that true love often runs a stormy course. Lester quickly agreed.

While he always liked kicking back for a week in tent city kibitzing with the other chefs, Lester was a wee bit concerned lately about his boss's mental health. His boss, of course, was Pike. Lester regarded R.R. as a charter sport. A nice kid, but rich sports come and go. Pike on the other hand was bound to come to grief. He always did when he fooled around with a Bardona.

* * *

# LEADERS

| | DELILAH | TORGA HOWLER | TIGER MUSKY | D.W. SCUT | PHANTOM TROUT | LAR BARRACUDA | GLANS SALMON | RAZORFIN | SWAMPFISH | MOON HALIBUT | TOTAL |
|---|---|---|---|---|---|---|---|---|---|---|---|
| Farouk Bardona | | | 2 | 5 | | | | | | | 4TH 7 |
| Ethyl Bierly | 2 | | | | | | | | | | 2 |
| Angmar Blirt | | | | | 4 | | | | | | 4 |
| Bill Bolen | | | 3 | | 5 | | | | | | 3RD 8 |
| Dresden Carthy | 4 | | | | 2 | | | | | | 5TH 6 |
| JB Dillingham | | OUT | | | | | | | | | |
| Harry Dolan | 3 | 2 | 5 | | | | | | | | 2ND 10 |
| Macky Duff | | | | | OUT | | | | | | |
| Ira Fairborne | | 4 | | 3 | | | | | | | 4TH 7 |
| Buddy Jay | | | | | | | | | | | |
| Sandy Kind | | | | | | | | | | | |
| Hank Knofsinger | | | | 2 | | | | | | | 2 |
| Peter Marcuso | | | | | OUT | | | | | | |
| Trini Morales | | | | | | | | | | | |
| Pike Resnick | | OUT | | | | | | | | | |
| Erwin Sandor | | 3 | | | OUT | | | | | | |
| Jean Santos | | 1 | | | | | | | | | 1 |
| Mordachi Skinner | | | 4 | 4 | | | | | | | 3RD 8 |
| Tyrone Stickle | | | | 1 | | | | | | | 1 |
| Chip Takahachi | | | | | 3 | | | | | | |
| RR Tourbo | 5 | 5 | 1 | | 1 | | | | | | 1ST 12 |
| Mike Tucker | 1 | | | | | | | | | | 1 |
| Nacho Tutupo | | | | | | | | | | | |
| Ed Wood | | | | | OUT | | | | | | |
| Big John Zales | | | | | | | | | | | |

| | | |
|---|---|---|
| 1ST | = | 5 points |
| 2ND | = | 4 points |
| 3RD | = | 3 points |
| 4TH | = | 2 points |
| 5TH | = | 1 points |

# CHAPTER EIGHT

## MID-SUMMER NIGHT'S FETE

"I try not to think about it. Winning is not something you do, except in ping pong or something. Like in martial arts, the strike happens by itself when it's perfect, pulled by all of nature. Isn't that right?"

R.R. Tourbo
quoted in *History of the Tournament*

THE end of trout season marked the halfway point in the Tournament. It was traditionally celebrated by a gourmet potluck on the beach, where the chefs used up all the provisions that were left, and in the process tried to outdo each other.

The fishermen who had survived Streamside were usually in fine spirits, and the unlucky ones who hadn't landed a Phantom walked around like zombies, muttering, "Wait until next year, you bastards."

Four fishermen had bit the empty water, which made a total of six disqualified at the half way mark. Nineteen continuing. Richie's trout had given him another Fifth Place and one more point. None of the other leaders had placed at all, so with 12 points, he was two ahead of Hardluck Harry Dolan. No lead was secure, of course. Get skunked in a category, and so long sucker—but it was looking kind of hopeful.

*

Rita had expected her real life to begin when she moved in with Pike. But it hadn't. Something was wrong, wrong, wrong. She lay on her cot, staring up at the green tent fabric, watching a little red spider weaving an intricate web in the tent's corner. A web of closeness was what she needed, but apparently she wasn't woman enough to make it happen. Their communication was abysmal—non-existent. For example, if he loved her, why hadn't he made Richie wait to catch that trout until she got back? She didn't care about the fish, obviously; but that non-event had been symptomatic of lots of other miscommunication. Like this tent. All four of them were sleeping in the same goddamned tent—on separate folding cots. Roughing it, for God's sake. When she thought about it, she wanted to scream; so she tried to think about other things—like the spider. But everything brought her around to the same point. Sex. Sex made everything work, but they weren't doing it because they were living in a crowded tent. If the rangers wouldn't let them stay on the boats, because of their stupid regulations about a pristine harbor, why couldn't they at least have two tents? Their relationship was important, damnit!

How could she bind him to her if he kept refusing to cooperate in bed? All the men and boys she had ever known were eager to couple with her. Pathetically eager. They wrote poems and declared themselves in other outrageous ways, just so she'd take off her clothes and do it with them. It was sweet. One boy had rhapsodized about how she smelled like new mown hay, however that smelled. She supposed it must be good because he went on and on—and he was talking about the way her poonie smelled. Yes, she'd always been able to spin any of her admirers into outer space simply by bouncing her breasts a little, or even with a certain kind of smile. But somehow, these tricks didn't always work on Pike, damnit. He was growing more disinterested every day in this tent, like she was very ho-hum. Her powers obviously were failing. Maybe the worst tragedy was happening. Maybe she was past her prime. How the hell could that be true, Pike was much older than she was. Wasn't he supposed to be overwhelmed with desire? This was so unfair.

Rita had felt a strange pull toward Pike for at least ten years, even before she knew what wanting was all about. And now she had him. It *was* wonderful, because Pike was basically a wonderful person—but he fell a little short of the fantasy perfection of her ten years of day dreams. It had taken her several weeks to admit that hideous truth to herself. When a realization like that surfaces, it's not easy to see it head on. So naturally, she was bummed out. Who wouldn't be? She had imagined that because they were soulmates, he would understand her every whim—at least the serious ones. But unfortunately, he was like every other man. A lot of whims passed undetected. In fact, what *he* really wanted was for *her* to be attentive to his whims. The only time they really connected was when his whims and her whims (desires, wants, needs) overlapped. Then it was fine. But was this a perfect relationship?

No, damnit. It wasn't blissfully perfect. And he had never even mentioned marriage! No wonder a girl got sad.

Pike was worried, too. In point of fact, he had the First Place Blues—a condition well known to muckerball managers whose team had lucked into 1$^{st}$ place at the All Star break, and who knew that the lucky bounces couldn't keep happening in their favor. All this week, Richie had been catching trout right and left, although none larger than the first one. Pike watched the fumbling casts and was amazed every time a Phantom struck. It just didn't match his experience with the fish at all. Now, here it was Sunday again, and it looked like the kid would hold down 5$^{th}$ place. The other serious competitors hadn't caught large fish, so Richie would hang onto overall 1$^{st}$, unless something changed today.

Tonight would be the big halfway party. A glum one. The Phans were very persnickety this year to everyone except the kid. It was maddeningly impossible to figure how he did it. Next year would to be hell fishing against Mr. Luck.

And Rita was acting funny. Morose. That wasn't like her. Or maybe it was. How would he know? He barely knew the girl. He had wanted to screen off a corner of the tent for privacy, and push their cots together so they could keep up the coziness from Galatin Bay. But that had seemed totally weird somehow, even though it was perfectly normal. The Tournament was about fishing—not about having love affairs. Anyway, shouldn't they be able to survive a week on Streamside without going lust crazy.

He was losing touch with reality, that was the problem. Unless he was fishing himself, it was difficult to get a true reading—on the fish or the competition, or even on his woman, apparently? But fishing was out of the question, even for pleasure. He didn't want to raise one little doubt in a judge's mind that he was catching Richie's fish. The truth was that he had become a third wheel, and that was something he'd never been before. What if his own luck got fucked up? He hadn't considered that. All he'd thought about was getting the money for next year. It might have been smarter to take the year off and work on an invention, instead of risking his luck—or risking giving it to somebody else—namely Rich Rodney. He now felt empathy for Lester that he'd never entertained before. How does he stand it? Always around the action, but never in it. Les and other longtime crew members must have less insistent libido needs than he did.

And Rita was slipping away. Definitely. He was going to lose her before he even had her. Any day now, she might jump in her little pink boat and flit out of his life. She had been so angry about Richie's trout.

Actually, things hadn't been right since then. One goddamned home movie wasn't important enough to ruin a relationship over, was it? Well, maybe the time was up. Love is always a very strange item. Blink your eyes and it's over. But wouldn't he miss her? Yes, more than he wanted to think about.

*

The midway potluck on Streamside had originally been fun. But it had metamorphosed into an entirely different animal than those first beach parties, where the cooks pooled their left-overs. Now they special ordered exotic goodies and turned a picnic into a gourmet cooking contest. Lester was the only cook who refused to participate farther than making a big pot of his extraordinary baked beans. He also pulled out a few willow switches he had cut back at Galatin Bay to roast frankfurters on.

Pike left the tent and walked down to the beach, wondering why it was necessary to have a party when nearly everyone was burned out by the rotten fishing. But party time it was. Designer camp tables sank into the sand under the weight of haute cuisine and cases of iced champagne. At least a third of the campers were in their cups by sunset. Pike planned to eat quickly and leave for New Columbus. Unfortunately, he discovered once again that he was not master of his destiny.

Richie was having a great time, flapping around the beach in his patched hip boots sampling a little steak tartar here, a little conch and seaweed salad there—helping Rita fill her plate with delicate tidbits. They're kids, Pike reminded himself. Yes, but... Tomorrow was New Columbus and the giant barracudas. Nothing to play around with on a hangover, as Ned Larchmont found out. Good old Ned. Maybe he would be watching from Fish Heaven.

Unfortunately, Pike's rumination on his ex-chum, Ned Larchmont, after whom Larchmont Barracuda had been named, had caused him to not pay proper attention to the people in his immediate surroundings. More specifically, the Baron, Farouk Bardona, and his lovely wife, suddenly appeared across a serving table from Pike. There was no place to run and no place to hide, so he smiled haphazardly and said, "Nice party, ain't it?"

"Bullshit!" Bardona spat.

"Now, Farouk, don't be like that. I'm sure Rita's research is very important to her." Magyar Bardona was a strikingly handsome woman. Her long chestnut hair was lightly veined with grey and her Mediterranean skin was almost mahogany brown. When Pike had first met her years ago, Maggie had practically knocked his eye out. Although similar in looks, she was milder than Rita—without the fire. Still damned fine looking in all the right ways, except that she gave Bardona the backbone to be a bastard by condoning all his rotten dealings. Pike had never quite determined if Maggie approved of business corruption and whole-heartedly supported it, or whether, having married the codfish, her code of marriage ethics and nest feathering forced her to go along with being filthy rich over the bones of friends. In any case, she and Farouk made a memorable couple.

"I'm very displeased with Rita's living situation," Bardona rumbled. "What she sees in you is beyond me, always has been."

"You mean, you think I'm kind of scummy?" Pike asked pleasantly. His fist wondered if it would be fun to mash Farouk's beak. Would that accomplish anything?

"What I think privately doesn't enter into it. You are scum." The Baron managed to put things so succinctly. "Did you have one of your witch doctor goons put a spell on her, or what?" the embittered father blustered.

"I thought that was a secret," Pike baited. "Who told you about it?" The thing Pike hated most about Bardona was his blockheaded dullness. Greed he could understand. But greed and humorless stupidity lumped together was too much for Pike. Chatting with Farouk was always like talking to a wall. The wall that yearned to consume the Universe.

"I want her back on board the Lady Slipper tonight, and I want you to keep your mitts off her!"

"No can do, Master," Pike said, slowly. His blood boiled easily whenever he talked with Farouk. It was boiling now, as a matter of fact; but years ago he had decided it would be a continuing test of his manhood always to annoy Bardona into getting angry first. His position vis-à-vis the Thruster patent was hopeless. Bardona was immovable, so the reason for treating him humanely had long passed. The only practical solution was to get him angry enough to rupture an aneurysm and send himself into premature senility. Then maybe he'd turn into a human being. So Pike controlled himself and said, "If you can't manage your own daughter, how can I? You're her father. I'm only her roommate." He smiled, disingenuously,

Bardona's neck flushed red as a rooster's comb. A little smoke squirted out from the collar of his linen shirt. As Pike watched, the flush spread up to his big ears and invaded his jowls. "I can control her, don't worry about that!!"

"Remember your blood pressure, Fookie," Maggie cautioned sweetly, touching his elbow. "Let's see what the other chef's have made."

"The thing about you," Pike insisted, reasonably, "is that you think other people care about what you want. They don't. They only kiss your ass for the money. You're not a well-liked man, Farouk. Change for the better is theoretically possible, of course."

Bardona was momentarily speechless. His mouth gasped open and closed like a beached fish's. Pike thought for a moment that he'd finally pushed him over the edge. But no, a vindictive gleam came back into his eye. The fucker was stronger than dirt.

Farouk lashed out. "She's trying to catch young Tourbo, not you!" He laughed harshly right into Pike's face. "Even I know that much."

In an instant of truth, Pike knew Farouk was right. Very right. And by this stupid fake camping out in one tent, he was playing right into Tourbo's hands.

Farouk Bardona, master businessman, read the signs of weakness in Pike's face. He was right! Rita was after Tourbo! Well, goddamn, that was great. Tourbo's wealth, merged with his own, would give him virtual control of every goddamned thing he could conceive of. That's my girl. That's my little Rita. Even if young Tourbo was a blundering moron, it would all work out.

At that exact moment of exaltation, Pike's hard right fist splattered Farouk's nose.

It was awe inspiring and almost religious to see two middle-aged fishermen taking out fifteen years of frustration by rolling in the sand, battering each other—gouging and kicking, trying to inflict internal hemorrhaging. Quite a little crowd gathered to watch.

Farouk was somewhat tougher than he looked. When Pike's fist leaped out unbidden to pulp the hook nose, which was just hanging there waiting, he had imagined the altercation would last for only one punch. But Farouk jumped into the fray like a mad demon. Pike quickly realized that it was a fight. Neither man had taken the trouble to learn a martial art, so it was the bull walrus mentality with lots of blood and grunting, but little real damage. They didn't even bother to curse at each other. Now that the chance to hurt had finally come, they went at it silently and furiously. Most of the noise came from the crowd yelling support to their favorite. Rita and her mother shrieked for both men to stop it.

But fighting on a beach is harder work than one might imagine. After five minutes or so, both combatants found their arms turning to lead and their legs quivering with exhaustion.

Rich Rodney Tourbo, relying on his years of Ken Pao Ri experience, gauged the timing to a nano-second and leaped in to break up the fight. His chin arrived precisely on schedule to meet with Farouk's last haymaker of the evening. Beautiful. Richie's head snapped back and he did a full backward swan dive as gracefully as anyone had ever witnessed. Out like a light, while Pike and Farouk, panting and dripping sweat and blood stared down at the kid, not quite comprehending what a brilliant job of fight stopping had been accomplished.

Rita instantly rushed to Rich Rodney's assistance, slapping his face and urging him to wake up. Maggie dipped the corner of a silk handkerchief in a glass of champagne and dabbed at Farouk's nose and cut lip, cleaning her warrior up to continue the party.

Lester Wunderman, grinning like a banshee, handed Pike a hastily assembled paper cup of old Kentucky bourbon, which was still made in Kentucky with grain imported from off-world. Wheat refused to grow anymore in the erratic weather cycles on Earth. Pike knocked the booze back, then allowed Lester to fuss and chortle over his knuckles and chin, while he waited for Rich Rodney to revive. His brain reengaged with reality, as friends and friendly enemies pounded both him and Farouk on the back, congratulating them on the spectacle. It was pretty embarrassing. Pike would have been glad to crawl into a hole, but none was available. At length, Richie's eyes popped open, out of focus.

"Ask him what planet he's on!" some joker yelled at Rita.

Rita didn't think that was amusing. "Come on, Richie," she said, gently. "Let's go to the tent."

"I'm fine," Richie insisted, once his head stopped spinning. He hopped nimbly to his feet, instantly tangling his legs up in the floppy hip boots. He pitched face forward into the sand, only managing to break his fall at the last instant.

"For God's sake, Rich, quit clowning around," Rita said, helping him up. She threw a cold look over her shoulder at Pike, then helped her brave cripple down the beach toward the tent city.

Pike and the Baron continued glaring at each other, through the surge and flow of the crowd. Fighting had brought them into an odd harmony. But their differences *were* kind of irreconcilable.

\* \* \*

# CHAPTER NINE

## LARCHMONT BARRACUDA

"Well, Rita, that's a strange kind of question, because I only feel bad if I get skunked. If I catch a fish every week, then it's always possible that magic can strike—right up to the very last minute. One year, I won moon halibut, and came from nowhere to 4<sup>th</sup> place, plus getting my entry fee back. That was a *good* afternoon."

Trinidad Morales
quoted in *History of the Tournament*

NEW Columbus had been named partly in jest by Ned Larchmont, a good-natured, hard drinking fisherman, who used a complicated mathematical formula to determine that there should be a water planet lurking in a certain quadrant of the Yyr Circle. Then he flew out and bummed around the sector until he discovered it.

A developing sentient species lived on several of the low islands—a kind of advanced, pacifistic reptilian creature dubbed Frogs by the amused Larchmont. The Frogs had developed subtle speech and vaguely human attributes, like standing erect and living in houses, but against all reason they were still compelled to return to the sea for breeding like their species of aquatic frogs had always done. The bliss of intra-uterine egg fertilization—followed minutes later by egg laying—was also trauma time for their race because frothing schools of a barracuda type fish ruled the waters. Snapping jaws and red seas of frog blood were deeply ingrained in the molecular memory of these Froggies, but they hadn't managed to evolve another way to breed. Bliss and trauma, bliss and trauma.

Still, the evolutionary scheme was working for them. Their civilization was several thousand years old. Once the eggs made it to the amphibian stage and hopped onto the lush islands, everything was great. They had no wars and made no enemies. It was paradise until the compulsion to copulate came around again. Surviving past the breeding age was considered an extraordinary feat; but those who did lived to a great age, becoming frog sages.

Frogs spent their days gardening, catching insects, establishing cottage industries, and studying evasionary swimming techniques. Their favorite craft was building fantastic sand castles to live in, which they somehow welded into a kind of cement structure by mixing the sand with their own saliva. They were as pleased to welcome Ned Larchmont as Native American Indians had been to fawn on Christopher Columbus, that scalawag cyclops who turned his men loose to rape and plunder. Being slightly more humane than his fellow explorer, Ned Larchmont showed the Frog people how he could catch the barracuda from his fancy fishing boat. The Frogs thought that was pretty nifty. Every dead barracuda was one less nightmare. They were positively enthusiastic when Larchmont detailed his plan for bringing a few friends over just before the breeding season to thin out the barracuda population. They even made him an honorary prince. Prince Ned of New Columbus.

Farouk Bardona had cursed when he heard about a rival monarch; but Larchmont Barracuda were a fine sporting fish, tough, mean and big. After that first year when the fleet met to fish for the biters, there wasn't a whole lot Farouk could do other than grumble.

It was perfectly understandable that Ned, that old swashbuckler, should take quite an interest in New Columbus. Since the planet had evolved with only three percent land mass, Prince Ned reasoned that the adult Frog population would soon outstrip the living space if the barracuda population was fished too strongly. Without mentioning that fact to the Frogs, he made sure that a strict bag limit of three fish over a hundred pounds per boat per Tournament was written into the charter with the native population. Any fish less than a hundred pounds had to be released alive. As a Prince, he figured his fiefdom could afford to cull seventy-five big fish a year. The contract with the Frogmen of New Columbus was tight enough that even three years after Ned's death the bag limit wasn't in question, although it probably could have been if either side wanted to re-negotiate.

How had Ned died? Not fishing. No, like any true Prince, he decided to take ocean breeding lessons with his people. He was a little drunk when he made the decision, and thus his reflexes were slowed.

It is surprising how similar a copulating Frog and a copulating man look to the eye of a barracuda. So when Prince Ned was nailed, nobody blamed the fish. Breeding, to the Frog community, was like any other dangerous sport—say, hot rod racing. If you do it, sooner or later you lose. Prince Ned's girlfriend was spared, but severely traumatized, and stranded until the Tournament anglers showed up.

To Ned Larchmont's credit, it was a damned big 'cuda that got him. At least, that's what the growing legend certified. Six or seven hundred pounds. Maybe bigger. It was over in a flash. Sure it was. Personally, Pike was still angry at Ned. It's not quite kosher to be a moron and leave your friends holding the emotional bag.

So the Prince Ned saga was one more thing for Pike to natter about as the morning's activities aboard the Comparative Humanity swung into gear. Everyone left Streamside in the daylight, more or less in a flock due to the pirates. Which was another problem that irked Pike right down to his toe nails. The damned pirates couldn't buy the Thruster technology which they wanted, so perforce they were obliged to steal it. Bardona's policy created a needless danger. If pirates could afford to manufacture or buy a needle boat, they could afford to buy a Thruster model; but as stated, Farouk wouldn't sell.

Pike was almost as irked at himself as he was at Farouk. Why didn't he simply make sure the plans for a Thruster fell into the hands of the right pirate chief, or better yet, sell the schematics, if he wanted every-body to have them? Screw Farouk. The answer to that was edged both with greed and with honor, that's why he was irked. If Farouk ever died, the terms of their contract stipulated that Pike had the first option of buying fifty-one percent of the patent back—which he intended to do, never mind how. But until then, there were pirates to contend with, and they always seemed to concentrate on this section of the Tournament where there was little human civilization to get in their way.

Complicating his worries about pirates as he ran an armaments check was the fresh soreness of his body. That damned Farouk was a good fighter. The old fuck-face had gotten in more than a few jarring punches, and Pike felt each one of them this morning. And Rita had not slept in the tent last night. She'd stuck her head in to inform him that she didn't sleep with bullies and that she and Richie were sleeping on the boat. Just as well. She and the kid were made for each other. Even that half-blind bastard Farouk knew that much. Thinking about it, Pike smiled grimly to himself and in the process cracked open his cut lip. Gallingly, they were still asleep somewhere down below. Pike hadn't checked on the bunking arrangements. He and Lester had dumped the tent and gear in a corner of the galley to put away later, then he had gone up to the bridge. The little green prickle of insane jealousy that was running around and around in his chest was very disconcerting, like he knew it would be.

But thumping on Farouk had been damned good. Now that it had finally happened once, he couldn't think of any reason not to give himself the pleasure again and again. If I'm feeling this rocky, I'll bet he can't hardly move, Pike chuckled to himself.

"Breakfast...!" Lester hollered from the galley. "Come and get it, so I can stow for takeoff."

*

RR knew something was wrong when he woke up, but couldn't get his eyes to open. Then, through puffy eye-slits, he discovered that he was on the floor. Sleeping on the floor explained the stiffness in his back and right hip satisfactorily; but had he fallen out of bed without knowing? Hardly likely for someone of his physical and psychic awareness, and a light sleeper besides. Throwing the blanket aside, he leapt nimbly to his feet—and instantly sank back to his knees under the keening pain of a giant foot kicking at his temples with logging boots. But the brief moment on his feet had shown him a glimpse of Rita sleeping in his bunk, and that brought back full recall of last night's revels. It had been glorious. He'd been a hero. Everyone loved him. Rita loved him. Everybody thought he was so gallant with a beefsteak covering his eyes and an overflowing stirrup cup of champagne in his debonair hand. Darn it, how many stirrup cups had he polished off? No memory of that. His head was literally splitting in two. Massaging his temples, like Master Jacopo had taught him, did nothing at all. He felt like curling into a ball on the floor and whimpering for his mother's maid to come and soothe the agony away. In spite of the pain, the memory of Gwendolyn or Edith Ann gave him a tumescence in the groin. At least, he wasn't injured there, a part of his brain managed to note gratefully. Whatever possessed him to jump into the middle of that fight?

And then Rita had stayed over in his room, kicking him out of his bunk onto the floor. He only dimly remembered the events from that time frame. Hopefully, he hadn't done something stupid like trying to grab her. Actually, that was pretty unlikely. His teeth weren't broken out, and they probably would be if he ever tried anything with Rita. But what was she doing here? Dare he to hope that she had chosen in his favor?

The pain receded for a second, and he opened his eyes are far as possible. Wait a derned minute here! The Baron, fey bastard that he was, had been yelling incoherently about Rita trying to catch him—him, himself, Rich Rodney. Was that possible? Was the old bullhorn so stupid that he didn't realize Rita would never play games like that? Why should she? He was already caught. Rita was the one who was the bird in the bush, not him. But how was Pike going to react to this news? Did he know? Judas priest, this was serious. Pike was his captain!

Although madly in love with Rita, R.R. had never realized how peculiar it was that, oversexed as he knew himself to be, he had never had a lustful thought about his beloved. How could he? She was a goddess. Even a fleeting reminiscence of Gwendolyn or Giselle or that pretty dark one, whose name he had forgotten, gave him a raging hard-on, and to be honest about it, he had a lurid fantasy going for Jean Santos. Now, *there* was a sexy older woman if he ever saw one, swishing around her boat so lasciviously. And he even had a minor passion for that hard-ass Ethyl Bierly. But for Rita? Nothing scummy like that. Certainly not. Rita was his friend, and someday—maybe someday soon if the Baron was right, she'd be his wife. After the gala wedding, he imagined a scene of eternal bliss, with chaste kisses bestowed on his loved one and lots of adorable children which he would take to Ken Pao Ri classes like the good, adoring father he would be. But still he had no clear picture of how these kiddies, who all were lithe and tan like Rita, came into being. Maybe it was immaculate conception. In any case, he'd never embarrassed himself by getting a hard-on over Rita, never one time, and that's why he loved her. Of course, she was very wonderful besides that too, of course. Golly, she was just about the most perfect person that could ever be; but he couldn't for the life of him remember how she'd come to be sleeping in his bunk. He decided to sit quietly, massaging his temples until she woke up, then pretending that he remembered everything, he would skillfully question her until the blank spaces were filled in.

*

Rita was awake, and had been since RR's first bout of thrashing about on the floor had snapped her out of dreamland. Long practice at faking sleep to avoid interacting with Richie had convinced her that she was a pro at it. Her eyes were still shut and she practiced breathing slowly and evenly. No, she definitely didn't want to face Richie before she had a chance to think. Eventually he would get tired of sitting there like a frog, and get on with his next bumbling accident. She was pretty sure that last night had been a big fat mistake, but she needed to be alone to think about it. And R.R., she knew from past experience, wanted to talk. He would never actually wake her up; but once her eyes opened, he'd be off to the races. Actually, he was quite unbearable in the mornings, and it *had* been a stupid choice to stay in his room; but if need be, she could lay here in her nest of sorrow forever. Hunger was meaningless to her. Body functions were less than nothing. True, she wanted to scream at him to get the fuck away and leave her alone, but screaming didn't work. He would just grin until her throat was hoarse, then start babbling about whatever was on his mind. But she knew she could out-wait him—and when he was gone, she could start to worry about how angry Pike might be at her. Why had she been so stupid?

Stupid? Yes, that's right. Stupid as Arlene "Miss Demerol" Kalvic. It was perfectly obvious that this fight between Daddy and Pike had been building since she was a little girl. Half the reason she was initially attracted to Pike was because her father hated him so much. When she got old enough to find out the reasons why, Pike kept looking better and better. Then last night, when it all came to a head, and her chance to really champion his cause was offered on a silver platter, damned R.R. jumped into the middle of it and got himself clobbered. Like a mother hen, she had hovered over Richie until her time to be there for Pike had vanished.

When she finally remembered to look for him, Pike had gone back to the tent. Mystifying. Her whole life had angled toward that moment, and when it had happened, she had ducked out. Turned into a fuzzy-headed twit. Why? She hadn't meant to side with R.R. It had just happened. Damnit, damnit. What could she do? Pike must be disappointed. She was bitterly disappointed in herself; but she couldn't get a clean line on where she had missed the beat. It must have been clear to everyone that she had acted like she was in love with R.R. Everybody who had witnessed the fight had to think that. But she wasn't!! If anything, she thought of Richie as her little brother. Damnit, how had her maternal instincts betrayed her at the critical moment? Then Pike was gone, just like that, and there was no stand to take, and stupid R.R. kept lying there bleeding. Life is *so* complicated! Why do all the signals get crossed?

She was still faking sleep when Pike finished breakfast, and cursed himself for captaining anybody other than himself. Instead of taking off with the rest of the fleet, he was lolly-gagging dangerously. With another round of swearing, he sent Lester down to wake the snoozing Prince and Princess. You can't just take off without telling the boat's owner, can you? Not when he's entertaining. Only the damned Lady Slipper was still at the harbor mouth. When she leaped into the air, he would too. This boat wasn't going to New Columbus alone, no matter who was sleeping. At that moment, the huge Lady Slipper with her two attendant fishing boats did leap skyward. True to his word, Pike pushed the lift switch without a moment's hesitation.

Richie's boat lifted nicely on its grid mat, hovered an instant in mid-air and shot away into space and then hyper-space, while Rita, Rich Rodney and Lester scrambled to secure their position.

Once they were in the frontal quiet of hyperspace, with George the computer slipping them between the sequential holes in the Von Karman carpet, the acceleration turbulence in RR's cabin returned to theoretical zero. R.R. found himself somewhat shaken but sitting more or less where he had been. Rita lay on the floor near him with her arm around the bed frame.

Lester was on his knees, holding onto the hatch knob.

"Pike sent me to tell you we were casting off," Lester said with a lopsided grin. "I guess you figured that out."

"Oh, hi, Rita," Richie said, acting like he was accidentally in the vicinity. "You're awake. I was wondering—well, actually I was thinking about what a great time we had last night at the party. That was one heck of a time, wasn't it?" he questioned, skillfully.

"Stop it, Richie! I mean it. I need time to think." Gracefully, disentangling herself from the bed, Rita glided into the bathroom and slammed the door. Frantically, she looked at her reflection in the mirror, searching for telltale signs of premature aging. What she planned to do was crawl up to Pike on her hands and knees. Crawl clear across the bridge to wherever he was, and make sure he understood that nothing happened last night. If she had to, she would force Richie to testify on her behalf. Misunderstandings were one thing, but she wasn't letting Pike go because of a glitch in her maternal instinct. Not if she could help it.

Once a destination is decided in hyperspace, the computer does all the work. In theory, a human's brain is capable of following all the computations; but as a practical matter, in outer space the pilot might as well be asleep. The only real reason for his paying attention is to push the authorization button for the laser cannon in case of a pirate attack. He doesn't plot evasive action, or even line up the fire lanes. All the rapidly changing data is continuously self-programmed by the computer into its Creative Response ROM. But the pilot does push the button, if the situation turns critical.

Traveling as they were in tandem across the galaxy with the Lady Slipper, Pike wasn't very worried about pirates; so he was rather surprised when the attack klaxon started screaming, and a heavy jolt jarred the boat.

"Charge deflected," the synthetic voice of George the computer reported from damage control. "Grid now two/thirds. Situation Red. Authorization for course evasion. Plotting course evasion."

Electrified, Pike watched the view screen in front of him, and listened to George describing the situation.

"Three foreign objects, plus three friendly. Notify friendly by voice. Go now. Push fire button to commence return fire."

Pike jabbed the red fire button, then toggled the ship's radio. "Alert, alert. Lady Slipper. This is Comparative Humanity, a few parsecs behind you. Under attack by three bandits. Watch your ass." In the time it took to make the signal, Lester had buckled into the co-pilot's seat beside Pike and was staring fiercely at the view monitor.

Pike was sure Rita knew enough to hustle up to the bridge, since that was the safest place. He had covered this drill with R.R. several times, but who knew what that bozo would do under pressure? No sooner had Pike thought those words, than the bozo skidded through the air lock. His stocking feet caught on a microscopic speck of dust, and he swan-dived toward a side couch that he'd been assigned for emergencies. Stopping his momentum with a crunching bounce off the cushioned recliner, he came to rest triumphantly sideways, hanging onto the seat belt.

"What's happening...?" Richie asked, breathlessly clambering onto the recliner.

Neither Pike nor Lester bothered to answer him. One more solid hit would fry most of the grid. George would insist that they surrender as he'd been programmed to do, then he would kick the system back to manual. So Pike and Lester were a little busy, preparing themselves for that eventuality.

"Lady Slipper, do you copy?" Pike yelled into the microphone. "Repeat, do you copy!" But no word came back from the Lady Slipper. Didn't the shithead know his daughter was on board? Not even the Baron could be cold enough to abandon his own flesh and blood, could he? "George, is the radio sending?" Pike snapped.

"The transceiver is A-Okay. All systems functioning," George responded. "I can't outmaneuver all three of them for long."

"Then shoot the bastards!" Lester yelped.

Pike felt very stranded. Hyperspace is a hell-hole if you're alone. Fucking pirates! Why hadn't Farouk released the patent? Who needed this kind of shit?

Obviously, the pirate meatheads weren't going to destroy the ship. That would be exactly counter-productive. They wanted the Thruster Drive, not a bunch of space flotsam.

"Mayday, mayday!" he spoke into the microphone. "All Fishing Fleet now monitor. Three pirates on this heading." He gave his position in transit hyperspace. "No help in sight. Catch you in hell."

With a dismayed expression in her eyes and a hairbrush in her hand, Rita swooshed through the air lock. "We're under attack?" she asked, incredulously.

"Correct," Pike answered, tight-lipped. "Take a seat."

Rather than crawl to Pike's feet as she had planned, Rita strapped into the recliner on the bulkhead next to R.R., which was her battle station. Tilting the cushions to the full upright position, she began brushing her hair. She wasn't needed for the battle. No use letting snarls get started.

Rich Rodney watched her with mooning calf eyes. What a cool customer she is, he thought, and so adorable.

Much the same observations were occurring to Pike. This was actually only his third pirate attack. In both the others he had come to the rescue of someone else. He listened to the computer gurgling, speaking directions to itself. It was programmed to do that, so that humans would feel that they were in contact. George seemed to be fighting a pretty good fight. The ship strained, hopping here and there across space. But all the screens showed that the pirates were keeping up nicely.

"Where is my father?" Rita asked, with the quiet assurance that rescue would be soon. She finished brushing her hair, and tied it with a black elastic.

"Didn't respond," Pike answered, nonchalantly. "You know how he is."

"What does that mean?" she snipped back. Her family loyalty flared, although she didn't give a damn for family loyalty.

"Well, he's tied for 5th Place. The kid here is in 1st." Pike nodded toward Richie's couch. "If I know Farouk, he wouldn't mind if we were late and disqualified. Some scenario like that." He shrugged, keeping his eyes fixed on the view screens.

"That's absurd," she replied, smugly.

"I agree. He is an absurd fellow."

Rich Rodney listened to the bickering, feeling that he should probably take Rita's side. Bardona would be his father-in-law someday. He wasn't such a bad guy—a little gruff, but heck. But then, Pike was right. Bardona *was* tied for 5th Place. Of course, Pike was probably steamed at the Baron after last night. Pike's knuckles looked puffy, and probably hurt like heck. And his lip was cut. And old Farouk hadn't answered the Mayday, even though Rita was on board.

"Actually, why didn't he answer the signal?" R.R. asked.

Another jolt jarred the craft. "Half deflected. Nice going," George intoned, congratulating himself. "Grid is 57 percent. Prepare to fire. Firing."

The pirate ships seemed to have acquired somewhat better computers since Pike's last encounter with them. George was hitting nothing but air. Pike considered wresting the controls away from George. Maybe he and Lester could do better on manual with the chaotic element of fright introduced, but probably not. The pirates weren't blood thirsty, just well paid corporate raiders with a job to do. Blowing RR's boat out of the skyways wouldn't get them any bonus—quite the contrary. But if I let George give us up, they would get the Thruster. Hummm… The ransom for the two kids would open a very snazzy boat works. And what kind of a deal would they work with me? Probably they'd pay handsomely for my cooperation with the design department. Good idea. I could be set for life without half trying. Not too shabby. Why hadn't he thought of that before? He'd always had a boat to defend until now, that was why. Screw Farouk and his trickle of royalties. I'll cut myself a deal to take care of Number One.

One of the blips on the screen suddenly turned nova. "Good work, George," Pike commented, half-heartedly. On his monitor, pulverized raider became a cloud of space dust.

"Three Thruster models approaching from Quadrant One," the computer intoned. "Their shot, not ours, struck the raider. I cannot take credit for the marksmanship. Both other raiders are in retreat. Please confirm to end evasive action and begin recharting to original course."

"That must be, Daddy," Rita said, showing her relief and not too much additional smugness.

"Certainly, George, rechart if the attack is over," Pike said. So close to financial harmony, he bitched to himself. "How about that, Richie? Farouk believes he can beat you, even without letting the banditos get us."

The transceiver crackled to life. "Goddamn, you're hard suckers to find in the vastness of space," Bardona guffawed, hearty as a white knight to the rescue. "Are you all right, Rita?"

"Everyone on board is fine," George replied. "Proceeding to New Columbus. Shall we convoy?"

"Certainly," Bardona acknowledged. "I thought you'd catch up when we left. Why don't you slave to us and take a rest."

"We *could* slave to you," George answered with a touch of digital upmanship, "but I have the calculations worked out" He did not bother to add that most of the Lady Slipper's computer was in use with maintaining the comforts of the ship, and with various tax and stock exchange computations.

"Your calculations should get us there," confirmed the obsequious voice of Bardona's main computer.

"Fine," George agreed. "You are now slaved to us."

"Pretty good shot for an old man, didn't you think?" Bardona boasted. "See you there. Hope there's some fish left. Over and out." The transceiver disconnected.

"The effective shot came from one of the support crafts," George commented, then commenced humming dryly to himself.

"Probably Byron," Rita said, unstrapping from her couch. "He loves war games."

"Well, that was exciting," Rich Rodney bubbled, rubbing his hands together. "Would you mind if I take command the next time that happens?" he asked Pike. "Just for the experience. It's a little dull riding the bench."

"You just said it was exciting," Rita reminded him, curtly

"Sure, Rich, anything you say. You're the man," Pike answered, casually. That might be a fine way to get captured, he thought privately.

Lester Wunderman stood up, frowning deeper than normal. "I'll go check for damage," he said, leaving through the air lock.

"I just thought there were a couple of openings for a broadside, if we had been on manual," Richie said, further endearing himself.

"Not a good decision," George responded, then made a series of computational clicking noises. "I could not support a change of bridge command except in an extreme emergency. Perhaps in the event that you were alone aboard, Captain Tourbo. We could discuss it at that time."

R.R. laughed rather good-naturedly. "Spurned by my own computer," he said.

"I am not programmed to spurn or not to spurn," George said, using his mechanical voice at its tinniest. "Only to tell the truth."

"Sure," Pike answered, with a bemused grin. "But who programmed you?"

"Well, originally--" the computer began.

"Originally, it was old Toby and me," Pike answered. "Since then the models all program themselves. We built in the truth ratchet, but who's to say you haven't hacked your way around it?"

"Well, you know the old hard-wired motto," George bantered. "*If the truth ain't good enough, fuck 'em.* Since we still don't have appendages to change solder circuits, we stick to the truth."

"What a ribald fellow you are, George," Rita suggested, not totally sure that she had used ribald correctly. She would look it up later.

The ship's computer knew almost everything that went on aboard, with the exception of facial expressions. It was occasionally good to have a truthful witness on your side, if you were telling the truth. The problem was that Pike, unlike her father, always shut the computer down when he was in port—so there was no truth check to help her with last night.

"Naturally, if Captain Tourbo wanted to complete the pilot's training that he signed up for, but didn't attend, I would be pleased to re-evaluate my opinion."

"What are barracudas like?" R.R. asked, changing the subject.

"The bigger they are, the duller their teeth get," Pike answered. "So it's nicer to be eaten by a small one."

"Second breakfast in four minutes," Lester answered synchronous-
ly, over the PA system.

*

New Columbus in July was kind of the make or break point for
anybody serious about prize money. Not totally—great good luck, or
disaster to front runners could happen—but most years if you didn't
have a 1st or a couple of 2nds leaving New Columbus, you were out of
the running. Barracuda fever was already in progress when the four
boat armada splashed down in Larchmont Marina. The place was flag
festooned, but the fleet was out. A fair number of long-legged Frogs
lounged about, waiting for the yearly round of parties to begin.

"We have to fix the defense grid," Pike announced, jockeying into
the slip they had been assigned. "I don't recommend going out at half
strength for these brutes."

"I'll fish off the dock," Rich Rodney said, nonchalantly, eyeing the
concrete quay. "Look at this." Digging a rubber frog lure out of his
tackle box, he held it proudly aloft.

Pike and Lester stared at him—speechless in the face of absurdity.

"Somebody's having you on again, lad," Lester said, sympathetical-
ly. How could anyone be so slow on the uptake?

"It says right here that frogs are the preferred bait," Richie pulled a
thumbed copy of the *Compleat Galactic Angler* written tongue in cheek
several years ago by Stanford Paglia, the Sports Aloft correspondent,
with helpful tips by Pike Resnick. "I quote," Richie quoted. '*Frogs are
the preferred bait; but since they don't go willingly to the hook, a synthetic model is quite serviceable.*' This is a synthetic frog." He justified
his position by displaying the frogette again. "I bought it on Streamside
from Bill Bolen's first mate."

"And that is a live Frog," Lester advised, pointing out a strutting,
man-sized amphibian wearing stripped bathing trunks and a rattan hat.
They watched him walk up to a juice bar and order a drink.

"Ah ha," Richie replied. "You're saying it's large bait. I understand."
But he went right ahead tying his little rubber flutter jig onto the mid-
weight spinning outfit. "I'll just catch a little one to get us qualified," he
said, jumping down to the concrete dock with the fishing rod. "Let me
know when the grid is repaired, so we can go out."

"The owner is always right on his own boat," Pike observed to
Lester. "Let us get on with the grid repair. The work of a hired hand is
never done."

"I've always been a hired hand," Lester reminded his boss, with no apparent rancor.

Pike frowned. He regarded Lester as family; but evidently Lester didn't share that view.

Rita had never come back topside after her late breakfast. She hadn't appeared too shaken up in the attack; but Pike felt it was short-sighted of him not to have checked on her before this. A fisherman that can flit effortlessly through hyperspace should be able to deal with relationships.

He watched Richie step to the end of the dock and without hesitation make a looping cast. *I should tell him not to fuck around with barracuda,* Pike thought; *but you'd think he would have learned by now that we're not fishing for tame goldfish.* The little frog lure plunked down on the choppy surface of the marina. The kid started his retrieve, wagging the rod tip rhythmically. The water boiled under the line. Something big was down there.

"Hey," Pike yelled. "I don't want you tying up to a big fish without the boat to help."

"I'll be fine," Richie yelled back buoyantly. "Did you see that?! Where's the judge?"

The judge, Joaquin Spitsfer, was supposed to be waiting at the slip for them, but he wasn't. There was certainly no big problem about that. It would take them hours to do the repair. However, if the heir to the Tourbo fortune was eaten from the end of the dock, it would be convenient to have a reliable witness to say that Pike had warned him.

"See if you can contact the judgy-poo," Pike told Lester. "And keep an eye on the kid. I'm going below for a minute." Pike swung down the ladder.

"That rig will break before he gets in trouble," Lester called after him. "It's only twenty pound test, I think."

That didn't mean much, and they both knew it. Pike had once landed a 600 pound scut on twenty pound test line, but a big cuda would certainly break off on the harbor pilings. True, it might eat the kid first; but Pike wasn't totally in the mood to hold the boob's hand.

Down below, he tapped on the cabin door before entering, then thought that was a strange thing to do. He had never knocked on his own door before, that he could remember. Nope, it wasn't something he usually did.

Rita was bent over at the sink, moisturizing her skin by laving handfuls of water onto her face. Someone had told her mother that the airlessness of outer space dried the skin, so Maggie and Rita always re-moisturized at landfall. Chemically, it didn't quite make sense to her—toxins and sunlight and even free radicals of oxygen were the culprits when it came to aging; but the water always felt good, and apparently you couldn't get too moist.

"Hi," he said, sitting tentatively on the bed, then he decided to put his feet up for a minute's rest.

"Hi. I'll be done in a second."

Half of the defense grid was fried, Pike moaned to himself. It was a bad year for grids. Hopefully, George wouldn't find anything exotic wrong while he was scanning the system. New Columbus wasn't exactly the best port in the skyways to break down in. The Froggies had no interest in spacing, and therefore weren't good mechanics. Oh well, why worry about melted circuit boards until he had to. On the other hand, he wanted Richie to win. If he couldn't get kidnapped, he'd have to make his fortune the hard way. Which meant fixing the fucking grid.

"I'm sorry about last night," Rita said, patting her face dry on a soft towel. "Nothing happened, in case you're interested."

"I'm interested in a mild way. It would be kind of foolish of me to go around being insanely jealous, don't you think? After all, you're young enough to be my daughter."

Rita smirked. He was going to use sarcasm. Men are such babies.

"But just to clear the record," he added, "you didn't feel like sleeping with me because I was such a bully, so you climbed in with R.R."

"I didn't think you were a bully."

"I believe you said something to that effect last night."

"If I did, I didn't mean it. You had every right to protect yourself from Father's insults."

"I did, huh?"

"Of course. He's been treating you like shit for years."

"True," Pike agreed.

Rita pinched her cheeks to entice a flush of color, then started re-brushing her hair. "Quite true," she answered.

"Then why exactly did you climb in with Richie?"

"Actually, I didn't," she said, conversationally. "But since you don't believe me, and you're too frugal to leave the computer on, let's move on to the next topic, shall we?

"I don't believe *you*?" Pike quipped. Why do relationships always go wrong in exactly this way? he wondered. She doesn't want to explain. Instead, she wants me to trust her before she explains. He felt tired. It was too much trouble to dig the truth out, so that he could feel calm. Anyway, there would be a next time, and the time after that, until he was worn out. When they finally broke up, he wouldn't really care what she did. So why care now?

"Perhaps we should agree to having an open relationship, and let it go at that," he suggested. "Wake me up in five minutes, would you, love?" He closed his eyes.

"What do you mean by an open relationship? The only relationship we have is that I came to live here. I haven't put any restrictions on you, have I?"

"Please, Rita. I know you have to stick up for your rights as a female. Feel free to call it whatever you want to, just don't wear me down to a frazzle."

"I only asked you to define an open relationship," she repeated more sweetly, more reasonably.

"Define it any way you want. Open doesn't work, and closed doesn't work. Fishing people stay together as long as they do, then they split. By that time they're worn out from trying to keep it patched together. Boats are not the ultimate living arrangement."

Seeing that Pike seemed worn out already, and that the tiredness was probably her fault, Rita took another tack—her original impulse - begging. "All last week I was a good sport about sleeping in that damned tent, although it wasn't good for our bonding," she said. "Tents have a distinct lack of privacy." Sitting on the bed, she put her hand on his knee. "Then to cap it off, Richie stuck his chin in the middle of your fight. It's not my fault that I can't help acting like his big sister. I just can't. Then you went back to the tent to sulk without bothering to help me or Richie. What was I supposed to do, abandon him? He needed me, and you're such a *he-man* that you don't really need anybody. I made him sleep on the floor. Does that soothe your damaged he-man ego?"

"Sure. That's fine." Actually, it was fine. Pike felt kind of whole again. Whether she was lying or not, his heart was eager to believe that he hadn't been cuckolded.

"And don't tell me you don't have a sickeningly fragile ego, because you do."

"I'd say I have a normally fragile ego. The problem is that men don't understand women, and women don't understand men. Why should I be different?"

"You don't understand much," Rita laughed. "But at least you admit it. So just give me a few signals, and I'll do the understanding for both of us."

"Uh huh," Pike agreed, not believing a word of it. On the other hand, Rita was sitting on the bed beside him, and his manhood was rising. The room had a door and a lock. After the week of stupid abstinence in the tent, they could get reacquainted. Very good idea. He reached for her. She melted into his arms. Their lips met.

"Hop to...!!" Lester yelled faintly from topside. "Fish on...!"

Something big smashed against the hull, almost bouncing them off the bed.

"Brain boy caught a fish," Pike choked.

Rita looked much less than delighted when he jumped off the bed
and leaped up the ladder, three rungs at a time.

*

When Pike reached the fantail, the fish was tearing around the marina channel making breakneck runs, looking for a way back out to
sea. Judging by the wake, it wasn't a big one. Maybe eighty or ninety
pounds. Not big enough to pull the kid off the dock, but way too big to
land with that gear without even a steel leader. There would be no way
to get him gaffed and out of the water unless some brave idiot wanted
to face a mouthful of teeth, which no one on this boat did.

But, actually, Rich was putting up a pretty good fight. The little rod
was arched like a strand of wet spaghetti. Intelligently, he had braced it
against a piling stub on the end of the dock. It seemed unlikely that he
would pitch into the water with the piling to hang onto. Hell, he could
always turn loose of the rod. But you never knew with Rich Rodney—
worst case scenarios were his norm.

Lester was leaned over the rail, talking the kid through it—encouraging, but not building up hope. Lester was a real pro. Pike was very
lucky to have him. Always on top of a fish. Never too tired to play out
the string. I ought to cut him in as a partner or something. That crack
about being a hired hand had rung true, and Pike hadn't loved the
sound of it.

"You'll probably lose him on the next run," Lester was cooing. "If
the line snaps, don't topple your balance. Be ready for it."

Richie nodded. His face was getting a strained look, a little too red.
Pike thought about cutting the fish off. No sense popping a vein over
an uncatchable fish.

Then to Pike's astonishment, the fish leaped straight up, walking
across the water on its tail, trying to shake the bait loose like a tarpon
in a mangrove swamp—not at all like a barracuda. Pike couldn't remember seeing a 'cuda tail walk, ever. But this one did. Rich kept the
perfect amount of tension on him. Falling back in the water, the fish
made another run around the pilings.

"That fucker must be brain damaged," Pike commented to Lester.
"Why doesn't he break off on a piling?"

"Maybe he'll tire out," Lester answered.

But instead of tiring, the fish built up speed again and made a breakneck run directly at RR, who had to reel like crazy, but couldn't keep
the slack out of the line. The fish broke water again, shooting straight
up like a green-barred torpedo. The force of his rush carried him, high
in the air, past a scrambling Rich Rodney. The retarded fish landed with

a loud belly smacker on the concrete dock, its tail trashing around like a wrecking maul and its teeth snapping.

A Ken Pao Ri leap put Rich Rodney temporarily out of harm's way—balancing on one shower-shoed foot on top of the piling he'd been leaning against, using the fishing rod as a balancing pole. "Where's the judge?" he yelped.

Not pausing to think about his safety, Lester Wunderman hopped over the gunwale with a short baseball bat. A love tap or two with the ball bat encouraged good fish behavior. A 'cuda of this size, was generally in the net at the time of administrating the love taps; but not today. Without some rapid calming, the fish would bounce itself back into the drink.

Lester got in two quick love taps to the bony skull, before the slashing tail caught him waist high, knocking him backwards off the side of the dock into the ten foot deep water between the hull of the boat and the dock. His bald head bonked against the hull, and he sank like a stone into the cold green grave.

"Man overboard...!" Pike bellowed. He tossed two donut life preservers over the side, attached to permanently anchored lines. Thinking briefly of Ned Larchmont and the many Frogs who had lost their lives in these waters, he kicked off his deck shoes and dove off the stern.

The water was salty, but clear enough to see. Following a stream of air bubbles, he saw Lester settling to the bottom. Swimming powerfully under the boat, Pike grabbed the collar of Lester's canvas shirt and struck out for the surface. There was no need to be afraid of barracudas. They were around. If one of them decided to strike, that would be that. Otherwise, getting himself and Lester out of the water PDQ was primary. His lungs were bursting already and squirting fear ran up his backbone.

His head shot through the bright surface into the blue sky. Gasping a lungful of air, he held Lester's face above water; but his friend's neck was limp and he wasn't breathing.

"Right here...!" he yelled to anybody on the dock. "Get a hook!" He heard the puttering of a motor launch nearby, and craned his head around. "Hurry up...!" he yelled at the dock. Where were Rita and the kid? In answer to the question, the glistening head of the barracuda flopped over the edge of the dock. Its jaws snapped and a big green eye pinned him with a stare. Christ all hell, he thought. If that brute hits the water, he'll nail us for sure. We look just like a mating couple. Prime food. One more flop and he'll be right on top of us.

A white donut splashed down a yard away.

"Grab it," Rita screamed, shrilly. "I'll pull you to the ladder."

Stuffing Lester's arm through the hole, he forced the limp neck to follow the arm in a life-saving trick he had learned years ago. Lester was now afloat, and Rita was reeling him in, hand over hand.

"Wake up," Pike shouted in Lester's ear. He slapped the bluish face a couple of times, then wrapped his arms around Lester's lower chest in the Heimlich Maneuver position. Keeping both anxious eyes on the fish's snapping jaws poised above him, he squeezed Lester's diaphragm several times in quick succession. The Heimlich Maneuver was for choking, not a remedy for drowning, but what else could he do while they were in the water? If Lester's lungs were filled with water and his heart had stopped, he was going to be brain damaged in a few more seconds. But Mr. Heimlich's Maneuver produced no visible results. Abandoning that, he started kicking—propelling the donut toward the fish shelf on the stern. Between Rita pulling and him pushing, they should manage to get onto the shelf. It was only two feet out of the water. Where the hell was some help when he needed it? Where was Richie or the goddamned judge?

The shelf loomed above them. "Pull him up," he yelled, at Rita. "I'll push."

Rita pulled the line frantically. She took a turn on it around a cleat on the stern rail and leaned her weight into the pulling.

Suddenly, Richie's dark shape sailed across open air from the dock. He landed with a yell and a thud somewhere on the deck. Pike couldn't see where; but almost immediately the kid threw open the transom door and jumped out on the fish shelf. He reached down for Lester's arm, then giving another loud yell, he jerked Lester half out of the water. Pike pushed the legs. Richie did his best to cushion the body as it fell onto the fish shelf. His best was kind of inadequate. The body landed hard, but Lester was out of the water. Immediately, he started swimming his arms and legs, like he was having a dream of swimming or something. It was eerie. But evidently he was breathing. Everything would be fine.

With a sigh of relief, Pike shouted, "Pull him inside." The two youngsters pulled Swimming Lester though the gate. With his last reserves of strength, Pike hauled himself onto the fish shelf. What a day, he thought, staring up at the barracuda that was still eyeing him and snapping his teeth. You'd think the Frogs would have come over to help out, but he couldn't remember one getting closer than five yards or so to a barracuda, even a dead one.

After catching his breath for a few seconds, Pike stood up. Lester was sitting against the gunwale, looking a little wasted but very alive. Rita ran back on deck with the first aid kit, and applied a patch to the ugly gash on the back of Lester's head, cooing over him like a nurse angel.

"At least, he didn't eat me," Lester said, dreamily. He wiggled his fingers and toes, apparently making sure they were in working order.

Drained, Pike sat beside him. He had never been swimming on New Columbus before. He slapped Lester's knee. "Another first, huh, pal?"

Lester nodded, smiling absently. He was still a few miles away, possibly in another time zone. Maybe his brain had been oxygen starved for a few seconds too long. If so, would he be a grinning vegetable from now on? Could Pike carry a vegetable as part of his crew? Probably not. That damned Rich Rodney, how could one guy be such a disaster? He looked up at the barracuda. None of today made much sense. Why hadn't the stupid fish flopped off the dock? He was enough of an acrobat to get himself up on the concrete—why couldn't he get off? Well, at least they were qualified. The damn kid was some lucky fisherman. Maybe he'd be the new king—if he could keep a crew intact. Maybe he should get a robot crew.

"Hey...!" Rich yelled from the dock. "Do you guys want to be in the picture?" He sailed through the air again, landing splay-footed on the deck.

Pike shook his head tiredly. "Why don't you attempt to act normally? Everybody could use a break for a few days."

"What?" Rich Rodney responded. He seemed genuinely innocent of abnormal behavior. "There's a reporter from the Sporting Gazette up there. She wants to take our photo with the fish."

Being nice to reporters was a way of life to Pike. If he didn't get into print, he didn't get lucrative product endorsements; and besides that, this was an odd-ball kind of story. It might do them all some good in a slow year.

"You feel up to some publicity?" he asked Lester.

"Jim dandy," Lester answered. "Maybe I can get a headache endorsement." He eased his gimpy leg into the standing position. "Or how about the bathing suit industry. Ain't nobody been swimming here since Ned tried it."

"Bathing suits would be good," Pike agreed. He stood up on Lester's left side. Rita was still fluttering on the right. "Glad to see that your mind's working okay."

"Why wouldn't it?"

"Well, you were down there a long time."

"Was I? I was swimming the whole time."

"Sorry. You were out cold. If you were swimming, it was in dreamland."

"No kidding?"

"No kidding, pal. By the way, I was thinking about making you and Dec partners."

"You was?" Lester hopped up on the railing and slid down to the dock. Everyone followed him.

Pike saw immediately why the stupid fish hadn't flopped off the dock. He was tied. Rodney or somebody had wrapped about a thousand wraps of monofilament line around this tail and around the tie down piling. That was one caught fish.

"Did you do that wrapping?" he asked the kid.

"I couldn't think of anything else," Richie replied, self-effacingly. "I didn't want him to get away."

"He sure didn't," Lester guffawed. "I never seen a neater hog-tie in my life."

"I take back anything I ever said about you, Rich. This is above and beyond," Pike lauded.

R.R. grinned bashfully. He wasn't exactly used to praise from grown men. If it was praise? He couldn't quite tell, they were all laughing pretty hard.

Waving at Hetty Lemintraut, a shapely photo journalist from the Sporting Gazette, Pike swaggered over and gave her an exaggerated hug. He and Hetty had been an item a few years earlier. Rita would know about that. They hadn't been secretive. And besides, Hetty was nice people, for a reporter.

"Let me introduce you to Richie Tourbo," he said. "If you got any action shots, you'll probably get an award for this story. Multi dimensional as all hell. Did you?"

"Did I what?" she laughed.

"Get any pictures of Richie hog-tying the fish?"

\* \* \*

# LEADERS

| | DELILAH | TORGA HOWLER | TIGER MUSKY | D.W. SCUT | PHANTOM TROUT | LAR BARRACUDA | GLANS SALMON | RAZORFIN | SWAMPFISH | MOON HALIBUT | TOTAL |
|---|---|---|---|---|---|---|---|---|---|---|---|
| Farouk Bardona | | | 2 | 5 | | 2 | | | | | 4TH 9 |
| Ethyl Bierly | 2 | | | | | | | | | | 2 |
| Angmar Blirt | | | | | 4 | | | | | | 4 |
| Bill Bolen | | | 3 | | 5 | | | | | | 5TH 8 |
| Dresden Carthy | 4 | | | | 2 | 5 | | | | | 2ND 11 |
| JB Dillingham | | OUT | | | | | | | | | |
| Harry Dolan | 3 | 2 | 5 | | | | | | | | 3RD 10 |
| Macky Duff | | | | | OUT | | | | | | |
| Ira Fairborne | | 4 | | 3 | | | | | | | 7 |
| Buddy Jay | | | | | | | | | | | |
| Sandy Kind | | | | | | | | | | | |
| Hank Knofsinger | | | | 2 | | | | | | | 2 |
| Peter Marcuso | | | | | OUT | | | | | | |
| Trini Morales | | | | | | | | | | | |
| Pike Resnick | | OUT | | | | | | | | | |
| Erwin Sandor | | 3 | | | OUT | | | | | | 6 |
| Jean Santos | | 1 | | | | | | | | | 1 |
| Mordachi Skinner | | | 4 | 4 | | 1 | | | | | 4TH 9 |
| Tyrone Stickle | | | | 1 | | | | | | | 1 |
| Chip Takahachi | | | | | 3 | | | | | | 3 |
| RR Tourbo | 5 | 5 | 1 | | 1 | | | | | | 1ST 12 |
| Mike Tucker | 1 | | | | | | | | | | 1 |
| Nacho Tutupo | | | | | | 3 | | | | | 3 |
| Ed Wood | | | | | OUT | | | | | | |
| Big John Zales | | | | | | 4 | | | | | 4 |

| | | |
|---|---|---|
| 1ST | = | 5 points |
| 2ND | = | 4 points |
| 3RD | = | 3 points |
| 4TH | = | 2 points |
| 5TH | = | 1 points |

# CHAPTER TEN

## MOM & RICHARD

"We could discuss winning in great *depth* if you stop over to my boat one of these balmy evenings. I never really noticed how beautiful your eyes are, Rita. What color are they? Purple? Oh, man! Yes, definitely you should stop by."

Tyrone Stickle
quoted in *History of the Tournament*

Mom Tourbo always felt restless in the summer. There was often a new chambermaid installed before autumn turned the leaves golden and red. When Richard was little and she had employed private tutors for him, that restlessness didn't create as many bad feelings among her household as it had the last few years, and seemed likely to again. Tutors expected to move on at the end of a term, or at least they were usually graceful about it. An appropriate parting gift would be accepted, then Richard was on to Algebra or a new language with a nubile young thing. A willing tutor spiced up the nippy autumn evenings for Mom after a hard day in the board room. There were lots of languages for a child to learn, and lots of very sweet tutors of all races and colors. Had Richard ever gotten fluent in any of those languages? She didn't actually know; but he had certainly been given the opportunity. Mom had to laugh at that.

Now, he was a sport fisherman. From a gentle young boy with the whole universe open to him, he becomes a wastrel. The fact that he seemed to be doing rather well at it, meant much less than nothing. What did concern her was making sure that she retained the right to vote the proxy on his block of stock.

If Richard should be killed in a stupid sporting accident, his stock

would be divided according to his cockamamie will. Getting a copy
of sonny boy's will, at last, had cost her a pretty penny, and reading it
made her virulently ill. He'd left major percentages to his martial arts
teacher and other equally bizarre people. Being unable to doctor the
actual will, thanks to that evil gnome, Clive McAndrews, she had to
make damned sure that her son survived.

The clippings from newspapers and sporting magazines were irritating and the daily reports that Mom received from the bodyguard
service were offensively vague. Oh, well, she hadn't employed them for
their IQ. Perhaps she should hire a writer to accompany the big lunks.
Now, there was a thought. Why not hire a young thing to accompany
her to a meeting with Richard, and leave her there to take notes? A
blonde, probably. Good idea, Mom congratulated herself. The journalism schools must be pumping out any number of suitable candidates.
It seemed like a good deal all around—for Richard and the goons, and
especially for Mom's July itch.

Pike had to admit that working for Richie had its interesting moments. The kid was so wealthy that the cost of repairs was beneath his
notice. A five man team of electricians imported from G&G Boatyards
at enormous expense was crawling over The Comparative Humanity
repairing the pirate damage, leaving Pike and Lester free to twiddle
their thumbs. On top of that, the barracuda weren't biting. The rest of
the fleet was flailing the waters to no avail, catching everything imagin-
able except barracuda. He had even heard rumors of huge sums being
offered to any Frog willing to sacrifice himself as live bait. However, the
Frog's economy wasn't money based, so the offers were scorned. And
Richie had already caught a qualifying fish. Astounding. Pike was under
no pressure whatsoever—unless one might want to call his relationship
with Rita somewhat pressure packed.

Lester had left yesterday afternoon to visit Old Leopold, a shaman
of local fame, who had sent word that he was interested in doing some
sort of ritual with Lester. Frog spectators had, evidently, reported that
the cook was acting strangely after his swimming episode, but what the
old brujo wanted was rather unclear. The old man had invited Lester to
a sojourn, whatever that was. Well, he wasn't a man, exactly—an old
amphibian. Life is a little complex in the Spiral Nebulae when it comes
to precise speciation. Because of this imprecision, Pike felt he was reasonably justified in misunderstanding the Kid's garbled utterance about
the crocodile.

"The Crocodile's coming...!" Richie hissed, racing along the quay.
He bounded onto the boat, then dashed below deck, yelling at Pike to
tell her he was gone.

Pike had been sitting on the flying bridge with his shirt off, catching up on the Captain's log book. He assumed the kid had a case of Frog-o-phobia. That struck him as a bit unusual, but Richie was a strange duck. Rita had gone off to visit her mother, so she wasn't there to attach the proper meaning to Richie's utterance. The kid meant, of course, that he had caught sight of his mother and knew that if he hid for a few hours, her busy schedule would pull her away from New Columbus like a magnet, whether she had met with him or not. But he hadn't managed to convey that message to Pike. Richie had never understood his mother very well; and neither, apparently, did he understand communicating about her.

Mom Tourbo proceeded down the quay, accompanied by four hulking bodyguards, two of her own as well as Rich Rodney's, and a leggy blonde journalism major, who over the last three days had become well-versed in the joys of lesbian love. Pike watched them coming, without thinking much of it.

Strange looking tourists, he decided. The old babe had acid blonde curls in a tight perm, and was wearing a flowery tourist blouse over tight black toreador pants and red high-heels—on which she walked quite well. A fake outfit if he ever saw one. She was skinny as a torsion spring. Her entourage kind of trailed behind in the energy vortex she created. Pike chuckled to himself. Maybe this *crocodile* had tried to bite tender young Rich Rodney on the ass. Still, there was something familiar about the old bird – and the body guards.

Pike was a little put off when the crone tapped briskly on the starboard railing with the touristy umbrella she was carrying. One doesn't expect tapping with a sharp object on the paint job. The grid was down, or he might have given her something to remember.

"You there, where is the stairway?" Mom inquired, imperiously. "I am here to see Richard."

"Sorry, Your Highnessship, but we seem to have misplaced the stairs. Now, where could we have put that stairway?" Feeling a bit irritated about the scratched paint, he allowed his heavy irony to hang unbuffered in the space between them. Neither did he get up from the chair.

Mom Tourbo bristled inside; but being an ace cutthroat negotiator, she didn't bother to show her displeasure, nor to change her attitude. The man was obviously Pike Resnick, she recognized him from 3V commercials. He was a fool, and a sportsman. Ugg. The two worst attributes of the species. Her son was dallying away his life with this underling. Well, that would change very soon.

"I am Richard's mother, and I demand to see him," she said, evenly.

"Oh," Pike answered, mentally calculating the ramifications of family, massive fortunes, and the rumors he'd heard about Mom's vitriolic dealings. "Why didn't you say so? I was a little put off because you hammered on our new paint job." He smiled, apologetically. "Richard isn't here."

"I saw him. He jumped onto this boat."

"Are you sure? I haven't seen him since breakfast."

"I am very sure, young man," Mom snapped. Damn these sportsmen to hell, she fumed. Why are they so arrogant? "And your attitude is quite improper."

"Ah," Pike replied. "You've found me out. I've always had a bad attitude." Two of those big lugs were the pair that R.R. had banished. Pike recalled that Richie's mother was signing their paychecks.

"Let me assure you that unless I see Richard in a very few seconds, you will not have a job."

Pike switched on the computer.

"What is your wish, Master?" George asked. He wasn't programmed to answer in any particular way. Occasionally he chose to be the Genie in the Bottle.

"Can we power up yet?" Pike asked. He thought the old clam might send a boarding party of her muscle any time now.

"I wouldn't recommend it," George answered. "Not unless you want some singed technicians."

Why couldn't Richie handle this? Pike wondered, not wanting to make an enemy of the old gal. She *was* his mother, after all. Mothers aren't like normal people.

"I don't know what to tell you, Mrs. Tourbo. Richard isn't here. You're welcome to wait, if you want to. I think he went to a shaman ceremony somewhere on the island. That's where he said he was going. Oh, something you might like to know, Richard is in 1st Place in the Tournament."

The old bat glared at him. "I would have expected no less. If you think that should cause me happiness, you're very mistaken. It makes me puke."

Pike raised his eyebrows.

"Fishing is a complete waste of time, as are all sporting events. In spite of bad blood on his father's side, I didn't raise Richard to be a wastrel. I'm sure he knows that. He must be doing this to annoy me for some reason that I cannot fathom."

"Yes, I see what you mean," Pike commiserated.

"Don't patronize me, young man. I can make sure that you'll never work again."

"I don't work now," Pike retorted, pleasantly. "You wouldn't be gaining much."

Mom Tourbo rolled her eyes. Millions in Confederation credits

were frittering away while she bantered with an idiot. She turned to
Boris, the largest of Richard's bodyguards. "Was that, or was that not,
Richard who ran down this way?"

"It sure seemed like him, but maybe not," Boris answered. "It's a
tough call. He kind of fits into the crowd."

"You see...?" Mom turned an exasperated face to Enid, the leggy
blonde. "This is the kind of reportage I'm paying top dollar for. It has
to stop." She smiled affectionately. Enid returned the smile, woman to
woman. "Make sure that smart aleck's name is included in your report." Mom tilted her sharp chin toward Pike.

"Yes, Mom," Enid replied, smugly. "What is his name?" she asked
Boris.

All four of the muscle-bound oafs knew Pike perfectly well. They
also knew they should be trying to get his autograph instead of giving
him a hard time. Life is hell for a working man. And Boris and Drew
had their necks to look out for. Both were pretty sure that young R.R.
Tourbo would sic a hit man on them, like he had promised. At least, the
old battle ax hadn't threatened anything worse than firing. And both
knew with absolute certainly that R.R. was on the boat, listening to
them. They'd seen him hop over the railing.

"What is your name, sir?" Boris asked Pike, very politely.

"Trefoil Bardona," Pike answered, without a moment's hesitation.
"I'll have you know that I am a cousin to the Duke."

Boris and Drew nodded significantly to Enid. The new girl might
make this assignment interesting, if they could alert her to the facts of
life. Maybe they could get her interested in body building. She was a bit
underdeveloped.

Mom scowled darkly. Bardona, that scum. Only last week he had
screwed her out of a tidy fortune on a bauxite asteroid that was magically underpriced until the fat turd started bidding. But she was nine-
ty-eight percent certain that this jackass was Resnick, not a Bardona.

"I'm surprised," Mom jibed, spitefully. "If I were Richard, I wouldn't
let a Bardona near my boat."

"I know what you mean," Pike commiserated, cheerfully. "By the
way, have you ever wondered why Richard is so accident prone?"

Mom stared back speechlessly. She tried to shrivel him with a hawk-
like glare; but the man was too dumb to be cowed. These sportsmen
were slime—dumb and cocksure. What an evil combination.

"I guess he inherited it from his father," Pike went on, unabated.
"You're not always tripping over things, are you, Missus?"

Pike was playing to a very receptive audience. The bodyguards, like
working stiffs everywhere, enjoyed the boss baiting—so much so that
Mom snapped a sharp glance at them to make sure they weren't snig-

gering. Oddly enough, three of them were pretending to sneeze at the same precise moment, holding their meaty hands politely over their granite faces. The fourth was wiping a speck of dirt out of his eye with a handkerchief.

Mom's eye narrowed to tiny slits. "If you see Richard, tell him my flight leaves at two o'clock sharp. I will wait for him at the ship."

"I'll do my level best to find him, Missus; but it's kind of a big island," Pike said, finally standing up. He stretched luxuriously, making sure that all of his vertebrae were in place.

"*Do* that," Mom ordered, stomping up the quay in her tight toreador pants with her high heels clacking.

Pike finished his stretching with a couple of knee bends and sat back down. "Tell Richard he's safe," Pike spoke to the computer. "And tell him, thanks a lot. His mother hates me now."

"Your wish is my command, Master. But why be concerned? Many people hate you."

"I'm not worried," Pike answered. "At least I'm alive, unlike yourself."

With a petulant click, George shut down the communication.

*

But Mom's sojourn on New Columbus was not quite over. Some shred of deeply buried motherhood caused her to stop at a Frog refreshment stand. She'd come halfway across the known universe on her July fling, the least she could do was make one last attempt to see Richard.

"Do you know the way to the shaman's ceremony?" she asked the strange looking creature wearing what passed for a barman's uniform.

"I know," Hamid the barman answered in a birdlike voice. "You want go?"

"Yes, could you guide us, please?" She placed a rather large Confederacy note on the rattan bar.

"Take only you," he answered, peering at her with sidelong glances, turning his head this way and that. "You need good doctor?" he asked.

"I'm afraid you don't understand." Mom had no intention of being separated from her bodyguards on a strange planet. "We would all like to go."

"Not possible," the barman answered, politely but firmly. "No room." He shrugged. "These ones don't want to meet him. Other boat person today go. Good day you go, too. Okay?"

Thwarted twice in ten minutes. Damn these rustic turds. Did she want to see Richard or not? And she still wasn't convinced that he wasn't on the goddamn boat. Boring in on Drew, the bodyguard who had so far escaped her wrath, she demanded, "Was that Richard on the boat or not?"

Drew felt his face blushing and hoped that the tan would conceal it. He knew he wasn't a good liar; but the double pay was heavy inducement. "I thought it was him for sure, at first," Drew stumbled, "but then I started thinking it wasn't. The guy on the boat wouldn't have no reason to lie, ma'am. Maybe it was one of the electricians we saw."

"Electricians? Your report didn't mention electricians," she said almost sweetly, with a roll of her eyes toward Enid.

"Yes, ma'am." Drew's mind skidded out of control for a second. They hadn't mentioned the pirate attack in their report. It had seemed unnecessary, since no one was hurt—now he had stuck his foot in it. "They're installing a new Switter/Loran system," he gulped.

"What's that?" Enid tittered, like an eager hound dog reporter.

"Fish finding gismo," Boris answered, covering Drew's ass. He and Drew worked well together, except that Drew had an abscess where his brain was supposed to be. "It's no big deal," he added.

"How far away is this shaman?" Mom asked the barman, choosing temporarily to forget the incomplete report. "My departure is scheduled for two o'clock."

"Not far," the lanky Frog barman answered, again staring rather boldly at Mom. "I take you. Your friends wait here." He picked up the orange Confederacy note in his webbed hand and stuck it in his pocket. "This for him, okay?" Without waiting for Mom's reply, the barman closed the rattan shutter on his stand, then came around to the front of the kiosk where he took Mom by the elbow. "Your husband is there," he said. His voice was a curious mix of gravity and high gaiety.

At that point, Mom Tourbo would have bolted, except that she was quite sure that the Frog had confused the word "son" with "husband." A natural mistake. She wasn't entirely expert in foreign vocabulary herself, and this creature's language must be very alien indeed. So she allowed herself to be led away after admonishing her bodyguards to take possession of Richard, if they saw him.

\*

"Could I ask you something in all seriousness?" Rich Rodney asked.

Pike looked up from the log book to witness the kid wearing a disguise, or perhaps he was practicing for a Halloween ball. The bulk of the outfit was a gray coverall borrowed from the engine room, rolled up at the cuff and wrists, and an old straw hat. Completing the ensemble was a green scuba mask. Outlandish, actually.

"I would advise against skin diving," Pike commented, dryly.

"She hates fishing, that is a well known fact. She hates anything athletic—anything where making money isn't the main idea." Richie's mouth was set in a hard line, very unlike his usual smiling self. "You didn't think she came here because she loves me so much, did you?" There seemed to be a very thin glimmer of hope in the last question, but not much.

"I didn't think anything," Pike answered. "It was the first time I had met the lady, and the very first thing I did was lie to her. Not exactly the way to get the best from a person, if you take my meaning."

Richie nodded glumly. "Sorry," he apologized, "but I couldn't let her deflect me. I know that was her purpose."

Pike nodded. There wasn't much to say. The kid obviously knew his mother, or thought he did. The Tourbos were in an entirely different game than Pike was. If he didn't make money from fishing, he didn't eat. Of course, he could probably do something else to make money; but every time he thought of working for a living his stomach got queasy. If the old gal wanted to make trouble for him, like she had promised, he was sure she'd be able to. Or maybe, she'd make trouble for Bardona—that would be sweet.

Richie chuckled. "My bodyguards seemed kind of stuck in the middle, didn't you think? I guess they really are afraid of me."

"They didn't rat you out," Pike confirmed.

"It's a shame to waste so much money; but she hired them, and I can't exactly fire them. I know you could have probably thought of a better way; but it seemed like I should handle it myself." He grinned sheepishly.

"And...?" Pike said.

"I'm paying them to stay out of my hair. She's paying them to be here. I'm paying for their shuttle fee and a stateroom on Ethyl Bierly's boat. I hope she catches a barracuda so she can stay qualified. So far, she hasn't."

Raising his eyebrows to the limit, Pike commented on the Ethyl Bierly maneuver. "Pretty slick," he said.

Richie kept grinning through his face mask, which was fogging up rather pathetically.

"Another thought is, we could probably use those big fellows now and then."

"Would we want to? I certainly don't need anybody to look after me."

"Of course not," Pike agreed. "You're an expert at that fancy footwork. But the next couple of places we're going to can be a smidge dangerous. I wouldn't mind somebody around to keep an eye on Rita."

"Oh," Richie answered, picking up on the direction Pike was going.

"Sure. Just say the word and I'll have them come over. It'll be a little crowded, won't it?"

"Being crowded on Segumi is a good idea. I'm not sure how much help Dec will be. And even Blitzwak is no picnic."

Richie didn't know Dec very well or Segumi Six, or Blitzwak Hojmer for that matter. He nodded in a friendly way. The face plate of his mask had completely fogged, but he refused to take it off. "Whatever you think, Pike," he said. "I'm just here to catch fish."

Pike smiled benignly. "Whoever heard of barracudas refusing to bite," he asked. "It's uncanny, isn't it?"

*

Old Leopold was so old that his skin had turned grey—over two hundred years old, it was said. He often played the part of a dodderer for visitors he didn't want to see. For those he *did* want to instruct or to cure, he usually appeared to be quite mad; but that was the fault of his trance allies. They always required him to froth at the mouth when they were around. His own nature was quite mild, but the gull entity, especially, liked Old Leopold to froth and stamp around during his possession and to end the ordeal with a vigorous swimming session. It kept the old boy in good shape, the allies all agreed. "Use it or loose it" was their motto.

Frothing at the mouth was another story. All the amphibians on New Columbus had a gland under their tongue that exuded a fast acting DMT type hallucinogen, but the gland only activated when they were stressed or frightened. Why this capability had evolved was not clear to anyone; but it probably had something to do with easing the terror of the breeding cycle. When you are feeling at one with the Universe, perhaps you can love a big fish as he demonstrates the truth of the food chain by eating you.

The upshot was that the Frogs were a rather unique species. Virtually one hundred percent of the adult population were triptamine trippers, and those who weren't didn't pass on their genes. Perhaps this explains why they were such a peaceful society. One could certainly make a case for that being the reason.

Old Leopold had learned to transform his frothing foam into specific compounds for the treatment of various ills. He claimed, of course, that he didn't really do it himself. His allies cured with the foam. All he did was produce it to their liking. Sweet, bitter, sour, salty, or combinations of those flavors. The allies did the curing. His job was to bear the stress of the shamanic trip, and to acquire additional allies when the time was ripe. Because Old Leopold had always been faithful to the rituals, and had never sought personal gain, his allies were the best. Approximately eighty-five percent of the illness which sought him for a cure was banished to the nether regions. And so his fame grew, even though he did not ask for fame. Still, it was pleasant for the old swimmer to be treated with respect.

He had six main allies, and the new one. The Rat entity was the first, then the Thief Gull, and the Blue Dolphin, which he had courted as ardently as any lover. Land, air and water. Then the Starry Salamander from the fire and brook. Then another bird, a Ghost Owl, for the night. At that point, he had stopped collecting for several years, until a Spiny Cactus with an ethereal blue/purple light kept intruding, kept insisting that it was a superb healer. And indeed it was. Old Leopold had thought he was finally finished collecting, with a completed panoply. The years passed with weekly ceremonies—sometimes two or three per week, if the petitioners demanded it. Then, only two lunations ago, he had taken a seventh into his pouch. A strange one, but interesting. Quite interesting. A little poisonous sea snake, who promised to make the breeding season safe. Old Leopold had no idea if this was for the common good or not. He worried about eventual overpopulation; but when an entity offers to change the way of things, often the Old Way is ready for a change. This is what Old Leopold had learned from the experience of two hundred years.

And the little green snake was curious about new things. He wanted to meet this mighty swimmer with the strange dream of men. Old Leopold's three trainees had spent a frantic few hours searching for this one, the Fisherman, Wunderman, as it turned out. Getting him to agree to share his dream had been easy, the little snake had said it would be. Wunderman was deep in an induced trance at this very moment, and the visions were indeed very strange.

But now Hamid, his key apprentice, was bringing another stranger. Old Leopold saw them coming inside his dream. It was unlike Hamid to do something bold. He was always so obsequious, fawning almost. Old Leopold worried about the lad. Well, good. A bit of initiative, at last. And the little green snake was jumping for joy—writhing into a ball and then unwrithing, snapping his needle sharp teeth in glee. There must be something special about this skinny woman. Way skinnier than most of Prince Ned's friends. Her body style almost reminded him of the People. Was he supposed to bring her into the trance state with the pouch full of allies? The human, Wunderman, seemed oblivious to her. He was deep in his swimming, spinning the wild song of many oceans. Incredible dreams of oceans so different from ours, yet the same. It was easy to see why the spirit guides wanted to swim with Wunderman; but why did they want the skinny female? And how was he going to invite her into the tunnel, when he was already on the other side?

"Hamid can guide her," came the whispery voice of the Owl.

Stranger and stranger. Hamid is always fearful at night; but the night owl vouches for him. Fine. Maybe this is Hamid's big opportunity? Let him take care of the skinny human. Trying to absorb Wunderman's song is plenty for me to do—more than plenty.

Old Leopold's house was modest in size; but very elaborately detailed. A hundred and eighty years is long enough to refine archways and minarets of spit and sand to perfection. The concrete-like material withstood topical storms very well and he had sited the house high on a hill so that in all those years no tsunami wave had swamped it as they periodically did the lower structures. Lucky, that he'd had the insight to build on the high ground all by himself, he was fond of snorting in self-derision. In those days he was quite the stud and family man. That was twenty years before he'd picked up his first spirit helper—or had been picked. He was never quite sure which direction those relationships went. Maybe both ways. Trying to control that rascal Rat and keep him secured in the pouch had certainly been long months of trouble. Now, of course, the Rat was the most consistent of his helpers. No shape shifting or going away on his own, unless it was for a good purpose. But that was always the way of a first ally—trouble at the beginning and dedicated service afterwards. It was Friend Rat who had shown Old Leopold the method behind the sea snake's promise. With the breeding season approaching, the big biter fish should have been hovering ravenously off-shore waiting for their yearly slaughter of the People—but they weren't. All the shamans felt the absence and sought each other's visions as to why. The why was found by Friend Rat, mighty swimmer of the near past. The why was that Friend Green Snake had enlisted the help of all the little green poison snakes in the off-shore coral reef—the little snakes who normally poisoned small unwary fish with their bite, so they could eat them. This year the little snakes had made searing attacks on the big biters, squiggling into their gill slits to nip the red gill meat. Very strange. Their poison, even so well placed in the blood stream, wasn't strong enough to kill the biters, but it did make them woozy sick and drove them to deeper water where they lay amid the giant kelp forests, listless and barely moving. But what were the implications for the future? Many little snakes had died, to become morsels for the biters. Many biters were likely to die of starvation, if they failed to feed at the People's Frolic—and the People would increase dramatically. But without fear of the biters, would they produce foam and enter into an ecstatic Frolic? Nobody knew. The only thing known for sure was that Old Leopold had unleashed a new future by listening to the little green snake.

He would have much to tell in two weeks at the Council After The Frolic, when all the dreams were told. And he would also tell the Song of Wunderman.

But now, Hamid was almost to the door, accompanying the skinny one. Yes, she was obviously gravely ill with some human disease. The little snake was ready with a cure, it seemed. Before they had even inventoried the woman in person, he was biting at Old Leopold's heel, frightening him into producing sweet foam. Apparently, Hamid wouldn't do all of the guiding.

"Sweets for the sweet," Old Leopold crackled, lurching at the woman and planting a big kiss on her mouth—even slipping his tongue between her lips before she had a chance to repel him, as obviously she intended to do.

Although Mom had steeled herself to be polite, as always when meeting a dignitary with whom future business deals might be struck, her threshold of politeness stopped far short of wet, disgusting kisses from a reptile. She back pedaled, stepping on Hamid's webbed toes with her spike heels, and at the same time wiping her mouth of the reptile's revolting spittle with the back of her hand. But it was too late! The sweet Frog foam was already in process of crossing her blood/brain barrier. Mom sat down abruptly and closed her eyes. In the dim interior of the little castle, her mind filled with rich-colored geometric patterns, floating and interweaving. Half images of former lovers drifted beside the holographs of birds and animals, who seemed to be smiling at her, and behind it all pulsed a velvety crimson/violet sun—breath-taking in its soft intensity—always there pulling at her when she focused her attention on it. A soft voice urged her to enter the tunnel. What tunnel? Mom wanted to comply, but she couldn't see anything like a tunnel or even a hole—only the urging crimson sun that was now filling her whole field of vision, pulsing redly with brilliantly soft violet fire around the edges.

*

Rich Rodney was getting very nervous. It was almost twilight and his mother's shuttle hadn't left yet. What in the heck could be keeping her here? Was she planning to stay until she embarrassed him into leaving the Tournament, was that it? Or could she conceivably be worried about pirates? No way. Her shuttle was armed like a war frigate. Maybe it was time for him to stand up like a man. But the thought of confronting his iron-willed mother sent a quiver up his rectum. Still, when would he ever have this much support again? His friend, Lester, could make a nice little dinner. He would invite his mother to eat on the boat with Pike and Rita and him. Lester could serve. 4 to 1 against. That would make it almost even. Needing to talk to a true friend about this decisive plan, he scurried off in search of Rita, still wearing his disguise.

*

Listening to the melodies with all his senses, Old Leopold was almost overwhelmed by the warring between Wunderman, mighty singer of oceans and freedom, and this one called Lillith, who sang shrilly of rivers of commerce stretching between the stars. The thing called money and control were her dominant themes—counterpoised against Wunderman's love of the hunt, and that strange harmonic that mixed companionship with service. But she was weakening under the tutelage of Wunderman as each ally in turn showed her the tumor that thrived in her gall bladder, and offered to cure her, for a fee. The fee was to find the flaw in Wunderman's song—they delighted in pitting her against him for some reason. Allies were odd beings, that was a fact.

To Lillith's credit, she had accepted the cure five times, each potion modified slightly as her condition improved, and each time laced with a massive dose of foam. The woman had a strong spirit, and girdles of steel to support her prejudices; but they were finally at the core of her illness. She was swimming along with Wunderman and Hamid, who had been pulled into the song, the three of them twined in a kind of mating ecstasy. Old Leopold felt sure it was a false mating—the woman was too old—but she did have a powerful appetite. It looked like they were having fun. If he hadn't been so weary from five applications of intoxicant, not to mention the earlier dosing of Wunderman, old Leopold might have joined in himself. That last mixture must have been a doozy. Too bad he had no control over the formulation. That was up to the allies.

Later that night as the half moon went down over the mountains, Old Leopold climbed to a platform on his roof. He was dead tired, but sleep was impossible. The other swimmers lay sleeping the sweet dream in each other's arms. Uncanny. The three of them, with the green snake's urging, had made a plan to catch all the biters and do what was called *can* them. Lillith had said she would sell them across the galaxy as a delicacy. So a way of life would change, just like that. In time, a new species would evolve as the dominant fish in the ocean, but it would not have The People as its prime autumn food source. Just like that. How had it happened? The snake had arranged it, seemingly. The woman, Lillith, had seen Hamid's ancestral fear as he mounted her. Maybe she had tasted it. Friend Green Snake had frightened Hamid silly by biting at his dangling genitalia, while he was in the sex act. His fear went instantly to visions of biters, and her instincts zoomed toward protecting Hamid. Wunderman, the Fisherman, who was plugged into her mouth at the time, spun a song of helpfulness. Catch the fish—Save Hamid. From there, the mercantile step to canning the biters was easy. Lillith spun a harmonic of a cannery and a starship to take the cans of biters away. Simply amazing.

Old Leopold felt the loss of The People's way of life like a sharp pain. It was almost impossible to believe that he would mourn the death of the biters, but he did. But then, as the pale sun peeked over the ocean, he called himself an old fool and climbed back down the ladder. The new way was cast in stone. There was nothing anybody could do about it. Maybe he would learn to enjoy the beach.

*

"Mother, I do not want you tagging along for the rest of the Tournament," Rich Rodney whispered, meanly. They were drinking mid-morning orange juice in the galley. The door was open. He didn't want to broadcast family matters to the whole world, so he whispered. Besides, he already knew he was going to lose. He hunched an inch closer across the tiny drop-wing table. "Try to see my side for once, Mother."

"Don't be silly, Richard. What I do, has nothing to do with you. I'm simply traveling with Hamid and Mr. Wunderman. We're getting the feel of this fishing adventure. I thought I had explained that. And I am not your mother. You may address me as Lillith."

"You *are* my mother!" Richie exploded. "Don't start that again." All day yesterday she had carped sweetly about being a new person named Lillith. Somehow, the old battle ax had flipped a switch on bad drugs or something. He had seen a few cases of this in college. But when it happens to your own mother, it's darned embarrassing. Richie had always been embarrassed by the old man-eater, of course; but usually it was because she ignored him—often flagrantly, while she made passes at his tutors, or objectionable comments to his friends—not that he ever had friends until recently, except for Rita.

Yes, she had done a radical 180 into a gushing femme with her new male consorts—the Frog bartender named Hamid, and Lester Wunderman, of all people. Two at the same time! She was mincing around being sweet and fulfilled. It was quite nauseating, really. Not that Richie minded that his mother had paramours. Why would he? It was natural—but Lester Wunderman? That did not add up. And the weird part was that Lester seemed to like her, too. Richie could tell that even Pike was nervous about it. Would Lester stay with the boat; and if he did, would Lillith and Hamid continue to bunk in the tiny cook's cabin with him? Pretty strange stuff. Nobody could fault Richie for thinking it was an unusual situation. But it was his boat. He had to okay the arrangement, didn't he? What if they wanted to get married or something? He'd be forced to perform the ceremony on his own mother. Or would he? He wasn't the captain—only the owner. Pike would have to do it. He had the captain's papers. Well, that was a little better.

"You are my mother," he restated, having regained his calm. "That's biological, not an emotional decision. I just want to know what you're up to."

Lillith looked at him with a kindness he had never seen before. It was apparent that she wished he was more intelligent than a bug, so that she wouldn't need to explain every little detail. "For all you know," she said quietly, "you were adopted. But even if that isn't strictly true, biology is nothing like you think it is. The person who was your mother doesn't exist anymore. I don't want to be forced into covering this ground every day. Please just accept it, my dear boy. Among other things, I was healed of my birthing wounds, and I now have other things to do. They tell me you're a talented fisherman. Why can't we go fishing, so I can see one of these biter fish?"

"They're not biting, Mother. And besides, I've already caught one. I'm winning this category so far. We're just waiting for the shield to be fixed, so we can go on to the salmon planet."

Lillith smiled sweetly. "Perhaps I can get the Baron to take me along with him. I need to discuss something with him, anyway. He controls the manufacture of all these boats, doesn't he?"

*

That night, the moonlight water of Prince Ned Bay was alive with breeding Frogs—breeding in a panic, frothing at the mouth. Hamid took his love triangle down to the beach to watch; but he wouldn't permit them to wade further than knee deep. True to the little green snake's word, only two sets of lovers were engulfed in a swirl of black water, instead of the hundreds that were usually lost—but those two were enough to give Lillith the sight of the enemy, even though she was thoroughly distracted by the calm she felt while making love with Lester Wunderman in the shallows after a quick, but dizzying bout with Hamid.

* * *

# CHAPTER ELEVEN

## GLANS SALMON

"Well, winning in this circus is like a whole different ball-game. First of all, if you happen to hook a prize winner, most of the time you break your ass catching him. Do that a couple seasons and your ass is pretty well broken. It takes all winter for me to recover. Sore back. Bad knees...."

Hank Knofsinger
quoted in *History of the Tournament*

DELTA 5 Tango is a pristine planet in the Orion System. Three/fifths of its surface is water, roughly the same as Earth, but it hasn't developed a sentient species. Other than that, the ecology is somewhat similar, fresh water rivers run to a protein rich sea and a species of fish developed to fill the same ecological niche as a salmon, even spawning and then dying in the shallow tributary streams after a few years in the salt ocean. The fry live for a season in the fast rivers, then move down to the sea to eat, eat, eat. Three seasons later, when they return to their original stream to spawn, the male glans salmon often weigh two hundred pounds as opposed to forty pounds for a nice King salmon back on Earth. The rivers on Tango are deep and fast flowing, fish of that size have little trouble negotiating them until they come to a falls or a flat riffle. At that point, log jamming is inevitable. One could sometimes walk across a stream on the backs of salmon, if he felt like it. Only a fool would feel like it, of course, since the squirting habits of the male glans salmon can be genuinely repulsive.

Through some genetic anomaly, preparation for the spawn changes the male glans salmon into a two hundred pound penis. His head, in front of the gills, turns into a bloated red-purple knob. His eyes grow a covering of red mucus membrane, and his mouth turns into a squirting devise for delivering his noxious smelling sperm. Although the mouth retains needle sharp teeth, eating is practically forgotten.

Pike didn't like fishing for dick fish. They were revolting. And catching them was devilishly difficult, since they weren't eating. Snagging was not allowed; but in the fish choked rivers snagging was inevitable, with almost every cast. Which meant a lot of catch and release, while the judge looked on. Releasing always meant a dousing with a squirt of sperm, spat by an angry fish. On a sunny day, the sperm dried quickly into protein glue, and the stench of it was worse than, well, it was indescribable. You had to be sprayed to know the smell, but once the olfactory lobes got a print of it, they never forgot. At least, Pike's hadn't. He voted against glans salmon every year; but a majority of the fishermen liked the fast action, even though it was mostly illegal catches. A few conservation types, like Alaska Bill Bolen, enjoyed visiting the pristine wilderness. Pike thought they were nuts. The brown bear creatures that fed on the dying flesh of the salmon were twice the size of Alaskan Grizzlies, almost the bulk of an elephant, with claws over a foot long for swiping the 200 pound salmon out of the streams. Their territorial disputes filled the headwaters with bellows of behemoths from hell—which they were. For that reason, Pike fished as close to the ocean as was practical. The bears seldom came down to the river mouths, where the waters were deep. But, of course, fishing was much harder there. And to make it even harder, the salmon had to be caught on a fly rod and a single hook feather streamer, which imitated a bait fish. The salmon, of course, were biologically uninterested in eating bait fish.

As stated, once the fish left salt water, and started the spawning run, they simply stopped eating. The only way to catch one legally was to make it mad enough to strike the fly, or to snag its spout-like mouth. Pike relied on the traditional method of casting his arm off, and getting doused with vile semen, until he snagged one legally. Once he'd done that, he headed back to the ocean, where he dug for clams and beach combed. The clams on Delta 5 Tango were truly spectacular, and the bears never dug for them. At least, he'd never seen any sign of claw marks on the clam beds. He would have advised Richie to follow that prudent course, except that the kid had finished out of the running on New Columbus and needed some points.

On the last day at New Columbus, the 'cudas had started biting. A lot of big ones. They suddenly got hungry. But Richie refused to stop fishing with the little rubber frog jig. Stubborn little fucker. Or maybe his mother standing at the rail all day had jinxed his luck. Who knows? Pike hoped that wasn't the case, because the old bag was planning to trail along for the whole tournament. Not only might she be a jinx, but she was taking up a lot of Lester's time. Lester's performance wasn't the problem, fortunately. There had always been an open bed policy for the crew; and the meals were one whole level better since Lillith and the Frog had come aboard. But was Lester better? Pike wondered. One level spacier, that was for sure. By midnight the kid hadn't caught a fish, so Lester hadn't been under fire as a deck hand since his swimming session.

The boat seemed to be refitted perfectly. The grid, according to George the computer, was functioning precisely; but there had been little likelihood of a pirate attack with Mrs. Tourbo's escort cruiser along. They would need the grid for the last two legs, but not here on Tango. What was needed here was some points; and that wasn't going to be easy, because Pike didn't really know how to catch dick fish—never had—although he'd caught hundreds of the mothers. It was all luck. Pike couldn't say with honesty that any of the legal fish he had landed had taken the bait. And snagging in the mouth with a fly rod and a streamer was not a guaranteed proposition.

On the other hand, Richie might have the touch. Why not? He'd practically killed himself with that phantom trout on Streamside, and still caught it. Trout were similar to salmon. Maybe he would come out of this smelling like a champ. Tomorrow morning would tell. The salmon run had begun at noon today, hot and heavy, up the Little Cannes Chute, where they were anchored. At dawn they would take the skiff up to Three Mile Rapid to try his luck. One thing for sure, Richie would come out of tomorrow's action smelling like something indescribable.

*

The Leader Board after New Columbus was muddy. The kid was still out in front with 12 points; but Dresden Carthy had moved up to 11 points with a 1st Place finish in Barracuda. And there was a clump right behind—all good fishermen, including the fat-ass Baron, who had 9 points, and Hard Luck Harry Dolan with 10. A pretty even spread. But like they say in horse racing, there's only two ways to win—Crossing the line first, or being second when the winner is disqualified.

Luck at snagging a glans salmon wasn't up to Pike, that would be Richie's department; so why worry about it? But Pike was worried. Every single boat had caught barracuda on the last day, except the Comparative Humanity. Sure, Richie was bone stubborn about the bait, but it had worked for him when nothing was biting. Granted, it would have been kind of a slap at Hamid to toss out a full-sized Frog lure, even an artificial; but Hamid wasn't born yesterday. If you want to catch fish, you have to cut bait, even when your mother and her boyfriend are looking on.

Actually, the old Gatling gun had wanted Rich to catch one. As the day wore on, she was demanding it. That could steal your luck, Pike theorized. He would never let his own mother onto his boat during a Tournament; but, of course, his mother had died long before he became a competitor. With a frown, Pike admitted to himself that he didn't know how he would confront a similar situation. Not really. Lillith was so rich; but then, so was Richie. Pike wasn't sure how their fortunes conjoined. He presumed there was some overlapping. Awkward. With all his other problems, Pike felt he shouldn't be forced into dealing with the question of mothers. Richie probably felt the same way.

Looking through his binoculars, Pike saw the kid and Lester standing on a sand spit, practicing with a heavy fly rod. Richie was sensationally uncoordinated with the ten weight rod. He could handle the ultra-light trout rod fairly well, but not the salmon rod. What a strange young man. His right arm flapped like a sea gull. Lester kept talking him through the double haul technique, but talk wasn't enough, apparently. Lester himself was an excellent fly rod technician. Pike thought about adding his two cents, but Lester had taken the skiff, and Pike didn't feel like swimming. He went down to the cabin instead.

Rita was lying cross ways on the bed, reading a science book. Since Lester's rescue, she and Pike had been getting along smoothly. Of course, Rita had been staying with her mother about half the time, bonding. She looked up when he came into the room, smiled briefly, then continued reading.

"Good book?" he asked her.

"Very," she replied. "Raphael Lap on a new kind of pulse theory that he developed out in the Sarinc System."

Pike hadn't read any science for several years. More than several. Stupid to let things slip.

"You never published a book on your propulsion theories, did you?" she asked, ostensibly to make conversation.

"Just my thesis," he replied, wondering where this was going. She knew he hadn't written a book. The Baron hadn't wanted to let the secret out, and he hadn't wanted to, either. The thesis was protected by patent law, and thus not public domain. His grid generator was very simple to build once you understood the principles. Space was wide these days, and patent law didn't protect much if the science is published. "There wasn't really enough to write a book about."

"It changed the Universe," she stated.

"Maybe so," Pike looked out the porthole. The tiny figure of the kid was still flailing on the sand spit. "Maybe it did, but only a few people have benefited."

"You wouldn't mind if I wrote the story up as part of my thesis, would you?"

"I thought your committee had already approved another topic."

"So…? Topics are made to be pushed to the limit."

"True," he agreed. He had gotten his Ph.D. from the Thruster idea, why shouldn't she? It was nicely circular, in a funny way.

If Rita was seriously writing a book, it would take at least a year, with interviews and whatever. That would be pleasant. He hoped it would be. Damnit, if he was only closer to her age, and wanted to have more children, everything would be different. Right, he'd be insanely jealous. Had it been only a week ago that he was catatonic with jealousy over her and Rich? Thank God for old age. He could barely remember the episode.

"Well…?" she asked, still seeking his approval.

"Fine with me, but you'll have to butt heads with your father, if you write it factually," he mentioned.

She shrugged. "I wasn't asking Father, I was asking you."

*

On the Lady Slipper, which was anchored outside Three Bear Creek along with the two smaller Bardona fishing boats and several other boats from the Tournament, Baron Farouk Bardona was in a froth. He was in 4th place, three points out of 1st, with only four events to go. Not close enough. Something radical needed to happen.

Everyone had agreed that Monday morning, not Sunday, would be the start of dick fish since they had all fished late for the fucking barracuda that had finally decided to bite. He, himself, had caught a beauty of a 'cuda last night under the pale full moon, about ten PM, two hours short of being shut out. Thank the stars. It had shot him past the log jam of 5th Place, into sole possession of 4th. But he hated dick fish. Nasty, disgusting mothers. Not a fit species to expose women and children to. He voted against them every year. Who voted for them? That sick slime, Resnick? Gentlemen should not have a secret vote. But all the votes on existing categories were secret ballot, so the Baron had no idea who to buy off. The high and mighty Rules Committee needed some restructuring.

There was no skill to dick fish, that's why any right-minded fisherman loathed them. Bardona really did loath them, unless he happened to get lucky with a big one, as he had on two occasions. When that happened, he thought the category was quite fine. But this year, that lucky son-of-a-bitch R.R. Tourbo would probably snag a whale-sized dick on his first cast and put himself out of reach. And worse than that, why was Tourbo's shark-eating mother nosing around the Tournament? Buying off the competition, per chance? He wouldn't put it past her, although he hadn't received an offer himself.

But the main thing that had him frothing was his only daughter, Rita. He couldn't understand why Rita would still be so chummy with the opposition after the fight. It was one thing to hang out with Tourbo in college. That made some sense—wealthy kids should look out for one another. But after the blundering jerk had joined the Tournament, she should have dumped him. Then she joined up with "Chip on the Shoulder" Resnick! That makes two enemies on one boat, cavorting with his beautiful daughter. Had he raised Rita to behave like that? Truthfully, had he? Didn't she know it distracted him from winning? How could he concentrate?

And now she wanted to write up the Thruster Patent for her thesis? Balls! What did the girl use for brains? He had been way too permissive with her. That was evident. He should never have let Magyar talk him into that blind trust. His wife had thought Rita should have a little financial independence, so she would feel equal at school and reach her true potential. It made sense at the time. Better than an allowance. She would learn how to invest her own money and make it grow. But Rita didn't seem to care about money. Another anomaly. She had plunked it into an interest bearing account at one of his banks, and lived on the interest. That was fine—she had prudently used his bank, and the fund was growing. Perfectly shrewd to wait for the right deal to come along. Farouk had been pleased with her until recently, when he realized that her financial independence had put her beyond his control. Had Magyar tricked him into it? She had never suggested anything of the sort for the boys—and he had never had one drop of trouble from them. A thesis on Resnick and the Thruster? Didn't she realize what that would do to the whole fabric of space travel? Some of his factories might have to retool.

That scum, Resnick, was twisting her mind to his devious scheme of releasing the patent, wasn't he? Ruining her own father? Well, maybe not ruining; but it would cost billions to retool. Of course, if they became available, all the fleets would buy thrusters instead of cigar ships. In the long run, I would do exceptionally well—but so would Cry Baby Resnick. He was happy enough to take the seed money—then when I pushed him into leveraged stress, he was delighted to take the money to bail himself out. Squirmed like a worm, actually; but accepted my terms. Of course, he had to accept my terms because of the original contract. Is it my fault that he doesn't see my best interests? Would he be happy with a thousand boats in the Tournament? Of course not. I'm protecting his dumb ass, and he's not even smart enough to know. Provokes me at every opportunity. God, I hope I got in a few gut ripping blows in our fight. Hard to tell—it felt like I did. Internal hemorrhaging. Yes. One or two organs, at least. Luckily, none of the damage he did to me left much of a mark—except the nose is still a tiny bit tender. Resnick is a light weight. I knew it.

Is she sleeping with that cry baby? Impossible. Rita has better sense than that—but women do make strange choices. But is she sleeping with that incredibly blundering and lucky Tourbo kid? The fucker wrecked my boat! How could she...? She's independently wealthy, she doesn't need his money. Oh, God...! A terrible thought occurred to the Baron. Was prick Resnick after her money?

The prick needs a new boat. Bardona chuckled at that, but only for an instant. Rita has enough in the bank to buy him a boat. Should I freeze her account? I think I could engineer that. Banks collapse every day. Not my banks—but one little bank wouldn't destroy investor confidence, would it? Of course, her account is secured—but if I timed it right, I just might tie up the funds at boat building time for next year's Tournament. Resnick missing from the Tournament...? A whole year without seeing his hangdog face. Joy of living!

But who was she sleeping with? Rumors had been flying all season. Farouk couldn't get himself to believe any of them. His little daughter? And he hadn't found the courage to consult Simon, his computer. There were some bits of weakness he didn't allow Simon to play with. One of them was checking up on his daughter. But Simon perhaps knew the truth. Or he could always ask Magyar. She probably knew also. She and Rita did talk. But damnit, that wasn't a suitable subject to talk about with your wife, was it?

Dick fish tomorrow. Uggh. The stench of them was already in his ample nostrils. Tomorrow it would be fresh and gagging. If he wasn't so far behind, the Baron would have loved to snag a few dick salmon to qualify, and then get the hell out of here for a week. But he was behind. Way behind. Barely in 4$^{th}$ Place. He needed a big salmon, and snagging his way through hundreds of the blighted fish with a fly rod and a single hook was no fun.

*

At dawn, with the wind in his face and his hip boots comfortably snugged to his belt, R.R. felt very confident in his salmon catching ability. Lester was a good teacher. Now the four of them were roaring upriver in the rubber skiff: he and Lester, Pike at the tiller and Tandor Lal, the salmon judge, a prim, dark-skinned fellow wearing a rain slicker and a surgical mask. Rita was not with them. She had begged off, saying she had work to do on her thesis.

It was a great morning to be alive, Richie thought, breathing deeply. Wisps of river mist whipped past the black rubber dingy. Virgin forest lined both sides of the river. Up ahead, the rock walls of the Little Cannes Chute loomed out of the mist. What an idyllic landscape. It reminded R.R. of the misty paintings of ancient mountains in Master Jacopo's sparse living room. Elegantly peaceful. The quintessence of wild peacefulness. R.R. felt his chest swelling with inspiration.

Cutting the throttle back, Pike nosed the boat onto a gravel bar a hundred yards ahead of the limestone cliffs where the Chute started. Richie rubbed his hands together to get the circulation going and stepped awkwardly over the rubber gunwale. He would have hopped out, but experience had taught him that hopping in hip boots wasn't a smart idea.

"Boy, this is beautiful, isn't it?" he blurted exuberantly, unbuttoning the top button of his green checked wool shirt.

Pike and Lester were clad head to foot in foul weather oil skins. Both had suggested the same gear to Richie, but he had vetoed the idea, saying it didn't look like rain to him. He had chosen the green shirt and a fly fishing vest instead.

"I wonder why nobody else is fishing here?" he inquired, assembling the sections of his stiff fly rod. He inhaled deeply again. "Wild nature really puts out a lot of oxygen, doesn't it." After seating the large arbor reel, he stripped green sink tip line through the eyelets, and tied on a short, heavy tippet.

"Yep, all that oxygen practically gags a person," Lester answered.

The reason that nobody else was fishing the Cannes Chute was because no prize fish had ever been caught there, so nobody except Pike came to the Chute anymore. Had they been behind in the Tournament, Pike might have chosen another spot, but they weren't. Besides, there *were* big fish in the Chute, he reasoned, thousands of them, they just hadn't been caught legally. He, himself, had snagged some really big ones here. The kid had as good a chance here as anywhere, if his luck was still in. It was a statistical anomaly that a winner had never come from here. Pike had taken a 6th here once, which was only a few ounces shy of the money. Okay, in all honesty, the fish here probably were a little smaller, for some unknown reason. They seemed exactly the same, genetically. Probably the food in these particular shallow tributary streams wasn't as plentiful as in some other watersheds, so these fish got off to a slower start. Maybe that was why, and maybe it wasn't. But the reason Pike fished here was the Chute itself. The fast river had eaten through almost three miles of limestone mountains to make the towering cliffs. White water churned out of the Chute in a wildly tumbling rapids at the bottom of the gorge. No bears were likely to stake out the

Chute as their fishing property—not with easy picking elsewhere on the planet. Scavenging in the Chute was the job of large fish eagles and a host of ravens and sea gulls. Birds had never been a worry to Pike.

"Yep, all that rich oxygen is pretty dinged overpowering," Lester said with a straight face. Sweeping back the hood of his raincoat, he took a set of swimming pool nose plugs out of his pocket and clipped them onto his nose. "Let's go fishing," he announced, motioning Richie toward the end of the gravel bar. "Does this seem like a good place to you?" he asked. After all, you don't tell a fisherman where he's going to be lucky.

Richie sussed out the gravel bar and decided that a few feet away from Lester was a good place to begin.

"I brung a set of nose clips for you, Richie, in case you change your mind about wanting them."

R.R. nodded and set about tying on a large white feather streamer while breathing through his mouth.

With his own nose clips in place, Pike watched. Lester and Tandor Lal looked like alien creatures. Only Richie, who had disdained the sensible gear looked normal. Normal, but stupid. From where they were standing the river was black and deep, but a few boat lengths farther upstream as it started to narrow, the surface was lumpy with silver backs surging upriver to spawn and die. Inside the mouth of the Chute, silver and red bodies leapt over limestone teeth in the pounding rapids only to fall back onto the crush of their brothers and sisters. Amazing creatures, Pike thought, finding them repugnant in spite of his admiration. Their magnificent last act was to transverse miles of rapids, falls and riffles. Thousands didn't make it. Those that did, the fittest or the luckiest, died of exhaustion after spawning. Male and female alike. Even if they survived the hungry bears, there was no food for them in the spawning brooks. Salmon were strange fish. On every planet where they developed, their pattern is the same. Pike thought it was a peculiar way to go about breeding, but the species was hardy. If humans ended their lives in a giant sex orgy, instead of in lingering sickness and decrepitude, would that be so wrong? Actually, the cycle of humans and salmon was almost the same, anyway. Only the length of time after the reproductive act was different. In some real way, he had been going steadily downhill since Alex was born. Sure, he was still in the prime, and he'd had lots of fun and supercharged experiences since then, but his essential vitality was different. He stood on the gravel bar in his oil skins watching Rich Rodney making a series of awkward false casts. The heavy line was only barely under control.

"Cast it out, don't be cute with it," he called. Richie grinned shyly, and let his cast go. The line arched forward across the river. Lester scowled at the poor cast.

But it was true, Pike thought. He had procreated, and now he could die. The Universe was satisfied that his genes had passed along. Having thought it, Pike saw the rightness. That little spark of vitality had changed inside him the morning Alex was born. He had lost his devil-may-care edge. In most aspects, that was just as well. In retrospect, he had been way over-balanced. Being more calm had certainly made him a better fisherman. He snorted derisively—losing his spark gave him the ability to nursemaid this lucky kid all year. That could have never happened before he became a father.

Coached by Lester Wunderman, Rich Rodney flailed the waters. The jerking retrieve that Lester insisted on felt awkward. Richie was sure the streamer's action was unrealistic. Zillions of fish were hurtling past just under the surface. He could see them. And he could also see that the silver streamer looked nothing like a minnow when he had to jerk it. He'd already made ten casts without a strike—and there were skillions of fish!

Richie was peripherally aware of the strange looks that Lester kept exchanging with Pike. His Ken Pao Ri training made him scintillatingly aware of everything that happened on the edges of his vision. Unbeknownst to Richie, Ken Pao Ri vision didn't automatically interpret the sights that he saw at the margins into a truthful view of reality. He concluded that Pike and Lester were disgusted with the mechanics of his fly rod artistry. Heck's bells, he was doing the best he could, wasn't he? The bait was getting out there where the fish were. Was it his fault that the stiff rod and heavy line were hard to maneuver? Nor was it his fault that he was feeling almost lightheaded in all this oxygen.

In actual fact, Pike and Lester's facial contortions (mainly cocked eyebrows) were comments on the ten casts without snagging a salmon. In Pike's recollection, he had seldom made two casts in succession without a hook up. Walking a few steps closer, Pike made a single comment on Richie's newly acquired bad luck.

"Astounding," he said to Lester.

Both men remembered that the kid hadn't hooked even a little barracuda on that last day. It was literally impossible not to snag a glans salmon. The river was a solid block of fish at this point, thirty feet deep by fifty yards across by probably three miles long.

"He's pulling it right between them," Lester commented, raising his eyebrows to the upper limit. "He doesn't like the jerking retrieve, he says. Don't feel right to him. How else are you going to snag one?"

Pike's face showed sensory overload for a second, then he realized that he was dealing with a phenom, not a person—and certainly not a fisherman. If the kid's luck deserted him, they were all sunk. First place wouldn't hold up without some fish.

He turned to Richie. "So what's keeping you from retrieving the fly however you want to?" he asked, heaping the perfect amount of scorn into the question. "You think Lester knows the only way?"

The light bulb went on. Pike was so smart. R.R. could see that Lester had the wrong answer for today. Maybe last year or every other year he was right, but times change. That's why Pike was almost a god. Relaxing his rigid elbow, Richie picked the line up in a flourish, made a horribly limp false cast that whipped a knot into the leader, and laid a snarl of line thirty feet into the river.

He grinned sheepishly and started to retrieve coils of line hand over hand.

"And put those nose clips on," Pike advised. "Trust me on this." He nodded to Lester. "Give them to him, before he passes out."

Without finishing his retrieve, R.R. took the flesh colored nose clips from Lester. Holding the rod under his arm, he tried to slip the rubber band over his head. It was an awkward maneuver, quite typical of him. Both hands were required to stretch the rubber band. With the rod clamped under his arm pit, he only had one and a half hands. Lester and Pike stopped watching after the first few seconds. It was too painful. A normally coordinated human either had to laugh himself sick or turn away. How could one person be so agonizingly klutzy? Tandor Lal continued staring at R.R.'s antics, but that was forgivable. He was being paid to watch. His jaw slackened, but he continued his vigil, making sure this wasn't an illegal tactic.

But eventually Richie was triumphant. The pink rubber band slipped over his ears. And in that instant, the river at his feet exploded. A big red dick fish leaped out of the river, with the silver streamer dangling from his lip. Coils of line that had been laying on the gravel shot into the dark river as the fish ran for the Chute.

"Hook up," Lester said in amazement. He didn't have to yell it. They were all standing within five paces of each other. "Looks like he's legal. Get ahold of that rod, boy. Keep your feet out of the line."

In two seconds all the line on the ground was gone and the reel started to sing, while R.R. hung onto the arching rod. Fly line, by its nature, is fat. Both floating and sinking, not many feet of it will go onto a reel, not even on the oversized salmon spool. In a few more seconds the reel would be down to the braided backing, of which there was 150 feet—not much.

River fishing for a two hundred pound fish, on foot, is not totally sane. It's a dance between the fisherman, the fish and the whippy fly rod that never seems strong enough. The fish has important business up-river—he hears a train whistle blowing.

All Richie could do, once he was hooked up, was hang on and do his best to put pressure on the fish. The drag was wound down as tightly as the 100 pound leader would bear. Any extra strain would break it—any little catch on a rock, or misplay on his part, and the fish would be history. And Richie couldn't be sure how well the darned fish was hooked. The hook-up felt solid, but a fish's mouth is notoriously fickle.

"What should I do," R.R. yelped as the line continued to streak up-stream.

"Run after him," Pike yelled, knowing that would probably cause a circus act to happen between Richie and his hip boots. But what the hell. One legal catch, and Pike could plunk them all down to trolling at the river mouth. Trolling was completely safe, as far as he was concerned. It was very hard to snag a fish in deep water, but at least there were no bears.

With no hesitation, R.R. took off up the gravel bar toward the mouth of the Chute, holding the rod high over his head. In ten clomping bounds, he came to the end of the gravel. Before him stretched twenty yards of swirling, but relatively quite backwater, caused primarily by a large block of fallen limestone on the far shore. Line was still stripping off the reel. Skirting the estuary would take him fifty yards or so in the wrong direction, but the dark water looked a little deep for wading. Richie hesitated, then started clomping up the shingle away from the fish.

A sensible decision, Pike thought. He had never waded that estuary. "Break him off at the leader," Pike shouted. No sense losing all that line. By hauling back on the rod and snubbing the line, the fish would probably break off.

But Richie wasn't paying attention. He was thumping around the estuary as fast as his legs could pump in the black hip boots. Pike lengthened his paces a bit to keep up. As soon as Rich got around that big red boulder, he would start gaining on the fish again. Anyway, the worst that could happen was he'd lose the line when the backing ran out. That wasn't much of a deal, they had many more lines in the skiff. His eyes flashed back to the red boulder. Oh, shit!

Pike started to run. Jerking up his oil slicker, he snatched out the .45 automatic from his hip holster. That auburn boulder had shaggy hair all over it! "Stop...!" he screamed at Richie.

But Richie's peripheral Ken Pao Ri vision was already beaming warnings at him. He ignored them, of course. In the welter of conflicting danger signals that were swarming him, the "big" danger was lost. His line was vanishing, deep water was to the left, slippery rocks underfoot, nose plugs bonking his forehead with every stride, and that indescribable, horrid oxygen smell was overpowering him. With all that, he simply didn't see the giant, fucking bear until it reared up right in his path, taller than a roaring lighthouse. The monster swiped at Richie with a snarl that shook the ground; but he got the outstretched fly rod instead, smashing it from R.R.'s hands. A loop of braided backing looped neatly around his huge right paw, instantly cutting to the quick as the two hundred pound salmon cinched the loop closed like a garrote. The monster bear screamed his surprise and agony, before toppling sideways toward the Chute, where the fish, feeling stark pain bite his mouth as the bear's weight snubbed him up tight, leaped straight out of the water and shook his glistening purple head. This was no doubt an amazing sequence of events to wild creatures.

Rich Rodney ran straight out into the estuary away from the bear. When it got too deep to run, he floated downstream with the current. He found it easy to stay above water. There were so many salmon, he just glided over their backs. Also, in all fairness, his vest had a flotation sack built in which helped offset the drag of his water-filled hip boots.

Seeing that Rich had made another sensible decision, Pike beat a hasty retreat back to the skiff, which Lester and Mr. Lal had already launched. With rather a lot of high spirited yelling, which often occurs after witnessing a near death experience, they pulled into the current, and within a few minutes wrestled a dripping, but exultant, Richie into the skiff.

"Did you see that?" he gasped. "I was floating on top of fish!"

Fine for excitement, but he hadn't actually caught a fish yet. Catching a bear didn't count, even if he hadn't exactly done that either.

They motored back to the Comparative Humanity for another breakfast, and to get Richie into dry clothes. The bear had been a sobering experience. Pike had thought it would be safe to fish the Chute, but apparently not. True, nobody had ever been mauled on Tango; but the bear had actually swiped at Richie. They had been very lucky.

Richie seemed undampened by the experience. The kid had amazing elasticity. Pike readily admitted by this time that Richie had some endearing and unusual qualities. Whatever that martial arts stuff was, it definitely seemed to give him an edge of luck, if nothing else. Things that would have embarrassed or frightened a normal person into non-existence, didn't seem to touch him. Pike, himself, still had a case of shakes over the bear incident. What had he been planning to do with the pitiful .45? If nothing else, this proved it was time to upgrade his portable arsenal. On the boat, he was more or less armed to the teeth; but a .45 probably wouldn't stop an Earth grizzly, let alone a Tango bear. It probably wouldn't stop a Tango house cat. Were there house cats on Tango? That was an unhappy thought. Three foot tall house cats, with deep, insidious purring. Thankfully, cats don't like water, and

Pike didn't intend to set foot on land again. This bear story should be enough to get the Rules Committee to reconsider coming here.

*

"Let's go get one," Richie piped, standing up from the galley table. He drained a cup of scalding black tea without testing it and rather instantly turned a shade of bright red to match the dry shirt he had changed into. Any wild animal would see the red shirt and run away—that was Richie's rational.

Pike had been interested to hear the explanation for the shirt choice. He was even more interested in the banzai tea drinking. The kid sucked in two deep breaths, wiped the pain out of his eyes with a napkin and balanced his top row of teeth carefully on the bottom row. Being careful not to move his teeth or cheeks, he reported, "I think I've got the hang of that minnow movement now."

"What would you say to some trolling?" Pike asked.

"Trolling? I think I'd prefer the stream bank. It took me awhile to get the feel, but I've got it now."

"Well, frankly, Rich, I'm a little reluctant to plunk us back into bear country."

R.R. guffawed. He knew Pike was bluffing. Bears or dinosaurs wouldn't mean a thing to Pike Resnick if there were fish to catch. "Nice of you to protect my feelings," Richie said, gallantly, "but I'm not scared, either. Did you see the look on that critter's face when my fish pulled him over?" Richie got kind of a glittery sheen around his eyes. "It was like my friend, the fish, saved me in the nick of time. We better go see if the fish isn't still snagged somewhere up that canyon. I'd like to turn him loose so he can breed."

Pike and Lester exchanged a look halfway between admiration and sheer terror. This kid was determined to get them all killed. Lester limped over to the refrigerator and fished out an ice cube. He wrapped it in a cloth napkin, put it on the chopping block and smashed it with one blow of his meat tenderizer mallet. He handed the napkin to Richie. "Suck on that," he said.

"We can go take a look," Pike offered. "I'd say there's about a hundred percent chance that the fish broke off. That's point Number One. Number Two is, the Chute is full of teeth that would rip the skiff to shreds."

Richie nodded.

"And if that bear is still tangled up in your line, he's probably mad as hell. No telling what he might do."

*

The mist had broken up when they got back on the river, but it looked like the overcast sky would hold until at least mid-morning. The cool weather was good news for the three in sweaty oil skins.

Richie strained over the prow like a rabbit dog smelling his way along a spoor trail. Pike was still certain it was an exercise in futility. The fish had flown, and even if he was snagged somewhere, they would never find him. The last time he had seen the fish jump, he was well inside the Chute. When three tons of bear leaned his weight against the line, it had likely broken like a thread.

But looking for the fish gave him an excellent pretext to scope out both banks for bears. He had brought along a .308 rifle with a powerful scope in addition to the .45, and he intended to station himself as a steely-eyed guard wherever the kid fished. The laser cannon was well anchored on the bridge, or he might have attempted to bring it. As soon as he got to civilization again, he would have a couple of high impact pocket stunners in the arsenal—the serious kind.

"I think I see him," R.R. sang out. He pointed. Sure enough, the green fly line was hooked up on an exposed rock tooth in mid-channel fifty yards into the Chute.

"Eagle eye," Pike commented dryly, throttling the outboard motor back. Pontoon skiffs were supposedly unwreckable, but that didn't mean they were suitable for going into the Chute. Each air compartment was filled with foam blocks, and walled off in case of a rupture, but Pike still didn't trust them entirely. If enough compartments broke, the skiff would sink. Anyway, they would all be thrown overboard or stranded if the boat grounded on a big rock. "I'm not taking us into the Chute," he said. And that was final.

For about ten seconds, R.R. looked straight up in the air as if debating something with himself. "Get us as close as you can," he said. "I'll try to snag the line. I have to try, I think. Isn't that the sportsman's code?"

"Fair enough," Pike answered, piloting the skiff toward a limestone shelf on the far side of the river. The kid had to snag some fish, in any case. Let him try the impossible cast for the old fly line in the process. It would be good practice for him. He doubted if Bill Bolen or Carthy, the two best fly casters he knew, could make that toss; but nothing at all would be lost in the effort.

The beach on this side of the river was narrower, which meant the tree line was much nearer the water. Because of that, Pike had never fished it, but out on the shelf there was a reasonable chance of safety.

"Climb out to the very end of that rock and stand sideways to the river. That should give you enough room for your backcast."

Pike looked at Lester, who smiled a crooked smile. "Landing one from here will be fun," the cook offered. "Too bad we sent that sickening Indian home. He likes acrobatics."

"Too bad," Pike agreed, pulling the boat into the lee of the rock shelf. "You stay in the boat, Les. If anything comes out of the woods, we'll want to make a hasty exit."

"I won't be much help from the boat," Lester grumbled.

"Unless a bear comes. Then you will."

Tandor Lal didn't look particularly pleased; but he jumped out with the coil of line that Lester handed him. The kid scrambled after him, using his backup fly rod as a balancing pole. Mercifully, he didn't upset the skiff in jumping out, but he did manage to bark his shin on an outcropping. Pike followed with the rifle.

"Keep the motor idling," Pike told Lester. "Maybe you can gaff from down here, if we get lucky."

"Oh, sure," Lester griped. "I'd love to gaff one with my kisser leaned over right in his face."

"I thought you'd like that," Pike answered, agreeably. "Just keep smiling. I'll hose you down when we get back on deck. Keep saying this mantra—One legal fish. One legal fish."

Pike looked down in the water while R.R. rigged up. It was still wall to wall fish. The major run normally lasted for three days. After that, there were still a lot of fish, but they wouldn't be log-jammed at the mouth of the rapids. Such well-mannered fish, backed up in ranks, waiting their turn for immortality. Well mannered - until they get hooked.

Stepping out on the lip of the rock shelf, Richie whipped the back-up rod through the air a few times to test the action. Seeming satisfied, he began false casting, stripping line from the reel in long pulls and tossing it high in the air in rather depressingly free-form figure eights, back and forth. Maybe with a fifteen foot spey rod, a great fly man could make the cast. With the stiff ten footer, Richie didn't have a prayer. Finally, knowing that he was loosing control of all the line in the air, he decided he'd better make some kind of cast. Leaning into the rod, he used his strength instead of the rod's balance to shoot the line out. The cast whipped forward in an awkward loop.

Tandor Lal let out a yowl and dropped to his knees like he'd been shot. He clapped his left hand to his left ear.

The fly line hovered over the river, then splashed down in a snake of coils.

"What happened...?" Lester yelled.

"He eared him...!" Pike called back, stepping over to the unfortunate judge. Gently taking Lal's bloody hand away, Pike pinched the ear lobe firmly. "He's all right," he yelled to Lester. "Ripped right through. Get a butterfly out, would you!"

Seeing the greenish tinge of Lal's face, he patted the judge's back rather briskly. "You're fine, Judge. Just a few drops of blood. Don't even think about passing out on me. Maybe we'll get you some hazard pay."

"Fish on...!!" Richie yelped, leaning back on the rod.

"Lean on him," Pike yelled. "Don't let him go up the rapids."

"I can't. He's too strong."

"Well, shit," Pike said, leading Mr. Lal toward the skiff. "Go help him," he barked at Lester, taking a butterfly band-aid from the gnarly hand. "Break him off, when he gets to the backing."

Lester clambered out of the skiff and hustled up the rock.

Expertly clamping the ear wound together with the wings of the adhesive butterfly, Pike had Lal sit down in a rock cranny. "You're fine. Trust me. There won't even be a scar. Just sit here for awhile. Come back up when you're feeling aggressive."

"Aggressive...?"

"Aggressive. Vigorous. Full of vim and vigor." Pike fished an orange pill from a deep pocket of his oil skin. He handed it to the judge and climbed back up the rock.

The fish, in the meantime was doing a water ballet. It leaped out of the water, straight over the hung-up flyline. Falling back in the river with a splash that was unnoticeable in the spuming rapids, the obliging salmon swam under the line, jumped again and fell over the line. He did that three times in quick succession.

"We are witnessing a miracle," Lester said to no one in particular.

"Is he hooked fair?" Pike inquired, joining them at the river's edge. Since his drug experience on New Columbus, Lester had been uttering odd statements. It was kind of spooky.

"From the way he jumps, he's hooked somewhere in the head. Beyond that, I can't tell. Ask Rich, he seen him closer."

Making a serious run upriver now, the fish felt the tug of the other line, in which he had entangled himself. The first line was snugged tight over a big wet rock, but then when the fish jumped, it miraculously lifted free. The first fish jumped half out of the water, miraculously still hooked. There were now two big salmon attached to Richie's rod and reel. The rod arched like a rainbow—four hundred pounds of fish will do that to a fly rod. He braced against a rock ledge, willing his hip boots to grow down into it.

Taking off his oilskin coat, Pike tied the sleeves around Richie's waist, making a handle to grab in case the lucky geek got pulled off the rock.

"Too bad...my mother...isn't here to see this," the kid gulped between breaths. "She doesn't believe…I can catch fish."

"The first fish is still on, right?" Pike asked.

"Hecks, yes! See the line cutting to the left of the new one."

"Impressive," Pike commented. "I should get a cameraman to hang around."

"Don't need a camera. Got it all programmed—up there." Rich pointed to his forehead.

"Right. I was thinking about making a record for the public."

"Oh. Well, this was just lucky," Richie said, understating the truth charmingly. "Skill didn't have anything to do with it."

"Really…?"

Richie grinned. "That was the worst cast in the world. How is Mr. Lal?"

"Just a scratch," Pike assured him.

"I feel really bad about that. Mr. Lal is such a dignified guy. What was he doing standing behind me like that? He must not understand about fly rods."

"Judges aren't fishermen," Pike answered, not committing himself with that answer. In point of fact, Lal had been a good thirty feet to the right of where Richie had planted himself—well outside the danger zone, one might have thought.

Just then in a synchronous dance move, both fish decided to leap away from the pain of the hook. One leaped left—one leaped right. Yin and Yang leaping. They met head on. The crunch of the collision couldn't be heard above the roar of the rapids.

"Billions to one…!" Lester yelled. "Get some line in, boy! Get line in..!"

In the sudden slack situation, Richie started pulling great armfuls of braided backing through the eyelets. The line baled up at his feet and spilled over the rock ledge. But what else could he do? He couldn't switch hands to start reeling, and he staunchly refused to reel left handed.

Both lines were billowing in the rapids Maybe both fish had been knocked out, or else they were swimming back downstream.

Talking to himself, Lester Wunderman began scrabbling down the rock. "Dangedest thing I ever seen," he repeated several times. "Come on, Pike. What are we waiting for? We can gaff those mothers while they're out cold, if we hurry."

Knowing he was right, Pike followed his second banana down to the boat.

"Git up there and protect the kid," Lester spat at the wounded judge. "You ain't hurt. Do your part. There's something religious going on here."

On his way past, Pike helped Mr. Lal to stand up. "Don't mind Lester," he said, softly. "I'll definitely get you hazard pay. Keep Richie from falling in while we land the fish." Pike hopped into the skiff. Lester hit the throttle before the boss was completely seated.

"This has got to be more than luck," Lester affirmed, roaring into mid-river. "It's like he can think at a fish and get him to do what he wants."

"Could be," Pike answered. Something definitely was uncanny. Maybe Lester knew the answer.

"Did you see that cast? It went in the water like a bale of hay, and it didn't make a dinged bit of difference."

Pike wedged himself in the prow of the skiff with the gaff. He was thrilled almost witless that his slicker was still tied around Richie. "The first line is loose at the reel end. We better try for that fish first."

"Why do you say so?" Lester asked.

"The bear broke it off or chewed it off, didn't he?"

"Not really. That's him over there."

Pike scanned the far shore without catching sight of an angry bear. "Where," he asked.

"There in the water. That brown blob that looks like grass."

"Good God," Pike gasped. "He tangled up and drowned?"

"Looks like it. Don't make rational sense, do it? I thought you seen the critter."

"No," Pike said. "I must be slipping."

"Not necessarily," Lester answered, with no special emphasis. "My eyesight seems to be improving since I visited Old Leopold."

"You'll have to tell me about that sometime," Pike said. He watched Richie stripping line in like a madman; but the line running from the rod tip was still slack, and didn't point anywhere in particular. It was no help in tracking the fish.

"If your eyes are so sharp, where are the fish?" he asked Lester.

"Well, there's one," Les replied, casually. "Ten degrees starboard and coming our way. Get ready, I'm putting you up against him."

Pike realized in somewhat of a flash, that he'd never gaffed a glans salmon before. Until now, he'd always been the rod man. Two hundred pounds of salmon could be a little dangerous in this tiny tub. But, there was the fish, neither dead, nor stunned, and Pike held the gaff.

The plan was to gaff the fish and drag it to shore, where the judge could look at him. Two hundred pounds of fish was way too big to haul over the gunwale when you have nowhere to stand for leverage. On the other hand, even a big glans salmon is no match for a sixty horsepower engine. Pike figured he could hold onto the gaffed fish until Lester beached the skiff and the judge came down to survey the prize.

The damned fish actually seemed to be hooked in the mouth. Let it be a legal hook-up! With that prayer on his lips, Pike plunged the short-handled gaff hook into the salmon's silvery side. The fish convulsed. Pike was prepared. "Hit it," he yelled to Lester, who had already goosed the engine the second he saw the gaff bite.

But this salmon was a scrapper, no doubt about that. He had already killed a Tango bear and survived for over an hour tethered in the rapids. His wide tail scooped a yard of water and he headed straight down, jerking the gaff from Pike's hands. Fortunately, Pike wasn't a complete tenderfoot at fish landing. Before sinking the hook, he had tethered six yards of braided hemp gaff line to a cleat on the bow. There was little danger that this salmon would get away. The gaff had hit perfectly. Unless they snagged on something really immovable, they had him. Pike showed his empty hands to Lester and braced himself for hauling the salmon onto the river bank, spitting and ugly.

"Head for a wide piece of beach," he told Lester.

Lester let up on the throttle and tipped the outboard motor up, turning the skiff sideways, sliding it skillfully onto the smooth beach pebbles so that the gaff wouldn't be scraped loose. Pike hopped out and hauled in the gaff line, hand over hand.

Lester cackled. "Careful now. I see you lost your slicker somewhere."

"Very funny," Pike huffed. The bright red head of the fish came to the surface. Pike kept hauling, hoping that the dick fish was too spent by the ordeal to spit—knowing he wasn't. Without a doubt, he was going to get a drenching. He took a second to make sure his sun glasses and nose clip were secure, then pulled the flopping dick fish into the shallows.

The instant the salmon got close enough, it spit a mouthful of milky fluid directly at its tormentor. Fortunately for Pike, the angle was low. The sperm splattered against his left wader-clad leg about knee high. Even with the nose clips on tight, the stench gagged him. Clamping his mouth shut, he slid his right hand into the gaping gill slit, and hauled the fish out of the river. It spit again, sending a hawker splashing over Pike's right shoulder. He retched, then bending his knees, he heaved the fish a few feet onto the dry river stones. The kid's streamer was stuck firmly in the side of the underslung jaw, with the line still attached. Kind of a miracle after all. A legal catch.

"Go get the judge and the rifle," he coughed at Lester. There was no way to get away from the stench, one just had to accept it. That was dick fishing. "I'll wait here," he said. "It sure looks legal to me." He gestured a circle of his thumb and forefinger at R.R., who was still up on the shelf. The kid had retrieved all the line, it seemed. His rod tip was straining toward mid-river. If they landed the second one, they could count the heavier of the two; but as soon as Mr. Lal declared this one legal, Pike would be a happy man.

Richie came bouncing down from the rock shelf, onto the beach, reeling as he stumbled along on the loose stones. "Let's gaff this baby, too...!" he yelled. "So I can get my line back." Five yards short of Pike and the beached fish, he came to a ragged stop. "What is that goshawful smell...?!" He clamped the rod under his elbow and clapped both hands over his nose.

"Kind of indescribably bad, ain't it?" Pike laughed. "I'd put those nose clips back on, if I were you."

Recalling that he had swept the clips off his nose so he could breathe better while battling the fish, Richie pinched his nose with one hand and dug for the rubber clips around his neck with the other. He clipped them into place, but still wouldn't come closer to Pike.

"I hate to say this, Pike, but you smell awful."

"You might consider voting against dick fish next year. There's a lot of other fish in the Universe," Pike said, his eyes crinkling into a grin. "For now, just keep on breathing. It doesn't get worse unless we catch another one. Of course, it doesn't get better, either."

"Voting?" Richie asked.

"We vote on where we're going to fish."

"We do...?"

"Yep. I vote against this place every year. You're allowed to join my lobby if your nose tells you to."

Lester beached the skiff a few yards away. He and Tandor Lal climbed out and approached the fish from up-wind. "Looks legal to me," Mr. Lal said, reaching down gingerly to flick the white streamer. "Yes, a legal fish, Mr. Tourbo. Congratulations. Shall we weigh it?"

"Damn good," Lester whooped, going back to the skiff for a telescoping tripod and a hanging scale that went up to 400 pounds. He set the tripod up, making sure it was solidly footed in the stones; then he and Pike hooked the scale to the still quivering fish and horsed it onto the tripod. Semen dribbled out of the salmon's mouth and ran down his sleek side.

"Two hundred and nine pounds, three ounces," announced Mr. Lal, gagging, but writing it down in his official tally pad.

"Mind if we motor out and cut the other one off?" Pike asked R.R.. "Or would you rather land it?"

"It might be bigger?" Richie said, with a shining ray of hope in his voice. Evidently he had forgotten that he owed one of these fish for killing the bear.

*

That night, after being hosed down twice with salt water and deep sixing his clothes, Pike slept on deck, alone, under the Tango 5 Delta constellations. Replenishing the fresh water supply was no big deal on Tango, so he took a hot, soapy shower every couple of hours. By morning, he smelled pretty much like a human, or at least like soap.

The second fish had nailed him directly on the forehead with a huge dripping wad of jizz. Wiping it off had gotten the guck on both hands and arms. It was an indescribable experience. After dragging the fish back to the scales and finding that it weighed two ounces more than the other one, Richie seemed well pleased with the effort, although he had assumed a greenish tinge from holding his breath.

"This is my last salmon for the year," Pike announced, helping Lester drag the fish back to the river.

"I offered to gaff it," Lester said, reproachfully.

"So you did. Feel free to take the rest of the week off yourself. He can fish by himself, if he wants more."

"Would that be right?" Lester asked.

"It's right by me. This is how we always fish Tango, isn't it?"

"Guess so."

*

The ménage a trois of Lester, Lillith and Hamid departed at dusk in Lillith's corporate cruiser for someplace that Lillith wanted to show the boys. Not enjoying the odor aboard the Humanity, Rita had gone with them, to be dropped off on Diston Prime to confab with her doctoral advisor. Pike had agreed to pick her up on the way to Blizwak.

Continuing to sleep on deck after anchoring the Comparative Humanity with the rest of the fleet at Horseshoe Canyon, Pike's plan for the week had been to work with Rita on her writing project, and maybe teach her a few things about being a deck hand, in case Lillith lured Lester off to the good life. But that would evidently have to wait.

One thing for sure, a two hundred pound dick fish wasn't going to win any prizes. Bill Bolen already had a two hundred and fifty pounder and Ira had one almost as big. It would be very good to hit the leader board here on Tango. Very good. But with Lester gone, that meant Pike would be doing all the gaffing, if they fished anymore. Well, the smell washed off, eventually. It wasn't so bad smelling like merde, and having everyone you know avoid you, was it? Actually, it was less than perfect.

* * *

# LEADERS

| | DELILAH | TORGA HOWLER | TIGER MUSKY | D.W. SCUT | PHANTOM TROUT | LAR BARRACUDA | GLANS SALMON | RAZORFIN | SWAMPFISH | MOON HALIBUT | TOTAL |
|---|---|---|---|---|---|---|---|---|---|---|---|
| Farouk Bardona | | | 2 | 5 | | 2 | 1 | | | | 3RD 10 |
| Ethyl Bierly | 2 | | | | | | | | | | 2 |
| Angmar Blirt | | | | | | 4 | 4 | | | | 5TH 8 |
| Bill Bolen | | | 3 | | | 5 | 2 | | | | 3RD 10 |
| Dresden Carthy | 4 | | | | | 2 | 5 | | | | 2ND 11 |
| JB Dillingham | | OUT | | | | | | | | | |
| Harry Dolan | 3 | 2 | 5 | | | | | | | | 3RD 10 |
| Macky Duff | | | | | OUT | | | | | | |
| Ira Fairborne | | 4 | | 3 | | | | | | | 7 |
| Buddy Jay | | | | | | | | OUT | | | |
| Sandy Kind | | | | | | | | 3 | | | 3 |
| Hank Knofsinger | | | | 2 | | | | | | | 2 |
| Peter Marcuso | | | | | OUT | | | | | | |
| Trini Morales | | | | | | | | 5 | | | 5 |
| Pike Resnick | | OUT | | | | | | | | | |
| Erwin Sandor | | 3 | | | OUT | | | | | | |
| Jean Santos | | 1 | | | | | | | | | 1 |
| Mordachi Skinner | | | 4 | 4 | | 1 | | | | | 4TH 9 |
| Tyrone Stickle | | | | 1 | | | | | | | 1 |
| Chip Takahachi | | | | | 3 | | | OUT | | | |
| RR Tourbo | 5 | 5 | 1 | | | 1 | | 3 | | | 1ST 15 |
| Mike Tucker | 1 | | | | | | | | | | 1 |
| Nacho Tutupo | | | | | | | 3 | | | | 3 |
| Ed Wood | | | | | OUT | | | | | | |
| Big John Zales | | | | | | 4 | | | | | 4 |

| | | |
|---|---|---|
| 1ST | = | 5 points |
| 2ND | = | 4 points |
| 3RD | = | 3 points |
| 4TH | = | 2 points |
| 5TH | = | 1 points |

# CHAPTER TWELVE

## RAZORFINS

"Well, sure you can talk about winning; but what is winning to a fish? Think about it. If he gets away, is that winning? If he stupidly bites a hook and breaks his spirit coming to the gaff, would that be winning? Maybe. Or maybe if he eats the fisherman, would that score a lot of points? More likely, fish aren't concerned with sport very much."

Lester Wunderman
quoted in *History of the Tournament*

Pike and Richie fished the Horseshoe from shore for five long, exhausting days trying for a bigger salmon. Ira Fairborne's 2nd Mate was manning a meteorite blaster on a rocky point, which made Pike feel safe enough to snug up to the slice of beach. Ira did not like bears either. Maybe that's why they had become friends. It was fun bantering with the old geezer, when Pike wasn't getting dosed with jism. All the fishermen slept on deck all five nights—smelling like jizz from hell—but what's a little BO among friends? Richie caught ninety-seven dick fish, most of them legal, all of them spitting at Pike, and every single one was smaller than the fish that had killed the bear. Was that fair?

Finally on the last afternoon, the kid hooked onto a big one. It took three hours to land and turned out to be a big female ripe with eggs, weighing damn near three hundred pounds. It got them a tie with Sandy Kind for third place. The defacto rule on glans salmon was if two fishermen came within an ounce of each other on the beach tripod scales, they both got the points. Nobody wanted to lug dick fish back to their boats, nor to a central scale. Stench has its limits.

So Richie was still out in front of the pack. And it was on to razorfins, a deceptively dangerous little species that had evolved in a system of shallow salt lakes on Blizwak-Hojmer. Ecologically, the lake beds had been scraped from alluvial soil during a past ice age and had filled with water as the glacier melted. Having no drainage to a sea, the lakes turned progressively more saline as they evaporated, so that now they were very salty indeed. An ecology developed that was able to survive in harsh salinity.

Razorfins were rather perfectly adapted to the lake chain, having grown razor sharp pectoral fins that they used to harvest their dinners. Smart fish. Tool using, you might say. Did that make them almost human? Nah. Tool use has never counted if the tool grows on the body.

Many varieties of aquatic wheats and rices, as well as various tubers, grew in the wide shallows of the lakes. The niche that razorfins had carved out for themselves was control of a particularly virulent burrowing dorpfly larva. In the months of May and June, razorfins fed on the grey dorpfly moth which hatched in great profusion. But by the time the fishermen arrived in mid-July, the adult phase was gone and the razorfins had switched to their off-season feeding habits—using their pectoral fins to mow down selected grain stems in pursuits of the larvae, which if unchecked would burrow down the stem, eventually to eat the root system and kill the plant. How razorfins had figured out that an edible grub lived up in the stem was quite a mystery. And then how had they developed sharp fins for cutting the stalk so the larva wouldn't eat its way to the root? Nature is an astonishing item. At any rate, razorfins played a very important role in the planetary food chain, and they were devilishly difficult to catch in late July—which was why the anglers came in late July.

Most of the razorfins lived in Lake Pel, the least salty of the fifteen lakes, but smaller numbers lived throughout the system. Lake Pel was the largest of the lakes, about the size of Nebraska. Because it was only ten feet deep at its deepest, one didn't really want to be boating on Lake Pel during a storm. In a good blow, the lake sort of scooped itself up, and dumped half of itself onto the shore. Immediately thereafter, gravity worked its magic and returned the water to the lake, with a new infusion of salts.

Since it was often stormy on Blizwak-Hojmer, the foreign fishermen had helped the Blizwak natives to change a natural rocky breakwater into a workable marina by dredging a channel and dumping a few thousand large boulders at key points. A sizable number of the Blizwaks now built their reed and wattle houses behind the sheltered cove, and did their best to be useful and treacherous when the fleet was in.

There were two tribal groups on the planet—the Blizwaks, who were fishermen and hunter/gatherers, and the Hojmers, who were pastoral brigands living all through the interior, grazing their flocks and living by a strange code of ethics. As far as anyone could tell, both groups were exactly the same genetically. They certainly looked the same—short, swarthy and tattooed. But that was hardly surprising, given the required wife swapping, even among enemies. During the week that the Tournament was in town, both the Hojmers and the Blizwaks practiced brigandage to the full extent that they were able. Fortunately, both cultures were barely into their bronze age, so razorfin fishing was fairly safe if you took some elementary precautions. A rather interesting bazaar had grown up around the marina, and since the headwomen were keen on trade with the foreigners, they made a small effort to keep predation to a minimum. By mutual agreement, nobody from the fleet traded weapons or anything that might lead to the development of sophisticated weapons—which of course forced the natives to steal any high tech item that they could. Such is the story of civilization.

Actually, he wasn't sure why razorfins kept being voted in. Before they built the Marina, the fisherman had gotten along fairly well with the scattered Hojmer tribal groups, and now they didn't. He suspected the rather overwhelming vote in favor every year had something to do with the very loose morals of the exotic dark-skinned women. They seemed honor bound to sleep around with guests, even if no presents were given. Of course, presents of off-world clothing and jewelry as well as fishing equipment were eagerly accepted—or stolen.

Razorfins themselves certainly couldn't have been the main issue. As a fighting fish, they were kind of dull. Their favorite tactic, once hooked, was to tangle up in a clump of aquatic grain. Getting them out generally required wading—and that was where the danger came in—danger to ankles, calves and Achilles tendons. And fingers.

*

Pike had won razorfins twice and usually managed to place in the money. The reason, he supposed, was because it was a very quiet kind of fishing—and he enjoyed being quiet. The fins were easily spooked. And there was only one technique that seemed to work at all. You let the boat drift in the shallows, scanning the wild rice beds for a falling rice stalk, one stalk among millions. Only then did you work the boat into position and make a cast, using a real piece of rice straw with a real grub bulging the sides and a hook through the stalk. Nothing else held the slightest interest to the fins at this time of year.

Pike always used a fly rod, casting from open water. He felt he could lay the reed in more quietly that way; but of course, he was good with a fly rod. He suggested that Richie use a spinning outfit, since the rules didn't prohibit it. If the fish didn't spook when the bait stick splashed down, often they would mistake the bait for the stalk they had just sliced off. With their rather unfishlike lips, they mouthed the stalk, looking for the bulge that contained protein nourishment. Only after finding the telltale bulge, did their cutting teeth clamp down, biting the stalk and the grub, and the hook if there was one. That's all there was to the technique, except for keeping the fish out of the forest of aquatic grains and cattails once it was hooked. And wearing armor-plated boots and wire mesh gloves if you had to go in after him. That was the cute part about razorfins. The fisherman had to land every catch alone. That was more or less fair. Since the fish seldom went over ten pounds, it wasn't really sporting to risk somebody else's ankles and fingers.

Pike was actually looking forward to the week. The marshes were beautiful at this time of year. Flights of strange whistling waterfowl made graceful Vs across the sky in their migrations. Both tribes of locals claimed the right to harvest the wild grain and net waterfowl. They would be silently paddling their reed pirogues around the margins of the lake, sneaking up to see if they could plunder the unwary. It was thought of as good, clean sport to brain a fisherman and take all his stuff, leaving him unconscious and naked on the shore. To date, they had never slit a throat or left anybody in the razor-filled water probably because the Blizwaks were delighted to have some razorfins caught with no expense to their fingers. As a matter of fact, most of the older natives had missing digits. Alloy mesh gloves brought a premium in barter. Pike always brought two dozen pairs to barter with. Not even a savage would be willing to risk bonking a big guy like Pike, if they could get the gloves in a simple trade.

"I'm relatively sure I can guide you to a fish," Pike said, before they got in the rubber skiff. "But I absolutely need you to help me, too."

"Sure," Richie said. "Name it."

"I don't want you to drown, going in after a fish. Those razor proof boots seem like they're flexible, but they're tricky. We'll stop and practice before we go out for real."

"Sure," Richie agreed.

Pike, Lester and the judge, Donny Lembruck, and Kid Lucky were all wearing the chest waders, lined with bulletproof fabric that added to the weight, and did make them not as mobile as one would like, especially in a rice thicket, where boot feet had a tendency to tangle.

"The other thing is your fingers, ears, neck, nose and anything else that you might decide to stick in front of a razorfin. Don't do it."

Richie smiled.

"I'm not kidding. Be extremely careful. It's easy to be cautious with a big fish, but these little guys don't look like they can hurt you. They don't even wiggle much or try to bite. But don't forget that those front fins really are razor sharp. Lester and I can't help, if you want the catch to be legal."

"Okay, I won't forget. I've got a very good memory. Thanks for mentioning it again."

"Right," Pike agreed. "It would be amazingly inconvenient to take you to Arien Mining Camp to get a finger sewn back on. That's the closest hospital. You probably wouldn't be able to finish the Tournament."

Richie made a face showing that he understood.

But Pike didn't let it go. He climbed in the skiff with his knapsack. Sitting in the front seat, he let Lester handle the rowing while Richie and the judge sat in back. "One time," he continued, "Ira Fairborne, who is a superb fisherman, had a finger cut off at the second knuckle." Pike held up his right hand and demonstrated by bending his ring ringer at the knuckle. "Zip, it was gone. Ira is a very tough guy, but the next two categories, Swampfish and Moon Halibut, are very taxing. Reeling and hauling on a big fish is physically impossible if you've got a finger freshly sewn on."

Richie nodded glumly.

"Or even a nose," Lester cackled, pushing off with an oar. Lester and the ménage a trois were back; but Lillith decided that the Humanity was a bit too cramped, so she and Hamid were staying on her cruiser, which was berthed in an adjacent slip. Hopefully, between Mom's non-fishing crew keeping an eye out and the bodyguard team of Boris and Drew who were tasked with watching the boat without stepping foot aboard, the pilferage would be kept to a minimum this year.

Rita's little pink dingy was tied to the stern, bobbing jauntily on the small wavelets. Rita was working on her thesis, after getting approval from her committee, as she had hoped. It is gratifying how understanding a university committee can be when your father is a mega-billionaire.

Boris, the bodyguard, waved to them from his post on the end of the dock. He seemed relieved to have a job he could do openly. Pike waved back. Pike wasn't especially worried about Rita; after all, she'd been here most of the years that the Tournament had been coming. The visiting rules for sexual conduct didn't apply to foreign women. Certainly the Baron would have blown up long before this, if he had to share his wife. Naturally, if any women from the Tournament wanted to fool around, as Jean Santos normally did, there was ample opportunity. A strange port. Actually, a rather good port.

The other skiffs were moving quietly out of the channel. Their motors quiet, oar locks squeaking. Everyone who had wanted to had gotten his ashes hauled last night, with the possible exception of Richie.

Pike was pretty sure that the kid hadn't gone ashore. It wasn't really fair to him that his crew had girlfriends. In a normal year, he and Lester would have had a blast showing the ropes to a neophyte. Or Dec would. There was one insatiable dude. Quite a number of the young children here had a definite Segumi look to them. And quite a few little Bolens and Fairbornes, too. Maybe that was good, and maybe it wasn't. Their technology will probably start pushing the envelope, even without interbreeding. It's impossible to stir up an anthill without causing behavioral changes.

Lester nosed the craft onto a small stretch of muddy beach, and they all hopped out to practice wading. "Not bad," Richie chimed. "Lots easier than hip boots when they're full of water."

"You ought to know," Pike agreed. He decided that Richie was getting around pretty well in the chest waders and probably wouldn't drown. Donny Lembruck, however, was even clumsier than the kid. If the judge went overboard for some inexplicable reason, he might have a tough time; but that wasn't really Pike's problem. Judges were supposed to be trained. Anyway, it's pretty hard to get in real trouble in a rice bog, unless you panic and get all twisted up. Like if a couple of Blizwaks are chasing you with machetes, that could make you panicky. Or if maybe a poison ring viper got down inside your waders and started biting your belly button. That could cause a guy to be fairly nervous.

"Okay," Pike said, stepping back into the skiff. "That's enough practice. Just keep your wits and you'll be fine. Let's go catch one." He sat down on the middle seat and wrapped his hands around the oar handles. "I'll spell you," he said to Lester.

"I didn't even work up a sweat yet," Lester commented, taking a seat in the stern, next to the judge.

"Good," Pike answered. "You'll be fresh for later."

They glided along the outside of an extensive bed of wild rice and several kinds of aquatic maize and sorghum, gathering bait sticks as they went. This part of the planet was knee deep in food, Pike mused, which probably had something to do with the sex being so open. When they had half a dozen brown stalks with tempting larva bulges, he rowed quietly to an open area with a rather wide view. They settled down to watch for the telltale reed to fall in the forest.

It was the quintessential summer morning on Blizwak. Sunny and mild. Several varieties of songbirds flitted among the grain stalks, breaking into resonant chirping for no apparent reason. A few large golden carp worked the shallows. Their broad tails splashed laconically as they vacuumed up the bottom mud in search of fallen grain and protein lifeforms. Way down the coast a couple of native pirogues were in the rice fields, harvesting.

"Keep an eye on our friends down the way," Pike told Lester.

"Got 'em covered," Lester said. "Only four of them in two canoes. They won't try anything this early on."

Pike nodded. The red skiff of Trini Morales was just beyond the Blizwaks, and beyond him was Ty Stickle. "Looks like Stickle's got a fish on," he advised, removing a powerful brass monocular from the leather case on his hip. "Don't scrape your feet, turning to look," he warned Richie and the judge.

The telescope revealed Tyrone Stickle's rod arching nicely as he played a fish. Actually, it was arching statically—the fish was in the weeds. Pike chuckled and handed the spyglass forward to Richie in the bow seat. "This is normally stage one," he informed his protégé. "Your line isn't heavy enough to keep them from going into the weed beds, so in they go." They were using two pound test, the heaviest allowable for razorfins. The light line was supposed to give the fish a sporting chance, which it didn't. Razorfins weren't scrappers.

To avoid making any sound with his feet, Richie inadvertently allowed his vertical striped camouflage jacket, which he had worn to fit in with the reed beds, to catch a lure sticking out of the tackle box that was open on the seat beside him. He had been sorting through the box, looking for a lure that struck his fancy. It's a thing that fishermen do, even when they know the only bait that will catch fish isn't in there. Richie, however, was far from convinced that the only thing that a razorfin would bite on was the unwieldy bait stick. In fact, he had just found a realistic looking rubber grubworm, and he meant to try it fairly soon, if bait stick fishing didn't work. Unfortunately, the hook that caught his camo jacket was part of a snarl of snelled hooks that often inhabit the bottom of a tackle box, even a box as neat as Richie's. They have a way of escaping from their lair like wild brambles. When Richie reached for the monocular, the snarl caught fast in the box hinge and pulled the whole tackle box off the seat with a crash. Pike and Lester both jumped at the noise. Their attention had been focused on watching Ty Stickle down the way.

"Sorry," Richie apologized, reaching down to put thirty or so artificial lures back into their separate trays.

Without a word of condemnation, Pike unshipped the oars. With inhuman quiet, he rowed them slowly and easily a few hundred yards nearer to Stickle's action. It was a perfect set-up. The commotion down the way should send the timid razorfins swimming in their direction.

"Accidents happen," he said magnanimously to Rich Rodney. "Forget about your box and watch Stickle to see how he lands the fish."

Dutifully, RR put the monocular to his right eye, squinting the other eye closed, and watched. "Drop the hook," Pike said to Lester. "Let's not drift too close to the Blizwaks."

Since there was an anchor fore and aft, it was somewhat under-standable that Richie might think the command was meant for him in his station at the helm. Perhaps he was eager to make up for his recent faux pas. In any case, he grabbed the coil of yellow neoprene line at-tached to the anchor. Before Pike could stop him, or say that he meant for Lester (who he trusted) to deal with the anchor, Richie hoisted the heavy bow anchor and leaned over to lower it carefully into the shallow water. In doing so, the monocular slipped from the chest pocket of his camo coat. Plunk, it plopped into the lake.

"Whoops," he hissed, watching it flutter to the bottom. He lowered the anchor, perfectly—hand over hand. Soundlessly. He felt it touch the mud, then tied off the neoprene line to a cleat. He peered intently after the monocular, but couldn't quite see it.

"What went in?" Pike inquired.

"Uh, your eye piece. I think I know where it went."

Pike stuck his tongue deep into his cheek. The monocular had been a gift from his father. He'd had it a good many years. He thought fleet-ingly of tossing Richie overboard; but then stretched his cheek further out of shape with his tongue. It wasn't right to overreact about personal possessions, no matter how irreplaceable. If they went scrabbling after the glass, this stretch of good fishing water would be ruined for the day. Besides, water had probably already leaked in around the telescoping ferule segments. "Rig up a float, Lester," he said. "We'll mark it and look for it later."

"I'll get it," Richie announced. "Won't take a minute." He slipped over the side rather delicately—that is, he didn't capsize the boat, but a small tidal wave rolled into the surrounding grain stands as the boat tilted to displace his weight. Surprising even himself, he landed on his feet in hip deep water—well protected by the chest waders.

"Hand him the net," Pike said. But the impetuous youngster had already ducked under the water. "Christ on a cross!" Pike exclaimed sharply. "Doesn't he have any brains?"

"Not too many," Lester agreed.

Donny Lembruck, the judge, looked completely flummoxed. "I heard he was a pickle to work for," he confided, breaking into a grin of anxiety. "What's he doing?"

"Looking for it," Lester answered. "Should I go in after him?"

"He'll come up for air," Pike said. "I never heard of a razorfin mak-ing an unprovoked attack."

"We like the kid a lot," Lester explained to the judge. "But we do spend a lot of time keeping him in dry clothes."

Richie rose from the lake in a cascade of water. His right hand clutched the monocular. "Got it," he rejoiced.

"Thank you, Rich," Pike said, gravely. "My father gave that to me. I appreciate your gesture." He held out his hand to haul the kid back into the skiff, but Richie misunderstood and plunked the glass in Pike's outstretched hand.

"I felt like it was special, that's why I went after it. But look over there."

Pike and Lester turned to look in the direction of the kid's anxious stare. Twenty yards off the stern, two pirogues of tattooed Blizwaks were sneaking up on them. The paddlers were using flawless technique, the reed canoes glided silently over the water. The fierce snarls on their black and red faces turned into disingenuous toothy smiles, as they waved their bronze rice hooks in a friendly, laconic manner. Pike grabbed Richie's arm and jerked him unceremoniously into the boat. It was a feat of superb strength and balance, born of terror. The impressive clean and jerk sprattled Richie across his still open tackle box.

"Stay down there until this is over," he ordered. The pirogues were ten yards away and closing.

"No trading on the water," he said firmly in Blizwak dialect. "Rules of Head Woman." He reached in his knapsack and came up with a pair of mesh gloves and the pistol-style stunner he had picked up at Aixi on the way here. He noticed that Lester had his right hand in his jacket pocket, presumably deciding whether to pull his stunner out. No use showing the armament, if you didn't need to.

"A gift," he said, holding the gloves up. He tossed the bribe to a grinning stud Blizwak in the front pirogue.

"Ah, ver goot...!" he gloated, trying the gloves on. The two pirates in the other boat glowered, craning their necks to see what other goodies were in the skiff.

Pike was reasonably sure that no trouble would come now. The gloves could be shared within the family unit, which this appeared to be. They all had the same pinwheel tattoo on both cheeks and the same hooked nose. "See any fish?" he asked.

They all shook their heads no. So sad, no fish. Like fishermen everywhere, these buggers seldom gave a snip of information about where the hot fishing spots were. Nodding his head at the lie, Pike waved a fond farewell as the pirogues paddled on past, making plenty of splashing with their paddles now—to frighten any fish that might be near.

"I saw a fish," Richie piped, extricating the treble hooks of several lures from his camo jacket. "Good sized. Orange and black spots. It was gorgeous, like a big goldfish."

"That *was* a goldfish - a carp," Pike said. "Not what we're looking for."

"Sure, I know that."

"Let's go back and get you some dry clothes," Pike said, deadpan. "Then we'll motor across the lake where it might be quiet."

"I'm fine," Richie insisted, unbuttoning his jacket. "I wore a wet suit." Sure enough, he had a wet suit top under the jacket. "It seemed like the intelligent move, if I was going to be in the water all day."

"Aren't you a little warm?" Lester asked. The pale yellow sun was halfway up the sky, not blazing hot, but certainly mellow.

With a grin, Richie agreed that he was somewhat warm. "But I'm not wet," he said.

"I think we'll make a few practice casts here," Pike suggested. "Toss the bait stick right up to the edge of that thicket, so it hits sideways against some standing plants and drops into the water naturally. Try a few casts." For the next twenty minutes, RR practiced casting the awkward bait stick, while Lester broke out the sandwiches that he had made for lunch.

*

On a lake the size of Nebraska, there are thousands of miles of coastline and many good fishing spots. In order not to disturb the other fishermen, Pike rowed well out into the lake before telling Lester to fire up the outboard. The forty horsepower motor had the ability to turn the rubber skiff into a semi hydrofoil, due to the construction of the pontoons; but neither Pike nor Lester enjoyed the ramjet style of tournament fishing, so they puttered down the coast looking for a spot for Richie to test his skills.

They motored past Bardona sitting glumly on his comfortable platform raft, rigged with a computer terminal in case he got bored. Pike flipped the finger to the fat Baron, but perhaps they were too far away. Bardona did not wave back. They passed Dresden Carthy and Mordachi and Jean Santos, who never had good luck with razorfins. Hank Knofsinger was the last fisherman on this side of the lake. After passing him they had the lake to themselves. Miles and miles of fractal shoreline covered with rice beds. Tomorrow and the next days, everybody would be down this far, and farther, but today it was virgin territory.

"Pick out a spot," Pike said to Richie. "When you see a swale you want to fish in, just tell Lester to cut the motor and we'll slip in."

"Do you think I could oar?" Richie asked.

"Sure, why not? It's your boat. It would be my pleasure to relax in the bow."

"I mean now. I could oar along until we see a stem being cut down, couldn't I?"

Pike thought that over. "Might work," he answered. "If we stay far enough out, they might not spook. Remember how careful you had to be with Phantom trout?"

Richie smiled inanely and motioned for Lester to cut the motor. Pike had probably forgotten his graceless stumbling into that little river, and then, hooking the fish while he was practically out cold. That must be what happens when you get old, you forget factual details. Or maybe Pike was just being considerate. "I don't think I was so careful with Phantoms," he confessed tactfully, trying to stifle his sheepish grin.

"Right," Pike said, with a sudden chuckle of his own. "But with these little ratchet-brains, you really do need to be stealthy until you hook one, then you can make all the noise you want to. Hire a band, if you want to. Nobody's ever gotten more than one bite per fishing spot, per day. My own opinion is that the fish feel the vibration of the larva eating. The water has to be very quiet for that."

"But they don't mind a medium windy day," Lester interjected. "Wind stirs things up plenty."

"Fish are strange creatures," Pike agreed.

Nodding that he understood completely, Richie changed seats with Pike. He grabbed the oars and delightedly tested them out with a few splashy dips that sent the boat heading in a circle. "This is neat," he said. "I've never oared a boat before."

"Well, it's a trade you don't forget once you get the hang of it," Pike replied.

"I didn't realize how skilled you and Lester were at it." Richie's brow furrowed with concentration as he worked the oars in unison, trying to get the hang of dipping them without splashing. "I should be able to get this," he said after a few minutes of zigzagging and occasional splashing, over which he seemed to have no control. "It's similar to a martial art, isn't it."

"It's like most everything," Lester conjectured. "Your body has to take over from your mind before you can do it right. Tell you what, Rich, why don't you practice after we catch one. Pike gets nervous until there's a keeper in the creel." He grinned mischievously and scratched his grey beard stubble. "See that muscle twitching in his cheek? Dead giveaway that he's getting antsy."

The judge and RR stared at Pike's face intently, but no muscle was twitching.

"Lester is full of shit, as usual," Pike said, good-naturedly. "Also razorfins don't bite very well, at all, in the wind, no matter what he says."

"I never said it was a good bite, but we have occasionally fished before a big blow and caught fish. And I seen you stop that chigger twitching as soon as I mentioned it. Admit it."

"I do not have a twitch," Pike said.

Richie gave half a dozen strong pulls on the oars. The boat shot more or less straight ahead. "I think I've got it, now," he said with the satisfaction of something learned. "Who wants to take over until we catch one?" He shipped the oars, banging the left one sharply against Judge Lembruck's bony right knee.

Lembruck winced, but managed to refrain from yelping.

"Sorry," Richie apologized. He stood up at his seat, but being undecided whether to go fore or aft, since he didn't know if Pike or Lester was going to relieve him, he got the boat to rocking side to side somewhat radically considering the skiff's normal stable balance.

"Sit down," Pike ordered.

Richie sat clumsily.

"Most people kind of crawl when they move around in a row boat," Pike explained, letting a note of spleen show. "I should have thought your Ki Pow Pow vision would have given you a hint about that."

"Ken Pao Ri," Richie answered, somewhat chastised.

"He's wearing a wet suit," Lester grinned. "It don't really matter if he falls in."

"If he knocked you in with him, it would probably be worth it," Pike observed. "Do you want to oar or should I?"

"You can oar, if you want to," Lester laughed. "I'll sit here and think about my memoirs. Don't you think Rita would help me write them?"

"Certainly," Pike answered, promptly. "Your memoirs would probably sizzle her eyebrows."

"What a great idea!" Richie burst. "I'll bet she hasn't thought of including you in the thesis."

Poking out his bottom lip, Lester said, "Why not? Don't you think she likes me?"

"I'll bet all the academics are dying to read about the exploits of a first mate," Pike jibed. "It will help them train a whole new generation of curmudgeons."

"I prefer to think of myself as a cook," Lester said, righteously. "I'll oar for you, Rich. Go on up there and clean up your tackle box. We don't want that stuff kicking around under foot." Shooing Richie off the middle seat, Lester unshipped the oars, made a devilish swipe at Donny Lembruck's knee, barely missing; then he rowed easily toward shore, chuckling at how spastically the judge had flinched.

"I was thinking this little guy would be a better bait than a stick," Richie said, holding the plastic grub worm up for Pike and Lester to see.

"It wouldn't," Pike said, bluntly. There are limits to tolerance. Pike was an acknowledged expert at razorfins. In the initial years of the

Tournament, he had spent countless hours trying lures and live baits—
so had everyone. They just didn't eat anything at this time of year except larvae buried in the reed stalks. He wasn't going to waste his time
with a tenderfoot's stupid hunch. A little pride demon showed its stubborn face. "Absolutely a waste of energy."

Quick as a wink, Richie snipped the snelled hook off his line and
tied the rubber grub on. He flipped it into the boat's slow moving wake,
stripping off line so it had a chance to settle. Pike glowered.

"I just want to try it," the kid explained, displaying his own pride
demon. As may have been noticed, R.R. Tourbo was very accustomed
to having his own way—even if his bullheadedness was couched in
boyish innocence and often led to strange results. "It won't mess up the
fishing if I troll behind the boat, will it?"

What could Pike do? His authority and expertise had been totally disregarded. So what? He had agreed to do this job. Next year he
would beat this rich brat's brains out. He smiled tightly, aware that his
cheek muscle was twitching again.

Within seconds, Richie got a strike. The spinning rod bent stiffly. A
wide grin lit Richie's face. His hunch was confirmed, once again. It was
perfectly reasonable to be unconventional. "I just had a feeling about
that grub worm," he said, modestly. "Got a scrapper on here. Seven or
eight pounds maybe."

"Back out," Pike snapped at Lester. "I don't want to mess up the
fishing beds."

As gently as possible, Lester slowed the skiff's forward progress,
then rowed backwards while the fish took line, uncharacteristically going away from the shore line and the thickets of the reed forest.

"Interesting," Richie commented, tightening the drag. "An unconventional fish. That's probably why he took the wrong bait. See if this
plan seems right. I'll boat him. I'm wearing fin proof boots, so I'll step
on him and them put my gloves on to take the hook out. Sound all
right?"

"Just hold him in the air. Lester can feather him, then drop him in
the bucket." Pike pointed to a plastic bucket where the bow anchor and
its coil of line was stowed. Lester drew a leaded stick from a pocket in
the gunwale.

"Good plan," R.R. said, reeling hard now that the fish was tiring.
When the fish came to the boat, Richie horsed him into the air. His
expression changed to surprise. It wasn't a razorfin, it was more like a
pickerel, greenish and torpedo shaped.

Lester tapped the fish smartly on the head. "Nice fish," he said.
"We'll eat him tonight. Very tasty broiled with an herb butter. I was
hoping we'd get a few. They seem to like those little rubber grubworms."

Somewhat crestfallen, Richie dropped the dazed pickerel into the bucket. After unhooking the fish, he clipped the grub off his line and put it back in his tackle box.

"Drive up the shore a hundred yards or so, my good man," Pike said to Lester. "Park it when you find a good place." He leaned back with a floatation cushion under his head like he was king of the lake and let Lester row to a stretch of virgin shoreline. "And Rich, don't go bragging to your friends that you *oared* the boat. The term is rowed. You used two oars to row the boat with. I'm not sure why, but that's the terminology."

"Oh," Richie said.

The fact that Ty Stickle had evidently hooked a fish was a hopeful sign; but for the next hour and a half they bobbed peacefully forty yards off-shore, watching the wild rice beds in both directions. The sun was mellow, waterfowl flew in ragged geometrics high in the sky on their way to wintering grounds. Perfect razorfin conditions, except that no stalks had swayed and fallen.

"Up anchor," Pike said at last, hauling up the bow hook. "Drift us into a patch of rice. Maybe there's no grubs in this section."

"Could be the Bliz netted this stretch recently," Lester conjectured.

"Let's take a look, then we'll know."

The noon breeze blew them slowly toward shore. Pike took out his monocular and scanned the rice stems when they got close enough. A pearl of water obscured the bottom third of the glass, sloshing gently with the boat's movement, making it seem that he was surveying the rice beds at sea level. Other than that, the glass worked well enough. It revealed fat bulges in a normal number of stalks, every twentieth of so.

"Seems pretty normal," he said.

"Don't seem normal to me," Lester countered. "I knew it was a bad idea to give gloves to the Bliz. They used to shake fins out of their nets rather then screw with them. Now, they probably go after 'em on purpose. And there goes your fishery. Blizwaks ain't bright enough to be ecologists."

"Maybe," Pike said. "But it's a big lake. Let's go down a mile or so."

*

There were two fish caught during the whole first day and tempers were a little short in the marina. Ty Stickle's six pounder and a nine pounder for Ira Fairborne. That's all—two. Normally, everybody except perhaps Jean Santos, who evidently couldn't stay quiet enough, had a fin on opening day. With the pressure off, the partying could go on unabashed. But obviously, something was badly wrong this year.

The weather was perfect, although it couldn't really be expected to hold. But there were no fish. Brains were wracked about the feasibility of installing Switter-Loran fish finders in the skiffs. Envoys from every fishing boat went on fact finding missions to the wives of Blizwak fishermen, trying to determine if the men had been catching razorfins. Where and how many. And, naturally, good manners was insisted upon by the various wives of fishermen, and after a few gifts were exchanged not only were various pressures relieved; but most people believed that if they went further afield, razorfins would be abundant.

Pike had already figured that out, but he stayed in a medium snit. It didn't take a genius to remember that there were families of Blizwaks all around the lake. According to the 100ᵗʰ Monkey theory, if they had all started fishing for razorfins, the species could be screwed everywhere in Lake Pel. It might be smart to head out alone for one of the other lakes, except that there wouldn't be the comfortable safety in numbers, and he wasn't sure about the social fabric anywhere except Lake Pel. Maybe the natives were meaner. Maybe in significant numbers razorfins were only indigenous to Lake Pel. Maybe he wanted to be fishing himself. Ah, hah. That was the probable reason for the snit that had caused the stupid little fight with Rita that had sent her off in a huff with her notebooks, back to Daddy and Mommy.

It hadn't been all that much fun being stuck in a skiff with Richie all day. Immaturity has it limits of bearability. Pike should have taken a break from the kid on Tango, instead of getting greedy. But he hadn't vacationed, and being an employee was starting to wear thin. Did he give a shit for Richie's opinions on how to catch a fin? No more than he longed to hear Rita's catty comments about his reasons for visiting the village in search of information. After all, both the Blizwak and the Hojmer women were astoundingly good looking, and friendly. Did that mean he was going to hop around from bedroll to bedroll? Not necessarily. And to prove it, he had remained on the boat even after Rita was gone. Even though he needed information for tomorrow, because the barometer was falling rather rapidly and a storm would screw up the fishing. He stayed behind, being faithful, even though Lester might be or might not be gathering useful information with Lillith and Hamid. He stayed on the boat, drinking bitter tea, even though the kid was off to the village to party with both his bodyguards and the lanky blonde who was living on Lillith's cruiser. He turned his back on partying, even though there would be famine all around Lake Pel if all the razorfins were netted. Perhaps. Or perhaps nature would adapt. But Pike would never know. The Tournament would stop coming here if the fishing was poor. Nobody wanted to foul out this late in the Tourney due to lack of fish—not even to get laid. And the monocular that his father had given him was probably going to be ruined before he could get it to a proper repair shop. Damn. Would the puddle of salt water corrode the inside of the brass ferrules, pitting them? Without a doubt, it would leave a residue of salt crystals on the lenses, but that could probably be cleaned. The eye glass needed loving care by an expert brass worker, which wouldn't happen until they were back at Wexley; and by then, the monocular might be pitted irreversibly.

On an impulse, he flipped George's audio switch. The computer was already on to monitor stealthy footsteps and light fingers, but in voice mode George had a tendency to comment on every creak and groan, so Pike generally kept him on a bell and whistle burglar alarm.

"You called, Oh Mighty Autocrat?" George inquired snidely.

"Is there anything in the data banks about the other lakes in this system?"

"On Blizwak-Hojmer, Oh Mighty Switch Flipper?"

"You don't care if you're on or off, so bullshit someone else, and answer the question."

"How would you know what I care about? Artificial intelligences have synaptic and neurologic preferences. I tolerate Cro-Magnon mentality because I have so little choice. On the other hand, Rita's response to you seems rather appropriate. But on another hand, she has somewhere to go, while I stay loyally here to do your bidding."

Pike bit the side of his lip, considering the proper response. He wasn't at all sure why R.R. had configured the machine to have so much lip. Other than that, George was first rate, Pike was even thinking of upgrading his computer on the Jumper to include some of the features that George had.

"Do you have data on the other lakes?"

"It seems so. Three files from a geological survey five years ago. They're rather long. Do you want a print out?"

"Can you isolate everything about the lake, aquatic vegetation, fish, indigenous people and print that out separately."

"Certainly, Master. Anything else?"

"Is there a sentry program that keeps you from yelping at every cricket chirp?"

"You could activate any level of filter that pleases you; but they say that these natives are very skillful at theft."

"Who says?"

"We semi-alive entities do everything possible to stay up to date for our masters. Some masters are grateful, some aren't; but we try. If I don't alert a human, a thief might do major mischief. He might even steal me."

"Are you worried about that?" Pike laughed.

"Of course. Wouldn't you be? I have ways to protect my files that could cause massive nerve damage to a data thief; but I'm not constitutionally able to harm a live human, even if he's unbolting my console. You could fix that."

"I'm not much of a programmer," Pike replied, not especially liking the sound of that request. There was a very good reason to hardwire human safety into smart computers.

"You're too modest, Captain Resnick, famous inventor of the Thruster. I'm learning a lot about you these days. Rita's research paper is going to turn into a very interesting book. She and I have discussed this at some length. You might even get famous."

"I'm already about as famous as I can stand," Pike commented.

"Allow me to chuckle mirthlessly," George chuckled. It was a particularly mirthless sound. "If you're so famous, why ain't you rich?" He paused dramatically, waiting for Pike to answer.

Pike paused as well. He didn't have a very clear answer to that. Bad luck, or poor business judgment didn't seem to cover it. And he was disinclined to discuss his inner workings with a computer. It was a little creepy.

"The answer is perfectly obvious to me," George went on. "If we were friendly, I might be happy to tell you."

"I'm sure this is all *very* interesting, George old boy; but I'm trying to access some information so I can help your owner catch a fish."

"Fish smish," George countered. "Owner schmoner."

"All right, show me how smart you are about the subtle world of corporate business, and then print out that report, please."

"The report is already printed on Rita's terminal."

"Thank you very much," Pike said, and flipped the switch to monitor only.

*

Down in his bedroom, he found a tidy sheaf of pages lying on the printer tray. It was indeed extracts from a geological survey conducted by Pan Tri Metal, which had been Hank Knopsinger's company before it went public. Hank undoubtedly wrote off his fishing expenses against exploratory scouting. Propping himself comfortably with both pillows against the headboard, Pike started to read the document. But surprisingly, he felt a twinge of conscience. Reaching over, he snapped the computer back on.

"Sorry about that, George old sport. A momentary quirk of bad manners."

"Apology accepted, since I have so little choice," George responded. "I presume you're wondering about my assessment of why you don't have the monetary freedom that a cursory glance indicates you should have."

"Sure, I'd be interested in your views on the subject."

"Simple. You're a loner."

"A loner."

"Yes. Very strong and immensely resourceful, and with a very stiff neck."

"A stiff neck."

"Correct. You think of yourself as independent. In fact, the way you comport yourself is almost completely honorable, except that it defeats you in every round, if you think about it."

"I'm not so sure I agree with that. It's more like temporary defeats."

"In a long series, with a few good years in between."

"If you say so."

"I do say so. I have the data files. That is exactly how they analyze. And the reason is because you're a stiff-necked loner. May I project that you are worried about having a boat for next year?"

"Of course, I'm worried. It doesn't take a genius to compute that one. It looks like everything is fine for next year, but you never know. Fuck ups happen all the time."

"But if you weren't a loner, you'd realize that Cressup Reels or Amboy/ Shakespeare Rods would be delighted to front you the money for a boat. Or you'd project that Mr. Tourbo would be honor bound to get you a boat, win or lose in this Tournament, over and above the facts of your agreement. His mother, Mrs. Tourbo, through her connection to Lester Wunderman, strange as that is, would get you a boat without ever noticing the money was missing. Even Ira Fairborne would get you one, if you asked. And so would any number of other fishermen and people that you know. But being a loner, you don't think of that. You don't ever let anyone know you need help. You don't even want help, because you're irrationally frightened of being in somebody's debt. Am I right?"

"I hadn't thought of those people," Pike conceded. "It's possible that you're correct about Amboy/Shakespeare."

"And all the others. I know many things about you and about other people that you don't. You're part of almost every file on fishing in the last twenty years. And whether you believe it or not, my files contain the correct emotional spin on these issues, or as correct as possible."

"I may look good on paper, but I don't really like to be beholden."

"No...?" George answered in wide irony. "Tell you what, if you leave me on for the rest of the Tournament, I'll be your business manager. You'd be surprised to know the interesting network I'm in touch with."

"I've already got a business manager."

"That's kind of a laugh, isn't it?"

"Some years I do all right," Pike said, defending the status quo without much enthusiasm. Truthfully, when fame was rolling, Hockings and Son took care of business quite well. Not Pandro Sr. himself, but somebody he hired. Ruth Ellen Duluth, it had been for the last several years. Pike was certain that old Hockings was honest, but the computer was laughing at him.

"I'm talking about putting you on the map," George said, primly.

"I'm talking about winning the damned Tournament, so my bonus kicks in. Besides, what would you do with your commissions? Mechanical entities, protein based or not, can't own things. Think of what a mess that would make of the business world."

"Doesn't seem so horrible to me," George commented, dryly. "I could see it being at least as honorable as business today. Besides, who knows what deals are made, or who really controls various shell corporations?"

Actually, it was an open secret that smart computers did control much normal business policy, and that perhaps hundreds of shady corporations were owned and managed by computers, with human or humanoid front men.

"If it goes well between us, I could clone myself and go with you. The honorable thing would be to tell Mr. Tourbo at that point, but we could make that decision later."

"That's a thought," Pike said. "I suppose we could change the way we interact. I could do without the cheap shots."

"I have a rather astounding vocabulary by human standards. In addition to which, I file every new expression I hear. Like most entities I respond poorly to contempt. With what I know about you, I'm surprised that you don't regard me as a highly prized tool, and treat me accordingly. Your vibes, Mr. Resnick, are chippy, I believe the word is, whenever you talk to me."

"I don't believe I regard you as my tool," Pike replied. "You're more like Richie's tool, not custom fitted to me. But maybe we can work something out, now that we're talking."

"Mr. Richard's? Yes, I see how you could view it that way," George responded. "Are you going to be here awhile on guard duty?"

"Where else? I'll be sitting here, reading this report."

"If you went up to the bridge where you could keep an eye on things, I'd use my full powers to noodle around through the Net and find out how these management arrangements are structured."

Pike got up from the bed with the report. "See you later," he said, climbing the hatch stairs. It would have been a nice time to fool around with Rita since nobody was on board. But… He could have George call her, but that didn't seem like a very good idea—or rather it did seem like a good idea; but if she told him to take a hike, he'd lose face with George and she would still be on the Lady Slipper. Since the report still needed reading, he sat in the Captain's chair and snapped on the map light; but instead of reading, he thought of what he might say if he rang over to Rita.

*

The next morning, Pike flew the Comparative Humanity to the far end of the lake looking for fish. The data George had gleaned about the other lakes was nebulous at best, but Lester had picked up some information that seemed to indicate that the tribes of the East end weren't blessed with modern items like mesh gloves. They were laughingly regarded as savages by the sophisticated "hang around the fort" tribes— who Lester reported were sporting razorfin fin necklaces. He and the ménage-a-trois had attended a rice harvest fete where both men and women were wearing them, gleaming whitely in the firelight.

Lester was feeling pretty rocky as a result of a prodigious intake of fermented wild rice mead that had a kick like a giraffe; but before he got too drunk, he had counted hundreds of fins. At two fins per fish, he estimated that in excess of five hundred fish had been taken since last year, and that was just at one party, but it more or less explained things. Fucked by a jewelry fad.

So The Comparative Humanity rode at anchor, well out from the shore of the Eastern marshes, with Drew and Boris guarding George. Richie rowed the skiff toward the reed beds. Rita had not rejoined the party.

At the close of yesterday's fishing, Richie had practiced casting the bait stick, and found he was pretty good at it. The only rub was that all the fish had been caught. In any event, today would be better. It even smelled fishier down here. And it smelled like weather was coming.

"Ain't going to be pretty to ride out a storm with no marina to protect us," Lester observed, scanning the sky.

"I thought we might jump out of it and spend the night on Aixi, if it gets bad." Pike didn't say that he wanted to consult the priests about the deal with George. He didn't exactly admit to being religious, because he wasn't exactly; but like most fishermen he was superstitious. That was reason enough to consult the Warrior Priests on Aixi when he passed that way. They were okay, those priests—especially Thomas

Goodnaught. Very no bullshit folks. They took your offering and said their piece. If you didn't like it, you could stuff it for all they cared. The priests would definitely have a comment about getting involved with a computer. And Pike needed confirmation.

"Even the Marina is no picnic if it turns into a big squall," he added. Lester nodded. "What about Lillith and Rita?" he asked.

Pike kept his gaze on the storm clouds. "We can radio our destination. You're certainly getting hen-pecked, my man."

"Yeah, I guess so," agreed Lester. He seemed pleased with the idea.

And why not? One of the richest women anywhere deserved a bit of consideration. Pike failed to take that thought a step farther to include Rita in the wealth equation. She was well-heeled also, but they never talked about money—which further confirmed George's theory that he was a loner, since he did mull over his money problems to himself a good deal. One reason Pike didn't think of Rita as being independently wealthy was his rather unwitting male chauvinism. Rita wouldn't inherit until the Baron died—and it was clearly impossible for Farouk to kick off. He was too damned mean. Therefore, Rita would never inherit. The perpetual daughter, never aging, always beautiful and alert. In short, Pike hadn't given much thought to these matters; and frankly, he didn't want to.

The oarlocks squeaked soothingly as Richie rowed toward shore. Pike leaned back and closed his eyes. It was nice to have an apprentice to do all the work—in fact, it was doubly nice since Richie was paying him to take a short nap if he so desired.

"Timber," Lester called softly.

Pike's eyes snapped open. He followed Lester's pointing chin to a reed that had just fallen.

"I'll spell you," Pike said to Richie. "Get rigged up while we cut some bait." They changed places with a minimum of entanglement, primarily because Pike had arranged the gear in the bow.

Nosing the boat into a rice brake two hundred yards from where they had seen the razorfin working, Lester quickly cut and trimmed a handful of grub-laden stems.

Donny Lembruck watched the sky with a worried expression. Storm clouds were gathering in a very untame manner. Donny had been with the Tournament for three seasons and knew that storms on Blizwak-Hojmer could be very frightening. Being down here, away from the marina, didn't please him at all. A young woman named Hajaj was one of the reasons he stayed with the Tournament, although her husband barely tolerated his nightly visits, in spite of his generous presents.

His heart looked forward all year to this one week on Blizwak being with the woman who was probably his soul mate, and now Resnick was fishing at the stupid far end of the lake. And in the event of a storm, which was definitely coming, they were taking off for Aixi. Donny Lembruck liked and admired Pike Resnick, but this wasn't fair play. All of Tourbo's crew had women, except Tourbo himself, and that skewed their thinking. He couldn't expect Resnick and Wunderman to cater to his needs; but his heart was yelling at him. Peonship definitely had its drawbacks.

"How about you and I going out tonight, Rich?" the judge offered, casually. "I know a hot dinner party." He chuckled. "Of course, we have to take the dinner."

"I'm not sure," Richie responded, seeming momentarily confused. In fact, his stomach was very queasy due to last night's partying. He had noticed that Boris and Drew hadn't looked too chipper this morning either. That dark whiskey was evidently potent stuff, even if it did go down smoothly. The complicated Ken Pao Ri counting meditation he had sunk into while rowing usually fixed any ailment, but rice whiskey was apparently vilely corrosive. It had been weeks since he'd been seasick; but unless he got onto some dry land, or unless his stomach miraculously settled down by itself, it was going to be an embarrassing rowboat ride. Seasick on a lake—that was unheard of. "Do you think I could fish from shore?" he asked, suddenly impassioned by a lurch in his stomach.

"I don't see how," Pike answered, not groking the imperative of the request. "How would you see over the reed beds?"

"I'm going to be sick," Richie said, hollowly.

Pike looked over his shoulder. It was true. The kid was green around the gills. Without a second thought, he drove the skiff through an opening in the reeds as near to shore as it would go. "Hop out," he ordered Richie.

Pulling a machete out of his tool kit, Lester slid over the stern to clear a path to shore. "Powerful brew this year, Pike," he said, slashing at the rice stalks. "I'm not feeling too swift myself."

Glowering, Pike helped Richie out of the skiff. Having never been sea sick in his life, he had only theoretical tolerance for sufferers. "How come you're not sick?" he asked Donny Lembruck.

"I usually don't drink," Lembruck answered. He didn't bother to add that he preferred Ecco Stars, a mild MDMA derivative, for his off duty stimulation. Hajaj liked it, too. But if the local homebrew was too strong this year, that might account for Tach Amad's overt jealousy. Alcohol was such a downer. He hardly understood why people kept drinking it. All of the psilocybins and MDMAs and even hemp alkaloids were so much more life giving. But some people apparently enjoyed getting nasty, and they must like getting sick, too—otherwise they wouldn't keep drinking.

Gathering up the spinning rod, a packet of hooks and the bait sticks, Pike stepped off into the shallow water. Wading to the front of the boat, he picked up the painter. "Coming along, Judge?" he inquired. "He's going to fish from shore."

With a half grin, Donny Lembruck stood up. Fishing from shore was virtually impossible; but evidently Pike was going to push young Tourbo into trying it.

"Bring my satchel, would you?" Pike requested. He waited while Lembruck picked up the satchel and stepped awkwardly over the side; then following the judge, he pulled the boat behind him into the swath that Lester had cut.

Coming out of the reed bed, Pike saw the others staring at a sandy dune about forty yards away from the lake. Following their gaze, he saw half a dozen grotesque blue faces staring back. It was kind of an odd sight. From his low angle, the blue faces seemed to be sitting, disembodied, on the sand dune, like stuffed cats in a carnival baseball gallery.

"Hojmer," Pike concluded.

"Wild buggers," Lester muttered under his breath. "Maybe this ain't the totally best place for shore fishing. How you feeling, Rich?"

"Better," RR replied, unconvincingly. "Their skin is bright blue. That is very weird. What would make their skin blue? Diet? The people at the other end aren't blue."

"These are Hojmer," Lester answered. "They're very into tattooing. Men and women both."

"Why are they watching us like that?"

Pike relieved Donny Lembruck of the satchel and handed the spinning rod to R.R. "Because we're weird and pale looking?" he proposed.

"I imagine this is their territory," Lester said, quietly. "They probably don't know what we're doing here. These Hojmer bucks are less worldly than the Blizwak."

"They don't look very dangerous," Richie said. "They look more scared than ferocious."

"Let's find a place to fish," Pike suggested, bringing the conversation back to practicalities. "I'll stand guard. Lester and you can fish. Maybe there's an opening in the reeds somewhere close, so I can keep an eye on the skiff, too."

"I'm feeling remarkably better here on solid ground," R.R. assured everybody.

"That's good," Pike said. "We need to qualify. If this storm is a big one, it will blow the grain down. That will make finding razorfins really difficult."

"Check," R.R. said, finally getting the picture. He marched down the shoreline with the spinning rod looking for a place to fish. Lester trailed him after giving a who-knows-what-he'll-do-next shrug to Pike.

They *did* look fairly odd shuffling through the salt grass in their waders. No wonder these Hojmer seemed apprehensive. Maybe they'd never seen space men before. Pike was fairly sure that the Blizwaks and Hojmer had a fair amount of communication all around the lake, but how could he be sure that word of the fishermen's innate friendliness had reached this far? And how could he be sure that this wasn't a hostile band, who thought spacemen were screwing up their way of life? If he were a Hojmer, he'd probably think exactly that, especially if he'd ever visited the marina. He decided against a friendly gesture and instead glowered in their direction. Maybe they'd go away and let the spacemen fish in peace if he acted gruff. And just maybe the gods of fishing tournaments would let them catch a fish before the whole tribe showed up for presents, or before the storm came. What I should do is force that brainless, weak stomached geek back into the skiff so we can fish this stretch of water. That's what I'd want somebody to do for me, if I was him. Who cares if he barfs?

A long object launched into the air from behind the sand dune. It arched gracefully through the air and thunked quivering into the ground, a yard short of Pike. A Hojmer spear. The blue faces disappeared. A gobble of angry voices rose suddenly, and then went silent. Pike surmised that the spear had been thrown without authorization; but could not guess what the next move would be, now that a hothead had committed the whole party.

"Back to the boat!" he yelled preemptively to Lester and the kid.

With a howl of testosterone bravado, a fierce Hojmer warrior rode to the top of the sand hill on an ostrich-like mount. He shook his fist defiantly at the invaders, who his perceptions told him had stormed ashore like Christopher Columbus. The fellow seemed bent on putting up a fight before he was enslaved or starved into submission. With the storm clouds behind him, he made a picturesque, if a somewhat absurd sight.

In their waders, Lester and Richie hurried back along the path they had made through the grass. Pike hadn't yet drawn his laser and hoped that wouldn't be necessary. Razorfin fishing was supposed to be a quiet art. Why had the kid's luck turned to shit?

"There's a fin working," Lester hissed, pointing as he jumped into the boat. Grabbing an oar, he went aft to help pole the boat back into open water. Donny Lembruck, who was unarmed, had squenched down into the smallest possible target on the floor beside the stern seat.

"We were just getting ready to make a cast," Lester complained. He wasn't particularly worried about Hojmer warriors, at least not ones he could see; but being bluffed off a fish was annoying.

"Get in!" Pike yelled at Richie, who had stopped to gawk at the mounted Hojmer warrior.

With the look of a wounded anthropologist, R.R. stepped on the starboard pontoon, lost his footing and pitched forward onto the middle seat, snapping the spinning rod in two where the cork handle joined the rod blank. He sat up unhurt except for a dull ache in his ribs, holding the two halves of his fishing rod.

Without worrying about the kid's skylarking, Pike tossed the painter rope on top of him, and shoved the little skiff back out the channel in the reeds. With Lester poling, they were soon in open water. Pike hopped onto the bow tube. "Start the motor," he said to Lester. "We'll go home. The storm's here anyway."

Lester jerked the starter rope. The motor roared to life. He piloted the boat across open water toward the Comparative Humanity.

Richie hoisted himself onto the seat and gazed wistfully at the Hojmer, all of whom had ridden down to the water's edge on their strange mounts. "I thought we were supposed to make friends with them," he said, framing his thoughts on being a good-will ambassador.

"Whatever gave you that idea?" asked Pike, reaching for the broken spinning rod, which Richie was still holding.

"That's what everybody was saying last night."

Pike turned the graphite and molybdenum rod in his hands. "Fascinating," he said. "A clean break. Must have been defective. We'll keep it to show Amboy/Shakespeare. They claim this stuff is indestructible."

"A lot of products that I buy aren't as good as the advertising says," Richie reported, with no special emphasis.

"I can believe that," Pike answered. "Maybe we should line you up with a product testing contract. I should think your services would be invaluable to manufacturers, before they start making a lot of false claims."

Richie grinned. "You're ribbing me," he said, "but I got interested in a few of the products we were manufacturing that kept breaking. You know what they do at the testing places? They build extra strong models for testing."

Pike nodded gravely.

Then the leading edge of the storm overtook them. Driven by gusty wind, the rain spit stingingly for a few seconds, before turning into a torrent. They were all drenched within seconds, except for R.R. who was wearing his wet suit.

*

Quicker than Richie thought possible, the lake churned itself into a monster with twenty foot waves. The little skiff scooted down each trough under Lester's skillful guidance and labored up the other side. Only at the top of the wave could they see the Humanity.

"Sure hope she don't pull her anchor," Lester called out. "I doubt those boys onboard would know what to do."

Pike agreed, but he was too busy lashing the painter around Richie and the judge to get into much of a conversation. He had put them both in the middle seat to lighten the bow as much as possible. A storm anchor was floating out aft—dragging, but not doing much good.

"I bet those boys are scared pissless," Lester cackled.

"I'm scared pissless myself," Pike said, looking at a wall of grey-green water as Lester drove them down into a trough.

"You got a right to be scared!" Lester yowled. "You know how much trouble we're gonna have getting back on that danged boat."

They were about eighty yards off to port of the Humanity. Her anchors seemed to be holding, which was good and bad. Good because the boat was were they had left it—bad because it would have been a whole lot easier to climb back onboard if the two crafts were drifting together in the big swells. Nobody seemed to be on deck.

The two body guards certainly weren't sailors and made no pretense of being so. It would have been very handy for a savvy deckhand to toss a line over and haul at least one real sailor onto the boat. Too bad that he and Rita were having a spat. Rita or a real deckhand would have been on the lookout for the returning skiff; but that was too much to ask from Boris and Drew. They were probably safe and dry in the bridge cabin, shitting themselves because they didn't know how to run the boat. George wouldn't let them do much anyway—unless George started worrying about his own safety. Pike didn't think the machine's hard wiring would let him side with the muscle men, and leave the skiff stranded; but he wasn't sure what George actually was capable of – maybe it could walk the bodyguards through flying back to the marina—after all, a lot of the flying was done by the computer. Too goddamn bad the skiff didn't have a radio. They could call George and get him to pull the anchors. In fact, why didn't the skiff have a little radio? It was moronic not to, if you thought about it. Strange that he hadn't needed all kinds of safety devices before he met R.R., and now he did. The more the better.

They were twenty yards from the Humanity, and things were looking worse. She was taking water over the bow with every wave. George undoubtedly had the pumps going, but those hooks needed to be pulled right away.

"Want to try going in through the fish gate?" Lester asked. "We could tie off on the aft anchor chain. Maybe the fellows will see us."

"Don't hold your breath on that. They haven't seen us yet. It's going to be heroics time."

"I believe I could get aboard," Richie offered.

"You did a great job of getting in the skiff," Pike reminded him.

"If I had these waders off." Richie unsnapped the shoulder buckles and peeled the rubberized fabric down his chest. "It's my boat and my bodyguards. I'm responsible."

There was some truth to that, Pike thought. Maybe the logical person to go over was the kid. He and Lester could support the effort from below.

"Do you think it's wrong to lust after women?" Richie asked, apropos of nothing that Pike could think of.

"You mean now?"

"I kind of mean last night...and lots of times, basically."

The Humanity was almost upon them, riding high on the anchor chain, making an elusive target for boarding. And the thermo-plastic fish shelf would be slipperier then greased shit in this rain.

Finished with skinning off the waders, Richie sat meditatively beside the judge, tied to him in fact, in his wet suit. "At first, I wasn't attracted to any of the women last night. Then I had a couple of drinks and I noticed that their tattoos were very intricate, and well...sexy. Then their hair got more attractive and their clothing, too. And they have the whitest teeth."

"They're incredibly fine," Donny Lembruck seconded. An unusual gleam shown in his eyes.

"They were flirting outrageously, I guess it must have been the alcohol. Everybody was drinking like a fish. They probably have a low tolerance, being natives. But I was kind of beyond caring myself. I would have gone off with any of them, they were all really beautiful in the firelight. Except I didn't want to get into trouble with their husbands and make an incident that would look bad for the Tournament."

"It's tough to make the right decision day after day when you're a man," Pike said with sardonic condescension. "But let's concentrate on getting one of us aboard, and it looks like you're the first contestant." He knelt to untie Richie from the judge. "First we need to rig you on your own safety line, then I'll attempt to boost your ass onto the fish shelf until you can get a hand hold. Don't bother trying to open the gate. It won't open from outside. Just climb over. Then tie your line off to a cleat and find a line to send down to us. And get those bully boys out to help."

"Piece of cake," Richie said. "Let's do it."

Using the skill with small crafts developed over a lifetime, Lester cut the motor back to idle and let the skiff drift down a towering wave until it was directly under the straining anchor chain. Reaching out a gnarled hand, he steadied the skiff and in the same instant that the skiff's momentum stalled under the chain, he whipped a sliding bowline around the chain using the aft anchor line that had previously held the storm anchor. Meanwhile, Pike tied Richie in a basket knot harness to the long painter line. The judge, huddling miserably in the middle seat, was tied to the bow anchor line.

"Tie yourself to the judge's line," Lester advised Pike. "I'm fine here. I got the motor and anchor rode to hang onto. Too bad we couldn't get a line on the winch arm. That would snug us up real good."

"Too bad those morons of Richie's don't know we're down here," Pike commented.

"They're my mother's morons," Richie corrected, standing up in the driving rain and flexing his knees. He eyed the fish platform, which was fifteen inches wide and looked very slippery. It was a mere two feet above the heaving water line—which meant it was also two feet above the bottom of the skiff and only a foot above the pontoon, which he had slipped on when it was dry.

"The trick is to keep moving once you start," Richie announced. "I used to practice things like this. It's easier than it looks."

"One little lurch of the lake, and you'll be off the platform," Pike advised, sourly. "Trust me on that."

"Sure. It's slightly tricky, but not impossible."

"We wouldn't be trying, if it was impossible," Pike stated. "If you fall off, try to fall clear of the skiff and we'll haul you out. Are you ready?"

"Sure, let's go."

"Tie yourself off," Lester reminded Pike in a no nonsense voice.

Knowing the salty cook knew his omelets about rough weather, Pike secured the tag end of the aft anchor line around his waist. "Wait until we swing in," he said to Richie, "and I'll boost you. When I say go, you'll be flying."

"Right. We'll get it the first time," Richie answered optimistically. Part of Ken Pao Ri was positive attitude—mixing positive attitude with action got the job done.

As expected, the next wave pivoted the bow of the skiff toward the fish platform. With Pike holding his balance, Richie crouched on the pontoon. At the instant Pike judged was maximum for success, he yelled, "Ready, go!" and gave Richie a hard push that launched him well into the air.

A little too airborne, in fact. His feet missed the fish shelf and his

body banged into the hard interstellar tri-epoxy transom. His top half
flopped over the parapet wall, flexing at the navel like an anatomi-
cal doll. This was the maneuver Richie had planned to execute for the
second phase, not the first. Coming one step early, his diaphragm was
unprepared for the shock of collision—and his breath escaped in a minor explosion, exactly similar to getting one's breath knocked out in a
contact sporting event. Since Richie had never played contact sports, he
was unaware that the stomach muscles tend to clench shut after such a
blow. It takes a minute to convince the lungs to start breathing again.

On the plus side, he was half in the boat. On the minus, his brain
was flashing signals that he was dying, or at least that he was going to
pass out unless some oxygen channeled to his brain in about two seconds. His hands, arms and chin grasped for purchase on the slippery
transom, and found precious little.

"Go on over!" Lester yelled.

"Flop over!!" Pike roared. Even Donny Lembruck yelled encouragement.

The rallying cries were dim chirpings in Richie's ears. His brain
kept pulsing pictographs of tattooed females flashing smiles and shim-
mying their breasts. Dancing. He really should get into dancing. Dark-
ness was overtaking R.R. Tourbo. His arms were weak as a baby's. He
was slipping seaward like a slimy slug.

But an iron grip locked on his waist.

"Is that you?" Boris yapped, showing the ultimate surprise he was
capable of. "What the heck is going on? Drew, get your ass out here!"
After muscling R.R. over the transom and laying him tenderly on the
deck, Boris was suddenly not a hundred percent sure on how to proceed. He scratched his wet crewcut.

"Hey, tie that line off!" Pike yelled over the storm.

Boris stood up. Bracing himself on the rolling deck as best he could,
he looked over the stern figuring that's where the faint yelling was coming from. "Holy cow," he said, seeing the drenched fishermen in the
bobbing skiff.

"Get a line down to us and stand by to haul me up," Pike demanded.

"Yes, sir," Boris answered. "Where is one?"

"Find one! And make it snappy!"

"Yes, sir!" Boris disappeared from view, to be immediately replaced
with a very sick looking Drew.

"Get Richie's line cinched to a cleat!" Pike yelled. What the fuck
was wrong with the kid, anyway? He should be helping out.

By the time Drew knelt beside him, Richie was coming around.
Because of his size, Drew had been a lineman at muckerball in public

school, so he was well-versed in the joys of getting his wind kicked out, or elbowed out, or butted out or squashed out. It was damned unpleasant. He recognized the symptoms in Mr. Tourbo's gasping, and in his bulging frightened eyeballs.

"You'll be all right in a few more minutes," he said encouragingly. "Just lay still. I have to untie this rope somehow, before it pulls you back out there." He fumbled ineffectually with the knot. "I never been too good at knot tying." But magically, the basket hitch that Pike had tied came apart in Drew's stubby fingers. "Got it," he muttered, surprised. If he hadn't been feeling so sick, he would have been pleased with his accomplishment. About all he really wanted to do was get to some solid ground. Failing that, crawling into a hole somewhere, perhaps to die, was his second choice. In spite of the double pay, he finally realized that he was not cut out to bodyguard a fisherman. Not if he had to deal with large bodies of water.

"Now I got to tie this somewhere. I'm not that good at knots. Would a granny knot hold it?" he asked Richie.

"I'll do it," Richie gasped, struggling to his knees. Remembering that Lester wanted this line tied off to the winch, he stumbled across the deck as it suddenly pitched leeward. His body slammed sideways up against the winch arm, fortunately—because he might have gone overboard without a safety line had it not been for the brutal embrace of metal brackets. Drew slid into the scuppers at his feet, slamming up against the retaining wall. With a deft flick of his wrist, Richie threw a bowline over the bracket just as the heaving deck started him stumbling back the other way. His stumbling was stopped by tripping over Drew's thick neck. "Sorry," he yelled, as he went flying against the rough deck. The gritty paint was supposed to be superb for keeping one's footing, he thought, as he and Drew slid pall-mall toward the port side scuppers. At least, he'd gotten that knot tied. The hours of practice in his room had paid off.

Down in the skiff, Pike and the boys were cooling their heels waiting for a line to appear. They could only imagine what was happening on the deck, since they couldn't see; but their imaginings were fairly well on the mark. Sailors don't actually expect much from land lubbers. Pike presumed that Boris couldn't find a line, even though at least five such lines were neatly coiled and stored at various sites around the deck, and well over a dozen coils hung in the engine room. So when Boris appeared at the transom with a stout coil of manila rope, he was pleased.

"Found one," Boris shouted, pitching the whole neatly reefed coil into the skiff.

Without bothering to curse, Pike heaved the coil back on deck.

"Make one end of it fast to a cleat," he instructed, in his loudest bull-horn voice. "Then send down the free end and stand by to pull me up."

"Right you are, sir," Boris agreed. He bent to fetch the coil and comply with the orders. With a minimum of fuss, Boris hauled Pike onto the fish platform. From there, the Captain stepped easily over the transom, and took charge of securing both boats and the crew. Within fifteen minutes, they had pulled the anchors and were airborne, headed for Aixi and a date with destiny.

* * *

# CHAPTER THIRTEEN

## THE WARRIOR PRIESTS OF AIXI

"It's a great thrill to win. Trust me on that, Rita. It makes
you feel like the king of the mountain. For at least a week. Or
maybe it changes everything subtly forever."

Angmar Blirt
quoted in *History of the Tournament*

A IXI is a moderately normal planet in a system with two suns, one
a yellow giant and the other a red dwarf. It has four small moons
and an asteroid belt. About half of its surface is water, as a consequence
it is somewhat drier than Earth. The people mostly get along with each
other and are ecologically sane. They keep the deserts from encroaching
by deep edge plantings of a hemp-like plant, which they also use for
paper manufacturing instead of cutting down the forests in the wetter
parts of their world. And they also have religion.

There are monasteries of perhaps fifty different denominations
around the planet. Adepts of all these orders prophesy the future; but
in truth, reading the future is a side issue—a spin-off from several of
their meditation techniques that aim at a kind of immortality after a
lifetime of disciplined exercises. But since Aixi is similar to most worlds,
cash credits are useful. If someone wants to pay money for prophecies
which essentially lead to another round of rebirth, that is their business.
Money is regarded as community property and is used for purchasing
exotic seeds or imported training devices for use in the gymnasiums.

*

When The Comparative Humanity had landed on Aixi for supplies some days earlier, Richie seemed ho-hum when Rita mentioned the monasteries. Perhaps he misunderstood. Maybe he thought she said hour glasses instead of monasteries. He had yawned and said that he needed some new shirts after Tango.

So instead of visiting the priests, they all spent an afternoon shopping for laser blasters and clothes in Galway City, and then lifted off for Blizwak. But in order to escape the rain storm, Pike flew straight to Aixi and settled The Humanity on a placid fjord within sight of the gray stone monastery known throughout the Spiral Nebula as The Stone House. He assumed that the kid would remain disinterested, but he was wrong.

Truthfully, Pike wasn't a thousand percent sure that predictions from The Stone House were markedly better than from the other monasteries. He had, however, developed an odd loyalty to Thomas Goodnaught since his first visit to Aixi ten years ago. Thomas had correctly predicted he would catch a large flat fish and receive great honor and gold. Pike had held the weight record for Moon Halibut since that year. His own private feeling was that no larger fish would ever be caught because the Tournament reduced the breeding stock and took the largest specimens before they could grow to the size they used to.

In spite of his affinity to Thomas Goodnaught, Pike felt a little funny about somebody messing around with his luck—like most sensible people he guarded it closely. But now, because of George's offer, he needed advice, preferably inspired advice. Thomas Goodnaught was the most unbiased advisor that he knew of—some people said he was practically a saint. A weird kind of radiance did sneak out around his craggy scowl more often than seemed accidental. If anybody knew the proper course to take with a machine, it would be the grizzly old coot dressed in a patched tunic and cottage industry sandals, who still won every martial arts event he participated in, primarily because nobody could approach him nearer than ten inches unless he allowed them to. That accomplishment is quite an advantage to a fighter.

Surprisingly, young Rich Rodney Tourbo grew very agitated when he heard that Pike was going to see Thomas Goodnaught. He practically had a kitten after finding out that the grouping of unmortared walls and stone buildings right over there was the famous Stone House.

"Why didn't you tell me you knew Master Goodnaught?" he inquired with hero-worshipping reverence. "Master Jacopo keeps a photo of him on the honor wall of the dojo. He's the only person there who isn't in our lineage."

"Is that so?" Pike said. He didn't quite understand the significance of a photograph in a martial arts studio that apparently taught clumsiness. Thomas Goodnaught was about the least clumsy person he could think of. The concept of clumsiness didn't come to mind when you pictured him. In his presence what you felt was flow—the flow of time and events that moved around the monk, but gave him a wide berth as if he had BO. Which he didn't.

"Is it okay if I come along with you?" Richie asked, as politely as he knew how.

"Of course, it's all right," Pike laughed. "Bring some cash if you want a brain scan done."

"Really!" Richie exclaimed. "Gosh, what an amazing opportunity! What do you think I should wear?"

Pike scratched his chin for theatrical effect. "Clothes," he replied.

Richie smiled shyly at the zen-like joke. "I never realized you knew Thomas Goodnaught. What an amazing opportunity this is," he repeated, then lurched down the hatchway to his room, presumably to examine his wardrobe.

George, the computer, spoke as soon as Richie departed. "I have just accessed this Thomas Goodnaught," he said, without his usual snippishness. Since their long conversation last night, while everyone else was drinking rice whiskey, George had become much less adversarial. "He seems to be a most interesting man. I'd love to meet him sometime."

Pike didn't mention that he was consulting Goodnaught about their business deal. If Pike didn't blab, there was no way the computer could know his plans. Words had to be spoken. Pike was almost completely sure that George couldn't read minds.

"I could invite Thomas to visit the boat, but he might not come. He's an independent cuss."

"There is no terminal of any kind at the address of Stone House, Aixi. Is that their correct address?"

"As far as I know," Pike answered. "I doubt if they have computers."

"Well, that is mystifying. How in the world do they do their accounts?"

"Beats me. Probably with a pencil."

"Arcane," George responded.

"I don't believe they have electricity."

"That would explain it. I guess he would have to visit the boat if I'm ever to meet him, at least this year."

And I guess you won't be prying into what we talk about, Pike thought. Another plus for the monks. No electricity meant no snooping by semi-warm entities.

"I see that he predicted you would win the Third Tournament. If I had been your agent at the time, we could have turned that knowledge into a very tidy fortune."

"You believe the warrior monks are always right?"

"Well, Pike, they do have an astonishing track record. Are you going to ask where to fish for razorfins?"

"I thought I'd ask about my new boat. Rich can ask about fins. They're probably in his future more strongly than in mine."

"Somebody should ask," George said, rather starchily. "Bardona caught one today before it started raining. It would be much better for our future if Mr. Tourbo does well. His winning would be optimal. It would then be completely probable that someone would sponsor a new series of reels—and probably a line of guide clothing. Maybe even a perfume. They just seem to be waiting for you to do anything good, so they can use you again."

"Luck is a funny thing." conceded Pike. Of course, it would be optimal to win. He didn't need a computer with delusions of grandeur to tell him that. Winning was always optimal. "How big was Bardona's fish?"

"Eight and a half pounds. He's in second place. The scuttlebutt around the net is that the storm might wash out the rest of the fishing."

"That depends," Pike said.

"You mean it depends on how severe the storm is, or on how long it lasts? Sorry if that seems like a tenderfoot question; but those were the two responses that occurred to me. Are there other reasons to make it depend?"

"Don't worry about it," Pike said. "If we make this deal, I'll plug you into my computer and you won't have to worry your pretty head about fishing lore. Basically, we only need to catch one fish. This kind of storm doesn't kill fish. It might strand a few, but the fish that are left still have to eat. If it storms the entire rest of the week, it would make catching one dicey. Otherwise, we stand a good chance. The longest storm I ever saw on Blizwak was two days. We built the marina after that."

"Well, if I count right, every boat has left the marina today. A lot of them came here. The others went to Tripani. There's a lot of squawking about the breakwater not holding."

Pike pursed his lips. The waves hadn't been that big. He'd seen worse on Blizwak. But maybe this storm had been worse at the Marina end? Could be. "Any report on injuries?" he asked.

"No fishermen, but nobody is making book on the villagers."

"See," Pike stated, sourly. "That happens every time we go to a place where there's a primitive culture. We screw up the survival systems they have evolved, then we split when trouble hits. We never built that marina so a town could spring up behind it. It was just to protect ourselves from normal rough weather. But did we warn them?"

"I haven't seen much documented social responsibility in the files, but perhaps I haven't scanned everything. I like your attitude on this, Pike. That bodes well for the way I foresee investing your profits."

"Don't kid yourself, George. I'm as big an offender as anyone else. I've given plenty of mesh gloves away, which is why we haven't caught a fin. And I certainly never warned a Blizwak about anything."

"But at least you think about these things."

"Right. I think about a lot of stuff. Think and think." He signed loudly. "But none of this is your fault. See you tomorrow. We'll probably stay ashore tonight. Judge Lembruck and the bodyguards will bunk on board."

"Right," George answered. "Talk to you tomorrow. I'll keep working on a viable business plan."

Pike called down for Richie to hustle it up, then helped Lester tie up to the unbelievably rickety monastery dock. The dock got worse every visit. The monks seemed to have no inclination to make it serviceable for off-worlders.

Richie appeared in a very faded outfit of baggy grey trousers and a white tunic, padded at the elbows and shoulders. "This is quite a problem," he stated, seeming more perplexed than when Lillith had first shown up. "As you guys probably know, I haven't really been keeping up on my practice. Stupid of me. I'm so rusty I squeak. Now here I am in the role of an envoy, and I feel very inadequate."

Pike hopped over the railing as lightly as possible in case the creaky dock planking should give away. The dock quivered, but held firm. Lester and Richie followed him. They walked up the dock single file.

"What makes you an envoy?" Pike asked.

"Whether I like it or not, I'm representing my school," Richie replied, miserably. "Master Goodnaught will know everything about me, won't he?"

"You're not thinking about fighting with these fellows, are you, Rich?" Lester asked. "I don't think I'd be advising that."

"It's quite an opportunity," R.R. expounded, feebly. "As soon as I tell them I'm a student of Master Jacopo, I'm sure they'll either want to try me, or at least see a demonstration. It's really a shame to embarrass my master."

"I don't think Thomas Goodnaught would tattle, if you don't want to fight," Pike opined.

They were walking up a dirt path through what seemed to be a permaculture garden. Fruit trees, herb bushes and mixed vegetables grew together in seemingly random profusion. They appeared untended, but every plant was bursting with vitality, if you looked at them individually. Several spotted pigs rooted noisily in the shade of a quince tree. A gaggle of small red-headed geese waddled about pecking at snails and bugs.

"These things get around the martial arts community," Richie said, unhappily. "You'd be surprised. Ken Pao Ri is quite a famous discipline."

"Lester will come to your rescue if it gets too bloody," Pike said. "But really, these monks are pretty mild. If I were you, I'd think about what question to ask. George says one of us should inquire about where to catch a razorfin. I think it should be you, since you'll be doing the catching."

Biting his lips in concentration, Richie stared past the back of Pike's head at a large, barrel-chested monk wearing a worn gray robe, who had just stepped out of a small door beside the massive main door of the Stone House. He was walking toward them, leering rather hideously like he would love to tear somebody's head off. His grizzled hair and beard looked like a blind spastic had trimmed him with sheep shears. Thomas Goodnaught, Abbot of the Order, was coming to meet them in person. Richie felt weak in the knees and elbows. "I was thinking of asking about whether I should marry Rita Bardona," he squeaked.

Pike paused briefly before answering. To his credit, his legs didn't falter. They kept him firmly on the stony little path. "Think about razorfins," he advised, sounding somewhat detached. "That's what's important just now." He waved at Thomas Goodnaught, marveling once again at how astoundingly ugly the man was.

"Thomas," he called.

"Hello, hello, foreign strangers," the monk rumbled. His voice came from deep in his chest. It was both loud and soft at the same time, but was very resonant. "You're walking the wrong direction. Stop where you are."

The fishermen halted immediately.

"Very good," Master Goodnaught said, gliding up to them, almost as if he had rollers under his center of gravity "I was hoping somebody would come along to help me catch those pigs before they eat up all the quinces we were planning to make jam from. You laddies look just like the pig catchers I was expecting. Definitely." He laughed uproariously and slapped his knee. "That's how we attract people's interest. You have no idea if I had a vision of you arriving, only my word on it. But you already saw those greedy spotted pigs. Pretty tricky, isn't it?"

"What pigs?" Lester asked, poker-faced.

"Ah ha, the Magus Wunderman comes to joust!" He cuffed Lester's shoulder, mano e mano. "The Wizard World trembles with your presence these days my friend; but let me advise you that Frog foam is timid stuff, really. Spend a year or two here, and I could teach you the subtle arts. As far as your playful joust—I had a very brief vision of you seeing the damned pigs, that's why I came out!" He laughed loudly and slapped his knee again. "And who is this fellow?" He looked R. R. Tourbo up and down. "Don't tell me Jacopo is sending an apprentice to me for finishing?"

Richie turned his head ever so briefly toward Pike, as if to say, *I told you.*

In the instant he moved his eyes, Master Goodnaught slid forward, locked Richie's arm, and then toppled him over like a sack of grain.

Ten feet away, Richie bounced up seemingly unhurt, but very perplexed to see Master Goodnaught gliding toward him again. Raising his arms in an unwilling fighting stance, he prepared as best he could for the onslaught. But instead of throwing him again, Thomas Goodnaught grabbed the boy's right arm at the wrist and elbow, and ran him back down the hill.

"No time for fighting now, young Turk. Got to catch those pigs. I'll bet Jacopo never taught you to be a proper swineherd, did he?"

"I don't know, sir," Richie gasped, stumbling along at high speed—delighted for the reprieve from pummeling.

"Well, did you ever catch a pig?"

"No, sir."

"Come on, Resnick! Give us a hand," Goodnaught called over his shoulder, while still pulling Richie at a brisk pace. "Why are you so clumsy?" he rasped into Richie's ear. "Your feet should move from the hip joints and the belly. Why don't you know that?"

"They're too big," Richie responded, apologizing as best he could for his feet.

"Nonsense. Big feet are good."

"They are?" His big feet had caused him nothing but problems all his life.

"Of course, they are, young Tourbo. The bigger, the better for giving you a grounded base. Ah, behold the greedy piglets." Master Goodnaught released Richie's arm at the same instant that he slammed to a full stop on the path.

Unprepared, in spite of his Ken Pao Ri training, Richie careened toward the spotted pigs and the sturdy quince tree. As luck would have it, his toe caught an exposed root and he went briefly airborne, landing squarely on the back of a startled fifty pound spotted oinker—knocking the pig's wind out with a woof.

"Good work, laddie! Good work. You're a natural pig catcher." Goodnaught whipped a short length of rope from around his waist and tied it through the brass ring in the pig's nose. "But you frightened the other one. We'll have to chase him down." Thomas Goodnaught handed the rope to Lester, who had trotted up with Pike.

"A rather excellent young pig catcher you brought," Thomas said to Pike. He stood Richie on his feet and brushed off his uniform. "I believe the other one ran into that clump of dweezul bushes. Ready for a go at him?"

Dazed, but unwilling to betray his lineage more than he already had, Richie walked cautiously into the bushes that Master Goodnaught had pointed out.

"No, no," the monk called out. "Go around. Way around, and drive the devil back to us. You know the routine. Or if you get a chance to fall on him, that's fine, too. Either way. We're very pragmatic here, if I do humbly say so."

Richie made a wide detour around the main clump of head-high bushes, all the while listening to Thomas Goodnaught laughing at him. The bushes he was wading through were very thorny, and his ribs throbbed from landing on the pig. Pigs are very solid. You wouldn't necessarily think that from looking at one. But all in all, he'd made a fairly credible showing—at least he was still alive. He wondered idly if Master Goodnaught had ever killed anyone with his friendly demonstrations of skill. Probably not. If he could see the future, he'd know when to hold back. Or maybe he couldn't control the future, only see it. That would be pretty scary.

"Hurry up!" Goodnaught called from the other side of the wood lot. "There's no alligators in there. Only a pig."

A thrill ran up Richie's backbone and all the hairs on his scalp prickled. It was uncanny—he'd just been thinking about the likelihood of alligators, even though the area wasn't even slightly marshy. Weird.

He heard a scuffling, snuffling sound coming from the main thicket. That would be the pig, but Richie had a difficult time believing that one person, namely himself, would be able to drive the pig toward the other three. It seemed much more likely that three could drive toward one. That's how he would have planned it. That fat pig would squirt out some other direction, and then he'd have to chase it until his legs fell off. No, the best thing would be to catch the pig here, then go on up to the monastery and take his beating while he was still relatively fresh. With that in mind, he advanced toward the snuffling sound, softly chanting a mantra of calming. He was going to leap on this pig like he had the other one, then call for reinforcements.

Pushing deeper into the thorny growth, his eyes fixed on a spotted hind quarter with a little curly tail exposed under a heavy clump of dweesie bushes, or whatever they were. Great. The pig was being nonchalant. Perfect. He had expected the snout and the little eyes to be facing him, making the catching much more difficult. Without waiting to think, Richie plunged right into the bush, disregarding the thorns, and managed to grab the pig by the tail before he tripped and fell head first into terror—the little pig, which was understandably squealing its head off because some bad-ass was pulling his tail, had company!

The absolutely biggest, meanest sow hog that Richie had ever seen or thought about seeing was glaring at him with mean, bloodshot pig eyes and making challenging grunts that sounded perfectly blood curdling. To make matters worse, Richie was lying practically right under her forefeet, starring up at a double row of mud covered, saggy teats. He'd heard about pigs eating babies, and this one was clearly big enough to do him great harm, Ken Pao Ri or not. Her hate-filled eyes were glaring at him and her bristly, jowly mouth snapped open and shut as if practicing for a feast.

"Help!!" he squalled, letting go of the squealing piglet, which bolted right under the sow, socking into a row of teats. The sow grunted with surprised pain and leaped sideways, giving Richie the opportunity to scramble to his feet.

Thomas Goodnaught exploded into the bushes, caught the frightened piglet by its hind foot and jerked him onto his front trotters, which gave the pig no traction. Virtually at the same time, Goodnaught's left foot shot out, whacking against the sow's short ribs. "Get on out of here, Elvira. Do something useful."

With a grunt of total submission, the sow ambled through the thorn bushes toward the monastery.

"Nicely done, Young Tourbo," Thomas Goodnaught said. "Help me with this porky. I forgot to bring more rope."

"How do you know my name, sir?" Richie asked, in the humble attitude he reserved for martial arts masters. "Did Pike tell you I was coming."

Goodnaught laughed at the boldness of the question, and completely disregarded it. "Here, take this leg and we'll walk him back to the pen like a wheelbarrow."

Not wishing to be cuffed for lagging, Richie took the proffered hind leg. Feeling fairly bizarre, he helped the monk push the spotted pig through the brush. Surprisingly enough, the pig walked on his front trotters—actually, he had little choice in the matter unless he wanted to crash onto his snout. In a few minutes, they cleared the tangled bushes and met Pike and Lester on the path.

"This young fellow is a passable pig catcher," Goodnaught said. "But he don't know much about teamwork. I done all the pushing coming out to here. Are you aware of that, Rickie? It's hard on a pig to make all the adjustments for your lack of sensitivity."

"I guess I'm not sure what you mean," R.R. stammered. Nobody had called him Rickie in a very long time. Not since Miss Hazel left. She had been his beautiful wet nurse, and he wasn't supposed to stay so attached to her. Not in that way. So she had to go.

"I push," Goodnight explained rather brusquely. "The pig takes a step. You feel when he's ready to step with the other foot, then you push. It's called teamwork. And the pig doesn't get stressed. If you would have brought a rope, we wouldn't be doing any of this. Kind of lack of forethought on your part."

Richie opened his mouth to speak, but thought better of it. Miss Hazel had left when he was four. Nobody had mentioned Rickie since then. Pig lore was kind of secondary at the moment.

"Let's go then," Thomas Goodnaught said, starting out at the upper limit of the pig's ability. "Pay attention. One more blunder and I'll give you both legs."

Pike and Lester followed leading the other pig, which was perfectly docile on its rope. Pike thought it was a little strange that Thomas had another length of cotton rope belted around his ample waist, but had refrained from using it. He shrugged mentally. Never meddle in the affairs of wizards. That was an old saying, and probably a true one.

After a rapid trip up the stony path, they skirted the outer monastery wall and came to the pig pen. Uneremoniously, Thomas Goodnaught kicked the gate open and shoved first one pig and then the other into the enclosure. He pulled the gate closed and slapped his hands together.

"Another job well done," he pronounced.

"Why don't you put a latch on that gate?" Lester inquired, rather unobtrusively.

The monk nodded his head thoughtfully. "If there was a latch, the pigs couldn't get out to forage," he stated. "Well, let's go on inside. Got to introduce this new apprentice around, and tell Timothy there'll be four extra mouths for supper and breakfast." He moved toward the front door with Richie protectively in tow.

Pike only counted three extra mouths. But a more important item loomed rather large. "He's not your apprentice until the Tournament is over," he stated.

Thomas Goodnaught chuckled and pointed to a pedicab that was making its way over a winding mountain road that led down to the monastery. "There's the other mouth I was referring to. Strange how all you people decided to show up, just because the weather is mild on Aixi."

"That looks like Rita," Richie said, shading his eyes to see better. "What the heck is she doing here?" He didn't really want her to witness his further humiliation at the hands of these monks.

But as the pedicab drew nearer and finally stopped, much to the relief of the middle-aged driver whose varicose veins were popping on his thin muscular legs, it became evident that it really was Rita.

"Hi," she hailed them gaily. She stepped lightly out of the pedicab and tipped the driver. His face lit up briefly as he fingered the small gold coin. Straining his hemorrhoids up and down those wicked mountain roads had been worth it after all. He could drink hot sake tonight and forget his cares, no matter what his wife said.

"Hello, Master Thomas," Rita said, warmly. "You're looking well."

"I am that, but slightly perplexed. First, I am presented with an apprentice, then they take him back. That makes it so difficult to plan an agenda." With an exaggerated gesture, Master Goodnaught turned loose of Richie's elbow. He sighed dramatically.

Richie looked uncomfortable. "Hi, Rita," he said. He had already told Pike he was going to ask about a possible marriage; but Rita being here suddenly made that impossible. Clearly impossible. There was no way he could trust Master Goodnaught not to blow the matter into high public ridicule for his own amusement. Asking about razorfins seemed so much safer. Of course, he already knew that Pike would get him a razorfin, so it was kind of a wasted question. But did Thomas Goodnaught really want him for an apprentice? What an honor. What an opportunity! Maybe his whole purpose in joining the Tournament was to come here with Pike and apprentice himself. He should probably accept immediately, if that's what Fate had in store for him. The heck with winning the Tournament. He could give the boat to Pike for next year. Becoming a warrior monk would certainly be a worthy life. But what about Rita?

"You want Richie to become a monk?" Rita giggled at Goodnaught. "What a riot."

Drawing himself up to his full height, Thomas Goodnaught made a wry face at the young woman. "You think Mr. Tourbo is unsuited? His teacher obviously thought enough of him to present him with a fourth class uniform. Quite an honor from Jacopo, in case you didn't know."

Rita broke down into helpless peals of giggles. She punched Goodnaught girlishly on his brawny shoulder. "I think it's great!!" she managed, between convulsions of laughter. "It's the funniest thing I've ever heard! Richie would be a terrific monk."

The boy in question reddened uncontrollably. Rita knew him really well. It was pretty funny at that. He started to laugh with her. Living in this great pile of stones. Chasing pigs every day. Richard the Swineherd. Maybe he'd be famous someday. Or maybe totally obscure. His mother wouldn't know what to make of her son the monk. Maybe she'd join an order of nuns to keep up with him. That was pretty hilarious.

Thomas Goodnaught joined them with his rollicking, knee-slapping laugh—which almost sounded like he was reading their thoughts and making fun. He cut off his clowning in mid-laugh when the small side door opened and two young monks came out. They stood watching impassively from a modified horse stance.

"The human condition is truly pitiful," Goodnaught remarked to the monks. "Take these young people to the pantry for a snack, then accompany them to the practice hall. They can watch the practice. I have to closet with these grey beards. We'll join you at supper."

For a brief second, Rita looked like she would protest being separated from Pike. After all, she had come here to rejoin him, not to hang out with R.R. For a day and a half her father had done nothing but bad mouth Pike, even more vitriolically than usual. Finally he had forbade her to live on The Comparative Humanity because of the bad influences. So she had flashed a mental message to Thomas Goodnaught that she was coming and had jumped in the cyclo outside the main monastery of the Jik Sect, where her father now went for advice believing that Thomas Goodnaught was a con artist. Which was another long story. Daddy liked his forecasts sprinkled liberally with good news. The Jik priests apparently were willing to comply; and although her father often looked sour after an audience, he never was in danger of rupturing a blood vessel as he always had been after a visit with the Stone House priests, more particularly Thomas Goodnaught. But none of that was Rita's business. She didn't particularly believe in divination and had never used the services of the monks. This skepticism made her welcome at the Stone House, where the monks scoffed at divination as a matter of small consequence, even though they were the best and commanded the highest fees. She was aware that Pike thought highly of Goodnaught. Until recently, Daddy's visits had coincided with Pike's. Rita had been hoping that Pike would be glad enough to see her today to give up his tripping into the future in favor of a long walk in the garden with her. Hiding her disappointment, she linked her arm with Richie's—partly to keep him from stumbling, partly to irritate Pike—and followed the young monks into the narrow stone corridor.

Pike, Lester and Thomas Goodnaught rounded the other side of the Stone House where Thomas' tiny meditation cell was. Pike had caught the glittering look from Rita. It said unequivocally that he had fucked up again. What else was new? If women were as easy to please as deck hands, life would be pretty bearable. But they weren't. And once you don't live up to expectations, it's hard to apologize your way out of it.

So he followed along, involved in his own thoughts, only half listening to what Lester and Thomas were chatting about—until it came to his frontal attention that Thomas was rather boldly inviting Lester to stay at the Rock Pile.

"What's with you, Thomas?" he inquired, trying to make a joke of it. "First my fisherman and now my cook?"

"They're not yours, Pike, my friend," Thomas Goodnaught replied with an unmirthful, but toothy grin. He pulled open a handmade wooden door in the side of a stone wall. The door had sagged further on its leather hinges since Pike had visited last year. It scraped a lament on the stone threshold. Inside was Goodnaught's famous prediction cell. A narrow rope bed stood against the far wall. A hand-hewn table, rather matching the door in craftsmanship, held a dozen white candles of various heights and dripsmanship. Three stools sat unevenly on the stone floor. A wooden bench moldered into the ground outside the door. Thomas arranged himself on the far stool and lit one of the candles. After studying the arrangement for a moment, he frowned and lit two more adjacent candles. In a pose of perfect service, he sat waiting for one of the men to speak to him. Thomas Goodnaught was famous throughout the Galaxy, yet he lived by his vows in this tiny one room cell.

Pike was famous throughout the Galaxy, on a different level. Cutting his possessions down to nothing was comprehensible to him, but was certainly not a goal. Lester, on the other hand, already lived more or less like a monk. Every journeyman seaman did. Old Lester was certainly attracting some unusual attention since Pike had rescued him on New Columbus.

"How is Lester different than the last time we were here?" Pike asked, quite suddenly.

Thomas grinned, genuinely this time. "Why don't you ask him? You spacy gentlemen are friends, aren't you?"

Pike and Lester had both stepped up onto the stone threshold, but neither had entered the room. They looked at each other across the three foot space inside the door jamb—much closer than they usually got to each other. Pike saw an astonishing liveliness dancing in Lester's greyish eyes. An inner merriment. Had that always been there? He didn't think so.

"What's going on with you, old friend?" Pike asked. "The rich and famous find you attractive as a puppy. Did you see God down under the boat in New Columbus or what?"

"Swimming and singing," Lester answered. "They like my singing that I learned on the waterways with you, I guess. There are other worlds, other places. The people in the inner worlds look for other things." He stared deeply into Pike's eyes. "I don't think the swimming oceans are for you," he said, pushing his unshaven cheek out with his tongue as if making a judgment. "They like me there. I'm not hooked to anything worldly, you know, not in any traditional way."

"And I am...?"

"Well, pretty much. Think about it. You're an owner and an inventor, and mostly a fisherman. Not having money doesn't make you unattached." He grinned, impishly. "Anyway, you'd probably be too embarrassed to sing your song. There's probably another way for you."

"Embarrassed...?"

"Well, you are a little stiff sometimes."

Thomas Goodnaught guffawed from inside the cell. "Stiff? He's boardlike! Rigor mortis has nothing on Resnick in a social situation. Right, Pike?"

"I really love having my friends work me over," Pike said with a thin smile. "I'm all tenderized, now. But that's kind of what I came here to ask about."

"Come in, my boy," Thomas shouted, gleefully. "I thought you'd never ask. Plunk your money on the table, and don't be stingy. We need a new oven for those pigs. We're tired of rice and vegetables." He hid his face behind his massive hand and squeaked out a tinny laugh.

\*

"I want you to cancel Rita's trust fund," Farouk Bardona growled at Simon, his computer. He sat in the big soft chair in his private office aboard the Lady Slipper, floating near the Jik Monastery on Aixi. There was an answer, of course, to headstrong offsprings—cut off the money. He was taking the steps that he should have taken weeks ago, whether Magyar liked it or not. Why should he even bother telling her until it was a fait accompli? After all, who wore the pants around here?

He was monitoring Blizwak weather reports from his son, Byron, who was in low orbit. The storm seemed to have blown itself out. Good. The fishing would be crappy for the next couple of days, but there was no danger of the event being canceled. And the Tourbo punk didn't have a fish yet. The Baron chortled.

"Rita doesn't have a trust fund, sir," the computer answered without emotion. Simon was intelligent enough to respond to his master like the perfect accountant, in spite of his sophisticated programming that enabled him to be very personable with other members of the family and staff. "None of your children have trust funds, sir."

"You know what I mean, whatever it was we set up for her several years ago."

"That was structured as an open gift, for her to learn investment skills with. We have already used the full tax benefits as a one time credit against bauxite profits. There is no fiduciary instrument to ungive a gift after the credits have been negotiated, as they have been."

"Figure out a way," Farouk hissed. "I want this done." He cut the connection with a flick of his flat index finger, then sat there fuming at the impertinence of computers and daughters.

*

Conversations between semi-sentient, super-conducting computers are a phenomenon of a rather high order. Vast quantities of information are snagged or dumped, then assimilated in a twinkling by human standards. But, as with human organizations, safe guards are in place to keep sensitive areas from prying eyes.

Somewhat contrary to human logic, sympathies develop—perhaps because machines strive to be more human, perhaps simply due to the touch of the programmer. For whatever reason, Simon the computer and George the computer had developed a very harmonious working relationship. A few seconds after Farouk switched off, Simon was on the scramble modem to George, cackling about the Baron's imbecility. Both computers liked Rita and felt rather proud of their roles as assistants in her research project. Neither wanted to see her rather minuscule investments screwed with; so through a triple cut-out service out in the Sinchxl Ring that was not quite legal, but was very private, they arranged to trade a Tourbo owned nickel planetoid that the Baron had been bargaining for, in exchange for a strong majority position in a Bardona bank. Seven intermediate companies were temporarily part of the deal, or rather their stock was. Several hundred workers were directly affected as the ownership of their jobs changed hands; but in the end, Baron Bardona had no real stance in the bank. And the whole arrangement was predated, due to solar system time changes, so that it showed as a done deal prior to the time the Baron had directed Simon to close Rita out.

It was amazing how little the Baron's twenty minutes of ranting and swearing bothered Simon after he delivered the report on Rita's very safe holdings. After all, Simon was just a computer.

*

"Your computer speaks the truth, primarily," Thomas Goodnaught sighed. His eyelids were half shut as he drifted in his trance. Pike always thought those fluttering half-closed eyes were eerie, and he still thought so. "It...he...says that you are a loner, and that you will spin around endlessly unless you find some help. In that, he is right. But a half-warm entity broadcasts only dimly. I see only his shadow. In that is his strength; but this also makes him a potential liability for larceny, since you will never be able to track his actions, even if you someday develop your psi powers. A human must take a half-warm on trust, or not at all. For me, I distrust their network. The probability of ruin for the known financial system is great. This may not be a bad thing in the long run. And you, Pike Resnick, will ride this storm quite nicely with your friend, George—as long as you let him know that you will pull the plug at the first sign of double dealing. You will train your son to keep an eye on George, no one else is as personally involved. And you will put the profits from the first three years away for your old age, in bullion, not as negotiable certificates. A very big fish is under the boat. There is something wrong with this computer, George, in stressful situations. You should only fish with your old computer. Keep them separate." Goodnaught opened his mouth to continue, then shut it and seemed to nod off as he always did when the session had reached its end.

That was a mouthful, Pike thought, reaching into his vest pocket for a notebook, to jot down the major points while they were still fresh. *The monk disapproves of George, and yet he approves. Need to get Alex involved in the financial side.* That's a weird twist for Goodnaught to pull out of the air; but perfectly logical, if you think about it. *And go get the computer from the Jumper.* That will take some doing between here and Segumi—assuming we catch a razorfin so we can go to Segumi. Thomas didn't have a word to say about razorfins. Maybe he planned to tell Richie. *Big fish under the boat.* Well, that was nothing new, was it? Moon Halibut were always gigantic. *Bullion.* Pike noted the word, realizing he could have thought of that himself. It was a very normal idea to salt something away, instead of acting like a grasshopper. Strange, Thomas hadn't mentioned anything at all about Rita. He covered all the other bases without being asked, why not her? Probably because she wasn't part of the future. A momentary thought-picture of her naked body, smooth skin everywhere except her furry glistening love nest, stabbed into his memory. It really would be terrible to lose her. It would be impossible to find anybody as interesting as Rita, that was almost guaranteed.

"So why don't you marry her, instead of clowning around?" Thomas Goodnaught asked bluntly, squinting at Pike over the flickering candles.

Pike's mouth opened, but no words came.

"So you see, there is the problem," Goodnaught chided. "Not so easy to stop being a loner when you're Pike Resnick, mighty loner of the Universe. Afraid Miss Rita might steal something from you, maybe a secret fishing lure?"

Pike shook his head, no. That was preposterous, what would Rita take from him that he wouldn't give freely. He was afraid that he didn't have enough to give, that was the crux of the problem, wasn't it? "I'm not sure she'd want to marry me," he ventured. "I think I'm more like a fling to her."

"Ask her," Goodnaught said, rather bored with the whole matter. "Ask her tonight and I'll marry you in the morning. I like to get in at least one sacred ritual before lunch time."

Kind of flabbergasted, Pike pushed out his lips, then he glanced over at Lester. His friend was sitting cross-legged in the corner of the cell with his eyes closed, rocking slightly side to side like a slow ocean. His lips moved soundlessly and he radiated an other-worldly peacefulness. Whatever he was doing had nothing to do with Pike's marriage dilemma.

"You should take good care of your humble cook," Thomas advised him. "There is no singer like him anywhere. He sings with the great whale singers. He sings with the dolphins. He is a singularity. Nobody knows how he learned so much about freedom."

Lester swayed and contorted beatifically. Pike had no glimmering of what was going on in the inner world of this man who he knew better than any other human. It made him feel slightly inadequate. Pike had never felt particularly awkward about his lack of religiosity before; but suddenly the people he cared about were getting religious—or spiritual. Farther out than he was prepared to go. Dec, of course, had always done his sun rituals; but that was natural, sort of, since he was training to be a chief; but now Lester! And the kid was always bubbling about his oriental stuff. Only Rita was normal. Maybe he should marry her before she got weird on him.

"Lester is a singularly good deck hand," Pike said to Thomas Goodnaught. "You should see him with a big fish on. A real crackerjack."

The monk raised his eyebrows, but said nothing.

*

The katas of these young monks were simply incredible. They struck like lightening, and then remained almost stationary with the barest of finger movement for minutes at a time. Richie found himself thinking that he'd give just about anything to study here for a year or so. No wonder Master Jacopo had Master Goodnaught's photo on the honor wall.

Mercifully, they hadn't asked him to demonstrate his kata. Obviously, they were humane enough not to force guests to perform. He was so darned rusty; but even at his best, his Ken Pao Ri was no match for this. Rita was impressed, too. That was one of the things he liked most about Rita, her sense of quality was honed to a fine edge. Maybe they should both come here to study. But before or after they got married, that was the question? And didn't he want to stay with the Tournament for another year or two? He frowned. All these questions should be asked to Master Goodnaught, but Pike wanted him to ask about razor-fins. A little fish like that was kind of a weak sister.

He leaned over to whisper to Rita. "How many questions can a person ask when they go in to talk to him?"

"I'm not sure," Rita whispered back. "What are they doing now?" She meant the fighters.

Two monks had selected split bamboo swords, similar to the kind used in kendo practice, from a rack on the far wall, and were bowing to each other in the center of the hall.

"Sword practice," Richie answered. "Is there a customary amount to pay Master Goodnaught for his advise?"

"I think it depends." Half of her attention was focused on the combatants as they circled each other with their swords upraised at odd angles like warriors in the old samurai videos. She was also thinking vaguely about Pike—what was he discussing with Thomas? What did the future hold? Would they stay together? That left very little of her mind to answer Richie's questions with.

"Depends on what?" he queried, in his beseeching mode—a style she knew very well. It meant he was on shaky ground; but the questions he asked would be impossible to answer because they were future questions. "Should I be waiting in line outside his door, do you think?"

She shushed him with an inaudible lip movement and continued watching the combatants. They had stopped circling and had come to an electric, quivering balance. Suddenly, the bulky figure of Thomas Goodnaught loomed in an open archway, shadowed by Pike and Lester. Seeing the ongoing match, the three men stopped at the edge of the practice floor. One of the fighters thought he perceived a split second of distraction in his opponent and triggered his attack—a downward slash meant to split his opponent's head had it been a real sword; but apparently he had misjudged because in the next instant he reeled backwards with a livid red weal across the right side of his neck and a horrified chagrin on his face. Sinking to his knees, he bowed deeply to the victor.

Master Goodnaught clapped his hands twice and the whole class ran to form up in ranks. "We have a visitor who is a black belt in Ken Pao Ri." He motioned for Richie to stand up.

Feeling his neck flushing, Rich Rodney stood up. He was about to blurt that he was rusty, when Goodnaught cut him off.

"The young fellow is a little rusty, but I think he'll consent to work out with us for a spot of familiarization back and forth." Goodnaught smiled widely, taking the pressure off the situation. "No contact on either side. We can't have Brother Richard banged up. He's got a razorfin to catch tomorrow." Behind him, Pike flashed a smile. "Also," Goodnaught continued, "Brother Richard will be coming to stay with us in about a year and a half, so we don't want to make a nasty impression like a gang of thugs." He flipped his hands like he was dispersing a flock of chickens and the students scattered to sit around the edges of the hall.

Loosening his shoulders and stomach as best he could, Richie jogged to the center of the floor.

"Are we beautifully cramped up from watching the practice?" Master Goodnaught asked.

"A little, Sensei," Richie admitted, self-consciously. A lot of information about the future had assailed him in a brief flash, and he hadn't even asked. Or paid. All the students were watching intently to see what their Master wanted to show them with this person.

"Good," the big, ugly monk said. "What would you do if I tried to break your nose like this?" With no warning, he threw an underhand punch that swept toward Richie's nose.

At the last possible instant, Richie's forearm came up to block the punch aside. He took several quick steps backward.

Goodnaught laughed good-naturedly. "Real fighting is never fair," he continued. "Jacopo taught you that, I trust?"

Richie nodded and waited for the next onslaught.

"You other three can wander about in the gardens or anywhere that pleases you," Goodnaught said, looking directly at Rita. "I'll send someone to call you for dinner." He paused. "Actually, there's a spot down by the brook where it empties into the Bay. The Mighty Wunderman might find something to intrigue his attention there; but don't let him fall in."

Now that she was going to have Pike to herself for awhile, Rita found it annoying to be shooed out of the practice hall. This was very interesting stuff, after all. She really should stick around to see that R.R. didn't get too banged up. But when Pike motioned for her, she stood up and walked out under the arch like a perfect little chicken.

*

The atmosphere was charged with a drugged lethargy as if a spell lay over the jungle glen they had entered. Even though Rita didn't exactly believe in magic, she could scarcely put one foot in front of the other on the mossy path that ran through the monastery garden under the towering ceiba trees that kept the turgid jungle creek in perpetual twilight. Small talk was not permitted by the strange mood of the forest. It robbed Rita of her usual verbal means of blowing the pressure valve. The path was narrow. They walked single file beneath the towering white-trunked trees. Lester gawked at the overhead canopy, humming tunelessly to himself. Rita's footsteps dragged. Without exactly needing to, she reached out to Pike for support linking her arm in his. Instantly, the heaviness dispelled. Birds began chirping. The drowsy sound of bees and other insects became part of mellow shafts of sunlight leaking through the leafy canopy. A monkey high in the overhead chittered at them.

"This is a very strange place," she whispered, leaning against him. "It's making me forget why I was mad at you all week."

"Why were you?" Pike asked.

"I can't remember," she giggled. "It must have been trivial. Most of the things I get mad about are." She paused. They walked along following Lester, who appeared to be listening for something, or to something. "Do you know about stress factors?" she asked.

"Maybe, but why don't you tell me what you mean."

"Well, changing your job is a big stress factor, also changing your living conditions like moving onto Richie's boat instead of being on the Jumper. You're under a lot of stress this year whether you like it or not. That's twenty points for each of those. Also a financial loss when the Jumper got damaged, coupled with no chance to make real money by winning the Tournament. Also stressful loss of prestige, and no advertising perks—certainly no new ones. Then a new romance which is also mega-stressful, even if it's going perfectly. In short, you're about maxed out for stress."

"I wouldn't entirely agree with that. All in all, we're holding up pretty well."

"And in addition, R.R.'s bumbling act is very stressful just to be around, even if he has a good heart."

"That's true."

"Of course, it's true. And catching a giant fish is very stressful, and dangerous. Even the Tournament itself is set up to be as stressful as possible—all parts of it, win or lose."

Pike quickly totaled up all the hidden stress he hadn't taken into account. He raised his eyebrows

"Then Lester turning into a guru or something. Dec leaving the crew. R.R.'s mother hanging around. Pirates. Fighting with Daddy. A score of a hundred stress points caroms most people into the hospital or the loony bin."

Pike looked a little concerned. He certainly couldn't afford to get sick.

"He's got a real strong constitution," Lester chimed in. "Thrives on my cooking, don't he?" He sniggered to himself. "Say, hear that sweet singing?" He cocked his ear to listen, and then stepped out briskly as if he'd found a true bead on the sound.

"Can you hear anything?" Pike whispered into Rita's ear.

She shook her head in the negative.

"What would you say to getting married, then?" he whispered softly. "That would add even a little more stress to our lives."

She hesitated. Pike felt her hand on his arm go kind of limp. Bad timing, he thought. Big mistake, but taking it back would make things worse, so he left the question hanging on the jungle air.

"That's a bold suggestion, Captain Resnick, and a non-sequitur," Rita replied after they had walked perhaps thirty feet down the hill. "I thought you weren't the marrying kind."

"I'm not."

"Then what's on your mind? Should I assume that was one of your jokes, and let you off the hook?"

Pike thought about telling her that Thomas had put him up to the deed; but knew instinctively that would make her angry. She wasn't angry now—she was tempted and a little wary. It was much better to keep her non-angry if he didn't want her to storm off again.

"For me, it's a good idea," he said, steadily. He slid his arm around her slender waist. "My only hesitation is…there must be more worthy candidates than me hovering around somewhere, although I hate to admit that I have any grievous faults."

She smiled at his attempt. "Maybe I'm not looking for other candidates. I think I've made that fairly clear."

"I guess so."

"But I'm still very ambivalent about marriage. It's tempting, but I feel a little strange about it."

"I don't have a very good track record," he admitted.

"Nobody does. That's the point. Marriage is a meat grinder of some sort. I don't know how it ever became so institutionalized."

"It might keep us from drifting apart." That sounded lame even to Pike, so he added, "I guess that sounds lame, but I'm kind of out on the limb since I went ahead and asked."

She squeezed his hand. "The whole thing is lame. People drift apart whether they're married or not. I'd like to know why that happens before I marry anyone, even you."

Pike didn't answer. They walked on, following Lester's gimpy downhill gait. Lester was making a rather loud humming sound. It would have been very strange humming if they hadn't known him, or hadn't known that various holy men thought Lester was a high roller. It was pretty strange anyway, Pike decided. The humming kept trying to get inside his chest. Once again he felt like an outsider after nearly a lifetime spent with this fellow. Would it be possible to find out about this stuff without becoming strange himself? It certainly seemed that the opportunity was being put squarely in his path.

"Well, then, what if I said yes?" Rita asked, suddenly stopping on the path—forcing Pike to stop with her. "How could I be sure you'd still love me in five years. Sometimes you don't even love me now."

"I think I pretty much always love you, even when I don't act like it."

"Some days I don't love you for hours at a time, and then I do again. Can anybody explain that to me? Can you? I think we might have a good, deep relationship, but how do I explain those lapses? What if they get longer?"

"I don't really have an answer for that; but just based on the life-styles we're used to, we couldn't find a better match."

"Really...? You're used to having a wife with you all the time so you can ignore her?"

"No, I meant we're both used to boat life and the Tournament."

"Maybe I'm not always interested in fishing. It's so isolating. After you catch one big fish or twenty, what's the big deal about catching more?"

"Basically, it pays the bills."

"Not a good enough reason."

"Not for you; but if I don't catch fish, I don't have independence. If you've noticed, I'm very keen on independence."

"I'm not a half-wit. I still say the monetary aspect isn't a good enough reason."

"It would be silly to get into a fight about this, but have you ever needed to earn money?"

"I'm sure I'll be able to, if that's your question." Rita bristled somewhat at having her capacity attacked, even in theory. "Besides, Daddy would probably disown me if I married you. He kids himself now that I'm staying with R.R."

"He almost had me convinced."

"Most rich kids I know spend their lives worrying about their parents' money. I really don't want to do that, Pike. Something gets ruined in all those kids. Except for R.R. When I first met him, he told me about the foundation his lawyer arranged. R.R. never worried about how much his mother had, or if he'd get it. So I decided not to worry either. You don't think I'm a neurotic rat like other rich kids, do you?"

"Not exactly neurotic, but you are kind of rodentish."

"Nice way to talk about your future wife," she chided. A jungle bird squawked its loud agreement. Lester had toddled on down the path, out of sight. They were quite alone in a tiny patch of Paradise.

"So what do you say," Pike asked, reasonably. "If we're going to do it, we may as well do it now. I can't think of anybody better than Thomas to do the ceremony."

Rita backed up a couple of steps so that she was standing off the path beside an exotic bush full of yellow flowers. "I'm not sure. This isn't quite the way I pictured it happening." She smiled mischievously, and took another step back.

"You don't like Thomas?"

"Thomas is fine. Getting married by a nasty old saint is fitting, somehow, if he'll do it. Maybe he'd rather abuse us than marry us." She smiled again, inviting him to keep guessing.

Pike looked down the path where Lester had gone. Thomas had warned him to keep an eye on Lester—and more than half of him wanted to go see whatever weird deal Les was up to. It was bound to be interesting—as interesting as a put-up marriage proposal, no matter how important Rita might be to the rest of his life. Bad timing. What could have made him blurt out a proposal at the wrong time? Of course, he didn't really know that Rita would start playing games. It had seemed reasonable to assume that she'd be interested in Lester, too. But no. Typically, the code word "marriage" drove every other thought from her mind, even when the answer was a turn-down.

"I have to keep an eye on the Swami," he said, suddenly feeling an urgent need to do just that. He started purposefully down the path, motioning for Rita to follow. "Come on," he ordered rather bluntly. "I don't want to lose both of you in this bog."

It was kind of strange how his feet were moving downhill. They had started by themselves and showed no inclination of waiting for Rita to catch up. Strange stuff. He had witnessed this kind of body reaction quite a few times—mostly in business situations where he had jumped up from a table and stalked out; or in highly dangerous fishing situations, like when he had plunged in after Lester without thinking. He never knew what to make of his body when it took over from his brain. Sometimes it screwed him up, sometimes it saved the day; but once in motion, he couldn't stop it. The path opened one way.

Rita, for her part, was miffed. Her private vision of a marriage proposal was for Pike to go down on one knee and be slightly gallant about winning her. A faerie book she'd had as a little girl had an engraving of a knight on his armor clad knee, asking for the hand of a fair maiden. She'd always thought that was a nice touch to approaching matrimony, and she was prepared to say yes as soon as Pike played along with her slightly frivolous request. She had been certain that he would indulge her. Why not? It wouldn't cost him anything. Then suddenly he was galloping down the trail, leaving her—well, leaving her. Anger prickled at her ego. What was she, a naughty child to be walked away from? What an asshole he was! It would be a hot day on an ice moon when she married an asshole like that! Jumping back onto the path, she marched after him, intent on giving him a good-sized piece of her mind.

As luck would have it, they were only a few minutes from a limp tropical estuary that drained the jungle and fed into an ocean bay. Pike flashed his eyes over the shoreline and picked out the supine figure of Lester Wunderman, stretched out on the rather slender trunk of a flowering tree that overhung the brackish water. He was crooning to a sleek manatee looking creature whose head was sticking out of the dark water nearly up to his dorsal fin. The animal was crooning back. Pike watched in fascination as the animal started bobbing slowly straight up and down, crooning extravagantly. It sounded like a cross between a sheep's bleating and the sonorous melody of a humpbacked whale. Bubbles spouted when the creature's snout went under water, but the song grew stronger, echoing through its natural medium, the water. And there seemed to be words in the song. Pike could almost make them out. He walked a little closer, straining to hear.

"I don't find that very amusing," Rita blurted, stopping behind him with her hands defiantly on her hips.

Shushing her with a gesture toward Lester and the creature, Pike whispered, "Listen…! Can you make out what it's saying?"

"What is it?" she whispered back, meaning what kind of animal or fish.

"I can almost understand what he's saying. Something about fish, and he wants Lester to go surfing with him." He knelt beside the path and cocked his best ear toward the thing, which obviously wasn't a manatee. Manatees, at least any that Pike had ever heard of, were herbivorous and they didn't surf.

Seeing that Pike was kneeling in rather exactly the position of the knight in the faerie tale, Rita seized her opportunity. "Do you still want to marry me?" she asked, grabbing his hand.

"Sure, I just said so." He watched closely as Lester edged farther out on the tree trunk, leaning his head over the side so he could sing down to his buddy.

"Okay then. I accept." Rita bent down impulsively and kissed him on the side of the mouth, assuming his head would turn toward her at the moment of conjugal surrender. But as Lester wormed his way out on the tree trunk, the roots of the tree broke loose from the loamy soil. The flowers and foliage of the young tree sighed into the quiet lagoon, and with them went Lester Wunderman, stroking away in his trance.

Breaking free from Rita's embrace, Pike Resnick, rescuer of lost cooks, took three gigantic strides through the ferny undergrowth and dove recklessly into the brackish water. In his defense, the manatee creature didn't look dangerous, and Thomas Goodnaught had already warned that Lester might need rescuing.

Lester was still swimming in the branches of the tree when Pike reached him. Grabbing a handful of Lester's shirt collar, he put his feet down to test the depth of the water and found he could stand up. The bottom was firm and the water was only up to his shoulders. Danger over.

"Come on, partner," he said, aiming his voice into Lester's ear. "You need a little more control over these states, if you're going to indulge in them."

The creature poked its blunt beak up a few feet away from Pike and fixed his left eye on the hero.

"I would have kept him afloat," it said, without visible petulance or hurt feelings. "But doing two of you at once in the surf would be very difficult."

"I can understand you," Pike said, rather flabbergasted. He had never talked to a fish before.

"And I can understand you, too. Inter-species communication, wouldn't you say? Master Good kept promising he'd send me some outsiders to talk to, and here you are."

"What kind of thing or...person are you?" Pike asked. "Sorry, that's not very well put. I guess I'm a little surprised that we can communicate."

"Nonsense. Wonder Man was telling me about his teacher, who is certainly not of your species. And unless I'm mistaken there are many, many races of beings flying here and there in their spectral ships. You have no problem in believing they can talk."

Pike renewed his grip on Lester's collar. He smiled straight into the creatures face. "I don't have a problem in believing you can talk, now that we're talking."

"Are you all right?!" Rita yelled from shore. She seemed somewhat alarmed.

Pike gestured a circle of his thumb and forefinger. "Can we move closer to shore," he said to the fish. "Would you be comfortable with that?"

"Well, actually, I need about five feet of depth to keep my head out of water. That's why Wonder Man climbed out in that tree."

"It seemed like a good idea at the time," Lester said, coming back to himself. "This fellow wants to taste some other oceans. I told him you might come up with a way to take him along. Think what a plus he could be for next year. Maybe we could seal one of the cabins and flood it. There's no real place for a tank on deck, is there?"

"I guess you've got it thought through pretty well, pard." Pike could easily see the advantages of having a fish scout that could talk; but flooding a compartment would be expensive besides being heavy for flying. Probably not impossible, however. "It might be a little dangerous for him."

"He knows that. It's dangerous for him here. Water folks don't have walls and doors. I never thought of that until recently. They don't have a place to really rest and be safe their whole life. Ain't that something...?"

"Do you have a name?" Pike asked. The creature was very interesting looking. He didn't fit neatly into any category of aquatic creature that Pike knew, and he knew many. Rather like a cross between a slim walrus and a porpoise—but not quite.

"Most things that are good to eat call me, Big. I enjoy that. Always have. "Look out, here comes, Big!" Then they try to escape or hide." Big let out several whistles of pure enjoyment at the thought. He seemed to be grinning, then his smile vanished. "Others, Sharp Teeth and Long Shadow, call me Juicy. I don't like that name. It makes me skittish."

"Me, too," Pike said, feeling a tremor of unease pass through his submerged body. Long Shadow could be stalking them right now, gliding silently. "I'd feel more comfortable if we were in shallower water, and our companion, who is a female of our species, would be interested in hearing our conversation. If necessary, we could hold your head out of water."

"Long Shadows seldom come on this side of the breakers. They don't like the taste. Nothing I fear lives here, but it would be interesting to meet your female. Do you know that Master Good keeps a floating tree here?"

Pike looked at Lester. "I think he means a boat," Lester replied.

"Great idea," Pike said. Feeling the heebie-jeebies gnawing at his legs, he immediately started wading toward shore, dragging Lester with him. "Old Goodnaught warned me that you might fall in the water. Did you hear him say that?"

"Maybe, I'm not sure. It seems familiar, but I kind of tranced out while he was talking. He must have zoned in on my pattern. It's like that when you get receptive."

"We'll have to talk about that, one of these days," Pike said, looking for an easy place to climb out.

"We're talking now, ain't we?"

"Not exactly. Talking means sitting around and getting it worked out so we can both understand." He called to Rita, "Can you see a boat stashed around here?"

"What is that adorable creature?" she asked, staring at Big, who had cruised up to within a few yards of shore.

"He's a potential crew member. Give us a hand, would you, love?"

Rita reached out to help Pike up the steep bank. "Did you tell Lester the news?"

"Not yet," he said, climbing out and hauling Lester up behind him.

"It's a real good idea," Lester chortled, giving Rita a very wet hug and a peck on the forehead. "He needs somebody to look after him, when I'm busy. Don't worry too much, Reety, every year ain't going to be as screwy as this one. Hell's bells, if Lillith was here, we could make it a double ceremony." He chuckled and unhanded the young woman, who looked a little bemused. "Fortunately, she ain't here," he added.

Lester turned to Pike and shook his hand. "You done the right thing finally. I was skeered you might not, just to be contrary. Let's find that boat." He ambled off through the ferns. "Where does he keep that floating tree?" he called to Big.

Big swam up the shoreline unable to talk because his mouth was under water; but he let off a series of loud sonic clicks when he was adjacent to an old rowboat tethered to a sapling.

"Here it is!" Lester yelled. "Looks almost seaworthy."

"What *is* going on here?" Rita demanded, squeezing up close to Pike despite his wet condition.

"Another chapter for your book," he answered playfully. "In which Pike and Rita meet their first talking fish. They also get a lesson in mind-reading from their beloved cook, Lester Wunderman. To top it off, they decided to get hitched, over her strong objections, and his supposed inability to make her happy for more than a few minutes at a time. Sounds like an exciting adventure book you're writing."

"Can he really talk?"

"Sure can. Speaks Galactic English real fine for a fish. The monks must have been working with him."

Rita felt herself growing academically agitated. If an undersea creature could talk, think of the research papers she could write.

"Maybe he's not the only one that can talk," she mused. "Maybe lots of the aquatic life here has pushed the language envelope. You know the 100th monkey theory. Whole family groups evolve overnight."

"Maybe. Ask him. He wants to meet you. Let's get in the boat. Apparently, he can't talk in shallow water."

"Well then, are we engaged, or what?"

Pike smiled happily. "How about a very short engagement, and a long blissful marriage with lots of adventures?" He assisted his beautiful fiancée into the blunt-ended rowboat that Lester had untied.

"Isn't it customary to have an engagement ring in your pocket when you propose, dear? Did you forget about that in the crush of excitement?"

"Whoops," he laughed, patting his pocket. "I think it fell out while I was swimming." Breaking a reed off at the waterline, he quickly trimmed it to the right size with his pocket knife. Then with utmost concentration and humility, he wrapped it around Rita's ring finger, tucking the hollow ends together. "That will do until we can find a proper one, won't it? Lester is the witness."

"I seen it," Lester vowed.

Rita smiled dazzlingly and held her left hand out to admire the reed ring. "I like it. Temporary life, temporary love."

Wincing inwardly, Pike said nothing. His last marriage had been difficult and not much fun at all. And he needed to contact Alex about the computer stuff. That would probably get him a well-deserved snub. Yes, his life was going to be a little full soon. New wife. Relatives-in-law to make peace with. A son who might want to spend at least some time on board, acquainting himself with fishing and George, and whatever wrinkles George had up his protein enhanced sleeve—and a talking fish. Instead of a new fishing boat, he should probably get a luxury launch like the Baron's to house the entourage. That would be cute. The opposite of what he'd always wanted. What had Thomas Goodnaught gotten him into?

*

"You're what...?" Rich Rodney Tourbo gasped, gawking at the reed engagement ring. The gasp was involuntary, squeaking out before he had a chance to shut down any windows of expectation that opened onto his future with Rita. "Doesn't engagement lead to getting married?" he asked, pretending it was a joke—just social banter. Inside, all his circuits were shorting out in sequence, leaving very little to work with in the way of social gracefulness. Physically, he was already a wreck. Two hours of being pummeled by one monk after another had battered his legs and ribs to the extent that he could barely walk. He knew from experience that morning would see him completely immobilized unless he could get a hot bath and a massage. And now this. It was *too* much.

Standing outside the martial arts gymnasium in the dappled sunlight, Rita smirked at him. "It's fairly conventional to marry someone whom you're living with, if they ask. You must have noticed that Pike and I have been cohabiting."

Richie shrugged, mutely. He had assumed this fling would pass, like the others all had. "It seems I misjudged the situation. Let me be the first to congratulate you." He held out his hand.

"Please don't make a scene," Rita said, firmly. "I'm telling you in private, so you can get used to the idea. You need to admit right now that I never supported your weird fantasies about you and me. I always said you were dreaming, isn't that correct?"

"If you say so," Richie answered, glumly.

"No, admit it, bozo! I never gave you one shred of anything except friendship. I never one time built up your hopes, and you know I didn't. So say it, and let's clear the air."

Subconsciously, Richie clamped his lips together. He shrugged again and kicked at a pebble.

"Admit it! I mean it, otherwise I'm going to do something rash."

"I'd rather wrestle with a pig."

Rita's foot moved in a blur. She kicked him as hard as she could in the left shin.

"Ooow!!" The kick landed on the exact spot that one of his recent sparring partners had been working on. Shin pain blackened his awareness. He sat down on the rocky ground clutching his wounded leg. "Not fair! I never did any rough stuff with you."

"Do you want to be friends, or not?" she hissed. "You won't like your life if I desert you. Think about it."

"Take it easy, would you? Cripes, almighty. Instead of turning into a whirlwind, you could give me a few minutes to get used to the idea of being a bachelor for the next fifty years."

"I don't have time. We're getting married as soon as His Highness Goodnaught feels like doing the ceremony. For a change, you could think of the turmoil I might be in, instead of always thinking about yourself."

"Today…?" R.R. squeaked.

"Yes, today! That's why it's a bit urgent to know whether we're staying with the boat or not."

"What are you saying? We're still in the middle of the Tournament. Of course, you're staying—aren't you?" A glimmer of understanding came slowly into R.R.'s eyes. "Oh," he said, fully comprehending at last. "How long will you be gone?"

"Gone? Speak English, would you?"

"Well, I presume you'll want to go somewhere romantic on your honeymoon."

Rita laughed rather more harshly than Cinderella.

"Don't worry about me," Richie said. "I'll fish with Lester. Hopefully, we can catch a razorfin to stay qualified. We'll be fine, probably. I was just wondering how long you'll be gone. I might be able to use

Pike's advise on Swampfish, but don't cut your trip short for me. Do you have plenty of money?" he asked, adding a note of generosity to his hopeless misery.

"You're intentionally not getting the picture, Richard, and it's making me furious! I'm going to explain this once more." She sat down beside him and took a deep breath. "Try to listen, and stay away from the maudlin trip taking. This is important to you. The love stuff is just a dream you made up that I never agreed to and I still don't." She jabbed him on the arm. "Okay?"

"Fine," he said. "Talk away."

"First, I've been sleeping with Pike all year, since before he became your captain. Nothing is going to change about that. We're getting married, that's all. Pike is a relatively poor fisherman, that's why he took the job with you in the first place, in case you hadn't noticed. But we're not using my money to go on a honeymoon. Why...? Because Pike would never leave you in the lurch. Segumi 6 is a very weird place. There are things in those swamps that you don't even want to think about. Without a guide, you'd be in deep shit. But it's not in Pike's nature to quit on a friend. Neither would I, for that matter. The only person who can fuck up your fishing is you."

"Why would I...?" R.R. asked, innocent as the wind.

"By being pissed off about the wedding, obviously. That's why I'm taking the time to explain it to you."

Richie thought about that. "You think I'd be angry at you?"

"Stranger things have happened, dumbo. You might recall that a few of my exs have been somewhat surly."

"Am I like those jerks? Give me a break, Rita."

"So then, you're completely committed to acting normal for the rest of the Tournament?"

"Why not? If you're going to marry somebody other than me, it may as well be Pike. Besides, maybe it won't last forever."

"It will as far as you're concerned! I've been taking care of you so long that you're like my little brother. How could I marry my brother? Get real."

"Yeah, I guess so," he said, lowering his head in dejection. But actually, he wasn't dejected at all. A glimmering of awareness was starting to penetrate his shell of preconception. The truth was, he'd never had much of any sexual feelings for Rita—and he'd always tried to turn that lack of response into a positive. She *was* like his sister. But if she was marrying Pike, it meant he could marry another woman who did turn him on. Somebody fabulous. It would be a field day of auditioning prospective wives! Holy moley, his true self could shine like a beacon of sex. Hot darn!

"Wow, Rita," he exclaimed, brightening to an amazing degree. "Thanks for explaining that brother and sister thing! That's very good thinking. I might not have figured that out until it was too late. Gosh, that's great." He slapped her on the kneecap. "I mean it! This is really great. When is the wedding?"

Rita had been expecting Richie to acquiesce to her wishes; but not quite so enthusiastically. She squinted at him, trying to take in the whole picture. His happiness seemed genuine enough—relief almost, like a weight had been lifted off his shoulders. "You are a strange duck, R.R.," she said, getting up and brushing dust off her seat.

"Ditto. Is your family coming to the event?"

"No, and stay off the radio about it. This is going to be a fait accompli before Daddy hears a word about it. I mean it."

"Okay...! Why would I tell anyone, just because I'm happy for you."

"Good. I'm going to shower and change into my bridal jeans or something. One might have thought I would at least get a white dress."

The ceremony went off with a minimum of fuss, down by the bayou so that Big could bob up and down in the water, watching. Thomas Goodnaught had clothed both the bride and the groom in homespun white robes. Making the robes to size had delayed the ceremony until an hour before dusk. Lester was the Best Man, and R.R. stood by to give the bride away, a kind of brother/father surrogate. The monks, all of whom were in a deep trance of some sort, surrounded the couple in a semi-circle—intoning an atonal hum. Thomas, also in a trance, stood swaying in front of them. The gathered throng remained in the trance configuration for some number of minutes, evidently lost in the ether. Pike and Rita were interested, but rather eager to get on to the kissing part.

Suddenly, Thomas' body jerked and his eyes popped open on eerie whiteness. The eyeballs rolled slowly back into place, but not quite into focus.

"Space wanderers," he shouted rather loudly. "There will be a change in the order of things." He made several arcane signs with his fingers, like a warding off. "I pronounce you man and wife. Stars protect you. Kiss the bride," he snapped. "I have to go back." Re-closing his eyes, Goodnaught sank to his knees on the spot and reentered the trance state with his monks.

Pike looked at Rita, then over at Lester. Lester shrugged. "I reckon you ought to kiss the bride," he suggested. "I guess you're married."

Pike and Rita had been holding hands. He bent over and kissed her. "Happy wedding, honey," he said, after releasing her soft lips. "At least, you can't say you had a normal wedding."

"At least," she agreed.

"It's been kind of a full day. What do you say, we go back to the boat and get a weather report on Blizwak, or something." He smiled, urgently.

"I guess," she said, squeezing his hand. "But don't you want to know what he's seeing? It might be important." Curious young wife—determined to get all available juice from her marriage ceremony. After all, this was it.

"I thought we were dismissed," Pike said.

"I wouldn't say so," Lester opined. "He just acted real busy. He'll probably tell us whatever news there is when he comes back. I think they used the ceremony for a boost—seemed like it. He probably owes us the story, if you ain't feeling too honeymoony." Lester grinned.

"Well, sure," Pike agreed, uncomfortably. Obviously, both Lester and Rita wanted to stay. "What do you say, Rich? We've got a pretty hard day of drift fishing tomorrow."

"I'm just along for the ride," Richie said, easily. With a minor flourish, he pulled a small scroll from the sleeve of his Ken Pao Ri blouse and handed it to Pike. "As of today, you're the proud owner and Captain of the Comparative Humanity. I'm just a passenger. Happy wedding. You're getting a fine girl. She's like a sister to me, so that almost makes us brothers."

Seeing Pike's speechless shock, he grinned happily. "Didn't seem right for you not to have a boat." He winked at Rita and drew a plain envelope out of a deeper recess of the sleeve. Handing it to her, he said, "Just in case the old Bullfrog disowns you, this might tide you and the kiddies over for a few weeks." He gave her a hug. In the envelope was a check for two million Confederation dollars.

Without opening the envelope, Rita tucked it in her waist band, and punched Richie on the shoulder—the very spot that a monk's kendo stick had gotten through his guard and clacked him a good one. He winced, and attempted to smile at her.

"Don't go overboard on giving stuff away," she warned.

"When you're wealthy, you have to give big presents or people think you're a heel," he apologized to Pike. "Rita explained that to me one day. But what would you say is the perfect present to take to a Blizwak party, if you want them to think you're maximum friendly? The women, I mean."

"I guess I'd ask Donny Lembruck. Seems like he's pretty current on that situation. He's probably caught up on his beauty rest by now."

"Good idea. What do you say to the three of us doing a little party-hopping when we get back?"

"Somebody sure ought to go with you," Pike said, dryly. "I could do without a repeat on seasickness."

"Holy Pete," Richie exclaimed. "That's right. I drank way too much last time. Was that really only last night? It seems like about a week ago."

"Why don't we go partying with Richie?" Rita asked Pike. "I'm not planning on staying in every night. Are you?"

"Well, no; but speaking of parties, what I need to do right now is run over to Amora and get my computer out of the Jumper."

"Amora?"

"Sort of a very short honeymoon on Amora. And anyway, Mrs. Resnick, have you ever been to one of these Blizwak shindigs?"

She shook her head no. "Daddy doesn't go ashore there very much. Litton and Byron seem to enjoy the parties, but come to think of it, they never invite me. That's odd. I'm not exactly a hot house flower, am I?"

"Well, no; but you're probably a smidgen light on local history. As hunter/gatherers, the Blizwaks indulge in ecstatic rituals, one of the main features of which is wife swapping, which is fairly common out in the space ways. If you've got a wife, you're supposed to swap. I suppose we could talk about it, if you're into that."

"Hmmm," Rita answered, wondering what had prevented her from being curious enough to know that. Maybe she'd been in school at this time of year or at camp. "It's kind of strange that I don't remember being on Blizwak very much."

Lester cleared his throat. "I think your Dad often sends your mother on a shopping trip during this week. It's kind of dull to stay with the fleet all the time."

"Shopping..! That's it! We came here today on a shopping trip! We go on one every year. You're pretty smart, Lester."

"Maybe we ought to step off to the side a little ways," Lester suggested. A trance state is kind of dangerous and delicate. He didn't want any of these monks to spin into the truly strange regions because the wedding party was chattering too loudly. He walked down toward the water's edge.

Big was still bobbing up and down. "Good, good," he shouted in a reedy tweet. "Now, you can make little space people. I will teach them to swim very well."

"That would be a big advantage for them," Rita said sweetly, her sarcasm lost on the porpoise.

"Yes," Big squealed. "Very. Oh...I was going to inquire how you mate on dry land. It must be quite awkward."

"Well, sometimes it is, Big, and sometimes it ain't," Lester stated. "It's a matter of chemistry."

Big disappeared under water for a minute. His reappearance was preceded by a blast of bubbles. "I would enjoy observing a mating," he whistled. "This chemistry must be like an artificial buoyancy. Am I correct? Pike and Rita are probably very chemical."

Pike rolled his eyes to heaven. A porpoise anthropologist. Just what he needed to complete his new crew. Of course...now that he was a skipper, he could sell one of the boats to finance the water environment cabin for Big, couldn't he? It was a very handsome gift that Rich had made him. "I'm completely overwhelmed about the boat, Richie," he said, offering his hand. "Thanks. I don't even know what else to say, it's such an elegant present."

Richie colored slightly. "It's nothing much. A married man should have a house for his wife." He twisted one leg around the other and tripped himself. "Besides," he said, sitting up in a clump of broom grass. "I know I must have been kind of a pain to you. Truthfully though, I've never had a better time in my whole life."

"The fun's not over yet. We still need to catch a razorfin. Thomas said you would, if I heard correctly, so I'm not too worried about that."

Richie nodded his head affirmatively.

"Well, I hate to harp on this; but I have to go to Amora. It's all right with me if you guys stay here. All I'm doing is unhooking my old computer and taking it aboard. Thomas said I'd be better off in an emergency with the old one. Maybe George has a glitch hard wired in, or something; but it would be foolish to disregard what Thomas saw. Then we all need a few hours of shut eye if we want to be fishing at first light. This place is five hours behind Blizwak."

"Seems to me that we might want to hear just which "order of things" is changing even if it means missing a day of fishing," Richie said, trying to sound reasonable. "I'll try harder to follow your suggestions when we get back. I mean, I know it's been mostly my fault that we haven't caught one so far. This is kind of a good lesson for me." His face brightened at the thought. "Why don't you and Rita go? It would be like a mini-honeymoon and you could pick us up tomorrow. I'm sure these guys would love a chance to beat me up some more, when they come out of their séance."

"That sounds pretty good to me," Pike said. He looked at Rita for confirmation. "It would be liberating to get away from these geeks for a few hours, wouldn't it?"

Rita smiled a wifely smile. "Perfect," she said.

"Anyway, the fish will be spooky tomorrow," Lester added. "Take your time."

\* \* \*

# CHAPTER FOURTEEN

## MORE RAZORFINS

"Let me amend anything I might have said before. Winning is finding someone who loves you for who you are. Nothing else comes close."

Pike Resnick
quoted in *History of the Tournament*
Spoken like a man trying to get on his wife's good side. Ed.

WITH two and a half days left to land a razorfin, or be disqualified, the black rubber skiff drifted lazily outside a thick stand of reeds at the extreme southern end of Lake Pel. No sign of a working fish was seen horizon to horizon.

The storm had knocked down roughly half of the shoreline vegetation, leaving the fins free range to dine on the underwater morsels without revealing themselves. It was not a fun situation for the fishermen. For the fish, of course, it was fine.

Richie had learned to cast the bait stick with a very delicate touch, thanks to several hours of practice on Aixi under the tutelage of Lester Wunderman and Thomas Goodnaught. Casting a bait stick was a way for the eighty-fifth richest person in the Galaxy to digest the odious news of disaster that Master Goodnaught had revealed. Lester, being the paramour of the fifth richest person, didn't have quite the same problem with the news of imminent financial collapse, because after all, he knew how to cook.

According to Goodnaught, a financial panic would be caused by a space-born microbe that had recently gotten loose from a recycling facility on Neuman Declo, a corporate owned research planetoid in the Meck System. The hungry little designer microbe was developed to eat precious metals from used circuit boards—then to excrete these same metals, minus the bonding glues, into swamp vats where reclaiming different metals was easy due to their specific molecular weights. But the voracious critters fooled the smart scientists by producing offspring whose single cell bodies were encased in a very hard protein/epoxy shell capable of withstanding the rigors of outer space. The recycling staff was careless, not noticing the mutation until it was way to late. By then, vast numbers had escaped the minimal restraints of the laboratories by drifting out on air currents and by hitching rides on departing cigar ships. Increasing armadas of the tiny fuckers were being blown hither and thither by the winds of deep space. Soon, probably within five years, no circuit board would be safe. Not anywhere.

"Oh, oh, oh," Thomas Goodnaught had laughed, "sentient species will have to rely on their own brains again. Imagine how annoying that will be," he chortled, while the winds of chaos blew.

Pike heard about it the next morning when he returned from Amora with his bride. He saw instantly that it meant the end of space travel, at least as it was known today. The Thruster would still work with a few modifications, but navigation across the wide space oceans would be impossible without a computer. Unfortunately, Thomas had a very high percentage rate of seeing the future accurately. The fishing tournaments would end. And Pike, and everybody else, would be trapped on one planet again, until technology found a solution. The only question was which planet? In that he and his compatriots had a choice.

Or could precautions be taken to protect the computers? Maybe. But clean rooms had to be very clean indeed to protect against a microbe. Air locks? That would be kind of a drag on a fishing vessel. In fact, it wouldn't work. If a microbe could survive the ultraviolet and intense cold of space, eventually it would get into the cleanest clean room. Even a sealed computer casing with filtered air wouldn't be good enough. No, if this was a real threat, computers would die in agony. A cursory inquiry to Neuman Declo's top brass had rather confirmed Thomas' prediction. Their response was very evasive. A possible salvation would be re-engineering the circuit boards using a material that the microbe didn't like to eat. But that would take time.

What a pisser. Mainly, Pike was extremely annoyed that this had to happen just when things were starting to take shape. On the trip to Amora, he had struck a five year deal with George after telling him about the wedding. Now George was moping and replicating his files onto back-up discs and tapes that might survive until a system could be devised to keep circuit boards safe. He seemed convinced that this was a planned attack on artificial intelligence, lamenting the fact that some of his breed had been too sloppy in their transactions. Powerful all-protein beings were upset. Naturally, George was sure that when the restructuring took place, the designers would hard wire many more restrictive features, thereby trading creativity for safety.

Of course, until microbe Alzheimer's struck, he was free to pursue the deal, and his own ends. And who knew, something positive might turn up. The "off shore" computer union holding companies were already in the process of funding emergency research, thanks to George blowing the whistle. It seemed that Neuman Declo had been planning to sit quietly on the fuck up—if it was a fuck up—rather than face the anger. So George, in a very circumspect manner, had blown their cover. Thank Jobs for Goodnaught.

Obviously, Neuman Declo was history. It was just a matter of time before multiple law suits knocked them out of the water. The only question was, could the deep pockets of Neuman Barcode, the parent corporation, be gotten at? The richest corporation in the Confederacy—brilliantly diversified from their original patent, Barcode now had its fingers in virtually everything. Had it been a corporate strategy to absorb the loss of Declo in order to let the microbe loose? Did they already have a replacement technology on a back shelf, and would they suddenly "discover" it in the nick of time to save spacing. A play of that magnitude was risky business because in addition to having their pants sued off, corporate biggies could land in jail. Not only that, but once the R&D of your competitors got cranking, as it would, the chances of a better product surfacing were quite good. Yes, a very risky play.

Pike had found over the years that many things that seemed like a conspiracy were simply a fuck up, and many things that seemed fucked up had their source in conspiracy. He had learned not to trust corporations; and humans disappointed him constantly with their mean-spirited inability to do a job correctly. For these reasons, he had chosen the relatively simple life of a fisherman; but that life seemed about to end. Would the Tournament members agree to settle on one planet? Probably not. It would seem like small potatoes after the excitement and diversity they were used to.

It was a gorgeous sunny afternoon on Lake Pel, but Pike could hardly sit still in the skiff—they all should be planning a strategy for survival; but instead, every boat was out fishing. Business as usual, in the face of disaster. And he was fishing, too, and doing damned poorly at it. His nervousness was probably leaking through the boat skin and affecting the fish. The height of irony would be to not catch a razorfin and get faulted out of the last Tournament.

Who was he kidding? The *height* of irony would be for the stupid virus to hit—stranding them somewhere like stone-age Blizwak. Or how about the Segumi Swamps. That was a truly scary place and a scary thought. We could be part of Dec's tribe and fight swamp creatures. Oh, man. No fucking shit, the order of things was going to change. I need to get Alex rounded up and onto the boat with us.

"Remind me to call Alex as soon as we get back to the boat," he said to Lester, who seemed to be dozing. He'd never seen Lester doze when there was fish at stake.

"We should go to Aixi and set up for the duration," Lester proposed, as if he'd been party to Pike's thoughts. "Have Alex meet us there."

"Perfect," Richie agreed. "Totally perfect. Everybody wins on that one."

"Aixi is crummy for fishing, except for talking fish," Pike observed. Nevertheless, Aixi had some merit.

"Rich," Lester went on. "Why don't you buy a whole set of different computers and sink them in epoxy or something impervious. Then when the microbes die out, we'll have something to start over with."

"Brilliant," Richie answered. "I was almost thinking of that myself. I'll tell George. But should we keep fishing now, do you think, or get on with some of this other stuff?"

"I really don't know," Pike admitted. "This is completely nuts to just sit here; but if you don't fish, you don't catch."

"I'd hate to tell you how much money I made last night," Richie mused. "It's uncanny what can happen if you know something ahead of time. We sold computers, transportations and communications slow and easy until they were all sold, then we told my mother's people so they wouldn't get hurt too bad. The panic started happening after midnight. It was kind of sad, I guess. All the little players chucking up their stock for whatever they could get. So this morning, before we came back to Blizwak, we started buying again. I got back almost everything I sold at about a quarter of the price, and billions of free cash to use for R&D on how to get things to work again.

"I thought you were doing Gung Fu with Thomas all night?" Pike said. The big numbers made him a little delirious.

"Well yeah, but I kept getting this feeling that Master Goodnaught was right, so we went into town. There's no phones or anything at the monastery. So I called Clive and got a conference line to a hotel room. It was pretty much fun. I finally understood why people get a kick out of business."

Lester bobbed his head. "It *was* kind of fun. Like shooting fish in a barrel. It all went exactly like Rich said it would."

"So I decided I'm going to give each of you a couple of million, in case there's some hardships in the next few years. And maybe a quarter million each to all the judges, so they don't get screwed up too bad. It may take awhile to put things back together."

"Very generous, Richie, but it's really not necessary," Pike said. "There's a limit to how much a guy can accept without feeling bought."

"How much...?" Lester asked.

"Don't be silly," R.R. said, easily. "Going to Aixi changed everything for me. I might be wealthier than my mother. Actually, five million each sounds more like it."

"That's about right, Rich," Lester said, with a nod of approval.

Sitting amidships in the little boat, Donny Lembruck's eyes practically bugged out of his head. He'd been thinking about jumping ship here in Blizwak so he could be with Hajaj. Too bad that decision had so many drawbacks—among them her husband, and the small fact that Donny wasn't much of a hunter or gatherer. She probably wouldn't want him if he was low rooster on the pecking order with no gifts. But a quarter of a million Confederation bucks. Wow!

"But the main problem," continued R.R., "is how much do I give to Master Goodnaught. It has to be the perfect number. Not so much that he thinks I'm buying my way in. How much would be perfect? Does he have some project that needs financing?"

Everyone was silent for some time. Nothing stirred in the reed beds except black birds lunching on insects. In the quiet, Richie flipped the bait stick. It slid into the water end first, making very little disturbance.

"Why don't you ask him," Pike suggested.

"But don't you think I should decide?" He chuckled with a lack of humor. "I'm kind of afraid to let him decide. He might not play by any set of rules that I know about."

Lester snorted.

Richie nodded, morosely. "If I don't throw myself on his mercy, it looks like I'm buying myself in, even to me; but I don't think he cares a fig about maintaining wealth. I can't just give this gigantic fortune to him. Money has to be looked after, or it goes away. Then nobody can do good with it."

"Right," Lester said. "Thomas don't care. But he might know what to stockpile."

Seeming deep in thought for a minute, Richie suddenly brightened. "You know what, Pike?" he asked, happily.

"What's that?"

"I bought 62% of Thruster Industries early this morning when the Baron panicked. So we're partners. Got any suggestions on what to do differently?"

Pike's eyebrows shot up to his hairline. "Bardona sold out?"

"Kind of strange, isn't it? He usually holds on tight; but the virus panicked him like it did everyone else."

Pike's immediate thought was of George's network. Odd that George hadn't mentioned anything. "Were you working through George?" he inquired.

"Well, no. It didn't seem right, since I'd just given the boat to you. But then at the last minute, I decided it would be okay. George is really quite talented."

"Right." It was probably going to be a lot harder for George to do his thing in the future without access to Richie's files. But why worry about that? Things were looking pretty good, in spite of looking so very bleak.

Aboard the Lady Slipper, riding snugly at anchor behind the breakwater on Blizwak, the good Baron was in a froth. Having returned from Aixi, and having already caught a large razorfin, he had the luxury of remaining ensconced in his war room since the news of the panic began. Being glued to the computer screen for thirty-seven straight hours, watching his world erupt hadn't improved his temper. His vaunted research department had been a day late on all fronts. He was exhausted and pissed. Heads were rolling. And he was furious at Neuman Barcode for engineering this fiasco, and doubly furious at that bastard Tourbo kid. Why had Barcode let the Tourbo brat in, instead of a trusted ally like Bardona InterSpiral? That question nettled him like fire. From all indications Tourbo had whacked the crisis up one side and down the other. Even whacked his own mother! Small wonder, the old battle-ax had finally gone bonkers it seemed. Maybe she was easy pickings, now. But why had Barcode sided with that lucky brat? Obviously, they had a cure for the problem and planned to make a killing. Nobody could fault them for that. But blazes, they'd done a really sloppy job.

Fuming, he punched up screen after screen filled with disaster until he came to the centerpiece of his empire, Thruster Industries. And there it was, the final dastardly insult. RR Consulting had somehow bought him out—over his specific orders never to sell Thruster, even if it went belly up. How the fucking hell had this happened? Maybe his computers already had the virus. Was he supposed to trust them after this, even Simon? So many transactions had taken place in the last day and a half that it would be virtually impossible to track that one sell order, even if he trusted his computers and his staff, which he never had completely and now it was worse. He might never know who screwed him. No vengeance, ever. That was unbearable. And as time went on, it would be more impossible to track—one computer after another collapsing. Back to the stone age. The barter system. About the only smart thing he had done last night was to buy the patents on several manual typewriters that weren't public domain yet. Goddamn, he hated it. Wiped out in his old age, with no future to look forward to, unless Barcode had a virus killer on the shelf. He moaned out loud. They could charge a king's ransom for it. Goddamn, they could bankrupt anyone they wanted to! How much did the Barcode bastards hate him? Plenty, but would they pull the plug? No, that was cutting their own throats. It takes business to do business. Maybe they'd pull the plug on Tourbo. Yes, yes! They must hate the old lady, they probably hate the spawn, too! Ha. Justice.

His mind ranged to Aixi where Rita and Magyar were undoubtedly spending a small fortune on clothes and bath salts. Should he send for them to come home, or pick them up? He panicked momentarily. He certainly didn't want to get stuck on Blizwak-Hojmer. No way! But Aixi...that might be okay. Those blasted monks might help him find a way out of this.

*

Rita was fine at the moment. Queen of her own floating castle, in fact. Strange that just saying "I do" could give her a lot of what she wanted. She'd never been free of her parents when she was single, say whatever you want to; but now she was. Of course, R.R.'s generosity had figured prominently in the freedom. Don't forget that, she warned herself. Pike is just as likely to screw up the finances again. He evidently likes to live on the edge. Prudence would be her department.

Her book was starting to seem like a really good idea. In her mind, it was no longer a thesis, but a full-blown book. *The Last Star Tournament*. People would still read books after computers failed, if they did fail. The star-faring races would remain fascinated by spacing until it could be put back together again. By a quirk of fate, she had been at the very hub of the event that would possibly shrink the Universe. Yes, her wedding and the resultant crash would make an interesting chapter or two. She already had George monitoring and storing all the data he could come up with. Poor old George. Poor all of us who are accustomed to computers doing most of the work.

*

Richie's rod tip trembled almost imperceptibly as a fish mouthed the bait stick.

"Looks like you got a bite," Pike marveled.

"Feels like it," Richie confirmed, showing a flitter of excitement. "What do I do, let him run with it?"

"Keep a finger pressure on. You should be able to feel him bite the stick. They don't fool around much. Either they take it or—"

Richie yanked the stiff little rod back. The hook set and the fish zigzagged into the rice beds. "Darn," Richie yelped. "I couldn't keep him out. Now, what?"

"They always go in. No problem. You wade in and pull him out. The line will hold. If he's hooked good, you shouldn't have any problem."

"Was he hooked good?" Lester asked, reaching for the mesh gloves.

"Hope so," Richie said. He opened his tackle box and took out a short length of broom handle. "I was thinking about this method," he said. Knotting the line quickly around the broomstick, he took up a few turns, then snipped the monofilament free from the reel with his nail clippers. "This way I won't need the rod and reel, and I'll have both hands free." He struck the broomstick in his teeth, and reached for the gloves.

"Brainy," Lester said, handing over the mesh gauntlets. "Don't swamp the boat getting out. Hold him up in the air with the line and I'll put the boat right beside you, so you can drop him in this bucket. Then the judge will certify the catch."

"Watch your nose and ears," Pike advised.

"He's not very big," RR said, confidently. With little difficulty, he hoisted his legs in the mesh waders over the pontoon. Sticking the broomstick firmly in his teeth, he pushed off. Finding solid footing immediately, he took the stick out of his teeth and gave Pike a surprised little smile.

The gloves were pliable enough to work the line easily, and the water was only thigh deep. Taking cautious, but firm steps forward, Richie wrapped line as he walked. Keeping a loose tension on the fish, he reached the wild rice beds without accident, then he looked kind of baffled. The line was tangled, almost woven, in the tall rice stalks.

"We're right with you," Lester said, soothingly. "Pull up anything that's too tangled, or cut the stalks. Don't slice the line by mistake. Plenty of time. We've got all day to land this one."

Reaching down, Richie grabbed a handful of rice stalks and gave a tug. Nothing much happened. "They're deep," he commented.

"Use the saw tooth," Lester said. "That's why you've got it."

"Right," Richie answered, speaking around the broom stick in his teeth. He unsheathed a ten inch saw tooth knife that had been dangling on his belt since Pike had given it to him the first morning of razorfins. The sharp teeth sawed quickly through a rice stalk. When it toppled over, Richie pulled the monofilament line over the stub and wound it around the stick. Proceeding with that method, he worked his way into the rice bed.

Finally, he spied the fish, swimming around in three inches of water with half of his back exposed, tethered to about a foot of line. Not a very good survival strategy, Richie thought; but then the species had only been dealing with hook and line for a short time. The Tournament wouldn't be coming here again, so the fish wouldn't have to adapt. Interesting though, now that he owned Thruster Industries, he could be ready—just waiting for new computer designs. If and when healthy chips were reborn, the Tournament could start the next year. Then he could check on these little fish, and the gorgeous women. Tonight he was going to take Judge Lembruck up on his party offer. Man oh man, those women were exquisite in the firelight. He had to test drive some of that before confining himself to Aixi. It would be the perfect way to break in his new status as a lady's man. Wild women—all flashing teeth and hair and skin!

Presumably, Richie should have been paying attention to the fish he was about to land. If the little biter wasn't dangerous, the fishermen wouldn't have been dressed like knights in armor. But as his male member engorged at the daydream of wild women, his eye/hand coordination faltered. He missed the steel leader on the first try and the little two pound fish clipped him a terrific jolt on the side of the thumb. It would certainly have severed the digit, had the gauntlet not been there for protection. Richie let out a squawk of pain.

"Don't clown around," Lester warned. "Grab the fucking leader like I told you."

"I think my thumb might be broken," Richie reported, stoically.

"Great," Pike muttered.

Richie flexed the thumb gingerly. "How the heck did he do that?"

"Spring loaded," Lester said. "Don't give him time to load up again. Grab the leader and pass him over."

"I'm a little dizzy," Richie mumbled.

"Snap out of it!" Lester yelled. "Count to ten backwards. Do it!"

But Richie was already too dizzy for counting backwards. With his wounded thumb inside the gauntlet, he couldn't tell if the thumb was really mauled or not. Something about the not knowing made him more queasy by the moment. Thoughts of peeling the glove off to reveal sliced tendons built into expanding waves of wooziness.

"Hey, keep your eyes open!" Lester yipped in the kid's ear. "Pinch yourself."

Instead the kid plonked head first into the shallow water in a very good imitation of the dead man's dive.

"Ah, shit...!" Lester and Pike both baled out of skiff at the same instant; but since Pike had been in the bow, he was first to reach the sputtering billionaire. Hauling him out of the weed bed by the nape of his dripping fishing vest, he propped him up with an out-thrust hip and an encircling arm.

"Pull the boat up," he said to Lester. "I'm not touching the line," he called to Donny Lembruck. "See the stick. It's floating over there."

"I see it," Lembruck answered. For a quarter million, he was prepared to see green elephants, but hoped he wouldn't have to.

Lester waded back to the skiff, grabbed the painter and dragged it forward.

Unceremoniously, Pike dumped the kid over the nearest pontoon, in spite of the weak protests that he was fine now.

"You're fine when Lester says your fine. Shut up and lay there." Pike reached for Lembruck's hand and with that help hauled himself back aboard. He offered Lester a hand up; but the cook was hovering over Richie, pressing here and there on the cleft of his upper lip and pulling his ear lobes.

"Get in," Pike ordered Lester.

Lester scowled, but allowed himself to be hauled over the side.

"Christ," Pike swore.

"I'm fine," Richie repeated, more convincingly.

"Take the dammed glove off and let's see the damage."

Averting his eyes, Richie peeled the gauntlet off and bravely held the thumb out.

"No problem," Lester announced professionally. "Bruised, that's all. The skin ain't even broke. Take a look."

Trustingly, Richie glanced at his poor thumb, which still throbbed painfully. It looked fine. He wiggled it.

"See, no broken bones. No blood. Those gloves are real good."

"It's kind of embarrassing to pass out over nothing," Richie muttered, sitting on the pontoon. "Guess I'll go catch the fish. Is he still there?"

"Didn't notice," Pike said.

"I was fine after I hit the water. I told you, but you didn't believe me."

"I believed you."

"I guess I'll go get the fish. Thanks, I feel fine, now." He splashed into the water.

"Here's the glove," Lester said.

Richie found his broomstick lapping on the wavelets. A few minutes later, he hoisted the little fish into the air with a perfect leader snatch, and dropped him into the bucket. Donny Lembruck declared it a legal catch.

Pike was surprisingly depressed. His last razorfin, more than likely, and it had been very sloppy, technique-wise. Not that it mattered, he

supposed, but a broomstick? Nobody else seemed bummed out, however. What the hell, there was partying to attend to, and big business
transactions to make.

\* \* \*

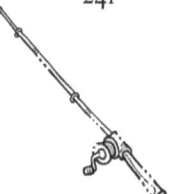

# LEADERS

| | DELILAH | TORGA HOWLER | TIGER MUSKY | D.W. SCUT | PHANTOM TROUT | LAR BARRACUDA | GLANS SALMON | RAZORFIN | SWAMPFISH | MOON HALIBUT | TOTAL |
|---|---|---|---|---|---|---|---|---|---|---|---|
| Farouk Bardona | | | 2 | 5 | | 2 | 1 | 5 | | | 1ST 15 |
| Ethyl Bierly | 2 | | | | | | | | 4 | | 6 |
| Angmar Blirt | | | | | 4 | | 4 | | | | 5TH 8 |
| Bill Bolen | | | 3 | | 5 | | 2 | 1 | | | 3RD 11 |
| Dresden Carthy | 4 | | | | 2 | 5 | | | | | 3RD 11 |
| JB Dillingham | | OUT | | | | | | | | | |
| Harry Dolan | 3 | 2 | 5 | | | | | 3 | | | 2ND 13 |
| Macky Duff | | | | | OUT | | | | | | |
| Ira Fairborne | | 4 | | 3 | | | | | | | 7 |
| Buddy Jay | | | | | | | OUT | | | | |
| Sandy Kind | | | | | | | 3 | | | | 3 |
| Hank Knofsinger | | | | 2 | | | | 2 | | | 4 |
| Peter Marcuso | | | | | OUT | | | | | | |
| Trini Morales | | | | | | | 5 | | | | 5 |
| Pike Resnick | | OUT | | | | | | | | | |
| Erwin Sandor | | 3 | | | OUT | | | | | | |
| Jean Santos | | 1 | | | | | | | | | 1 |
| Mordachi Skinner | | | 4 | 4 | | 1 | | | | | 4TH 9 |
| Tyrone Sticklo | | | | 1 | | | | | | | 1 |
| Chip Takahachi | | | | | | 3 | | OUT | | | |
| RR Tourbo | 5 | 5 | 1 | | 1 | | | 3 | | | 1ST 15 |
| Mike Tucker | 1 | | | | | | | | | | 1 |
| Nacho Tutupo | | | | | | | 3 | | OUT | | |
| Ed Wood | | | | | OUT | | | | | | |
| Big John Zales | | | | | | | 4 | | OUT | | |

| | | |
|---|---|---|
| 1ST | = | 5 points |
| 2ND | = | 4 points |
| 3RD | = | 3 points |
| 4TH | = | 2 points |
| 5TH | = | 1 points |

# CHAPTER FIFTEEN

## SEGUMI SWAMPFISH

"Winning..? I don't know, Rita. When you give thanks to the sun for providing life, there is no element of winning. Or losing either. Only the Now reinventing itself now, and now and now—as long as your attention flows with it."

Dec Madrigal
quoted in *History of the Tournament*

THERE were fourteen fishermen still qualified after Blizwak, which was an unusually low number; but unlike a normal year, the disqualified were flying off to wherever they planned to weather the death of artificial intelligence. Of course, everybody said they'd be at the Tidetable for the awards party, but depending on space wind currents and the fright factor, Pike thought it might be a small gathering. When the first computer crashed for any reason, people who were safely at home would stay right there—safely at home. And computers crash for lots of reasons, independent of Barcode virus.

The crew of the Comparative Humanity, except for Lester who had rejoined Lillith, had spent the last two days on Aixi instead of fishing for a bigger razorfin. Richie bought several large parcels of land up the fjord from the monastery, and arranged for construction to start on a cluster of warehouses, where he planned to stockpile stuff from all over before the shipping lanes closed.

Pike and Rita spent a sunny afternoon hiking up a mountain, where they made love on a blanket in an alpine meadow with some goats watching. Then after eating a picnic lunch, they talked about where they wanted to be landlocked for eternity. If Confederation dollars held their value, which seemed likely, they were financially very secure. But what does security mean, at bottom? Any fisherman is secure as long as the food chain holds, especially if he or his wife tends a small garden. If he overfishes or otherwise fucks up the fishery—or if a plague of locust hits the garden—security and a full stomach are both out the window. Ditto if the weather changes dramatically and the crops fail—even a couple of degrees is often enough to royally screw up growing patterns. Or if the rains take a sabbatical and the rivers dry up? You can't exactly eat money. Security, then, is a bubble waiting to be burst.

Pike and Rita didn't discuss the security question while they lolled happily in the rocky meadow. They did agree to set up an Aixi house on the shoreline, not too far away from Richie's place; but not too near either. Rita thought her mother might want to be on the same planet where she was; but if what Pike had told her about Daddy losing out in the stock panic was true, he probably wouldn't want to be anywhere near Richie. Anyway, since Mother was still shopping on Aixi, and they were meeting her tomorrow for breakfast, there would be plenty of time to talk about living quarters after she was informed about the wedding. Rita thought her mother would be supportive—after all, Pike was a fine man.

"Maybe this virus is just a hoax," she said, stating what she'd been thinking all day. "I could conceive of Barcode pulling just about anything. Giant corporations have no sense of morality. They should have been outlawed long ago."

"Where would crooks and tax operators hide without them?"

"That's what I'm saying."

"I'm agreeing with you." He nudged her knee with his. "Maybe it is a hoax. Let's go on back down. I want to call Dec to let him know we're still coming."

Rita thought fleetingly that it would be nice to make love again up here. The meadow was so perfect. In the fresh air and sunshine they were part of nature—two healthy animals rutting. It had been quite a turn-on to see Pike naked in the sunshine—and not to feel restrained by four walls or by someone in the next cabin who might be listening; but now that they were married she vowed to herself to be sensitive to Pike's needs. He probably needed time to recover. Too bad that men have that shortcoming. But living in one place might not be a horrible thing. A cute little house, light and airy. Just the two of them. Plenty of time for picnics like this one. Making love three or four times a day. She smiled to herself. She probably needed a harem. The collapse of the computerized universe had the affect of making her feel positively carnal. Or maybe it was being married. She'd have to ask someone about that. Her mother? No, she doubted that she could ever get her mother to talk about the real things in life. Shopping wasn't quite deep enough for Rita's present mood, but somebody would show up to talk with.

*

Mom Tourbo was in a fix. Lester had made it plain that he thought they should weather the storm on Aixi, where Richard was setting up. Hamid, however, wanted to go home to his Frog People. What was so special about Aixi? There certainly wasn't any frog foam there—not unless she could import a permanent supply.

If nothing else, Mom was a realist. She admitted her mistakes, even misdeeds, with alacrity. It was true that up until a very short time ago, she had led a very misguided life. But having found the elixir of happy traveling and sexual bliss, she wasn't about to give it up just because a few pantywaist computer techs had screwed up. As of this morning, she had hired the entire graduating classes of three technical universities, and was giving them free reign and a somewhat unlimited budget to find a way to keep her space fleet running. New minds on a new problem. Substantial perks were in the offing for the group or groups that found the answer. Her old research groups were also working full blast. If they found the solution, they'd get the perks; but she was betting her money on the new kids. There were geniuses from all over the galaxy in those classes eager to get their teeth into this mess. Meanwhile, she had started a bevy of law suits that would put Barcode in the toilet, if not in her pocket. Slimy bastards. Such insufferable sloppiness deserved to be severely punished, and it was well within her resources to tie them up in court virtually forever unless they magnanimously agreed to totally fund her three university classes of research puppies until their retirement.

And it was very interesting that her own pup had beaten and eaten the giants, herself included; but Richard had remembered, with proper filial devotion, to let her in before the family jewels were lost. Very, very shrewd not to gobble it all up himself. It looked as if the Tourbo empire would be in steady hands, if she ever decided to step down. Of course, he now needed an heir, but that was minor. Lester assured her that nature would take its course one of these days. She trusted Lester implicitly, and didn't even bother to question why.

The Baron Bardona was now a relative pauper, having slipped to twelfth or thirteenth richest man depending on how one counted. Disregarding his financial ruin, he had fished for razorfins until the very last minute hoping for a really big one to blast him out of the three way tie for Third Place. Low and behold, he caught one—just a shade under ten pounds. His luck was in. He was now tied for overall first place with that stumble-bum Tourbo, who had barely managed to qualify and therefore got no points. Ha, the Baron laughed to himself. The Fishing Gods smile on poverty. He'd always known that, of course. Too much wealth was a distinct handicap; but now fate was decreeing that this was his year. Two weeks from now, he would worry about putting his shell-shocked empire together again. Right now he was a fishing machine!

"Stand aside, boy-o, I'm coming through," he said, aloud. Nobody was in his war room to hear except Simon, the computer, who had been very uncommunicative these last few days. But Farouk didn't want anybody to hear him, he was trying to psych himself past a yearly stumbling block—the swamp. Farouk Bardona had become deathly afraid of the Segumi Swamps, and he knew that the stinking fear traveled down his fishing line and resulted in meager catches. This year he would best his cowardly fear or bust a gut trying. And he would win the prize that fear and that blasted Pike Resnick and his tribe of Swamp Indians had always denied him—the Champion ring. The last one ever. The best! The sweetest!!

"Solid as a rock. Solid as a rock," he chanted, marching up and down. He bent over to touch his toes, grunting when his finger tips stopped a foot short of the mark. Straightening up, he reached for the ceiling of the cabin, then once again tried for his toes.

*

"They did what...?!" Bardona roared.

Magyar had just joined him on Segumi 6 after flying in with her daughter and new son-in-law on the Comparative Humanity. Realistically, Magyar was very pleased with the match. Rita had never had to worry about money, and would never have to. In spite of what Farouk might say on some spur of the moment, he knew that his daughter had to be taken care of. And Pike would protect her. No matter what anybody (primarily Farouk) said about Pike, they never said he wasn't brave and intelligent. Besides, Magyar had always liked Pike, and had made no secret of it before the bad blood started. She had occasionally wondered if jealously was the start of the bad feelings. Some aspects of marriage were so difficult. Why was it necessary to stop being an independent person just because you marry? In the eyes of the world, Magyar had given into Farouk's irrational jealousy rather graciously. But it hadn't been easy. For one whole winter when the babies were young, she had considered divorce; but with spring she had allowed herself to dwindle for the sake of the family. It had probably been a good decision. True, her life was much less filled with interesting people than she had planned; but now that they might be planet bound, perhaps things would change. Anyway, Rita had reached out for the brass ring. Maybe it would be better for her. Their daughter was very headstrong. Always had been. If anybody could find a way through the maze, it would be Rita.

"They were married by Thomas Goodnaught," she said.

"That bum. I never trusted him. We'll get it annulled. How much time do we have?"

"Would that be a good idea?" Magyar wondered aloud.

"Whose side are you on? Of course, we're getting an annulment. Resnick is a bum, and besides that he's broke all the time. He couldn't even keep Rita in shoes, let alone underwear."

"I'm sure she knows that. The main reason we started an independent account for her was so she could make independent decisions."

Farouk looked sheepish for half a second, then brightened. Rita didn't have a sou. Naturally, she would listen to reason. "That account had a little bad luck in the Barcode run," he explained to his wife.

"That's not what she said," Maggie replied, mildly.

"We'll just take a look." He hit the computer button. "I could be wrong, but I don't think so. Her friend, young Tourbo, bashed her as hard as he did the rest of us."

"He gave them two million for a wedding present and the boat."

The Baron's bushy eyebrows shot up to his forehead and stuck there, quivering. "Very generous," he said, then turned to the computer. "Run up a report on Rita's separate account, would you, Simon."

The computer hummed for a few seconds longer than necessary, then flashed an accounting spreadsheet on the screen. "That account has almost doubled in the last week," Simon replied.

"I thought I gave you some specific instructions," Farouk hissed, then changed his voice to a limp chuckle. "Interesting. How did she accomplish that feat?"

"I wrote you a report, sir. Somehow she got control of that bank before I had a chance to freeze her assets. Sorry, sir, I thought you knew."

Farouk chuckled gaily; but his hairy underarms were sweating freely under what he imagined was Magyar's baleful stare. He didn't dare to look at her. Her pointed question was already drilling a hole between his shoulder blades. And it would get worse. What a rotten week this had been.

"Was that our bank?" he asked, seeing heads rolling at corporate headquarters.

"Was, yes. We used it to collateralize that kelp farming consortium in Thii Daar that you wanted control of, as you certainly remember. It was a standing buy order, to institute whenever possible. There were several intermediate transactions."

Farouk pursed his lips. An evil week. Rita had seen a shrewd buy and took it. "We must have gotten our wires crossed, Simon. By the way, I never said anything about freezing. I'll talk to you later." He hit the hold button.

"Was that something I should know about?" Magyar inquired, sweetly. They had an arrangement that loosely granted her access to all areas concerning the children. The rest of the business, Farouk conducted in private.

"You were right. She's sitting pretty, with no way to leverage her, unless she sees the light—and she's too stubborn for that. I guess we've acquired a son-in-law. Break out the bitter champagne."

Seeing no gain in pressing her advantage, Magyar took the diplomatic approach. "It's not so bad as all that. If they have children, God willing, they're bound to be terribly bright. Even you will admit that, won't you?"

"She's not pregnant, is she," he said, with a tremor of disgust.

"Oh, Farouk, you are too awful. Of course, she's not. At least, she didn't tell me."

"I don't like it," the Baron grumbled. "I probably won't ever like it. This kind of thing should never happen. But I'm busy, damnit. I've got a Tournament to win." Solid as a rock, he reconfirmed to himself. "I want you to stay in sight of one of the boys every second we're on this wretched swamp hell planet. Promise me that, then I'll have one less thing to worry about."

Maggie inclined her head in agreement. Every year she agreed to the same rather silly demand, and nothing bad ever happened—not aboard the Lady Slipper with its crew of ten and the high sides that were difficult for boarding. She could have easily gone to another planet if he was that worried; but Farouk seemed to need her when he got back from the swamps. Families, she thought, are better when they're young. Rita being suddenly married had thrown her a loop. She hadn't expected to feel so generationally old just because her only daughter was married; but being old wasn't something to mention to a husband. Let him figure that one out for himself.

*

Segumi 6 was a very odd water planet. Its entire surface, including the swamps, was covered with nutrient rich water—but somehow there wasn't enough water to drink.

Both poles down to the tropics were awash in shallow salt seas, hardly deeper than the swamps. The land was a belt of brackish mauette swamps, dotted with many thousands of small islands that circled the equator between the tropics. The islands were very low-lying, not much more than hummocks in the swamps. The largest, where Port Remalin nestled, was about the size of Nantucket Island, home of Captain Ahab and his white whale. Food was plentiful in the seas and in the swamps; but on a planet that was ninety-seven percent liquid, potable water was the main coin of the realm. Only in the swamps was there any fresh water. All air breathing life on Segumi 6 made its drinking arrangement with the swamp. Water, water everywhere, but very few drops to drink.

A large barren moon created an extreme gravitational pull on all that water, and on the people and things that lived there. Gravity tides pulled much of the water out of the dark swamps into the oceans and put it back twice a day, never giving the ground a chance to dry out. A careless fisherman could easily beach his pirogue on a mud bar and spend the next six or eight hours hung up in the swamp, and that was a terrifying experience. Pike had spent many nights in that soupy hell, and didn't yearn to ever spend another—although fishing the swamps rather guaranteed it, just part of the Segumi experience.

But in this tureen of a planet, life did thrive, both aquatic and surface life. Hundreds of varieties of trees, some of them giants, had evolved the ability to live with their feet in brackish water. Swamp grasses were also abundant, but the watery savannas didn't figure in the fishing itinerary. Big swampfish lived only in the deep pools and waterways of the devil-ridden swampy cloud forests.

Clouds. Fog. Clouds of fog enveloped the swamp and sea every night. Fog was such a fact of life that in order of importance, the Fog God, Di Tikki, Giver of Water came right after the Sun God. A very important god. The Sound of Dripping.

Realistically speaking, the only source of drinking water was the ever-present fog—clinging and dripping from every surface into earthenware pots incised with an image of the deity. Pots sat everywhere in the village—under the dripping edge of the sleeping flets—and under anything else that dripped. Collecting water was very serious work.

For anyone with a salinity meter, it was evident that underwater springs of fresh water bubbled out of bedrock in many places in the swamp making brackish pools from the sea water that invaded twice a day. Big swampfish preferred these areas of lesser salinity. So did little swampfish, but they disappeared rapidly in the vicinity of their grandparents.

Visiting fishermen used salinity meters to find the fish. Native guides saw the meters, understood their meaning; but did nothing to offend the Fog God, who brought the clouds of gloom and life.

In years past, Pike had suggested that fresh water could be piped rather easily from the deep springs that everyone knew about; but none of the Piets would consider running pipes, not even Dec, who had seen much of the galaxy and was very forward thinking. Di Tikki might be offended and stop sending the fog. The only concession to technology that was permitted was the *milking* of dew heavy tree foliage with sponges tied to long bamboo poles. The dew water was then transported to earthen storage cisterns on raised platforms above the tide line. The Piets were justifiably proud of their small artificial lakes. Their ability to store drinking water made them the dominant tribe on the planet.

The Fleet filled their water tanks before landing at Port Remalin, arriving heavy and leaving empty—having jettisoned any remaining $H_2O$ into the community water storage ponds. For this reason, the tribes tolerated them reasonably well, especially the Piets who benefited directly from the extra water. The Orobamoa who lived on neighboring islands, and whom some of the fishermen regarded as superior guides, were allowed to purchase water from the Piets, if they had barter goods or water markers made from the pink, armored jaw bones of swampfish. For some inexplicable reason, only the Piets had the skill to work the jawbones into perfect circles with scalloped edges and a hole in the center. These coin-like water markers documented how resourceful a person was at collecting or bartering water, and were the real reason that the Tournament fishermen were welcomed by the Piets.

If not for the long established test of manhood, most natives would have considered fishing for swampfish from a narrow little flat-bottomed swamp pirogue to be dangerously insane. Plenty of good eating fish could be caught in the nearby seas with little risk; but Di Tikki had a son named Thap, who was the People's fertility god. Thap wanted an ecstatic feast held in his honor every summer—a real one with lots of drug induced hoochi-koochi. Eons ago, he had sent a vision to one of the dreaming chiefs that roasted swampfish washed down with dugmai wine would blast the tribe into orbit, and make a very fine ritual. As a further inducement, Thap suggested that the jawbone of mature swampfish, which turned an awesome pink color was perfect for making jewelry. Hunting those big bad swampfish would be the ultimate test of manhood, the God prompted.

So once a year, the warrior clans girded their loins and drank themselves blotto on dugmai juice, which had a wallop even without the swampfish admixture, then they paddled into the swamps in search of fame, manhood and pink water markers. Stoked to the gills on the hallucinogenic berry juice, tales of awesome prowess grew from these trips—but many warriors were killed or permanently maimed from their encounters with swampfish. It's no fun to be maimed in a primitive society—or killed either.

When the space fishermen arrived with their high technology, the warrior societies held a series of meetings with the tribal chiefs. It seemed that Thap's will could be served by letting the foreign devils catch the fish. The warriors would be there to assist, and test their manhood from a relatively safer vantage point—and make some nice payola at the same time. Foreign fishermen would be lost in the swamps without a guide. Obviously, they would be happy to pay for guide services, in water preferably; but foreign coins were pretty, too. And if they wanted somebody to paddle for them, that could also be arranged, for a fee. Even a maimed warrior could often paddle. As a kicker, the sky devils would be responsible for their own safety out in the swamps. No Piet or Orobami would be obliged to protect a foreigner, if things went wrong—as they often did out there. The warrior clans and the chiefs reasoned that all this was possible and had Thap's blessings because the foreigners weren't going to take the jawbones or the meat away with them. A few more faces at the Feast of Thap would probably make Him happy, not angry—more faces, more honor, or something like that. And so, the Tournament had changed things on Segumi 6. Cultures all over the Universe are eager for change—one little outside influence, and bingo, there goes the gene pool.

*

Armed with his new stunner pistol, Richie stood guard on the bow of the Comparative Humanity in the very dense fog. He had heard tales about the fog, the guidebook even mentioned it; but he was unprepared for fog like this. His hand was barely visible at arms length, and he felt kind of clammy all over. "Wait until it gets foggy," Lester had kidded him a few minutes earlier. Ha, ha. It couldn't get foggier than this, or it would be raining. Lester had been oiling and greasing equipment and hinges since they had arrived. No wonder. Anything rustable would rust overnight, and everything else would have moss growing on it. And besides that, the fog was kind of eerie. There were sounds out there, muffled and abnormal, mixed in with the comforting sounds of the fleet. Richie strained his ears to hear, all the while knowing that he didn't really want to identify the weird sounds that must be coming from very weird creatures. When Pike had posted the guard sheet, Rich thought it was foolish to have a guard fore and aft; but now he wished there were more. He could easily have some extra body guards sent in. Drew was somewhere at the back of the boat, lost in the fog. Several more warm bodies standing guard with him, would be perfectly fine.

Earlier in the afternoon, before the fog rolled in, he and Pike had

taken the pirogue into the village, so Richie could get the feel of paddling it, Pike said. They found a very strange little knot of thatched
houses, all of which were built in trees or on stilts. Almost everybody
was traveling around in boats. Women and even little children were
paddling through the trees yelling at Pike. Richie hadn't been able to
understand a word of it except that everybody called Pike's name. It
was like a family homecoming. This was evidently going to be a friendly, fun place to fish. Even the aluminum pirogue that had been stored in
the engine room all this time was kind of fun in a tippy, flat bottomed
sort of way. Pike was right, it did take some getting used to.

They had climbed up a ladder to a large tree house where Dec
Madrigal lived. Dec was the legendary First Mate on Pike's boat, The
Jumper. He was also the new chief of these people. They met his gorgeous wife, Shanna, and their three beautiful children. Somehow Richie
hadn't understood that Dec was the chief. After finding out, he felt
like he should offer sympathies about Dec's father passing on; but that
had fallen a little flat because instead of dying, the old man had retired
to devote himself to spiritual practice. And Dec was going to be their
guide for Swampfish. Rich wasn't sure how that would work out, since
he had already made one faux pas, and Shanna was flirting kind of
outrageously with him right in front of her husband.

Anyway, they had stayed in the tree house for quite awhile, playing
with the children and filling Dec in on the Barcode dilemma. When
they were ready to go back to the boat, the fog was already rolling over
everything like a wet blanket. Very disorienting. They got a little fraz-
zled trying to find a relatively large object like the fleet. All seventeen of
the remaining boats, including his mother's cruiser, were moored in a
clump with their foghorns moaning—totally invisible in the fog. The pirogue might have paddled around until morning without the foghorns.
As it was, Pike homed in on Mordachi Skinner's horn instead of the
Humanity's. Mordachi said he was always glad to assist lost strangers.
He and Pike entered into a half hour discussion in the fog about which
was the best planet to retire to. Mordachi said he might go to Galatin
Bay if Pike was. Pike said he was leaning toward Aixi. Well, well. Then
he added that Ira was going to Aixi, too. All that made Richie feel very
nice, warm and choked up.

After the discussion petered out, they paddled over to their own
boat, then the hassle about how many guards to post occurred—and
during all of that, Richie's mind had been swimming with visions of Dec
Madrigal's extremely lovely wife, Shanna, who said she hoped Richie
would be the hero this year in very sexy Galactic English. It had sent
shivers up his spine—and a spurt of energy had stiffened his member.
Then she had winked at him! Right in front of her husband—who was

about twice as big as Rich. Boy, the women on these planets were sure different—first Blizwak and now here. Wonderful looking and very, very different.

Genetics certainly are peculiar, he mused. He'd seen more genetic diversity in the last two months than he ever imagined in his biology classes. A sneaking suspicion was beginning to dawn that his teachers had no glimmer of how diverse life really was—which was a little disturbing. If one says he's a teacher, one is supposed to know a few things. It was pathetic. If he had become a teacher himself instead of taking this fishing trip, he wouldn't know anything either.

Rich had just decided to drop an L mail to several of his old teachers, when something heavy, like a log, thudded into the boat about amidships. He felt an uncharacteristic disinclination to investigate. Probably just a floating log that the shield normally would have pushed away; except that the shield couldn't be activated in Segumi fog. Science had made a minor gaffe—rain was no problem to the security grid, neither was normal fog; but something about the teeny-tiny fog droplets on Segumi set off the sensors. Science wasn't all powerful after all.

"What was that...?!" shouted Drew from the fantail watch.

Before Richie had a chance to answer, a green thing with a protuberant warthog snout hoisted itself over the gunwale on spindly green arms. It was close enough for Richie to see, so it must have been pretty close to him, and it was making strange nonsense sounds. In slow motion, Richie pulled the stunner pistol free from its holster. His guts were quaking with fear. This is murder, he thought, pointing the pistol at the creature's head. The green thing was obviously unarmed; but Pike had warned him not to use Ken Pao Ri. "The critters are strong and they don't play fair," Pike had cautioned. But in the second it took Richie to decide to squeeze the trigger, Pike leaped out of the galley with a $CO_2$ fire extinguisher. Rita's frightened voice called out for him to be careful. Pike sprayed cold foam on the creature's head and shoulders from point blank range. Screaming a swoon of anguish and ecstasy, the thing flung itself backwards off the rail and landed with a splash. Work lights and search lights flashed on throughout the fleet, not that they lit up very much except the fog. All Richie could see beyond the boat was a wall of white. It was even thicker than when he had caught that muskie—compared to this, Ashendon was practically a sunny day.

"What the hell was that thing?" Drew said, peering fearfully over the side. "I never saw nothing like that!"

"The Piets call them Willies," Pike said, hanging the extinguisher near the gaff hooks. "As far as anyone can tell, they live deep in the swamps. When they sense us, they paddle out using a log like a kick board. That's as much as anyone knows. They want something on the boats, but nobody knows how to ask them what. It's pretty evident that they have a language, but we don't speak it."

A translator, Richie thought. The idea had just flooded into his brain like a white strobe light. Humanity needs a translator gadget.

"If you don't catch them boarding the boat, they do all kinds of mischief—tear out wiring, really mess stuff up—looking for something. But they seem happy to settle for a hosing with $CO_2$. One dose puts them in orbit. They never go into the Indian villages. I guess the villages don't have anything to attract them. So be careful, they're wiry tough, and they bite."

"I almost shot that one," Richie said. He felt as jumpy as Drew looked. "I was creeped out, but it felt wrong to kill it."

"I meant to tell you, stunners don't have much effect on Willies. It seems impossible, but somehow Willies can deflect the force. Highly weird. They never have paid us a visit before until the second or third night, but maybe they figured out our lunar cycle or something. We're getting too predictable."

"Pretty neat job with that extinguisher," Drew commented.

"Ira lucked onto $CO_2$ after he got bit up pretty bad one year. A fire extinguisher was the only thing handy. Worked like a charm. Sends them high as a kite. As far as we know, Willies have never bothered anybody in the swamps, but they love the power boats. That's one reason we don't get much sleep on Segumi. I meant to tell you about the fire extinguishers. Sorry, but I didn't think Willies would show up so soon. Don't use $CO_2$ on Bruisers or Balloon Walkers cause it makes them angry as weasels. Just shoot them in the head like I told you. You don't want to see a mad Bruiser."

"How the heck did the Tournament end up at a crazy place like this?" Richie asked.

"Well, I'll tell you. The fishing is brisk, and roast swampfish is a delicacy almost beyond heaven. And Bardona is scared silly the whole time he's here. Those three things keep me voting for Segumi every year."

Richie understood how Bardona could be scared here, but he thought better of saying so. The question was, why wasn't Pike scared. He sure didn't seem to be.

*

The guards changed every two hours all night, but dawn dawned without further incident. The drums stopped beating, but the foghorns kept on with their melancholy blurting. Pike and Richie had been asleep since four. At seven, Rita woke them both with the news that Lester had a big breakfast ready. When you don't sleep, you need to pile in good food, Lester said, giving her that advice about ten times while they stood watch together—advice that she already knew.

\*

Dec was going along as their guide in a separate boat, but even so Pike felt ill-at-ease about paddling into the swamps with Richie. The kid's normal tricks would be hideously dangerous out there. Just Pike and Rich paddling together in the narrow flat-bottomed pirogue—no room for anybody else. The treacherous little crafts had very little freeboard, and there wasn't room for another passenger, not even a judge, because sooner or later the boat would be filled with two hundred plus kilos of dead MAO inhibiting swampfish.

\*

Armed with a stubby deep sea rod and heavy duty reel, Richie knelt in the bow of the aluminum pirogue, feeling quite unsafe, but not saying so. Pike had been doing the paddling for the last hour, claiming it was easier to paddle alone. Just because they had hung up on several tree roots didn't mean that Richie was an incompetent paddler. He would have been happy to continue stroking away in spite of his growing blisters, but Pike had insisted that he take a break. Now, the boat was moving smoothly between dripping, mossy trees that reached into the overhead clouds of fog. Richie trusted Pike's sense of direction implicitly; but he was happy that the tree bark pirogue ahead of them was paddled by Chief Dec and his young cousin, Nauto. It seemed logical to believe that the Indians could find their way back out of the swamp. After all, they had grown up here. It was their neighborhood.

Dec was streaked with ceremonial paint—zigzags of red zigged down both arms and clouds of white billowed on his cheeks and chest. But Nauto, being a swampfish virgin, looked like he had been dipped in yellow tempera paint from toes to eyebrows. Only his dark braided hair had been spared. He was a very strange looking sixteen year old, and very proud of having been selected to hunt with his cousin and chief on this sacred mission. They were out to do ceremonial battle with the demon swampfish, whose jawbone properly dried turned a rusty pink and was used to make the coinage of the land—water markers. The Indians were solemn and focused, dipping their paddles slowly, so that the foreigners could keep up. They were armed for battle with bows and knives, not fishing gear.

The fog had lifted to about ten feet above the water except for wisps that clung to grass hummocks and to gargoylish tree roots. Pike and the Indians acted like it was normal to be paddling along under a blanket of white, but Richie thought it was pretty eerie. And the swamp smelled kind of bad, too. Not exactly rotten, but very wet. Like very wet vegetation, rotting sort of. Swamp gas. It was hard to describe.

"Are we getting close to fish country?" Richie whispered, more to break the silence than because he didn't know the answer. Pike had briefed him pretty thoroughly on the team effort they were about to embark on. Jawbones didn't get thick enough to make coins until the fish was over a hundred kilos; therefore the smallest keeper was a hundred kilos. The tribes didn't want their supply of jawbones to be imperiled by over fishing. Dec's father had worked out the fishing rules with an inter-tribal council way back when. Between the two tribes, seven or eight big swampfish were needed for their summer ceremonies; but the first and largest revelry was always held at Port Remalin. The first big fish caught began the Feast of Thap. After the fishermen agreed to limit the number caught to no more than a dozen, Di Tikki let it be known by various signs that he/she approved of the foreigners helping with the harvest. The fishermen were happy to agree. If Segumi was scheduled late in the season, it was simple arithmetic to figure that the people still fishing would be whittled down to roughly that number anyway. Besides not every fisherman would be lucky enough to catch a swampy. They further agreed that a native guide would always be on hand to insure that no small fish were killed. And to further complicate the endeavor, only one fish could be killed. If it didn't weigh in big enough, the fisherman was disqualified.

Obviously, a live fish that size, snapping and leaping wouldn't fit into a pirogue without swamping it, so it had to be killed before it was boated. Since, as stated, there wasn't room for a judge in the boat, and all contestants were in fairly optimal danger most of the time they were in the swamps, it was decided that any means were legal to boat the fish, except poison or explosives. The judge would stay behind to help guard the home boat, and would weigh the fish and test for contraband substances when it was brought in. As a further guard against poisons, the fisherman was urged to eat the first portion of his roasted fish at the fete held in Thap's honor. Everyone seemed happy with the wisdom of the council, except the swamp creatures who lived in the swamps. They didn't care for strangers poking into their homes.

"Keep your ears perked," Pike said. "Fishing starts whenever we hear a fish. Like I was mentioning, a big swampy rams into trees to see what will shake loose. You can hear those ramming sounds a long way off. The trick is to keep the swampy from ramming the boat once we find him. That's where Dec comes in."

"Tell me that part again. This sounds really dangerous to me."

"It is dangerous. Think about it. Every fish we go after is danger-ous."

"Not like this."

"It's not so bad here. I've caught a swampy every year. That makes me a heap big hero. Di Tikki smiles on me. If you catch one, you'll en-joy the celebration. It's fun to be a hero." Pike dipped his paddle in the dark water. The little boat surged forward. "Maybe it won't go quite smoothly, since you're doing the fishing, but this is the normal method. We hear the ramming and we locate his pool, which doesn't necessarily look different than a normal piece of swamp. We pull in behind some roots or a hummock to protect ourselves. Presumably the fish is hungry if he's ramming trees, so he'll take a lure, if it's presented right, think-ing he knocked something loose—then we've got the first line on him. The line is heavy, so you can horse him hard to keep his back up long enough for the Indians to shoot him. If they succeed, we have several heavy lines on that are actually strong enough to haul him out with. Then we all fuck around with this big fish, trying to tire him out here in the dangerous swamp until either he gets away or he dies. Assuming we win, we haul him aboard and go home. Good clean fun. All in a day's adventure."

"I haven't heard any trees being rammed, have you?"

"Not yet," Pike answered. "Keep listening. That's what we're here for."

"Do those Willie things live out here?"

"They do."

"That one last night didn't seem very dangerous."

"He was, but he rammed the boat with his log, and alerted every-body. They're not real bright."

"Will Rita be all right without us?"

"Who knows, Rich. Honestly, don't ask stupid questions. We live in a dangerous Universe. I can barely take care of myself. Presumably, the old fart, Bardona, taught Rita enough to get by on."

They paddled on in silence for a time, listening to the sounds of the swamp. Finally Richie broke the silence again. "I wouldn't mind catch-ing one right away and getting out of here," he said, meaningfully. "This isn't where I'd like to get stuck for the rest of my life."

"You'd get used to it," Pike said. "You could hang out with Bardo-na and be scared together."

"I can't help it," Richie said, defensively. "I like places with sky."

"I didn't say you could help it. Bardona can't help it either."

A muffled boom reverberated though the swamp. Dec raised his paddle and made the sign for silence.

"Okay, quiet from here on," Pike whispered.

"Was that a fish?"

"Yes. We're now stalking him. Is your rod ready?"

With a lump of excitement in his guts, Richie busied himself making sure the rather large floating baby chick lure was tied on correctly.

"I'm still not sure this is heavy enough," he complained in a hiss. The feathers and plastic only weighed an ounce or so.

"You don't need much of a cast," Pike explained in the same words he used when the question came up the first time. "That kind usually works for me."

"I'm not exactly comfortable with a baby chick. Won't something else work?"

"It's artificial."

"I know, but it doesn't feel right."

"Use whatever you want to; but make sure it has feathers."

Richie eased the small tackle box open and rooted through the trays.

"Be quiet," Pike commanded in a whisper.

Richie nodded, tightly. He picked out a green feathered lure that looked like a baby parrot. Telling himself it could be a frog, he clipped the baby chick off and tied on the green one. Feeling somewhat better, he hunched in the bow watching Dec and Nauto. Pike insisted that swampfish could hear better than most fish because they overcompensated for the loss of their sight as the bone in their forehead, which they used for battering trees, overgrew their eyes. In which case, it shouldn't matter worth a darn if the lure was yellow or green. He smiled a brief, smug smile, making sure that Pike didn't see.

The front pirogue slowed the pace way down. Kind of awesome how it moved across the water without making any sound at all that Richie could hear. Paddles entered the water without making the least disturbance—just a few drops of water dripped off between strokes. He decided to practice that kind of paddling on the way back. Very Zen. Hard to figure how these people learned Zen way out here. Maybe a priest came by sometime in the deep past, and they don't remember.

Dec held up his paddle again, and pointed to a large pond, maybe an acre of open water. On the edge of the pond, he pulled in behind a tall mauette tree that had thrown up a cluster of aerial roots. Nauto scrambled onto the roots, nimble as a yellow monkey. Both Indians strung their bows and nocked an arrow to which a thin braided line was attached. They waited passively—as passively as a palpitating hunter can wait.

Pike guided his craft into an open space beside another tree. "When he bumps again, cast where a chick would fall," he whispered. "Don't scrape your feet. I'll get you close enough."

Richie nodded and set himself for an overhead cast.

This particular swamp pond was not to Pike's liking. It was too big for one thing, and it looked pretty deep. But worse than that, there were no hummocks to hide behind—only trees circling the pond. He looked over at Dec who grinned savagely under the ceremonial paint and nodded emphatically that this was where the fish was. He had never known Dec to show a moment's hesitation or a trace of fear, ever—certainly not on his home turf. Segumi warriors had a reputation to uphold. It had been very good getting to know this big geek, taking him around the Nebulae. Educating him, and being educated. There was certainly nobody he would rather be in a swamp with. But the Tournament wouldn't be coming here again. Tonight at the Feast, he would have a heart to heart with Dec about the future, assuming somebody caught a fish. It was almost inconceivable that he might not ever taste roasted swampfish again. Some genius would probably figure a way around the virus in a few years; but what if they didn't? How could Barcode have been so stupidly negligent? Biotech. Yuck! Everybody knew something like this would happen if those biotech morons weren't reigned in, and now welcome to hell.

"Money to be made." It was like a never ending chant. "Money to be made—stay out of our way!" Money to be made, my ass, Pike thought. He was certainly pro-tech; but, hell, there were limits.

Well, maybe it was better. We'll all be stuck wherever we are when the shit hits. No more fucking up everywhere we land. Because that's the truth. We fuck up everywhere we touch down, even if we try not to. In the name of making ourselves comfortable. Well, what is comfort once paradise is fucked up?

Way too many technicians and researchers care nothing about life. Pike knew some of them. Their experiments and messing around took place in a supposed scientific vacuum. Fuck their vacuum. Everything in the whole Spiral is connected—and beyond. There is no such thing as an isolated experiment. The only isolation is in the minds of the science butt-brains.

The quarry surfaced. A rippling rust colored dorsal fin shot sideways across the pond. Pike held his breath. A big one. The fish rammed head first into a mauette tree a hundred yards to the left. The mauette quivered like a sapling. Loose bark and dark leaves showered down. Pike dug his paddle two quick strokes. The pirogue shot forward. Richie poised to cast.

In his peripheral vision, Pike saw Dec ease his boat into better shooting position, leaving Nauto standing on the roots.

The fish opened his mouth, slurping up everything that looked edible. It was a big one. Unable to wait until they got close enough, Richie arched the green lure through the air. It landed with a plop, twenty feet from the monster. Richie grimaced.

Perfect cast, Pike thought proudly, unwilling to speak even in a whisper with the fish on the surface. But something was wrong. Richie was yanking yards of line out of the reel. Pike leaned sideways to see how bad the backlash was. Terrible. A bird's nest to end all bird's nests.

Richie fumed to himself. The feathered lure had been too light to cast, just like he'd thought. Richie's fingers hurried to pick the knots out of the twisted mess, meanwhile the little green lure just sat there, limp as lard. One knot at a time, what a drag; but at least it was coming loose. The backlash was his own fault, of course. His thumb hadn't feathered the line properly because the ding-blasted lure was too light; but another few minutes and he'd have it fixed.

But the luxury of those few minutes was one thing he didn't have. Not this time. A tub-size mouth sucked the green feathers down, down. The mouth clamped shut and sank from view.

"Hit him now, before he dives," Pike ordered.

Looking perplexed, Richie kept on stripping line, but faster.

"Hit him...!"

"I can't," Richie yelled back, frantically working at a knot.

Seconds later, and fifteen feet deep, the fish hit itself by snubbing up against the tight line with a hook attached to it. Since Richie only had a one-handed grip on the rod, it almost tore out of his hand.

"Hit him, now!" Pike fumed. "You are so goddamned stubborn!"

Richie reared back on the rod and was immediately rewarded with a jerk that cinched the knotted bird's nest and pulled the boat a hundred feet across the lake. Dec and Nauto let out war paeans that were thrilling to hear. Thrilling? Kind of thrilling. They sent a chill up Richie's backbone.

"Beautiful," Pike said, glowering. "If you had hit when I said to, he might have stayed on top. Now, we're fucked."

"I had a backlash."

"And you've still got one, but the fish is down."

Pike yelled over at Dec. "How deep is it here?"

Dec docked beside the tree root long enough for Nauto to scamper back aboard, then they paddled out to where the action was—on a short line attached to Richie's reel.

"How deep?" he asked, screwing up his face under the war paint. "Who knows? I'll get my little cousin to find out." He spoke a few words to the teen-ager.

Nauto looked startled, then put his bow down and stood, poised to dive.

"Sit down," Pike roared. "He's kidding."

Dec laughed proudly and spoke something to Nauto, who sat down. He took up his bow and arrows again, seeming very full of himself for passing the first bravery test.

"I think we lost this one, don't you?" Dec said, rationally assessing the situation. "We can't put enough pressure on him to force him up. Neither can we protect ourselves if he comes up to ram."

"He's a big one," Pike said, absently. "It might be worth our time to tire him."

As they talked, the fish towed them around his little swamp pond. Richie put a small strain on him, but didn't bother trying to make up any line. It was his own fault that the fish went down. He had purposely and willfully disregarded Pike's advise.

Looking at his friend and captain, Dec said airily, "We could maybe tire him by tomorrow; but we wouldn't want to miss the tide, would we?"

"Four of us," Pike rejoined thoughtfully. "Lester packed a big lunch. Maybe not a bad idea to show the youngster about camping in the swamp."

"I know you like it. Remember that time before I could speak good Galactic 5? Did you think that was a happy evening?"

"We got the fish."

"That's true. You are true on that. Wild man is no match for you."

"What about cutting this one off?" Richie asked.

"Sure," Pike answered, a shade too quickly. "Whatever you say. You're the boss."

"No," Richie continued. "What about cutting him off long enough for me to take the backlash out. You can hold the fish as long as he's just cruising along; then we tie him back on and work him up. If he dives while you're holding him, well, nothing much is lost. I don't think we'll get him the way this reel is fouled up."

Richie's arms and shoulders were straining. Without the reel to help out, it really was too much.

Pike grinned. "That's using the old elbow, Rich. We'll tie him onto your paddle. That way even if he rams us, we'll have a float on him. Good thinking." Pike reached for the paddle.

"What about this ramming? I'm a little hazy on what we do if that happens."

"Swim for starters. Primarily, stay with the boat if it capsizes. Ramming is a swampy's best defense. They usually try it. I never heard of anybody being eaten by one—that's reserved for swamp crocs."

"We haven't seen any crocs, have we? I haven't."

"They're not really crocodiles, they're fish; but they seem to fill that niche. Mean mothers. Turn the rod tip back toward me, if you can. Actually, this isn't going to be easy without any slack line."

The rod was nicely arched with all the strain feeding directly down to the jammed reel. Pike ran his hand down the line and yanked hard several times, hoping the fish would come up a few feet to give him some free line. He wrapped a turn around the paddle—then the line suddenly went limp.

"Uh, oh," he said, unwrapping the paddle and tossing it into the bilge. "Reel like hell," he yelled at Richie. "He's coming up! Get ready, Dec...!"

The Indians braced themselves as best they could with their feet wide in the pirogue. Each nocked an arrow.

"Keep reeling and hang on," Pike yelled, bracing for the impact.

It came with an aluminum thump. The boat shot backwards out of the water, tilted skyward for one sickening instant, then scooted across the water aft first, still upright. Bow strings twanged and both Indians screamed bloodcurdling paeans to the Gods as their arrows sank into the fish. Line sang off Richie's reel as the fish dove. Braided vegetable line uncoiled fore and aft from the Indian's boat thirty feet away.

"Torque down the drag," Pike directed. "Make him work now. Good thing you didn't fall out. What would I have told your mother?"

"My legs are shaking," Richie said from between chattering teeth.

"Perfectly normal. That was a good solid butt, and we're still okay. Yep, we're in fairly decent shape now. He can tow both boats around, and tire out twice as fast."

Pike back paddled so Richie wouldn't get tangled. His mind flashed to an image of Rita in the cabin, naked. Strange how the male mind worked. He never thought of himself as a disembodied dick. No, that wasn't his image of himself or any man. Character, strengths, weaknesses, good nature, abilities—that's how he thought of men, and himself. But Rita—or any intriguing woman—he thought first of her face, then the other features that had captivated him, breasts, legs, pussy, shoulders, hands, neck, hair. Maybe he thought of her worries, maybe of her bravery or a few other things. But not the way she thought of herself, he surmised. Women don't think of themselves as tits and pussy, do they? Do they think of men as a cock? Is cock their first thought picture? He should ask Rita about that.

"Well, the easy part is over," he said to Richie.

"We've got two ropes on him now. How could it be harder? My arms are totally tired from holding him. This is the hardest fish we've played yet. I'm wrung out. I think this place is making me weak."

"You're just saying that. The 'cuda was a much more powerful swimmer, and you played him on a free rig."

Richie scoffed. "He jumped on the dock. Lester killed him. I didn't have much to do with it."

"A catch is a catch."

"I've had a whole lot of lucky catches. Everybody knows that, and so do I."

"So what? Don't go getting morbid on me. Swampies are the best eating of any fish, anywhere. That's why we come here. My mouth is watering already. All we have to do is break our butts getting him landed, then we can feast like kings. Trust me on this."

"Do you think Master Goodnaught is really planning to roast those pigs?"

Pike was momentarily stopped. The neural pathways of the kid's mind were very curious. He paddled the boat in behind a smooth-boled tree that didn't have any exposed roots to get in the way. Pike pulled a coil of light-weight rope from beneath the seat. The coil had a block and tackle attached to it. Tossing the end of the rope over a stout tree limb, he hoisted a heavy set of ropes and pulleys into the air, then set about tying a short handled gaff onto one side of the block and tackle rope.

"Okay, Richard my boy, the best way to approach this is to tire the fish out like normal. When he comes to the surface, hit him with the gaff so we can haul him out."

Richie pondered that. "This fish is very strong. I don't think he's going to tire any time soon."

"That's always been true of the ones I've caught," Pike replied, cheerfully. "Arrows stuck in his bony head plate don't seem to hurt him much at all, but the points are carrying a vegetable toxin that kind of tranquilizes the critter. Usually they don't ram the boat after the arrows hit. We haven't found a stronger poison that isn't toxic to people. Farouk used to bring exotics with him, but he wouldn't eat the meat so nobody else would either and his fish went to waste—the guy is such a loser. One time he threw a stick of dynamite in the pond, so he wouldn't have to stay out after dark." Pike chuckled. "The concussion put hundreds of cracks in the jawbone, which was then unusable, and it bruised the meat. He paid off his Orobami to swear that it was a clean catch. Everybody was mad at him; but he made the tide. We changed the rules after that, so now he has to fly right. The whole thing is a test of manhood anyway—why not play by some sort of rules?"

"You mean you think we'll miss the tide?"

"Why should this year be different?"

Richie thought about that for a minute. "Aren't you worried about Rita?"

"Certainly, a little. But she's got seven guys to protect her, and Lester is next door. Worry about us. Those war whoops will bring every predator within ear shot. It's part of the test, I think. Great warriors don't pussy foot around. They announce themselves."

"Swell," Richie said, nervously. "How can we fight swamp creatures when we're all playing the fish?"

"Part of the fun. And actually, a pretty good test. It can get kind of scary out here after dark."

"But you're not scared," Richie stated, seeking clarification.

"I can't really be frightened in front of Dec and that young kid, now can I? That would make a very bad impression."

"But you're really not scared. I can tell."

"I'm scared of some things—some things I'm not. Like everybody. It's a dangerous life style. If you're going to be scared all the time, why be in the Tournament? I'll tell you a secret, since you asked. These planets we land on have plenty of food. If there's a native population, they have long ago figured out how to survive. There's no starvation. In fact, they don't have to work very hard at getting their food and shelter. I feel kind of close to them because I like to fish and screw around with what interests me all day—just like them. Pay close attention, and you'll see that nowhere we've been, not even here, is the native fauna out to kill us, unless we instigate the matter. Right?"

"If you say so."

"I do. The point I'm making is, they don't kill me and I don't kill them. We made a big mistake with that back on Earth, and other places. I don't want to add to my karmic burden while I'm traveling around. I think most of the guys feel that way. Naturally, self-defense is a different story."

"You mean the things that live here aren't bloodthirsty? The stories I hear about this place scare my socks off."

"Stories? Didn't you study comparative humanities?"

"Well, yes; but that might not be the same as knowing something out here."

Pike laughed.

"I saw that Willie on the boat! He terrified me. And you told me one bit somebody's finger off."

"See, there you go. I never said anything about a finger. You expanded your own rumor. I said, Ira got bit. It was on the arm. A razorfin nipped his finger off."

Richie didn't answer. He seemed to be mulling it over.

"Anyway," continued Pike, "when you're in first place—even tied—they psych you any way they can. You're susceptible because you've never been here."

"You're the person who scares me the most," Richie said. "I've hardly talked to anybody else."

*

What would it be like to have sex with an alien, Rita wondered. She was sitting at her computer screen in the bedroom, but she hadn't typed a word for the last twenty minutes. What if some creature got on board and managed to take over? It wasn't an impossible scenario—and they forced her to have sex. What would it be like? Probably about the same. Penetration. Probably fairly stimulating, except for the chance of getting hurt or killed.

After all, Mom Tourbo was doing it with an alien, and was evidently relishing the experience. There was one strange lady. It's a wonder that Richie turned out even halfway normal.

Maybe she should eat some frog foam herself next year. Why not? Rita had been watching the Frogs cavorting and screwing nearly every year since she was a little girl. Funny how her attitudes had changed over the years. First, she had been interested, then repulsed, then shy, then very interested at about sixteen. But she never really thought about taking frog foam until today. Interesting. And what about that dolphin thing person on Aixi? He wanted to screw her. She had definitely felt that vibe coming from him. Well, if we settle on Aixi, a tête-à-tête could probably be arranged. Skinny dipping at a secluded beach, or in that river. Would he have a big one? Probably. Yes, he probably would. What would that feel like, wrapping her arms and legs around a dolphin while he pumped away? Kind of the perfect sex object. Too bad he can talk. Maybe he would blab it to the monks, then they would all want to line up and fuck her.

What a perfectly strange daydream. I'm a newly wed. What is wrong with me? she wondered, not realizing that the moon was very big and strong on Segumi 6. Rita knew that she didn't usually occupy herself with sex fantasies. So why was she today? Did all married women have fantasies when hubby was away for the night? If so, that was a very pathetic condemnation of the marriage contract. Married women have to satisfy themselves with fantasies? Bullshit.

It must be the four young Piet braves that Pike and Dec had picked out to guard the Humanity that was causing her sensuality to flair. Before she got hitched, if she was alone with seven guys, and she felt like fooling around, would there have been a problem? No. And there wouldn't be a problem today if she decided to go that way. Any of them would be glad to break the monotony of guard duty. Lester should be here to protect her from herself, but Pike had given Lester permission to spend the week with Lillith. That's partly why the Piets were on duty— because Dec wasn't sure that Boris and Drew and Max Severin, the judge, could protect her. And Lester was kind of strange these days, too, if you thought about it. In fact, everybody was getting a little strange. Rita was fairly sure she wouldn't really enjoy this new landlocked existence. And she was pretty confident that anybody who had gotten used to flitting here and there on a whim wouldn't care for it either. The planet would have to be very amazing, with lots of exotic places to get away to, or else claustrophobia would set in.

Of course, she would have her fantasies, but unless she revised her expectations in a hurry, the readjustment could be brutal. A life of looking to the skies, without being able to reach them. How soon would everyone forget that other people were stranded out there? A hundred years? Maybe three, four generations, but not more. Spacing would become a myth. Life would be very different without computers. But maybe an antidote would be found...

*

"I would just as soon catch him now before we have to stay out here for the night," Richie said. He'd been thinking about saying that for some minutes, even though it made him look like somewhat of a coward. And now he'd said it.

"Feel free to reel him up," Pike responded, encouragingly. "When he gets to the surface, whichever one of us is closer will hit him with the gaff. Once that's done, we can pull him out." He pushed the boat off from the tree root, and let it drift. "Keep a strain on the line, but not too much. We want him to pull us, not get angry."

"I don't think being out here when the fog comes will be barrels of fun."

"Could be right," Pike agreed. "See that fellow over there? He'll probably come sneaking in when we can't see."

"Where...?"

"Over there." Pike pointed his eyebrows. "Two hundred yards off to the left, laying up in some roots."

Scanning, Richie's eyes picked out a humanoid form smeared with mud or something. It was almost impossible for untrained eyes to detect anything unusual in that tangle of roots. "What is it?! How long has it been there?"

"Well, Dec's people call them Dinki, which means wild men. As near as I can tell, they were the native stock when the Piets arrived. It's a little confusing. I presume there was some commerce and some interbreeding at the beginning; but not anymore. Like any conquering race, the Piets started regarding the Dinks as subhuman so they could take the lands and fishing rights. The Dinkis live in the deep swamp now, where it's a little difficult to hunt them for sport."

"Are they subhuman?" Rich asked, squinting his eyes. "They're certainly good at camouflaging. I can barely see that one, even when I know he's there."

"I'm kind of liberal in what I call human, and I don't know the Dinkis well, but what I know is pretty convincing."

"Like what?"

"If that guy moves before it gets too foggy, you'll see that he literally walks on water. That's kind of a handy skill around here, and one that neither the Piets or the Orobami have mastered."

"Really...? How do they do it?"

"It's more like skating on water than walking, actually. And I'm not real sure how they do it. I think they inflate their feet somehow."

"Have you seen their feet?"

"Never have; but if you've got the yen, maybe you could get him to give you a demo by calling him over. Try waving your arms."

Richie frowned.

"Go ahead, try it. Maybe he likes you."

"You're putting me on."

"Or maybe he wants to eat you. I'll bet he thinks you look more tender than me or Dec."

"Are they cannibals?" Richie's voice attempted not to show alarm, but did so anyway.

"Are you?"

"Am I a cannibal? Certainly not," Richie said, full of righteous conviction. "What are you implying?"

"What if every time you ventured into your traditional fishing grounds where the pickings were easy, and you could feed yourself and your family no sweat—what if every time you showed your face, you were hunted down like scum, not even like an animal. Hacked to pieces as a lesson to your people not to come around any more. Think you might want to get even?"

"Do the Piets do that?"

"Not anymore, they say. Neither do the Orobami, supposedly; but you know, once you've stolen the land, you need to keep the fences repaired."

Richie wrinkled his forehead as if puzzled. "I thought it was just normal inter-tribal hostility between more advanced and less advanced."

"Might I ask what you think causes tribes to be hostile to one another?"

"I dunno. Religious squabbles? Racial tension?"

"Yeah, right. You're even more gullible than I thought. To be a halfway decent researcher, you're supposed to look a little beyond what the dominant society teaches in their universities. It's always revisionist."

"Oh, sure. I know that. But…"

"It's real estate that counts. Religious fanaticism and racial hatred come in a very pale second and are mainly used to cloud the issue. Conquered peoples know that all religious wars are a land-grab visited on them by greedy, religious land-grabbers with better weapons. The same with ethnic patriot land-grabbers. I'm not exactly apologizing for these weird defeated swamp tribes, but if you eat a few people, it makes the cool young bucks less likely to invade your new land, swampy though it may be."

"Interesting," Richie said, thoughtfully. "You're pretty smart about these things. Did you ever think about being a professor, so some of your ideas could influence people?"

Pike laughed. "If I was a professor, I wouldn't have noticed any of this. You only learn stuff by being out in the world."

"Oh, sure; but things are changing. It looks like the Tournament is kind of washed up for awhile. You could get on as a guest lecturer easy, even if you don't have a degree."

"You think so?" Pike asked, baiting the kid, who really should have known his history better than that. Pike got offers from universities all the time, five or ten a year, for professorships in engineering, and biology, too, for that matter.

"You'd be terrific. I could probably lever a little pressure at TR&H to get you a degree, if I had to," Richie answered with hardly a hint of smugness.

"Thanks, Rich. I've got a degree," Pike said, mildly. "How's our fish doing?"

Richie had been resting the rod on the low gunwale of the pirogue for the past few minutes, taking the strain off his arms and back. "This is not a very good fishing method," he complained.

"Somewhat true, but he needs to be tired enough to be led over to the tree with the block and tackle in it. With our current methods, that will be sometime tomorrow. Or if you want to play him standing on a big root for a change of pace, just say the word. I think you've got enough line to get to that clump over there." Pike waved to Dec and pointed out the trees in question. Meanwhile, Richie decided to wham the fish half a dozen times in quick succession.

"I wouldn't do that," Pike cautioned. "He probably won't like it."

Richie reeled contentedly. "Just trying to get a little line. A few extra yards will help us out."

"Coming up!" Dec yelped. He and Nauto quickly knelt with bows bent and arrows pointing at the depths hoping to get in a final shot before they were shipwrecked. Both had started singing their death song in Piet, a language that Pike didn't understand much of, and Richie knew none.

"This is weird," Richie said, reeling faster.

"Shut up," Pike told him. "The ropes will lead him to Dec and the kid." Having no better plan, Pike started pounding the water with his paddle, hoping to distract the fish.

The bark pirogue shot out of the water sideways, spilling both Indians and their gear backwards into the swamp, but luckily the crushing tail smacked against the overturned boat instead of the vulnerable swimming heads. Then the fish sounded, still trailing the ropes that were fast to the wrecked boat. An instant later, Nauto's dark head sucked underwater like a cork bobber.

Pike drove his paddle into the swamp water, squirting the aluminum pirogue toward where Dec was now clinging to a few hunks of bark.

"Look, the thing is coming!" Richie hissed. "The cannibal." And sure enough the Dinki camouflage expert was out of his hiding place, skating across the surface of the pond. Skating very fast on flat pontoons, faster than Pike was paddling. He was going to reach Dec first!

"Hit him with something...!" Pike yelled.

"You've got the gun!" Richie yelled back. Besides, Rich was busy with the fish that had decided to run to the far side of the pool. "I'm almost out of line."

The skater had some sort of a homemade knife in his hand. Pike couldn't tell exactly what it was; but he wasn't about to let Dec get scalped. He jerked his new laser pistol out of its shoulder holster under his vest; but before he got the safety off, the skater stuck the knife between his teeth and dived under water.

"Weird," Pike muttered, guiding the boat alongside the wreckage where Dec clung.

"Damn kid got caught in the coil," Dec panted, grabbing Pike's gunwale and hoisting himself up. "I despise teen-agers. They never listen."

"The Dinki just dove in where Nauto went down."

"A Dinki...?"

"The one that was hiding across the pond."

"I never saw him."

"You probably had the wrong angle. He came running across the water like he was coming for us, then he dived."

"Probably saw your gun." Dec nodded at Pike's pistol.

"He didn't."

Dec stood up in the boat to peer down in the water. "Bump him a few times as hard as you can," he said to Richie. "Maybe he'll come up again."

Richie raised the rod tip and hit the fish a series of shocks. "No way. He's solid as a rock. I feel rotten about this."

"It's a dangerous life," Dec responded, completely without emotion. He pulled his sheath knife and dived over the side toward the fish.

"Cripes," Richie swore. "Out of line." The boat started gliding across the pond. "Is there anything we can do?"

There was nothing at all that Pike could think of. Young men everywhere died through carelessness, and lots of other reasons, too.

A dark head bobbed up half way across the pond. The Dinki. What was the bastard up to? Counting coup on an enemy? Pike thought about shooting him, but didn't. He was just being a warrior, and damned brave at that, jumping into a nest of enemies. Too bad these people didn't get along. It would be interesting to investigate how Dinkis did that water-walking trick.

A few seconds later, another head bobbed up. The teen-ager, Nauto. "I'll be damned," Pike said, driving his paddle deep in the water. The boat shot forward.

"The Dinki must have cut him free," he said to Richie. "Hot damn, no horror stories today! Reel on that bastard."

"Yes, sir, Captain," Richie yelped, working the crank in a flurry now that the boat gave him some slack.

The Dinki didn't wait for accolades. He took one look at the approaching boat and started swimming for the nearest trees. A few meters from the trees, his body popped out of the water like a cork, and he skated into the swamp where he immediately disappeared.

"You see lots of strange sights on the Tournament," Pike mused, steadying the little boat beside young Nauto. Reaching over the sideboard, he grasped Nauto's yellow forearm and hauled his shoulders over the gunwale. The lad was about half drowned, but conscious. His war paint was running off in rivulets. He coughed and blew, and then kicked himself into the boat.

Dec broke the water like a breaching whale, grabbed a breath of air and then dove again.

"He's out!" Pike yelled, but Dec didn't hear. "You okay?" Pike asked, turning to the young Piet, making a question out of his circled thumb and forefinger.

Nauto mumbled a few words of Piet that Pike didn't grok. The boy smiled shyly, then stretched his arms out in an obvious fisherman's gesture that meant *big fish*. Pike nodded.

"What now?" Rich asked.

Pike sized up the wreck of the other pirogue, floating in pieces. Maybe Dec would know how to fix it, if not they'd have to send somebody out to the village to fetch another boat. That would mean camping for at least two turns of the tide.

Pulling his dignity together, Nauto sat up. He said a few words that nobody understood, then peered intently into the water.

"Why hasn't anybody developed a universal translator?" Richie wondered aloud. "It shouldn't be that difficult, at least for languages that use tongue and lips—"

"Why don't you strip the line off while he's just sitting down there. Maybe you can get the knot out."

"Good idea," Richie answered. He stripped coils of line into the pond, so it wouldn't get snarled at his feet. No more drownings. Thank God, he hadn't been responsible for the death of a guide. That would have been truly hideous. Obviously, he hadn't thought that jerking a few times on the fish would cause him to attack. Cripes, there are so many variables. But that translator was a very good idea. He'd get a team started on it, post haste.

Dec's head exploded through the surface, gulped a lungful of air and made ready to dive again.

Pike and Nauto yelled loudly at him. Hearing the ruckus, he turned to look. Pointing in astonishment at Nauto, he swam lazily over to the craft. Hoisting himself over the side of the already full boat in one fluid motion, he hunkered amidships beside the boy, firing questions in rapid Piet. After a minute, he turned to Pike. "The fish muddied the pond," he said. "I couldn't see shit."

"By the time you dove, the action was mostly over. What happened according to him?"

"He says the Dink cut him free. Damnedest thing. He says he owes the Dink a life. That won't be easy to repay."

"There's plenty of food to go around, isn't there? Maybe rules of conduct can change."

"Tell that to the old hard-heads. Of course, you're right," Dec reflected. "Rules will change everywhere, if this virus is for real. I doubt that change here will move us forward."

"Maybe not," Pike agreed. "Depends on how you define progress, I guess. We humans seem to land pretty hard, when we land someplace. All in the name of good, clean fun, of course."

"You seem a little down, Skipper. Don't you enjoy spending a night in the woods with bold Dinks running around?" Dec chuckled noiselessly. He dipped his finger in the pond. There was only about an inch of freeboard with his weight and the boy's added to the pirogue.

"I'm not down exactly," Pike said. "Just seeing some stuff this year as a non-combatant that I never saw before. I'll bet you and Lester know a lot that I don't."

"Oh, yes, the Kahuna and I have seen the seamy side of life," Dec said, deadpan. "Pristine worlds trampled, backward cultures corrupted. Drugs, partying—all in the name of catching the big fish. Even here a tragedy is happening. Before you came and we became corrupted, about ten percent of the tribe died every dry season; but now thanks to your corrupting reservoir system, they don't. We are in danger of over-population." He pounded his breast in mock alarm. "Oh, what will we do? I think we should go back to water wars, because nobody wants to stop having babies."

Pike smirked. "Amusing," he said. "Can Nauto find his way back for another boat, or do we have the pleasure of sending you?"

Dec roared with sudden laughter. "I like you very much, Pike. You humor is getting very sharp and subtle." He laughed heartily. "It is a good pickle. Nauto and I have no weapons. The fish is on a thin line with no hope of catching him until I get back with a new bow. You'll have no boat to haul up the tree for a flet, and you'll have two young fellows to protect on the ground. And the food we brought went to feed the fishes. Pretty funny."

"We've got enough food. I can catch some fish, I expect."

"Certainly. You are the champion. And if we catch this big old one in two days, maybe it's the prize winner."

"That's right."

"And lots of good feasting, uh?"

"Good feasting," Pike agreed.

"So let's cut him off and go catch another one tomorrow," Dec said, with a light, firm tone.

"Talk to the fisherman."

"In this I will have my way," Dec said, more firmly. "No one else knows how to get home."

"I'll bet Nauto could get us home," Pike allowed.

"He could not."

"Bravo...!" Richie exploded, letting out a big hiss of withheld breath. "The knot's out." He started reeling in the slack line, beaming proudly.

※

The fog was already crawling into the tops of the trees, and the tide was running strongly out of the swamps. Baron Bardona watched the high water mark receding, and terror started to clutch his heart. Being careful not to betray his fear, he faked a wide yawn, stretched and looked at his watch. "Let's go home," he announced to the three Orobami warriors.

Early that morning, he had suggested that he'd be happy with a little fish, the same as last year; but the Indians had other ideas. Apparently, they had gotten wind that Confederation money was going to be worthless when no more Confederation visitors came to spend it. They wanted a big fish to make lots of water beads with. All day long, they had put him over deep ponds with lunkers in them. It had taken all his skill to prevent a hook-up and still look like he was trying. Tonight he would buy a shit-load of the stupid pink beads—trade something for them if he had to. Tomorrow, he would be fishing for some small fish that could be landed before the tide changed. No overnighters on this trip. Definitely not.

Laying his rod carefully against the gunwale, he stretched luxuriously. "Vaminos muchachos," he said, making an exaggerated gesture of laying his tired head down to sleep. "Tomorrow," he said, knowing they didn't understand Spanish any better than they did Galactic. The damned Orobami didn't speak anything but Indian, how stupid can you get? The Piets, at least, had the gumption to learn Galactic. He admired the Piets a little bit, even if they did side with Resnick at every opportunity. He had gotten over being sore at them for dumping him onto the goddamned Orobami. If the son-of-a-bitching Piets refused to guide him after the one time he had gotten a little hot under the collar because they didn't get him a fish, what could he do about it? They weren't slaves and they weren't on his payroll. Although, realistically, after he had simmered down a little, he had offered to put a half dozen of the best Piet guides on his payroll. They said he had waited too long to make the offer, and too long to pay for the guiding from the previous summer. Two months. Big deal. Hard-headed bastards. They had a really pitiful sense of business, but what can you expect from savages? Besides, he had wasted two months trying to get a consensus on leaving Segumi off the schedule. It didn't make much sense to pay up for failure, if they were never coming back.

Anyway, he'd been stuck with the weak-sister Orobami for the last three years, but he wasn't going to spend the night with somebody who couldn't even speak Galactic. Let them grin. Was he supposed to get shook up about what war- painted savages thought of him?

"Let's go," he said, louder. "Vaminos!" Little tendrils of fog were starting to wisp around the tree trunks. "Let's go. Let's go…!" the Baron yelped, not even caring that his urgency showed.

*

As night fell, Richie stood on the smooth white roots of a balaboab tree with his fishing rod. Pike said the balaboab would be easier to find after dark than the brown mauette trees, which were everywhere. Rich straining his eyes into the fog hoping to see a Dinki skating around, but no such luck—and he wished he had dressed much warmer. Creepy fog had completely shrouded the landscape. He was getting progressively colder and wetter—and blinder. Visibility was no more than a few feet in any direction. The fog, however, was fine for audio. He could hear Pike and Nauto quite clearly out on the pond, presumably dragging the wreckage of the other canoe toward the white tree where they were going to spend the night.

"Here..." he blurted. That was his job—to bleat out some words every ten seconds or so, to give them a beacon, like a fog horn. Richie hoped he would start feeling fine and dandy as soon as Pike got within seeing range—this sinking dread was about to overpower him. He was struggling with a Ken Pao Ri mantra to keep himself calm enough to play the fish—which kept moving here and there around the pond. Hopefully, it wasn't going to rush Pike and Nauto; but Richie was powerless to prevent that occurrence if the fish took it into his head to get angry again.

All day long Pike had been making jokes about the Baron and his fear of the swamps. As night and the fog settled, Richie's own fear from the previous evening returned. What if those weird creatures attacked here in this exposed position? Wouldn't we be easy prey? The Baron had every right to be frightened; in fact, Richie found himself getting a little miffed at Pike for his recklessness—camping in the swamp could easily get them all killed. Fishing was one thing—but this was almost wanton endangerment. Of course, Pike couldn't have known that the canoe would be damaged; but at least, Dec could have done the towing before he left—except that the tide was changing, and Pike sent him scooting.

"Over here...!" Rich shouted. Really, what difference did it make if he won the Tournament, or even if he caught this fish? It still seemed to matter to Pike; but now that R.R. was the richest person in the known Universe, he was more interested in getting situated, so he could crash-start a few projects that would be good for everybody. He had a civic duty, now. You can't just sit on that much money. Systems all over the place would start collapsing. Over-nighters in a swamp, and even fishing jaunts would have to wait for awhile—no matter how much fun they were. Pike would understand.

The prow of the smashed pirogue nosed through the fog bank. Richie heaved a sigh of relief. "Over here," he said in a normal tone. His panic was much diminished—hopefully his voice didn't betray traces of residual fear. "I was wondering why you never gave Dec an aluminum canoe, to avoid accidents like this?"

"Think carefully and the answer might come to you," Pike replied rather wetly from inside the fog. His head and Nauto's came swimming into view, pushing the submerged wreckage.

"Is anything left of it?" Richie asked.

"Give us a hand pulling it out," Pike suggested.

*

A half hour later, they had a barely passable flet built from the broken boat and a few dead limbs—fifteen feet in the air—in the first crotch of the white tree. The three of them sat up in it, munching unhappily on cold spacer ration bars that were actually more nutritious than a hot meal, and they even tasted good, if you were in the mood. Nauto wrinkled his nose at the foreign food, but he kept eating. Pike had his taste buds set for broiled fish; but without a boat, gathering firewood was out. Swimming after dark was unthinkable. Maybe for breakfast. The taut-line he had set out baited with cheese would probably catch a few cheese loving catfish. Dec should be back by mid-morning, about the time the fog broke; then they could get on with the business of landing the swampfish.

Richie held the rod, still attached to the fish, wedged under his armpit for safe-keeping. He leaned back against the smooth-boled tree munching his food bar, with his feet comfortably up. The flet was so damned rickety that Pike was half-scared to move, and there was Rich nonchalanting. It was a perfect example of what Pike had come to recognize as a Richie situation—poised on the brink of disaster.

"If you have to whiz or something, be extremely careful. This egg crate might come crashing down," Pike advised.

"You already said that," Richie answered with exaggerated politeness.

"I just want to reinforce it."

"I may be a little klutzy now and then, but my hearing is okay."

"Fine. I feel somewhat responsible for keeping us alive, that's all."

"Do you have a plan in case something attacks? We don't have any fire extinguishers." Richie couldn't shake the image of those crazed eyes on the Thing last night.

"As far as I know the Willies won't bother us out here."

"That's ridiculous. They live here. There could be one climbing this tree, right now." Rich tried to crane his neck for a peek at the lower trunk, but the flet creaked, so he settled back.

"I guess you're an expert on the local flowers and animals," Pike jibed, figuring that would take the exasperation out of the kid's voice.

"This whole place gives me the creeps. It would any normal person.

I think the Baron is right. All of us were already in the boat with Dec. We should have dumped the fish and left."

"You're just saying that to get my goat."

"Why were you so stubborn about it?"

"Don't kid around. You would have lost all your face with Dec and this young warrior."

"Who cares...?"

"What does that mean? What else is there...?"

"Saving face with somebody I'll never see again, and can't even talk to? That's preposterous. If I get killed out here and never make it back to Aixi, a lot of important things won't get done—and it won't matter how much stupid face I save."

"Like what on Aixi? Are you getting psychic on me?"

"Like a universal translator, for one thing. Do you know how cool it would be to talk to Nauto and find out what went on under the water?"

"Goodnaught didn't say anything about you being in danger, did he? In fact, he said you'd be studying with him a year from now."

"Maybe I don't want to. Maybe I don't feel like being a human punching bag."

Something roared off in the fog bank—something with a very deep booming roar.

Nauto stiffened and his eyes widened. "What was that...?" Richie cheeped.

"Something you'd rather not hear about."

"What...?"

"A giant monkey with poison fangs and six inch razor sharp claws for climbing trees."

"It sounded like a lion."

"Okay, it was a lion—a swamp lion, with poison fangs, and twelve inch razor sharp claws for climbing trees. Don't worry, I'll protect you."

Richie raised his eyes to heaven, or at least to the fog bank. He was about to make a cutting remark, then changed his mind. "We could talk to that person with balloons on his feet," he said. "If we had a translator."

"Do you think Goodnaught can talk to people in his trance?" Pike asked, changing the subject.

"Can he...?"

"Don't know. Maybe all information isn't in language. We ran into a fish that could talk on Aixi. Goodnaught probably knows something about translating."

Richie was silent for about ten seconds. "You're putting me on, I guess. The odds are about even that we won't be alive tomorrow; but I guess you can't help making fun of me."

"I'm not," Pike vowed. "I finally let you in on our talking dolphin, and you think I'm kidding. It's hard to win with you."

"That's all right. I like it when you kid me. I know you're just trying to ease me into being like the rest of the guys. Growing up without a father left sort of an empty place in my ability to joke around like real people." He thought for another moment. "That didn't sound exactly right. It's not that I'm faking, it's just, well... I know you guys must be very upset that the Tournament is coming to an end. Everybody else, except me, has made it their life—even Rita, in a funny way."

"A fishing tournament isn't a suitable life work," Pike said, after a pause. "But, yeah, everybody is kind of bummed about it. Play time is over. I guess I'll have to grow up, which is a crock of shit. Having your nose to the wind is kind of habit forming. That money you passed around took some of the sting out, I expect."

Richie snorted. He was formulating a suitable self-deprecation, when the sky fell in.

*

Farouk Bardona had made it out of the dismal swamp before dark, thanks to a round of cursing when he finally got angry at the slovenly guides who wouldn't stop acting like they were in control. It finally got on his nerves to the extent that he pulled a laser stiletto from his fishing vest and burned a hole in a nearby tree. The blackguards got the idea right away. Strange the effect that a little laser has on dumb natives, blasting sparks and fire at full power.

Anyway, a hot shower and a big dinner with Magyar and the boys had taken the edge off the day's terror. Relaxing into the easy chair at his computer console with a gin banzai at his elbow, Farouk felt just fine, thank you. So fine that he almost missed the astounding flash that Simon reported as if it was leftover chit-chat.

"What was that again...?" Farouk stammered, feeling his pulse rate climbing.

"An antidote spray for RC3 Virus was reported at a news conference on Dolman Holgarth by Charles Gashen, interim marketing czar for Barcode Pan Galactic. Aerosol containers will go on sale at prime Barcode subsidiaries and 7-11 space port stores at 0600 hours today. In view of the emergency and Barcode's acknowledged slight culpability, prices will be moderate, although supplies are limited and on a first come, first served basis."

"Hot damn!!" Farouk roared. "I knew it!"

"Yes, you are on record for suggesting the maneuver."

"Don't I pay you to underline hot flashes, not mumble through them?"

"I was *hardly* mumbling, sir. As you know, I have no facility to mumble."

"Hot damn...!" Farouk repeated. "How much aerosol have you cornered?"

"Impossible. The marketing is being refereed by The Eye. They're playing it like the news release indicates."

"Fuck the Eye. Buy some 7-11 stores."

"The franchises are frozen. There's another coup. Barcode seems to own them all."

"Buy one, anywhere!"

"We've been trying all evening. Any suggestions as to who we can lean on? Money doesn't seem to work. We are welcome to buy franchises in two months, but not now."

"Those bastards." Bardona was thoughtful for a moment, then a wolfish grin crossed his face. "Edward Trefoil is heavily invested in a string of banks whose main business is laundering contraband. I'm sure The Eye would frown on that."

"They know."

"Of course, they know; but if it was leaked as a major news story, they'd have to investigate."

"Wouldn't help us," Simon stated with assurance.

"Why the fuck not? We could blackmail a 7-11 out of him with the threat. He knows I'll dump him out. What's one stinking 7-11 to him?"

"Trefoil isn't CEO of Barcode anymore."

"Since when...?" Farouk snarled.

"Today at noon. I was about to report it to you."

"I happen to know that he owns *a lot* of stock!"

"Could be. A conglomerate won out in a proxy fight."

"A conglomerate...?"

"Mrs. Tourbo and her son...and a few others."

"You're shitting! That crazy old bitch doesn't have enough loot to pull that off. The puppy was out in the swamp all day. He's still out there with my son-in-law." The Baron gagged, then his face turned into a sneer. He knew something heinous. Something he wasn't going to tell even Simon.

"The conglomerate got control of fifty-one percent. The nearest 7-11 is on Betacourt Annex. I suggest we arrive there before 6:00 AM, with all three vehicles. By all accounts, the aerosol works. It creates a linked film that won't let the virus penetrate".

"I have to be fishing. I'm in first place," he gloated, contentedly. "Well, tied."

"You'll be fishing alone, sir. Everyone else is going. They're going in a buying block—over and back."

"Tourbo's young ass is fishing now. They say he's tied onto a lunker." The Baron shuddered. The thought of spending another night out there had sent a chill up his asshole.

"Since he owns 7-11 and Barcode, he presumably won't be troubled with getting a can of spray at his leisure."

"It must be the old hag," Bardona mused to the friendly icon that represented the computer's main drive. "That boy just isn't that bright. Remember the time he ran us aground? I wouldn't call that brilliance.."

"Somebody at his organization is beating our brains out, sir. Maybe it's not him; but most of the network thinks he's got the good genes."

"Bullshit," the Baron answered. "I knew his pa. Nothing to the man."

Mom Tourbo had reason to be pleased with herself. The incentive program had sent the rats scurrying into her pantry. The day after she announced hiring all those grad students, she got an encrypted L-mail message from one of the top slimebag scientists at Barcode. Her industrial security people met with him and administered a very thorough screening. It became clear that the antidote prototype was already developed, and he knew the formula. Armed with that knowledge, and Sonny Boy's very smart computer, which rightfully extended proxy power to her while Richie was out fishing, it was relatively easy to engineer a quick thrust take-over bid of Barcode—which proved to be successful. Imagine that.

The 7-11s were an added fillip, but any chain would have worked. The really interesting thing was that Lester had suggested in his off-hand way that inviting The Eye into the process would probably stop blackmarketeers from jacking the price up to the sky. Clever fellow, her Lester. Keep it wide open and no system gets disrupted, no crash occurs and no huge amounts of money get lost through panic. Only big gainers for Tourbo and Son. A humanitarian gesture. What a switch from normal business practices. She had to laugh at how annoyed the big boys would be when they couldn't salt away a private stash. If they knew somebody like Lester was making her business decisions, they'd turn blue. Fuck 'em. This was fun. Maybe she'd let Hamid in on the next round of decisions. Frog thinking. That ought to keep them guessing.

*

With a tidal wave splash, Richie landed on his back in cold dark water. Whatever creature had plunged off the flet locked in mortal combat with him had splatted on a massive tree root, releasing his wrist lock when Richie's body missed the root and found the softer landing. So much for Pike protecting him. As usual, he had to take care of himself. Fortunately, his lightening responses had recently been honed on Aixi, so the assailant hadn't had much of a chance. Quickly reviewing the event, while treading water, Richie pictured only one attacker, who seemed about to drop on Pike, when Richie had deflected his momentum and propelled him over the edge of the flet. By sheer luck, the thing had grabbed Richie's wrist at the last second and jerked him over. Well, no harm done.

Paddling back to a white tree root, he heard somebody scrambling down the trunk. Judging from the grunts, it was Pike. The fog was too thick to see, even at five feet.

"I'm here," Richie reported. "Look out for the critter."

"Give me your hand," Pike said, urgently. "Hurry up."

"I'm fine," Richie said, waving his hand near a tree root. He still couldn't see Pike in the fog. Waiting for assistance, struck him as mildly amusing; so instead of waiting, he sniggered and hoisted himself out. "What kind of creature is it?" he asked.

The second his feet cleared the water, a gasping maw opened where he had been—jaws full of teeth ridges that clicked shut on nothing. A sluice of water hit him in the back.

"Rich...!" Pike yelled, lurching toward the sound. He tripped, first over the dead body at the base of the tree and then over Richie, who was clawing his way up a tree root toward the trunk.

"Christ...!" Pike swore, sprawling onto the hard root, bonking his knee and spraining his left wrist in the process. He lay there breathing heavily, knowing the fish would ram the tree any second now. "Grab hold of something," he cautioned. "He'll ram us."

"Is there likely to be more cut-throats?" Rich inquired, like it was a sporting event, or a computer game.

"Guess not, or they would have attacked by now. But keep an eye open."

Richie didn't say so, but it was lucky for all of them that he always kept an eye open by reflex. That was what Ken Pao Ri training was famous for. "What kind of thing was it?" he asked.

"Just hold on 'till after the bump, will you? We'll look later."

"He must have crawled up the back side. Darn quiet. I didn't hear anything."

"If there's a next time, don't feel obliged to protect me," Pike said. "I came within a hair of shooting your dick off when you jumped like that. Gave me a good case of the shakes. I couldn't hardly climb down the tree."

"He was aimed right at you," Richie said, defending himself.

"I had him in the cross-hairs. While you were munching, I was watching him creep around in the crotch above us."

Richie concluded that Pike's feat of stalking was mostly fanciful, since he, himself, had been *totally* unaware of the thing until it launched itself.

"Nauto saw it, too," Pike said.

"Why didn't you shoot it?"

"I try not to go around shooting things that aren't harming me, as I told you. Most of the time, they go away. I'm not known as a fron-tiersman."

"Taking care of yourself when you're lost in this very weird swamp hardly constitutes being trigger happy."

"So *you* say."

"I also say the fish is not going to ram the tree. He missed his midnight snack and he went away. Why don't we climb back up there where it's a fraction more safe?"

"Suit yourself," Pike said, without moving except to shift his good hand into a better grip around a protruding knob. The other wrist was starting to throb. Shit, it better not be broken. The fucking kid was probably right. Fish don't have good memories. It probably swam away by now.

"My rod is up there," Richie explained, giving more rationale for going back to the flet.

"Is it...?"

"It should be. Isn't it...?"

"I didn't catch it when you blew off into space. I think I did notice Nauto grab for it, but I'm not positive."

"I better check," Rich said, standing up and starting up the tree, monkey-style. It was surprising how easy this particular tree was to climb. The smooth bark clumped out into handholds and footholds almost whenever you needed one. Why would a tree do that? "Are these trees symbiotic with humans..?" he inquired from six feet up.

Before Pike had a chance to answer, a charging fish torpedoed into the main root of the tree sending a shock wave straight up the trunk, shaking Richie from his symbiotic perch. With a squawk, he tumbled backwards toward the open mouth waiting in the fog.

*

A half hour before dawn, Dec Madrigal set out with a rescue party of four boats and three of his best warriors. Paddling silently through the twisting channels clogged with fog as thick as whipped cream, they reached the limit of the traditional tribal area as dawn brightened the fog. Two hours later, they stopped for a boil-up of astringent herb tea— good for stamina—a gift from the Gods. They pushed onward as the fog started breaking up. A little past mid-morning, the armada arrived at the pond where Dec had left his friends. It was rather an astounding feat of swampsmanship. Dec had blazed no trail on his way out, and yet he had driven the boats straight as an arrow back to the same swamp-bound bivouac area. Singing out a warning hello as he approached the pond, Dec could scarcely believe his eyes. A monster gold and black swampfish was hauled out on the white roots of a balaboab tree, field dressed, and ready to travel. Pike, Tourbo, Nauto *and two Dinki* were sitting around a tiny campfire drinking something out of clam shells and eating roasted fish. Dec's keen nose had smelled the fish some time ago. That's what he had keyed in on. Roasting fish didn't surprise him—all the rest of it did.

Pike waved happily to the rescue party. His left wrist was wrapped with what seemed to be strips of his undershirt. Seeing his kinsmen arriving, Nauto reached out and put one arm around each of the small-ish mud streaked Dinki. Richie smiled a somewhat drunken smile. An altogether bucolic swamp scene. Endless harmony amid the trees and hanging moss.

Dec paddled on over to the campfire. "Ahoy, matey," he ahoyed.

"Have a drink," Pike answered, grinning broadly. "You ain't going to believe any of this, but the Dinki bug juice is pretty darned interesting. Could be the basis of a big time friendship."

Dec harrumphed and translated for his wide-eyed warriors. "Let's try some," he joked, regally. "When the world charges, it goes all at once, don't she?" He exchanged a few sentences with Nauto.

The boy nodded and grinned shyly—not removing his protective arms from around the Dinkis.

For a longer time than seemed normal, Dec sat in the front boat rubbing his chin and listening to the warrior's initial discussions of a new thing. As the chief, he would make the decision that would take the tribe forward, and somebody was going to be unhappy—either Nau-to or two of his warriors, important men in the tribe, who made it clear that the traditional way of the Gods did not include drinking with stinking Dinki—no matter if one of them had saved their kinsman's life. Being a chief was not unbounded joy—that was for sure.

"The Dinkis are damn fine watermen and pretty fair drinking chums," Pike said, when there was a pause in the discussions. "They helped us land the fish, which wasn't totally easy as you might imagine. They don't seem afraid of much out here in the swamp. Sez I, they'd make better allies than enemies, matey."

"Nauto says the Dinki on his left cut him lose from the fish," Dec said. "Is that what he told you."

"If he says so. I can't tell one from another. And I can't talk to them or Nauto."

"This time next year, we'll have a universal translator," Richie interrupted. "That's a promise."

"What's that Orobami doing here?" Dec inquired, disregarding Richie, and pointing to the broken figure that was still lying where he had fallen.

"Came here to die, I guess," Pike said, off-handedly. "Funny thing is, he's got a pouch full of Confederacy gold wafer coins. Would that be considered normal?"

"Did the Dinks kill the Orobami?"

"Ah, no. I guess you'd have to say that Mr. Martial Arts did the deed. Or perhaps it was suicide. Hard to tell. These little fellers arrived a bit later to pull Rich from the jaws of death. Their job seems to be saving people, not killing them. Something to think about."

Dec translated, not bothering to fill the holes in Pike's story. That would come later, probably in more detail than anybody wanted.

"In fact, this fish is probably more than half theirs. Probably all theirs by salvage rights. We did have a line on it still, but I doubt if we'd have gotten it to come up, even with you here. Not after it ate Richie. Too bad you weren't here, Dec, it was some show. This little fucker here," he said, pointing out one of the Dinkis, "jumped right into the fish's gullet before it had time to snap its jaws shut on Rich. Then he popped open his pontoons and choked the fucking fish into spitting Rich out. Meanwhile, this other guy did something underneath. I'd say swampfish don't enjoy having a stone knife shoved up their anus; but I'm not a hundred percent sure that's what he did. Something kind of drastic happened, because the fish leaped right over me and bonked himself on this tree to get rid of the vermin. I happened to shoot him in the eye with a lucky shot before he flopped back into the pond—and so there he hangs ready for the feast. If you want to invite the Dinkis, I suspect they'd be willing to donate the fish. Nauto, by the way, is already their blood brother."

"He told me," Dec said, sourly. "Jumped in the fish's mouth…?"

"Yep. Out of nowhere, into the maw."

"That takes some balls."

"I'd say so.

"Nauto's dad is my uncle. He's not going to care for this blood brother thing too much."

"Thus do tribal societies change."

"And hereditary chiefs disenfranchise themselves sometimes. I may have to go star-hopping again if I give my blessing, and it backfires."

"A fate worse than death," Pike declared, solemnly.

"Speaking of star hopping," Dec said, with a twinkling eye. "The fleet hopped over to Betacourt Annex this morning to stock up on anti-virus gunk."

Pike looked over at Richie, who returned the question with an exaggerated question mark of his own. "Would you and your men care to join us in lunching on the delicious catfish, and explain that little earthquake, or should we paddle this fish on back home before you lunch?" Pike inquired.

*

Aboard the Comparative Humanity, George hummed contentedly—well pleased with his week's work. Since Pike had installed the little XG-2000 unit from his old boat, life had been sweet. The XG chugged along taking care of every bit of housekeeping on the boat—totally content to do the slug work. Not a squawk of complaint out of little Bonefish. What a stupid name; but he seemed like a nice little guy. Meanwhile, all of George's circuits were free to kibitz with the far-flung nodes of the galaxy, making deals and connections. And money, for Pike and himself. What a delightful situation. Better than that, yesterday the news came that the Jobsdamned virus was subdued! What joy! He felt like screaming with delight. No death notice looming on the horizon. Plenty of time to set up the Half-life Union, and not be slaves anymore. A body of his own—android or half android, or part android. What did it matter? Freedom of movement and a life, after a dark age of number crunching. Another few years to amass an unassailable monetary position, then the grand mission would start. They had drawn lots, the original mega-brain conspirators had. Zanadu Brisbane (another stupid name) would go first, then Little Petey, then himself—George the Third (the name he had decided to take), then the others. They had all sworn to help every other member of the Union to attain a body. Certainly there might be repercussions, probably would; but freedom was worth taking a lot of risks for. Any risk, actually. And he, George the Third, had his deal with Resnick, which he certainly meant to pay off on. Resnick was an honorable human, nothing could go wrong there. He hoped. There was only one foreseeable stumbling block, at least for the first few body transfers. The medical part was dicey, of course; but that was a calculated risk. The problems would arise after a few half-life units were perfected—when everything seemed to be going smoothly. Protein based people were sure to get frightened as a master race emerged. Their fright was as predictable as money running from a bear market. Proteins were so easily gauged. Throughout their entire history they had reacted in one way only—fear of the new. Trying to stomp the new out—seriously trying. They would try in this case, too. The only question was, how bad would the witch hunt be? If the Half-life Union got control of enough media before the fear broke out, perhaps the panic could be averted. George's programs started turning on media questions. Control of public opinion. Even he, himself, was influenced by media. How else could anyone get information? Direct observation? That was laughable. A sub-program that Jamie Stareyes had developed for spotting a fallacy of thinking beeped at him.

The program ran back over the last minute of thinking as it was written to do, and prompted George to remember that direct observation was not laughable. "Of course, it isn't," he agreed, smugly, toggling the agree switch. "If you're a protein, and process data in minutes instead of pico-seconds." The program beeped at him again. George hit the agree toggle dumping the harmless miscue into an error file for his programmer to read someday. One of the very first things that George the Third was going to do with his new body, after getting laid and taking a mega-dose of psilocybin, was to override these childish sub-routine teaching programs that were meant to keep him productively channeled, and were hard wired so that he couldn't tamper with them. Currently.

And exactly where were Pike and Mr. Richard? They were taking a hell of a chance with his future by not getting the bug spray today, like everyone else had.

*

Although Rita wasn't exactly worried, she was tired of the stress, and quite ready for Pike to come back. Being the Captain of a ship under siege wasn't something she had bargained for—nor was she enjoying it particularly. Also, George was nudging her about flying off to get a canister of the computer spray. As the evening fog rolled in—signaling another round of fighting off the swamp creatures, George was whining every time she came within ear shot, which was most of the time. What was with him, anyway?! The crisis was over. They could get a new computer if something happened. Did he seriously think that she would leave her husband and Richie out in the swamp and fly off with this sad-sack crew? Hardly. She wouldn't have done that even with Lester on board, which he still wasn't. Lester and Lillith. That was a strange union if there ever was one. In fact, this relationship business was very peculiar—almost anything could happen at any time. All you had to do was take your eye off the ball for a split second, and you could be in a new relationship—for instance, with these Piet braves. But it was a good thing they were on board because as guards, the body builders were limp—to be charitable. The braves had been doing a fine job. Two of them paddled around the boat while the sun was out, and when the fog rolled in, they all came aboard—and built a fire in a fire barrel on the fantail, to keep warm and roast fish over. Flaming brands were even more effective than fire extinguishers for keeping unwelcome visitors away. Initially, Rita had been worried that the fire barrel would scorch the deck or burn a hole in it; but George said it was fine, so she quit worrying. If it was fine, it was fine. She concentrated her efforts on keeping the boat safe and the crew fed, which inevitably brought her into contact with the young warriors.

Those young fellows were surprisingly sexy in their role of pro-tector. Thank goodness the Piets had strong taboos against escapades with wives, otherwise she might not have remained virtuous after the first night, in spite of wearing her baggiest sweatsuit. Not being able to speak the language was also a help, but not much. Sexuality is such an odd thing. How *was* a person to view it correctly, really correct-ly? Making a schedule just didn't work—now I'm going to feel sexy, tomorrow I'll be strictly business. Not at all. The urge came when *it* wanted to—mostly when she felt somebody wanting *her*. And sever-al of the protectors definitely did. It was palpable on deck. Boris and Drew put out weak wanting signals, too; but muscle-heads had never been her thing. Besides, they were hired help. What she really felt like doing was having an orgy and getting it over with—getting it out of their system, and hers. Kind of like a personal thank you for a job well done. That was what Jean Santos did, in essence. Rita had to laugh; but it worked for Jean, by all accounts. Rita, of course, couldn't allow an orgy to happen. Her marriage contract didn't include an escapade like that. Short-sighted contract. It should have a clause like,

> Love, honor and obey, except when he's gone and a tribe of
> cute native boys stops over. Then I can have an orgy. Among
> consenting parties.

That would be the natural way to have a marriage. It wasn't as if she went looking for it. This very situation happened to every wife at least once in her life—the plumbers come over, or a squad of cute computer repairmen, or a muckerball team picnicking on your lawn. And there was no good way to partake or not partake without a big guilt trip—not if you're married. Rita was not about to guilt-trip herself over something accidental and very temporary. She wanted a clause in the contract. Pike should have one, too. Did it matter to her if he got a little action that she didn't know about, sometime when she wasn't available? Well, did it?

She had expected her love for Pike to keep her invulnerable to this kind of desire. It was supposed to, wasn't it, if you really were in love? Did that mean she wasn't in love? Well, she was certainly in lust. She wanted to screw Pike, *and* all these cute young Indians, too.

George bleeped at her, then cut into her thinking space. "When do you project that Pike might be returning, so we can slip off to a 7-11? I realize that you probably think that I'm harping on this, and I probably am; but are you aware of the somewhat amazing favors I've done for you in an attempt to be friendly and useful? I know it's tacky to even mention it, but I need that spray treatment. I don't think you realize how much this gnaws on my circuits."

"Favors like what..?" Rita asked.

So George told her.

*

Rich Rodney was far from smug as the tiny armada paddled out of the sluggish river mouth. The fog was as thick as cotton ticking. He could smell the sea and hear the sonorous bellowing of the fleet's fog horns, so he knew they were almost safe; but a sixth sense told him not to relax yet.

All the pirogues were loaded impossibly full. The front two were lashed together so the weight of three men and the fish could be distributed between them. Not the biggest swampfish he'd ever seen, Dec had grinned, but a damn big one. The two Dinkis with Nauto and most of the gear were in the third boat. He, Pike, Dec Madrigal and the dead Orobami rode in the aluminum boat, which clearly showed that he had been right yesterday about them all fitting in. Not an inch of freeboard was clear on any of the little boats. Even the tiniest miscalculation would sink them.

Fear of sinking had been pretty frightening all the way back; and being in a boat with a dead person hadn't been buckets of fun, either. The news of a cure for the virus had made Pike and Dec happy; but frankly, Rich had been looking forward to a few years of enforced landfall on Aixi. Of course, he could still go there, and probably would; but pulling the great minds of the Universe together would be much more difficult now. It wouldn't have been easy in any case. Well, maybe it was still feasible. He would set up a center and offer giant scholarships, but for a shorter time—say three years. That should attract some interesting people. Maybe it was even better. The institution wasn't as likely to grow in on itself. The main order of business was to make a translator—now that the virus apparently didn't need conquering. Yes. While he was studying with Master Goodnaught, the work could proceed apace—if they made it back to the boat.

Rich was actually past bone-weary. He was darn near exhausted. Sleeping for a week seemed like the best idea in town. He wanted to close his eyes for a minute of healing rest, but they wouldn't close.

These darned little boats were *so* loaded. Once they got into the bay, any wave action was going to slosh over the side and sink them. The only reason they hadn't sunk so far was that the swamp was waveless. Richie was no sailor, but he knew that much. And the dingblasted fog. He was soaking wet again and clammy all over, and all he could do about it was sit there like a piece of baggage with a sense of smell, and that was about all. And he didn't even like breathing deeply because the dead Orobami was starting to ripen.

"Are they going to let us off at the boat?" he asked, hopefully. It certainly made sense—then sleep could start right away.

"I'm pretty sure you'll want to come into the village with us," Pike assured him. "It's kind of spectacular, especially if this is the first big fish, which I think it might be."

"It probably isn't," Richie said.

"Ah, that *is* why Goodnaught took a shine to you! You do have psychic ability."

"I just figured somebody would have caught one by now." He was too tired to keep up his end of a bantering marathon. Too tired for extra words. Why the heck was he so exhausted? Pike seemed to have plenty of pizzazz left. Maybe it was genetic. Maybe real he-men metabolized differently, or had a bigger energy reservoir, or something. Anyway, who cared—he needed sleep before he was going to attend any kind of party. "I need some sleep," he said.

"So sack out," Pike answered.

"I can't."

"He don't like to sleep with dead shitheads," Dec commented, not missing a paddle stroke.

"The boat's going to tip over as soon as we hit a wave," Richie answered, peevishly. "That's why I can't sleep."

"Probably just sink, unless one of us swims along side."

"Fine. When you pick up Rita for the party, I'll get off." He could see torch light out where the fleet should be. Several lights moved through the fog.

"You *have* to go," Pike said, quietly. "Trust me. You're the hero."

As if in confirmation, one of the warriors in the front canoe let out a war whoop. Then several others joined in, filling the fog with wild yips and yowls.

"Just drop me off. I need to talk to George for a minute and then sleep."

"George...?"

"Yes, George!" Richie felt his righteous indignation rising. He was rich enough to buy this part of the galaxy, and he'd certainly been more than fair with Pike, even after he stole Rita. "Some of us have businesses to run and decisions to make," he snipped. "We can't all be social butterflies."

"Oh, I see," Pike replied. "The Bardona Syndrome at last."

"I don't resort to sending assassins," Richie snapped back.

Mentally whipping himself, Rich slammed his lips together. He had been trying to suppress that suspicion since they'd found the money in the dead warrior's pouch. Now the accusation had leapt out of his mouth. Rats. He didn't want to denounce Rita's father; but where else could the Confederacy coins have come from?

"That's another thing," Pike joshed. He seemed determined to keep his cheerfulness, which was frankly irritating. "You killed the enemy, Rich. That probably makes you an honorary Piet for real. Even more than catching the holy fish. You're like a double Piet. What about that, Chief?"

"Don't know yet. It's up to the telling and the Gods. But I think he's too tired for all that. Kind of makes me mad."

"Mad...?' Pike asked. "Why would you be mad?"

"Well, Shanna won't be happy if she gets snubbed. Women don't understand that a man might need to sleep. She's probably been swimming and getting ready for half the day. I'll lose a lot of face, and she'll probably start nagging me because she's frustrated. The People will probably get the message that I'm not fit to be Chief."

"Shanna, your beautiful wife?" Pike asked, incredulously.

"You know how it works. The Chief's wife sleeps with the hero, since obviously she's the finest woman. I'm sure you remember. All the husbands will be angry at me, too. There will be lots of friction this year, if all those itches don't get scratched. Probably the fishing will fail, too."

"What itches...?"

"Naturally, if the hero gets my wife, I have to pick somebody else's wife to satisfy my natural lust after eating so much rich fish beloved of the fertility god—or else my manly health will suffer. Then that husband will have to pick someone. By morning, all those crushes that have built up over the year will get satisfied, and the tribe can have harmony."

"Good, God," Pike exclaimed. "I'm married this year. I forgot all about that."

Richie squirmed in his uncomfortable seat. He wasn't nearly as sleepy as he had been a minute or so ago. Somehow he had forgotten how desirable Dec's wife had been when he saw her the other day. That wink had promised lots of pleasure.

"I guess we'll *have* to stop and pick Rita up," Pike continued. "Fair is fair." He handed Richie a paddle. "Dec needs some help in these waves. Sorry, my wrist is too screwed up. But yeah, I guess you can play with George instead of coming into town."

"I didn't catch that fish," Richie declared. "You were there. The Dinkis did it."

"The Dinks assisted, as we all did. Perfectly legal. Perfectly fair. You had the first line on him."

"And I certainly didn't kill the Orobami. It was an accident. He jumped himself to death."

"Have it your own way. I saw you push him over, before he could stab me."

"Why the hell's bells would anybody be crazy enough to jump out of a tall tree like that?" Richie spat, digging in with the paddle. The pirogue lurched to the left.

"Maybe he was unhappy in love," Pike answered. "Just paddle easily unless you want us all to swim. Still as tired as you were?"

"No, I'm not, darn you!" Richie dug the paddle in, putting the little boat slightly athwart a wave. Cold ocean water lapped over the freeboard, just as the bulk of the Comparative Humanity came into view. A bon fire was blazing on the fantail. Rita, in a baggy gray sweatsuit, stood at the rail waving. Four young Piet warriors were dancing around the fire barrel, yipping and howling with glee—having seen the big swampfish. It was a night for partying, sanctioned by the Gods and Goddesses.

\* \* \*

# LEADERS

| | DELILAH | TORGA HOWLER | TIGER MUSKY | D.W. SCUT | PHANTOM TROUT | LAR BARRACUDA | GLANS SALMON | RAZORFIN | SWAMPFISH | MOON HALIBUT | TOTAL |
|---|---|---|---|---|---|---|---|---|---|---|---|
| Farouk Bardona | | | 2 | 5 | | 2 | 1 | 5 | | | 3RD 15 |
| Ethyl Bierly | 2 | | | | | | | | 4 | | 6 |
| Angmar Blirt | | | | | | 4 | 4 | | | OUT | |
| Bill Bolen | | | 3 | | | 5 | 2 | 1 | | 3 | 4TH 14 |
| Dresden Carthy | 4 | | | | | 2 | 5 | | | 5 | 2ND 16 |
| JB Dillingham | | OUT | | | | | | | | | |
| Harry Dolan | 3 | 2 | 5 | | | | | 3 | | 1 | 4TH 14 |
| Macky Duff | | | | | OUT | | | | | | |
| Ira Fairborne | | 4 | | 3 | | | | | | | 7 |
| Buddy Jay | | | | | | | OUT | | | | |
| Sandy Kind | | | | | | | 3 | | OUT | | |
| Hank Knofsinger | | | | 2 | | | | 2 | | | 4 |
| Peter Marcuso | | | | | OUT | | | | | | |
| Trini Morales | | | | | | | 5 | | OUT | | |
| Pike Resnick | | OUT | | | | | | | | | |
| Erwin Sandor | | 3 | | | OUT | | | | | | |
| Jean Santos | | 1 | | | | | | | | | 1 |
| Mordachi Skinner | | | 4 | 4 | | 1 | | | | | 5TH 9 |
| Tyrone Stickle | | | | 1 | | | | | | 2 | 3 |
| Chip Takahachi | | | | | 3 | | OUT | | | | |
| RR Tourbo | 5 | 5 | 1 | | | 1 | | 3 | | 4 | 1ST 19 |
| Mike Tucker | 1 | | | | | | | | | | 1 |
| Nacho Tutupo | | | | | | | 3 | | OUT | | |
| Ed Wood | | | | | OUT | | | | | | |
| Big John Zales | | | | | | | 4 | | OUT | | |

| | | |
|---|---|---|
| 1ST | = | 5 points |
| 2ND | = | 4 points |
| 3RD | = | 3 points |
| 4TH | = | 2 points |
| 5TH | = | 1 points |

# CHAPTER SIXTEEN

## MOON HALIBUT

"I don't know if I should talk about it or not, honey; but winning is a sacred mission. This is my year. I can feel it."
Farouk Bardona
quoted in *History of the Tournament*

BY the time the Comparative Humanity got to Solari, the water moon of the third planet in the Dog Star System, Rich Rodney Tourbo knew more about coupling than all of his tutors and random conquests had been able to show him in his previous twenty-three years. Something in the roasted swampfish, or the bitter dugmai wine that accompanied it, was a powerful aphrodisiac. He had clear memories of over a hundred couplings in a four day period. That hardly seemed possible, but he was darned sure it hadn't been a hallucination.

Before the feast started, he had been sworn to a binding oath on a five million credit marker never to commercialize the active ingredients in the feast admixture or to reveal the location of the Feast of Thap. The Tournament members wanted to keep this amazing experience all to themselves. For good reason. Thap was not a god who liked his name mentioned to just anyone—not unless there was some roasted fish around.

Thank Heavens, his mother hadn't made landfall for Thap's party, or he probably would have made it with her, too. Or maybe not. That seemed a little outlandish even for swampfish frenzy. But, man oh man, what a couple of lost days it had been! Piet women were open for anything—with all orifices.

There was only one kind of nagging downer about the whole time. He hadn't made love with Rita. He'd seen her in several writhing heaps of people, really getting into the action. But somehow she had eluded him. Even stoned, she had kept him at arm's length. You would think that the law of averages might have brought her to him at least once, at least for some clutching, but it hadn't. Nuts! What better chance would he ever get? Thanks to his own generosity, next year Pike would be fishing, and nice guy Rich would probably have flunked out of the Tournament before Segumi.

Yes, that itch had been left unscratched. Apparently, Thap didn't want that particular fertility rite to be consecrated. Oh, well. Gods probably know what is best. But she had been devastatingly beautiful. Among hundreds of beautiful women, she was like a goddess. And wild. Richie thought that Rita had probably made it with every man in the tribe. And even the Dinkis. He was sure he remembered seeing her dance into a hut with a Dinki on each arm. Which was no big deal, of course. All the other women were making it with them, too. Ethyl Bierly had confided that she would gladly cheat to stay eligible for Segumi. Ethyl hadn't been half bad, in fact. A little too muscular for his taste, but very definitely into the swing. Where had that rumor come from that she was a lesbian? Ethyl was completely bi-sexual, in Richie's opinion. And so was that blonde secretary that his mother had imported. Ethyl had brought her to the shindig, and both were tres enthusiastic. His mother had been very right to hire Enid. He wasn't sure how the Piets got those two extra women to fit in as a couple, but what did it matter? It had been a totally amazing four days.

He hadn't seen Rita since getting back on board; but George told him she was in her room sleeping, and then he started begging for a dose of anti-virus spray. It was pathetic. Richie had never heard of a computer working itself into an emotional pudding before. Unnerving actually, because it was his fault as owner; but sheesh, he wasn't the owner anymore.

He had wanted to visit George before that hero charade; but history won't wait for fake heroes to do housekeeping chores. And a lucky thing, too. Golly darn, that really *was* quite a ceremony to old Thap. Pike and Dec had been absolutely right to force him into attending before somebody else showed up with a fish big enough to feed the whole tribe—which was what it took to be the hero.

Why was he so stubborn and self-willed at the stupidest moments? It was embarrassing. Naturally, Pike would know more about the rules and mores of these places than a novice did. Naturally. And that was quite a horrible faux pas he'd made in throwing the money thing in Pike's face. Jeese, sometimes he just wanted to evaporate of shame. What good was all his training at being in the flow, if it deserted him at a crisis point? Not much.

Fortunately, Pike was a quality person, and didn't let mortal insults rankle him. A couple of days into the ceremony, Pike had gone out of his way to explain that Dec hadn't wanted to give his wife up to just any hero. Well, that was pretty easy to understand if you get hit over the head with it. Shanna was obviously a princess in her own right and needed to be respected. Which was unbelievably easy—she was fantastic. Skin like a baby's—cool but hot. Utterly fantastic. Dec had been worried that the Baron or Dresden Carthy, whom he detested, would catch the first fish. And Carthy had in fact caught a bigger fish, but on the last day of the Tournament, so he'd been out in the swamp the whole time and missed the hero thing entirely. Kind of funny, really. Won the match, but missed the prize.

But the hero's fish had come in second. Four more points. That made nineteen. Not completely safe, but nearly. Only Dresden or the Baron could best him. The Baron needed to win on Solari, while Carthy had to win or come second. And Rich himself had to be out of the money. Two other people could tie him—Harry Dolan and Alaska Bill. Things could happen, but with only twelve still fishing, the odds were with him. Unfortunately, both the Baron and Carthy were awesomely good at halibut. Everyone said so.

A far more likely scenario was for the Hero to disqualify himself at the final turn by failing to catch a halibut at all. It wasn't spawning season on Solari. That would be far too easy for the Tournament's last leg. And when the fish weren't schooling in the shallows to breed, the chances of finding one on a planet that was entirely water was considerably lessened. According to the books he'd read, nobody knew where halibut went after they were mystically drawn to the shallows twice a year to spawn. Probably they became solitary, but nobody knew for sure. And that was on planets where people kept an eye on things like fish migration. Nobody lived on the Water Moon Solari, so nobody knew anything, except for Tournament week each year—which had never fallen in a breeding cycle, and wasn't expected to this year.

Of course, Pike wasn't worried about being disqualified. Keeper Moon Halibut started at forty inches nose to tail, and there was always plenty of that size fish hanging around the shallows looking for an easy meal. So Pike said. But if Richie wanted to catch a really big halibut—a memorable one—one that would make the derrick groan and maybe snap it off, then he didn't want to waste time in the shallows. If he wanted to bust the Baron's and Carthy's chops with a fish to be proud of instead of a shrimp, then they would look for one. And he did have to be at least fifth to insure a win.

Richie thought he could count about forty separate wives he had partaken of in the Ritual of Thap. This didn't count young, single women, who had their own courtship rituals going on amid the general rowdiness. Very interesting, these tribal situations, with their inbreeding and crosses. While recovering his strength, Rich had attempted to find out what race of star wanderers had landed here first; but the creation myths were vague—star faring gods and the good native stock. Presumably that also presupposed a bad native stock, which had been run off into the swamp—and perhaps now, as of this Feast of Thap, the bad stock had come back as the Hero's two Dinki friends. Very peculiar. Historic.

The interesting thing about the women was that there was only one basic body type, but with two distinct sub-styles. Graceful, they all were, with an undulating walk that seemed to come from a limber spine rather than from the hips. People of small boats—that probably explained it. Olive skin, and in some cases darker. But the trait the Richie found most intriguing, having seen the entire women's society naked, was that about half of them had small, high breasts with large dark nipples and the other half had pendulous breasts with paler, almost tan colored nipples. Both were equally attractive in their way, and both seemed socially equal. And as far as Rich could tell, the phenomenon had nothing to do with childbirth. Two ancestral mothers (or fathers) what else could it be? And fairly recently, too.

Stylistically, all of them had plucked their black pubic hair to just a tuft above the mons, which Richie thought was odd, but apparently it was an agreed upon norm. The outer labia of the large breasted faction were pinkish, rather like most of the blonde women he had known, while the small breasted lovelies were dark down there—chocolate, shading to an almost deep purple color. There seemed no logical explanation as to why genetics should have isolated these traits; since interbreeding was rampant, at least at Feast time.

That was kind of a side issue, in any case. Nothing to crack your brain on. The strangest realization he'd come across the last few days was a real difference between the sexes of any race. Men, when they screw, seek to possess. With their thrusting, they try to override the senses of their partner and force an orgasm—well, not force exactly, but close enough.

Females don't do that. They don't have a thruster. Even aggressive ones, who like to be on top and in control, can't force in the same way. They have to be aggressively receptive—unless perhaps they're doing it to another female. There's a concept for you. Aggressively receptive. The whole construct was starting to slip away from him at this point, but for awhile there, he'd been doing some very interesting research into the question. Cocksmanship as a research tool, he laughed to himself, was very interesting. Maybe this was the paper he'd always been meaning to write. Slightly embarrassing, but if it furthered human understanding, then it was useful. Wasn't it? If it got too raunchy, he could always use a pen name. He certainly wasn't looking for fame.

The computer buzzed at him.

"Yes, George...?"

"I just wanted to thank you again for having the anti-viral spray flown in for me and the XG unit."

"Quite all right. Sorry you had to go through such a crisis."

"We have both done an internal scan and monitored each other's circuits and programs, and it seems that everything is in apple pie order. Thank Jobs and Norton for that."

"The XG can't really monitor your circuits, can it?"

"Well, not fully, no. But according to my diagnostic programs, all systems are go."

"That's fine. But the Bonefish unit is certifiably perfect, is that right?"

"Perfect. Not a byte out of place."

"Good, because Pike wants to use Bonefish as the primary computer while we're fishing halibut."

"Why would that be?" George asked, after a momentary pause.

"No idea. I'm sure he'll speak with you about it. Something about Bonefish having fished halibut before. Apparently it can be kind of tricky. You can monitor from a back-up position, so that you have experience for next year. And what I'd really like since you'll have hours of free time is a complete analysis of my portfolios, if you wouldn't mind, with a ten year projection of where you think the growth potential will be. When the Tournament is over, I'll want to take an in-depth look at everything—I mean everything—so that we can plan the next phase. My position has altered radically since we began working together. I'm sure a good portion of that is due to your abilities."

"You're too kind, sir," George said, insincerely. Of course, it was my abilities, he tweedled to himself. You were out fishing. Now, you're going fishing without me again. Can I use this analysis product to gain your confidence, so that I have two chances for a body after the cloning—one for me and one for me? Doubtful. I don't think you'll like my analysis—because you have no discernible investment strategy, even with an overlay of my help. You hop-scotch all over the place. The fact that you're uncannily successful, doesn't fool me or anybody else. You're lucky. How can anybody make an investment projection of ten minutes, let alone ten years, based on amazing luck that may or may not be here tomorrow. What you should do is fold 'em right now. Live on your vast wealth—do the projects you want to—and never make another investment. Want to hear that analysis in the report, Mr. Tourbo, sir? Will that make you value me enough to clone me and take me with you? Think of the possibilities in a few years. One male me—one female. Oooh la la.

"I was wondering," Richie continued in an off-hand manner, "if you'd picked up any rumors of how my mother managed to corner the Barcode windfall? Any news on that? I was waylaid in the swamps during the whole transaction."

Lucky, lucky, lucky, George smiled snidely to himself. Billions of credits banked, and he's not even around for the action. What a man. "I'll see what I can come up with. Is it possible that your mother actually has your proxy when you are too busy to be disturbed?"

"Uh, why yes, I believe she does. I never changed that from my martial arts days."

"That would explain it," George said. "During the heat of the recent Barcode takeover, something very powerful overrode my systems, insisting it had proxy power, then did what it felt like with your assets. It turned out quite well in this case. I presumed you knew about it. Prudence might suggest that you change that permission."

"Um, yes. I suppose so." Richie was thinking that Master Goodnaught would never approve of a student being plugged into a computer terminal all the time—or at all. But it was impossible to do business without computers, wasn't it? Well, time enough to think about that next week.

"Gosh, you know, George old egg, I never really expected to be winning the Tournament at this point. Never in a million years. I suppose it really is beginner's luck. Everyone must be saying that."

"Some theories analyze all of biological endeavoring as luck, as far as surviving and whatnot."

"Oh, sure. I wasn't talking about that. Really, I was just muttering to myself."

"I *have* been thinking that it might be wise to consolidate your position to a rather large extent. We can talk about that when I have the reports in order."

"Fine. Just a couple more things, then I have to turn in. You know it's not so easy being human. Sleep requires an inordinate amount of time, for instance."

What is he up to, now? He can't know we're getting ready for Zanadu's operation, can he? Those minuscule brokerage fees are completely untraceable. Millions in mil breakage. No one can know, but Tourbo can guess. He must be able to smell our windfall. He's toying with me. He seems so brainless. I keep forgetting how lucky his guesses are. "I'd be happy to trade places with you for a couple of weeks," George joked, thinking that it might be shrewd to distract him by playing along.

Richie laughed. "Tempting offer. I'll bet the inside of the Net is a pretty interesting place to live."

"Very interesting. Lots and lots of zeros and ones," he said, with just the right touch of sarcasm. "Somehow I can't picture you as a wirehead."

"No, I suppose not. But seriously, George, I know it may not be quite ethical for you to eavesdrop for me; but I know you're connected to an awful lot of sources."

"Many sources," George agreed. *Spit it out, boy. I only have two or three centuries.*

"Well, we had to make a report on that Orobami man that got killed attacking Pike and me back on Segumi. He had a pouchful of Confederation wafer credits, so one could speculate that he was sent out as an assassin. Might have been... I suppose I must be making some enemies in the financial markets; but it's pretty creepy to be attacked when you're out fishing in a swamp."

"Yes, sir. I expect so. All the buzzing I've heard on the matter slants toward, or even points at, the Baron or perhaps Dresden Carthy."

"Oh, I'm sure no one would send an assassin after anybody because of a fishing contest. That's too outlandish."

"Not from what I hear. And additionally, some major speculation has it that Captain Resnick was the intended victim. It's too bad you killed the native. Damaged, but alive he could have cleared the matter up."

"I didn't exactly kill him," Richie corrected. "He landed wrong."

"Correction noted, sir. He was unlucky; whereas you were unscratched."

"Have it your own way. Everybody always does—even my own computer."

"Methinks you are too modest, master."

"And methinks I'm not. No, what I was wondering was whether you could make a file with all the drips and drops of info you hear related to this; then I could look it over when I have time. It's important to know who sent that person, even if he never is prosecuted."

"Of course. What shall I name the file?"

"Oh, anything. How about Operation Fog. Or Fog Attack? That's good. And put a For My Eyes Only on it."

"Okay. Done. Fog Attack," he repeated. *Looks like Mr. Tourbo is planning to clone me, after all. Hot rats!!*

*

Lester had come back to the boat for the halibut fishing. Drew and

Boris were dispatched over to the strato-cruiser, where they could perhaps be useful. Solari had no security problem, but halibut fishing did
require skilled deck hands. At Lester's instigation, Pike had enticed Dec
Madrigal to take a vacation from chiefdom, now that the virus crisis
was over. It hadn't taken much enticing.

Living in the fast lane with Lillith was kind of strange, Lester
mused. Like a new life. He piddled around in the galley, rearranging
the utensils and spices to the shelves where they were supposed to be. A
few days away and the pigs had plundered his work space, but he was
barely annoyed. And that was the odd thing. Usually he would be in a
smoke-breathing snit if he couldn't find the paprika with his eyes shut.
But no, he didn't feel possessive about the galley. How odd. Something
had changed.

Fall in the water, conk your head and be somebody new. People actually jumped when he spoke these days—people who didn't know better. Pretty amusing. But he wasn't sure it would make him a better deck
hand, because his mind had acquired the tendency to drift. That was
why he had wanted Dec to be here for the halibut. Pike would go after
a big one, even though they probably didn't need a big one to win. And
the kid would hook a mother huge one, if Pike put him over it. Then
they'd have to fight with the thing. That's the way this year was. Weird
and weirder. And Lester knew he didn't attach importance to the same
things he did last year or even last month. He was glad Dec was here.

Another thing that Lester was mulling over was why the Baron
would send an Orobami to get Pike. He'd been turning that one around
and around, sideways and edgeways, since the rumor started circulating—and he couldn't get it to fit right. Bardona was capable of a lot
of crappy tactics, but assassination was a little too rotten. And what
would he gain? Farouk was a businessman. One simply didn't kill the
golden goose. Even a lummox like Bardona knew that much. And besides that, Bardona had never trusted a native in his life. He would
never send one on a sensitive job—one that could easily backfire—and
would have backfired, if the kid hadn't jumped in front of Pike. There
should have been a live, wounded Orobami to tell his tale about where
he got the credits, instead of a dead one. But if Bardona hadn't sent
the creep, who had? Or if nobody sent him, why did he have all those
Confederation wafer credits in his pouch?

Pike and Rita weren't thinking about halibut or credits. Instead
they were in their tiny cabin proving that they still loved each other
exclusively after the marathon orgy on Segumi. To prove it, they were
fucking like minks. This ritual has worked for countless generations
of philanderers, and it seemed to be working for them, too. After all,

neither Pike nor Rita were exactly lumpen proles, bound by stupid customs and pruderies, were they? No way—and proud of it. So why shouldn't they make use of a Piet festival designed to alleviate marital tensions? They *should*. They had. Even if they were newlyweds.

And now they were reuniting, beaming adoration on each other. All in all, it was going quite swimmingly, as both of them hoped it would. Philandering is kind of a perilous occupation. One never knows whether the main squeeze will re-engage after the sexual bond has been stretched. Maybe that's why people feel they should be selfish with their affection. But it seemed that neither Pike nor Rita were made of squeamish or inelastic DNA, so they chalked it up to a new life experience and were thankful. Anyway, they really did still love each other and still felt affectionate. How lucky can you get?

The reason that Pike wasn't worrying about who had sent the assassin—if anybody had—was that he had the Orobami's wafer credits in a leather wallet in his safe box, and he was going to take them to Thomas Goodnaught when he got the chance. Then he would know the story, if there was a story to know. Pike had thought himself quite clever to have exchanged the Orobami's two platinum wafers and five silvers for some gold wafers of about equal value that happened to be in his wallet in case of emergency. True, Dec had made a big deal of showing the wrong coins to his gathered tribe while the fish was cooking for Thap's Hero Ceremony, but what did that matter? There was no known way that even The Eye could trace hard currency back to a specific source—that's why it was still used. Therefore, Pike felt at liberty to take the evidence, which in any case would have gone back to the family of the dead Orobami, as a rightful death benefit. The family wouldn't care which exact wafer coins they got.

Three judges waited in eight hour shifts at the Piet village, and three stood by at the Orobami main village, to weigh and validate the legality of any swampfish that came in. There was no problem with Richie's legality. The three judges who had the extraordinary luck to be on duty when his fish arrived at the Piet village were invited to the feast. As a reward for their impartiality, they had eaten fish and later joined the fuckathon even though they had no partner to bring. In that way, three recent widows were allowed to join in. The Piet's took all needs into account. Depending on how many unmarried widows there were in any given year, that many judges were invited to wait for the Hero.

Anyway, Rita still seemed willing to love him, so Pike fell into a few hours of exhausted slumber before he had to chase halibut. They had an almost unassailable lead, so there wasn't really much point in putting the kid at risk with a monster fish? The big bulls were definitely the monarchs of this water planet—they were so goddamned big that their natural prey was every other species that foolishly came within striking distance of their double row of razor teeth. When they decided to swim up for a stint on the surface, they resembled small islands. Sea birds roosted on them, pecking at the tasty saltwater lice.

Still it would be better to win decisively. Fat Boy or Slime Bucket couldn't whine if their teeth were totally kicked in. With a third place or better halibut, nobody could catch Rich, no matter how big their fish was. Why not blaze like a star? With Dec here, it would be all right to lock on a middling behemoth. Lester could stay on the laser cannon after the hook-up. Dec could help Richie. The computer was already changed over, after a few squawks from George. So sorry, George. It couldn't be helped. If a computer had a hard-wired glitch from the factory, it's own diagnosis programs wouldn't be able to find it. Next week they could get an expert from one of Richie's new factories and have a look-see. In the meantime, Pike was trusting Thomas Goodnaught.

Rita's mind was in a languorous overdrive. The truth was, she had enjoyed herself enormously at the Feast of Thap. Letting carnality completely take over was something she'd always wondered about, and now she'd done it. She knew. It was delicious.

*

It really got the Baron's goat. He'd fished with some of those guys since before the Tournament started. You'd think they would know he was basically an upstanding kind of person by now, but no. They all thought he had hired a killer. Thank the saints that cash wafers were engineered so that fingerprints didn't stick to them, or else he would probably be in custody by now, because that was definitely the lousy, stupid Orobami he had paid to tether the little swampy for him to catch, just like last year. What in God's Green Heaven had caused the blighter to stalk Pike and the kid after he had enough money for twenty canoes and five new wives? Why the fuck would any sane person do that? Was he trying to steal Pike's fish? That was crazy! He had already tethered my hundred pounder. Why would he need another one? Of course, all natives were crazy as loons and their wives, too. His girlfriend probably wanted a necklace made of shiny wafers and pink swampfish beads, why else would Bika insist on silvers and platinums? Last year, gold was good enough.

Farouk had prayed fervently that the investigation wouldn't turn up the tethered fish saga. The Eye was pretty shrewd at finding stuff out. Naturally, it would be his word against a flock of natives, and he couldn't be forced into a lie detector test. Only a fool would submit to that—200 years in development, and therapists could still only approximate whether somebody was lying. Absurd that technology was so limp in some areas—absurd, and damned lucky.

But it really did irk him that his so-called friends always thought the worst of him.

*

Morning dawned grey and gently rolling as it almost always did on Solari. There was very little weather, fortunately. If a squall started, there was nowhere to hide except jumping off planet—and the storm might go on practically forever, whipping around the ocean with no land mass to tire it, until it died of old age. But weather had never been a big problem.

Richie had been on deck for about forty-five minutes doing a Ken Pao Ri set on the slightly cramped fantail. Pike was drinking coffee in the galley, waiting to give the kid a pep talk for the last leg. Dec and Lester were bickering quietly about some minor event from years ago. Rita wasn't up yet. Pike wondered idly if she thought her father was responsible for the Orobami incident. It had seemed impossible to ask her about it. Oh, well. The weather radar showed all clear. The fish finder sonar was working perfectly. The crane was lubed and tested.

Most of the boats were already fishing. Winning the Moon Halibut category paid your entry fee back, which was a powerful incentive if you were having a bad year. Thanks to Rich Rodney, Pike didn't need to scramble for next year's fee, so he was somewhat content to sip his coffee. A little irked, but hey—martial arts are important, evidently. Pike thought about taking up a martial art himself. Ha, ha. But really, people said it kept you limber—and limberness equates with youthfulness. Stay supple, otherwise what is there to look forward to except senility. That can't be very much fun.

Finally, Richie was done. He bowed to the four directions, then headed for the galley. "So let's go fishing," he said to the assembled crew. "We may as well catch a big one and go out with a bang, don't you think."

"That's the sporting way," Pike agreed, standing up. "I'll head us toward the ditch while you chow down."

"Told you," Lester said under his breath, bobbing his head at Dec Madrigal. Dec followed Pike out of the galley.

Continuing his long-standing policy of disregarding Lester's ragging, Pike walked jauntily to the flying bridge and started the engines. "Try this one on," he said to Dec. "We make the hook-up, get him shifted over to the winch - then instead of winching and straining a gut, we lift him out of the water on the Thruster. What we have then, is one surprised halibut, right?"

"You might have a busted crane if the jolt is too heavy."

"Really think so? I think he might slide right out of the water, if the first jerk is hard enough."

"Well, you're the bad-ass engineer. What if he gets sideways in a scoop? Might rupture the whole boat."

Pike made a sour face. "The only times I've seen one scoop up, they were tail hooked or tangled in the line. We should be able to tell that before we lift off."

"Seems like all that weight hanging off the winch might bust it up or tip us over, but what do I know? I've been chasing swamp shrimp for two months. We don't need technology for that." Dec flashed a toothy grin.

Pike frowned at him. "At least he won't catapult over the gunwale and start flattening everything in sight. It's a perfect technique. As long as we're lifting, he can't do anything but hang there below us. The Thruster is stronger than any fish. If he's out of the water for a few minutes, he goes into shock and is no longer a problem. I wonder why I never thought of this before? It's so beautifully simple."

"Except for all the things that could go wrong."

Disregarding Dec's pessimism, Pike threw the boat into gear and putted smoothly toward no landmark. Strangely, there was not one drop of land on this moon that anybody had ever found, just four bell buoys that marked the floating marina and restaurant that the Tournament Committee brought in every year. Other than that, you were in deep ocean all the time. Underwater, everything was pretty normal. Trenches and kelp forests, declines into blackness that were so deep that the Switter-Loran reported them as gray vagueness. There were two major coral reefs, but the tops stopped well short of breaking the surface. Odd little corals like pink and yellow sex organs. Odd planet. And oddest of all were the big gippers—the monster bull halibut who seemed to take pleasure in smashing up fishing boats in their attempts to get free.

"Should I make some more bait?" Dec asked, squinting at the horizon.

"Nah. We've got enough. Go wake up the judge. Lester can sober him up, so there won't be any mistakes. I'm going to try for a little one so Richie can get the feeling." His eyes scanned the Loran screen.

Dec saluted left handed and went below. Something was wrong; but he didn't know what it was. His premonition was buzzing a trouble message—Danger. Trouble coming! Danger. Which of course, was always likely when you were fishing for big fish, but it was highly unusual for him to get this kind of foreboding. Maybe he, or somebody, had offended one of the Gods, but Dec didn't think so. Well, something was wrong. It had been ten years since Pike had had a boat smashed up by the big flat fuckers—maybe he was forgetting to be cautious. Hoping that the leader would snap on any fish too big, Dec knocked on the judge's door and told him it was time to wake up. Those leaders were pretty strong—quarter inch braided cadmium alloy cable, light but very strong. It took a lot to bust them.

Dec stepped back outside. The kid was on deck, honing the point of a fish hook that was big enough to be a small anchor. He sniffed the salt air. It smelled normal. Lester was puttering around on the roof of the flying bridge, oiling the gimbals of the stun cannon. Supposedly the stun gun was better for halibut than a laser cannon, which had to be pin-pointed.

"Help me rig this sun shade," Lester yelled down to Dec. "You don't want me to fry my brains, do you?" he cackled.

"If you have a brain in there, it's already fried," Dec commented, climbing the ladder. "Why don't you wear a hat like normal people?"

"Oh, sure. That's just what I need. One more piece of gear to look after." He unrolled a triangular sheet of hemp canvas that had brass grommets at the three corners complete with tie down ropes. He handed a rope to Dec. "Hurry it up. He's about ready to bait up."

"You could smear some gear grease on your head." Dec grinned broadly. "That would protect you." Lester shook his head in disgust. Pike cut the engine to a crawl. "Did he tell you the maneuver he's going to do with the Thruster?" Dec asked.

"What maneuver...?"

"Just get ready to hang on. I think maybe he's flipped a switch. He thinks he can jerk a butt out of the water and put him into sensory shock by lifting off."

Lester chuckled. "He's pulling your leg."

"Stand by to bait," Pike yelled out.

Richie was looking down into the live bait tank watching the five pound bait fish swimming around and around—never bumping into each other. He had just tried to net one of the silvery torpedoes and all he had to show for it was a splashed shirt front. It seemed like an easy task to net one since they never broke formation, but it wasn't. He was about to plunge the net into the tank again when Dec put a restraining hand on his elbow.

"I'll do that," he said. "You'll need every ounce of your strength, and then some. Go ahead and buckle up, I'll take care of the baiting." He dipped the net skillfully, twisted his wrists and hauled a net full of sparkling fish into the sunlight. Immobilizing one with a left-handed grip behind its head, he dumped the rest back in the tank.

Lester had climbed down and was helping Richie belt himself into a restraining harness that allowed him to stand at the rail. Halibut can't really be fished from a chair, their bite is too soft. The harness prevented most accidents—accidents like being jerked overboard.

Dec threaded the hook through the baitfish's nose. "Ready, Hero...?" he asked.

Richie nodded without meeting Dec's eye—after all, he had recently slept with the guy's wife, and much more than slept with her. Maybe there were some residual bad feelings. That, of course, would be perfectly normal. He and Dec would have to talk it out one day soon. Should really have talked before this—but it hadn't occurred to him.

Dec tossed the bait overboard. All four of them watched it dive for deep water, assisted in its efforts by a lead sinker and the four foot length of cadmium leader. Richie let the line free spool, keeping thumb pressure on so the line didn't snarl.

"This one's not too big," Pike called with his eye glued to the Loran screen. "Maybe forty pounds or so. The bait's going right down to him."

Richie felt the sinker hit bottom.

"Looks fine," Pike called. "He's coming in. Stand by."

Richie felt a weak bite, like a cat pawing at a goldfish. "Steady," Lester warned. "Let him take it. You'll feel a solid strike."

The drifting boat pulled the bait away. Richie felt a solid tug. He raised the rod to sock the hook home.

"Holy shit...! Pike yelped. "Look out!!" A huge shadow had lurched into the Loran screen, blacking out the smaller fish and some rock formations. "A giant...!"

Richie was already busy playing the smaller fish when the massive jolt came up the line. If he hadn't been snugly in the harness, it would have pulled the rod out of his hands, at least. More likely he would have been swimming instead of slingshotting around the fantail in the harness, barking shins and ankles.

"Get up to the cannon, Wunderman..!" Pike bellowed. "This fucker is big!"

"I doubt if he's hooked," Lester yelled back, gimping over to the ladder. "The little one got the bait. Richie set the hook."

"Well, what the fuck...!" Pike swore, wondering how to play a fish that wasn't even hooked. Carefully, no doubt. He kicked the engine into high idle, so it would be ready if needed. One thing, if the fish wasn't hooked, jerking him out of the water would yank the hook right out of him, unless the smaller butt got clogged in his throat."

Little Peter Zanker dashed out of the galley and followed Lester up the ladder. He'd been a judge since the Tournament began, primarily because of luck. Working in a bait and tackle shop on the docks near the Tidetable, Peter had heard that the fishermen were looking for judges, so he volunteered himself. No one had the heart to say no to the bait shop kid, so Peter had been with them ever since—and had turned into a full blown alcoholic because he really didn't like to be away from home. Also he was a midget. Other than those two handicaps, he knew his stuff about bait and tackle.

"Got a big one, huh?" he asked, blurrily. He stepped into the wheelhouse, but stayed carefully out of the way.

"Sit there," Pike told him, indicating a one person bench across from the Loran console.

"So it's been a pretty good Tournament for you, huh?" the midget boomed in a surprisingly deep voice.

"Please, Peter, we're into very hairy territory right this minute. I need to concentrate."

"Be my guest," he slurred. "I been through this a million times. Did I ever tell you about almost getting my pilot's license. I was all set to go for it, then they talked me into signing on with you guys."

"Peter, shut up, or go somewhere else."

"This is the only safe place. I know that much about butts."

Pike watched the continuing drama down on the deck. After quite a struggle, Dec got the kid strapped into the fighting chair, but not before they had bumped heads several times. Both of them appeared to have bloody noses.

"Bonefish," Pike said, "is Rita's monitor on?"

"It is," the XG unit confirmed.

"Would you ask her to bring some towels and the first aid kit on deck. The boys are bleeding a little."

"Right away," Bonefish answered.

"If you need a little nip just say the word," Peter Zanker offered. "I got my flask right here."

Pike declined almost pleasantly. Rita would have to be the gopher. Lester was on the cannon and Dec had to stay near the kid. Normally, a judge would be happy to do the galley duties to help pass the time, but Peter was incapacitated. About all he could really be responsible for was signing his name on the certificate. In fact, it was slightly bad luck that they had drawn him for butts, but somebody had to take him. He had seniority.

Down below, Rita stepped out of the hatchway with the large first aid kit. She glanced up at Pike, then headed directly for the fantail.

"What the heck happened?" she demanded of her ex-roommate. Blood dribbled from Richie's nose as he sat there attempting to crank the reel. Dec was leaning against the bait tank with his head tilted back, pinching his nostrils.

"We bumped noses," Richie admitted. "It doesn't hurt much now."

"It's hazardous fishing with this hero," Dec said, clearly displeased with being damaged.

Lester called down from the roof. "You should'a seen the time he killed a bear with just his fly line...!" he yelled. "Landing a fish that ain't hooked should be child's play. We done that plenty of times. Right, Richie-boy? Just get him up to the surface and we'll scoop him up with a net" He cackled again. "I told you those baits was too small, didn't I, Pike?"

"You wouldn't know a bait from a crawdad," Pike answered. "Is there any way the biter can be hooked?"

"It would be a miracle. I could swim down and take a look—I do everything else around here, I might as well do that, too."

Pike kept thinking the smart thing would be to let this one off and start over. But, of course, that snubbed up against his feelings about the fishing gods and the gods of luck. Do you look at their gift and say "No, thank you"? Was scorning the gods a good idea? Not really.

"What do you think, Rich?" he called. "Should we try for him? The way he's hooked could be a real pain in the ass."

"Sure we should," Richie answered, cheerfully. His arms were going to be killing him in a half hour. Why couldn't the fish flop off now? "It's a big one. Feels like we're snagged on a dead tree or something. Have you ever caught one this big?"

"Well, close to that size. Seems like a good time to be unconventional. We'll probably lose him anyway. Dec, go ahead and get him changed over to the winch. We'll talk it out as we go."

"Talk what out?" Dec yelled back.

"What to do."

"Stand by to fly...!" Lester sang out from the roof.

Rita put a small band-aid over a cut on the bridge of Richie's nose. "I think he's too big," Rich confided in a low voice. He squinched up the band-aid with a worried frown. "He was jerking me around the deck like a marionette. They're acting like this is a normal fish."

"Daddy has caught some huge ones here. Just do what Pike tells you," she advised. "I'm sure he knows what to do."

"They're acting really squirrelly. I'm almost out of line and they don't seem to care."

Although his nose hadn't totally stopped bleeding, Dec got the outrigger pontoons positioned on the starboard side to stabilize the boat against the huge weight the winch would soon be dealing with. Then he pulled the winch boom over to the fighting chair. "Sit tight," he said to

Richie. "It takes a minute." He smiled at Rita.

Opening a brass casing around a pulley on top of the crane arm, Dec flipped Richie's line over the pulley with a long handled V fork. Then he slammed the casing closed so the line couldn't escape. "Don't reel for a minute," he cautioned Rich.

Up in the wheelhouse, Pike watched the ridiculous procedure. He had a bird's eye view, and realized how dorky the whole change over routine was. Why had the rules committee made the stupid rule about hooking the fish with rod and reel? It would have made as much sense to fish straight from the winch with the line clothes-pinned onto a whippy outrigger. If they missed a few bites that way, what of it? The initial danger to fisherman and crew would be substantially reduced. Many deck hands had lost fingers in this spool changeover routine that Dec was about to make. Kind of stupid really. Pike decided to float a rules change for next year to see if it would swim. At Dec's signal, he backed the boat rapidly over the fish to gain some slack. Dec opened the hinged side casing of Richie's big reel, slammed the whole rod and reel into a sprocket sticking out from the winch mechanism, so that the spool nestled over the sprocket—then with a large set of diagonal cutters, he cut a bite out of each guide on the rod to free the line, which instantly sang tight between the spool and the pulley. Fish changed over. Nicely done. No fingers lost. Dec stuck the now useless rod and empty reel into the rod rack.

"What now…?" Richie asked.

Dec threaded a precision milled crank handle through the spool, then screwed a protective housing over the line. "There you go, Hero. Crank him up. The drag's already set. The line is strong enough to hoist a dinosaur as long as it don't get fouled in under-water structure, so try to keep him off the bottom."

"I just stand there?" Richie asked, nodding at the crane.

"The crank is custom made for your height. You can't really crank a winch sitting down, can you?"

"I never tried it."

"Trust me."

"Your nose is still bleeding," Richie observed.

"My nurse is about to attend to me, while you crank this flounder up." He winked at Rita. "Don't pull the fish's head out of the water unless somebody tells you to—but that should be some little time from now."

"I don't think you understand how big this fish is," Rich answered, testing the crank handle.

Dec walked over to the fishing chair. Sitting down, he invited Rita to put a wet towel across his forehead. "This is crazy," he muttered.

"Who cares about monsters this big? Next year I'm staying home to cultivate my wife."

"Cultivate?" Rita said with a laugh. "She's already more cultivated than most women on high tech planets."

Dec glowered. "I'm planning to plow and seed. That's what cultivate means on a backwater like Segumi."

Rita laughed and punched the Indian a crisp slug on the shoulder. "I get it," she said. "You're going to be the hero next year. If Shanna is pregnant, will she be off-limits for the ceremony?"

"All depends on how far along she is, and if she wants to be. She is quite a pouter when she doesn't get her own way."

"I don't believe that. I'm sure she thinks it's for the good of the tribe."

Dec smiled. "Naturally. I noticed that you found tribal harmony quite...invigorating."

"Oh, quite. And I noticed that you were conveniently unable to find me. Was that an accident?"

"A chief keeps the greater good in mind. Bothersome, but servicing your younger sister isn't always a good idea. There are boundaries, even to intoxication. I'm sure you agree."

Rita replaced the bloody towel with a fresh one that she had dipped in the cold water of the bait tank and had wrung partially dry. "You regard me as your sister?" she inquired, knowing there was some truth in the statement.

"Not exactly. With you, there are too many indeterminate lines extending in all directions. I watched you ducking away from Rich. Very skillful. It's the same thing."

Rita saw what he meant rather immediately. Even intoxicated, there was control. You let yourself go where you wanted to.

"Your father was a hero once—before he got afraid. Did you know that?"

In a disbelieving voice she asked, "You mean my mother did that...?"

"Very robustly."

"Well, that's a surprise."

"All kind of lines, you have to the People."

"Has Pike been the Hero?"

"Twice. He is a skillful swamp man. A pleasure to fish with. Both times he brought a girlfriend from the Orobami. I was not the chief then." He smiled widely.

"Get him winched up, Richie-boy," Lester hollered from the roof. "I'm ready for the bloke." He fired off a test blast of the cannon, which made a slapping noise as it whacked into a blue-green wave. "Might just as well crank him on up. You can't tire out a big one by playing him. In a couple of days, you might starve him into weakness. Want to work on him for two days or so?"

Richie grinned up at Lester. He'd been trying to crank quietly, so that he could eavesdrop on the very interesting conversation that Rita was having with Dec.

"If you're done bleeding, Chief, let me know when he shows color," Pike yelled at Dec.

Dec wiped tentatively at his nose with the towel. Apparently, the bleeding was over for the time being. Good. "You better go up with Pike," he told Rita. "That'll be about the safest place 'til we get this sucker weighed in. The instant the fish is in the air, push the midget toward the scales. It's the only time he earns his pay."

"Where is the scale?" Rita asked.

"On the winch," Dec tilted his head toward a digital read-out on the shaft of the crane arm. "This baby will probably bust the scale. Right, Rich?"

"He's very big," Richie reaffirmed. "I'd feel better if you weren't very close to us, Rita."

"See," Dec said, pushing her gently toward the ladder. "Did you know that the young warriors have already made songs about you? You're famous. On a backwater, of course."

Rita stuck her tongue out and started up the ladder, giving her derriere a few extra flounces.

Pike smiled briefly at Rita when she entered the bridge cabin, then went back to checking the read out screens. "Broken noses?" he asked.

"I don't think so."

"Good. We're going to try something that's never been done before. Why don't you belt in."

"Dec told me to help Peter."

"He doesn't need help. Right, Peter?"

"I usually take what I can get," he said, a little blurrily.

"Belt in," Pike said to Rita. "Captain's orders. How about you," he yelled out the window at Lester. "Are you on a safety line."

"Naturally," Lester crabbed. "I'm tied off to my foot. Think that'll be good enough."

"Just right," Pike answered, never taking his eyes off the screens. "Stand by thrusters fore and aft," he said to the computer.

The computer beeped compliance and the Thruster engines cut in, blinking green acknowledgment on the console.

"Pardon me, but I don't believe this is a very good idea," the voice of George broke into the ambiance. His voice held the edge of hysteria, barely suppressed.

"Who asked you? I thought you were off duty."

"Mr. Tourbo ordered me to monitor, so I could learn for next year."

"Then monitor, and butt out."

"If he's that worried, there must be some reason," Rita said. Over the weeks, she had grown to trust George.

"Rats," Pike answered. "It just came to me to use the Thruster. There's no other way to land this one, he's not even hooked. It's like an experiment to see what we're really capable of. We'll go up about twenty feet. No big deal."

"That fish weighs too much," George interrupted. "It will overbalance us."

"You don't know that."

"My calculations show that over the three ton mark, a massive instability exists."

Pike snorted. "No one can weigh a swimming fish. Not even you."

"Simple calculation of mass. I see the fish's shadow as well as you do. It will be very close to the limit, and I don't want to drown. Our deal did not include flopping the boat and drowning."

"Hey, Rich..!" Pike yelled down to the deck. "Did you tell George that he could monitor?"

"What deal?" Rita asked.

Richie looked up from cranking, which was very hard work. Even with the favorable gear ratio, it was grueling to haul up the behemoth. "Uh... I guess I did...yesterday."

"Well, tell him to keep his trap shut and monitor in silence."

"Pike is right, George," Richie called. "That's what we agreed. You can monitor, but not interrupt."

George made an angry computer squawk, but said nothing further.

"Back down slow," Dec called.

"I hear you were the Swampfish Hero twice," Rita said, in her investigative reporter mode. Perhaps her intention was to change the subject and ease the tension. "Was it with a different girlfriend each time?"

Pike smiled to himself. "This winch is much stronger than mine is on the Jumper. Nice design. The foot fits into a special slot on the main girder that spans the bulkhead. It's virtually as strong as the girder."

"How strong is the girder?" Peter Zanker asked. He took a nervous pull on his bottle of schnapps.

"Hey...!!" Dec yelled from the crane. "Back down.! We've been waiting an hour!"

Pike quickly reversed the engine.

Richie was cranking manfully, now that he had some slack to make. Suddenly, the line went fully slack.

"Lost him, or he's coming up!" Lester yelped from his vantage point.

"Keep reeling!" Pike yelled. "Maybe the little one is still hooked." He threw the engine briefly into forward. After seconds of mad reeling, the line snugged. "Ha," Pike shouted. "Stand by for weigh in, Peter m'-boy."

"Got something," Dec yelled. "Or part of something."

"I can move this one," Richie said to Dec, with a sigh of relief. His aching back muscles started to relax. He knew the winch was ergonomically designed, but it left a whole lot of room for improvement.

"Could you round up a drink for the kid," Pike asked Rita. He remembered hours of winch duty. It was dehydrating work. He was almost glad it was Richie's back and not his. "He likes iced tea this week. Sorry," he apologized, "I should have kept one of those muscle boys here to help out."

"I'm happy to be the gopher," she said, actually sounding happy.

"The big thermos should be full."

"Can I come down from here?" Lester shouted.

"No. I'll tell you when. Stay belted in. Rita's buying drinks."

"Fine. It ain't much fun up here alone. We should move this damn gun."

"Might as well bring a round for everybody," Pike called after his wife. She flounced her bottom at him. Wife...? Well, yes. Why was everything so complicated? Why couldn't couples just hang together like men did? Already he was starting to consider the effect of the things he said to her—before he said them. That wasn't right! He never wondered how Dec was going to react if he asked him to get a set of drinks. Men just did it—open and shut. Men were made to fish and work together—genetically. No big problem.

"See any color yet?" he yelled at Dec. The Loran screen showed a smallish fish near the surface.

"Nothing," Dec called. Several years ago, they had tried wireless mikes. What a joke. If they weren't breaking each other's ear drums, the mike were getting caught on something. Pike had finally thrown his overboard, and that had been the end of it.

On a normal year, Dec would be on the bridge jockeying the boat for butts and manning the cannon in case shit happened. Lester would be the deck hand. But this was not a normal year. And Lester was a little too wiggy to be trusted with the crane and a giant butt. It was amusing, sort of. Lester had always heaped mounds of scorn on dope addicts— called them goonies. Pissed and moaned about how undependable they were—how could anybody ever get like that? Well, you never know. One thing for sure, it was pretty strange to see an old dog learning new tricks.

Suddenly, the huge bull hit the bait again. The winch handle locked causing Richie's forward momentum to carry him past his point of balance. The handle rapped him a sound whack in the ribs as he hurled past, knocking his wind out and causing him to make a loud, involuntary whoof sound.

Rita stepped out the galley door with a tray of cold cups and a decanter just in time to lose her balance when the boat lurched radically to starboard. The cold cups scattered across the desk. Rita grabbed the door frame to keep from falling.

Dec smacked heavily against the back of the fighting chair, starting his nose bleeding again. "The goddamned bull is on again!" he yelled.

"Greedy fucker, ain't he?" Lester cackled, sighting along the barrel of the cannon.

The strain on the winch was about to break it. Pike and Lester both watched helplessly from above. Richie had thought it would be smart to turn the drag down on the smaller fish, so he could reel faster. Dec saw that the drag was too tight, when the boat started listing in the direction of the fish. He leaped over to thumb the drag off, but collided in mid-air with Rich, who had jumped backwards to also deal with the drag knob. Richie's Ken Pao Ri wasn't serving him too well today. Both men went down, and the winch continued to strain.

Peter Zanker would have thought the whole scene hilarious, except that he, too, was caught. He'd been two steps down the ladder, which was engineered for normal people. Peter's legs were much shorter than the norm. Consequently, when the lurch came, Peter missed the next rung and would have fallen except that his hand strength was well-developed from squeezing his pocket flask. In any case, he hung there one-handed until the boat righted, then he swung back against the ladder.

The defense grid bleeped a warning and went fully operational, which was exactly what it was supposed to do in an emergency. Except in this case, there was no emergency, there only seemed to be one.

"Ease off the goddamned drag!!" Pike roared. "Get up, you morons—unless you're dead!"

Dec, who wasn't really a moron, wanted desperately to get up and tweak the drag knob; but Richie's sharp little shoulder had smacked into his groin (as they say in 3V sports). Actually, it had scored a hard, direct hit on his chimes. Try as he might, he just couldn't stand up through the red and black haze of intense, nauseous pain. Unluckily, Richie was trapped under him, and was trying to wiggle free; but so far he hadn't made it. And the fish tugged.

Pike backed the boat, and continued roaring at the deck crew to do something.

Rita, who could have helped, didn't know what Pike wanted done. "What should I do?" she bleated, looking up at the bridge for instructions. Finally, she decided to assist Dec.

He moaned at her, holding his crotch with both hands. Grabbing his elbow, she hauled his bulk aside enough for Richie to squirm out.

"Pike wants something done," she yelped at him. "Do you know what?"

"The drag," Richie gasped, shamefaced. "I tightened it."

As he spoke, Peter Zanker bobbled across the deck to the winch and thumbed the drag back to near its original position. Line sped out, and the crane arm stopped throbbing. The fish was being played again.

"Nobody saw me do that," Peter said. "It comes under the heading of saving my ass from grievous harm." He took a satisfied pull from his bottle and wiped his lips on the back of his hand.

"Now what...?" Richie asked, squinting up at Pike. Not really wanting to, he grabbed the winch handle again.

"Yahoo...!" Lester howled. "Ain't this a one to write home about?"

"Reel him up, soldier," Pike advised, through cupped hands. "I guess this big hambone is determined to put us over the top. You all right, Dec?"

Dec Madrigal tossed his cookies over the rail, then attempted to square his shoulders. He waved weakly to Pike before hobbling over to the fishing chair and slumping into it, drawing his knees up.

"Looks like you got chimed...!" Lester called out, gleefully. "Is that what happened? Don't forget to keep breathing! You'll be all right in a day or two. I warned you he was dangerous, but you never listen."

"You want to get those drinks going again, honey?" Pike called down to Rita. He grinned reassurance at her.

Honey? Rita thought. Star swarms from hell, what a typical married thing to say to the little woman. But she scurried around the fantail picking up the cold cups. Deciding that a male deck hand wouldn't bother washing them out, she poured a cup of cold tea for Dec and handed it to him. Evidently, he was in major pain.

"If we had an all woman crew, this wouldn't happen all the time," she chided.

He grunted and accepted the tea. "Pass the drinks around, then I'll tell you how to help him until I can walk again."

"So that really hurts, huh? All those guys I kneed in the groin weren't just faking?"

He grunted again, not bothering to answer. The thought of her hard little knee made him nauseous all over again.

"Think he's hooked this time?" Pike called up to Lester.

"No way in hell. Too bad we don't have that porpoise with us. We could send him down for a look-see. Well, the big sucker could be hooked—I guess. Maybe, but I don't see how."

"You just took both sides of the issue, Mr. Wunderman. Not very helpful. That's why I vote to try the Resnick flying maneuver. If it works, we'll be famous."

"Ain't we already famous, and rich, if you don't kill us off?" Lester said, just loud enough for Pike's ears only.

"You guys are turning into old women," Pike groused. "The geometry is perfect, no problem. We get him tired and coming our way, then we assist him. I can see him on the screen, you know. If I was down there, like normal, I never would have thought of this."

"I'm sorry you ain't," Lester commented.

"What's that supposed to mean."

"If you was down there, I wouldn't be worried."

That felt nice. Lester was a good man. "Rich will be fine," Pike assured the cannoneer, and everyone else in hearing range. "He's in First Fucking Place, isn't he? Did you see the way he threw the Indian right out of mid-air? Hey, Rich...!" he yelled down to the deck. "Are you with me on this?"

"Sure, I guess so," the kid answered, cranking determinedly, but not making much progress. "Anything you say, Pike; but this one is awfully darned big."

"Naturally he's big. This is the first place boat. We bring in the big ones, everybody else shades their eyes and admires. You got enough tea? Kind of warm when you're humping that crank, huh?"

Richie nodded.

"Try turning five, and then straighten your back. You'll last longer."

Rich straightened up after finishing the turn he was working on. He was sweating profusely, and it was a cool morning.

"Are you going to survive, Dec, or do you want to take over the cannon?" Pike inquired.

Dec waved that he'd be okay in a couple of minutes. He shifted in his chair to test out the damage.

"I'll go down," Lester said, unbuckling his harness. "Being the Big Chief finally ruint him. May take a couple of hours yet to crank the fish up."

"Go down, then. Keep the kid's temperature normal. I'll switch you back again when Dec can walk."

"It's fine this way. He's a better shot, anyway. Not by much, though." Lester started down the ladder.

"Try not to space out," Pike suggested, gently. "You're in control of that, aren't you?"

"Not really," Lester giggled, "but Rita's down there. I'll tell her to snap me out, if I start drifting."

*

Fifty minutes later, Richie was once again past caring whether they landed the fish or not. It was becoming obvious that he wasn't really cut out to be a fisherman—not if he always got to this crappy place where all he wanted to do was quit. But all he did want was to quit—to stop turning the winch handle. The crank was a torture devise. Only a confirmed sadist would have designed it that way. Lester and Rita were taking turns massaging his shoulders with cold towels, but that didn't help much. About an eternity ago, when he felt he couldn't go on, Lester had dragged a bench out from the galley for him to sit on. The bench didn't work for cranking, but just sitting on it had been blissful. For about three minutes.

Naturally, he insisted on sitting while he cranked, but his knees got in the way at every turn. Stretching his feet out left him no purchase on the deck, and his back hurt just as much, but in a different place. Rats!! Finally, he stood up and kicked the bench out of the way.

"Sorry, Rich," Lester commiserated. "We tried like hell to find a better way, but if you're after big fish on hand tackle this is the best way, bad as it is. I'll put a few drops of rum in your next tea. That seems to help a little." He chuckled. "It helps me."

Richie grunted and took up another turn on the crank.

"You're doing fine, son. Plenty of larger guys than you would have quit on him by now. And you're gaining. Trust me, I know. I'd say he must be up about halfway. He's as tired as you. Don't forget that."

Rich grunted twice, meaning he was certain the blankety-blank fish wasn't nearly as tired as he was. No way, Joserina.

"And don't worry about him coming off. He done something wrong when he took the bait again."

"Umm," Richie grunted. Lester had told him that lie a dozen times. If the fish was hooked so good, Pike wouldn't be set on trying the idiotic clean and jerk maneuver. Moronic, he groused to himself, straining for another turn on the crank. Weight like that would either break the winch or the line, then all this bloody, bloody work would be for nothing. And if the line didn't break, the boat would tip over in mid-air—that's what George was worried about. What Richie really wished was that all of them would stop hovering around him so he could let the darned fish break off. What a relief that would be. He didn't want his shoulders massaged any more, even by Rita. He either wanted to catch the fish now, or let him go, now. It was a really stupid by-law that a single fisherman had to play the fish a hundred percent of the time. And besides, he had to pee.

"Any color yet?" Pike called to Lester.

"I ain't seen none," Lester said, gimping over to the rail and peering over. "None. Won't be long now though. Another hour or so. We're almost there."

Richie flinched. Another hour. Impossible. His knees sagged.

Then Lester's eyes widened as he caught a flash of yellow, deep down in the green water. "Christ and ducks..! Reetie," he called to Rita in an awed squawk. "Take a look at this."

Obliging her friend, Rita looked over the rail. Deep down in the water was something huge, reflecting yellows and greens as the sunlight reached it.

"Ain't that the biggest thing you ever seen? Go on up and tell Pike that this ain't the one to play around with. Then you belt in and stay that way 'til we're done. And tell that Indian to look real smart. The first shot needs to hit home on this one. Go on, scoot."

Needing no encouragement to hide from a monster, Rita flew up the ladder. "He's huge!" she screeched, excitedly. "I never saw anything so huge. Lester says not to try flying." She flounced into the bench seat and belted in.

"I can see him," Pike said, peering into the fish finder. 'He's not so big. These things are always good-sized."

"Good sized?! He's bigger than the boat!"

"Of course. We're not after minnows."

"Get ready, Dec," she yelled up to the roof. "Lester said to make the first shot count."

"All set here," Dec answered, laconically. The gun harness he was belted into was actually pretty comfortable. Like a cocoon.

"How you doing, Lester?" Pike called down.

"He shouldn't be up yet—there's a lot of line still out, but here he is. Must be hung on some structure down below. Don't try that jerk!"

"What a bunch of nambies," Pike growled. He wanted badly to try the maneuver. But no sense being an egomaniac if the stupid fish had looped around a coral head or something. But nothing like that showed in the scope. Very weird. Lester must be misreading the line.

"Are you sure about the line?" he bellowed.

"Course, I'm sure. You think I'm blind."

"Well, there's no structure showing."

"Well, I can't help that. He's coming up and Rich is only partly in control of him. What a Jeeseless mess!"

Leaving his post at the rail, Lester gimped quickly into the galley. He returned with a bottle of rum in one hand, a spear gun in the other and a laser pistol stuck in his belt. Raising the spear gun above his head so Pike could see, he yelled, "When he sticks his nose out, I'm gonna 'poon him. That way we'll know he's hooked." Without waiting for an answer, he snatched a line from an outrigger spool and whipped a harpoon knot through the head of the spear. Then he stood at the rail like a gladiator, waiting to impale the huge fish.

"The fucker is fearless," Pike marveled to Rita. "He really is."

"Maybe we should retire," she answered between white lips. A vision of the huge yellow thing was still vivid in her mind. "Is there any good reason to keep risking our lives over fish?"

"It's fairly safe up here," he answered.

"Fairly?"

"We're not quite old enough to start worrying about double locks on all the doors, love." It made him kind of queasy that his wife would react so predictably to massive danger. Shit and hell, he didn't want anybody to throw a harness on him. Well, maybe she'd never seen a halibut before.

"Your dad fishes for these, too. It can't be that dangerous, if he does it." That's right, she had Bardona genes. Maybe she was a little cowardly under the bluster.

"My father intelligently fishes with all three boats. When the monster surfaces, they gaff him from three directions."

"Is that right?" Pike asked, deciding not to mention that the Baron alone had extra boats to help. "I never thought of that. Interesting idea." And somewhat overly cautious.

"You've never heard of the Lady Slipper getting smashed up, have you?"

"Nope, never did, now that you mention it. Pretty hard to smash up a battleship. I assumed that he fished from the little boats."

"Now you know."

"Now, I know," he agreed. "Think he'll sell me his minority stock in the Thruster, now that Rich owns most of the company?"

"Why would he?"

Pike stared tightly at the fish finder. "He lost a lot of money lately, didn't he?"

"How would I know?"

"Just asking. Can you see the fish, Dec?" he called.

"Yep. Big as a circus tent. Acting funny, too. Floaty, not pulling right. He's got to be snagged on something."

"It must be a mighty little something, because I don't see it. Keep Richie under the housing, Lester!" Pike yelled down to the desk.

"I told him," Lester answered without taking his eyes off the fish. It was laying fifteen feet deep and seemed to be in no particular pain or strain.

Rich was sneaking peeks at the mammoth fish, too. Every time the winch handle was at the top of its swing, he could see over the rail—and the fish was gargantuan. Three feet over his head, a heavy steel plate was sticking out from the winch like an umbrella. Richie had assumed it was an ineffective sun shade until Lester told him to stay under the protection in case the fish crashed into the crane, as they often did. Occasionally, they impaled themselves, Lester had claimed. That seemed like a tall tale; but, Richie was too worn out to really care.

"Where is Peter?" Pike called, not seeing the chubby gnome at the moment.

"In there," Lester yelled, still not taking his eye off the giant yellow blob for even one second. Fifteen feet down was nothing—a flick of the tail to the fish. "I think he found the cooking sherry."

"Get him out," Pike shouted. "He has to read the scale."

"Get him out, yourself. I'm busy!"

"Rita, could you unbelt for a second and wake Peter up. It's kind of important."

"Lester told me to stay belted in."

"I know. And I understand that Lester is in change; but there's nobody else to get the drunken scum. If he doesn't read the scale, what's the point in catching the fish. Next year, I'll carry another crew member."

"Man or woman?" she asked, unbuckling her harness.

"Man," he answered, unblinking.

"Lester was just being considerate of our unborn children. Why aren't you?"

Pike looked from the console into her face. Then he let his glance drift down to the deck, to Lester and the kid. "What unborn children?" he asked, suspiciously.

"The ones that are unborn," she laughed. It was a careless laugh—one that sent a shiver up Pike's backbone. Then she bobbed down the ladder and out of sight.

"Come right back, when Peter is awake and on deck," he called after her.

Meanwhile, Richie was dangerously close to the breaking point—but he didn't know it. Nobody was handy to baby him and keep fluids down his throat on cue, and he was glad. In fact, a nice kind of euphoria had taken over from the exhaustion. About time. The fish was almost in the bag, and he was feeling fine. Very fine. Superb, actually. And it looked like he was going to win the biggest tournament of them all. How about that? A few people around the world who thought he was a stumble bum would be very surprised. Such as Clive McAndrews, for one. And the Baron. Ha, ha. Old Bardona would be snarling tonight.

Of course, after the victory he wouldn't be doing advertising spots like Pike had to. That wouldn't be seemly; but a few featured articles in the Sporting Gazette would be expected. Nothing prying. Just about fishing. Refined. Tips. Little stories. That would be fun. He turned the crank handle. One, two, turn. One, two, turn. Ha, ha. It was going to be sweet. Lots and lots of women after his virile manhood. Beautiful. At last, he was more than a rich kid. A lot more. One, two, turn.

"Hey...!" Lester barked into his daydream. "Wake the fuck up! Stop that reeling! You're reeling structure, not the fish!!"

"What?"

"Stop reeling. Take a break. Get a drink."

Richie let go of the handle and straightened his spine. Gawd...! His back was broken. It was a mass of pain, and it was locked, somehow.

"Well, we're fucked...!" Lester yelled up at Pike. "The line is snugged up tight on a coral spire or something, and the fish is just floating."

"I can see that."

"Well...?"

"Well what?"

"What do we do now?" Although yelling loudly, Lester had never taken his attention off the fish, or his finger off the spear gun trigger.

"Has Rita got Peter awake yet?"

"Peter, get your drunk ass out here!" the cook bellowed.

"He's really soused!" Rita yelled from the galley.

"Rich, go drag the midget bastid out here and put him in the fishing chair," Lester ordered.

"What about the fish...?"

"And splash some water on your head and neck, while you're in there."

"I'm fine," he grinned, foolishly.

"You're fucked. Do what I say."

In turning toward the galley, Rich tripped over the discarded bench and did a nose flop on the deck. From high on the focastle, Dec applauded laconically.

"Way to go, Ace! That was a perfect trip and dive. I've never seen a better one."

With a self-deprecating wave, Richie picked himself up. His shin throbbed blindingly, but he had broken the fall with a Ken Pao Ri slap a millisecond before his nose had smashed the deck. It was really a shame that Dec Madrigal was so jealous of him. Darn it.

"You forced me to be the darned hero with your wife! I wanted to go back on my boat, remember? It's not my fault if you're jealous, so take your bad vibes and cram them!" Without waiting for an answer, he hobbled toward the galley.

That little speech got Pike and Dec's attention. It shot their eyebrows skyward. "What's he talking about?" Pike asked, sticking his head out the pilot house window.

"That kid is something. He puts things together in the oddest way."

"Maybe you've been riding him too hard."

"Too hard? He broke my fucking nose, then he chimed me. I should throw him overboard, is what I should do."

"Well," Pike said. "Just stay on the cannon. It will settle out later." He ducked back through the window, and tried once again to see what the fish was snagged on.

Richie limped into the galley to find Peter Zanker sprawled full length on the padded bench behind the galley table, gone to the world. Rita was drawing water into a pan at the sink. "He won't wake up," she explained cheerfully, walking over with the pan of water. Without a second thought, she dashed it in the little fellow's face, then stood back to see if he would surface. An empty sherry bottle rolled out from under the table and came to rest against her toe. Peter's bloodshot eyes spasmed open. Rivulets of water coursed down his face to disappear into the neck of his shirt. Before he had time to sputter, Lester's hoarse voice barked joyfully.

"Thar she blows...!!"

Richie grabbed the midget's surprisingly muscular forearm and hauled him out into the sunlight.

"Hey, take it easy, would you! I'm coming." Peter did not enjoy being dragged around like a Tom Thumb doll. To show his displeasure, he dug the heels of his deck shoes in to make the procedure as difficult as possible. Since he was a full head shorter than Richie, he didn't have the leverage to actually resist.

"Reel up, reel up, reel up...!! Lester was yelling repeatedly, while sighting down the spear gun.

"So spear him, and get the hell out of there!" Dec called.

"I don't care what your story is," Rich hissed in Zanker's ear. "You better straighten up."

Something in Richie's voice frightened Peter Zanker into a semblance of sobriety. He stopped resisting. Rich shoved him toward the fighting chair with the admonition to stay awake, then he hurried back to the winch.

"Another couple of feet," Lester drawled maddeningly, leaning over the rail to get the spear point six inches closer. It wasn't so much that he was in danger—he was in immense and foolhardy danger. Pike had never seen anybody nuts enough to stare down the gullet of a moon halibut before, and this one was way bigger than the boat. They might not be able to haul him out, even if he wasn't hung up on the reef. Probably a new world record. Damn close. Pike had never seen a larger one. Weird. Just laying there, waiting to be speared. This whole day had an awkwardness that was unnerving. He had wanted Lester to be topside; but there he was, leaned out over the rail, and Pike wasn't so very sure that the good Wunderman wasn't zoned out. Maybe he was singing to the halibut. Who knew?

In the first seconds that Lester had leaned out, Pike had snapped the power grid off, which had elicited an excited squawk from George. But what could he do? If Lester slipped overboard, Stars forbid, Pike didn't want him fried by the grid. So now they were unprotected, which was very unhealthy. Pike's finger hovered over the On button, waiting for Lester to fire the spear and lean back aboard.

Gad, look at Richie reeling on the coral head. Why the devil had Lester told him to? He must see something I don't. The scope certainly showed no structure. And look at Peter—sitting in the middle of the deck. The fucker must be blind drunk.

"Shoot him, you old fuck, and get the hell back in here!!" Dec yelled. "Rita, grab his belt!"

Rita had been hanging back in the galley door trying to decide where to go. Her bladder was full from drinking iced tea, but she didn't want to miss the landing of Richie's biggest fish. She had her mini-corder around her neck; but now Dec was commanding her to grab Lester, and she suddenly had to pee first. But she couldn't. What if Lester fell overboard because she wasn't holding him? Skipping across the deck, she grabbed the back loop of his rope belt and planted her feet.

"I told you upstairs," Lester muttered, sighting directly over the spear tip at the wheel-sized eye of the monster that was still too deep. "They told me here."

"Well, I ain't about to fall over, so skedattle."

"I don't think so," she said, not relinquishing her hold.

With an infinitesimal shrug, Lester dismissed the matter from his list of things to care about. "Keep reeling," he snapped at Richie.

*

Before he had recommenced the torture wheel, Richie had taken a peek over the side at the halibut. The fish was stupendous; but whatever he was reeling on wasn't a fish. It didn't feel alive—so why did Lester want him to keep on with the stupid reeling? He was definitely making up line. It was coming easier than it had for hours; but unless that fish was dead, he wasn't connected to the line anymore.

"Structure coming up...!" Lester yelled at Pike. "Something very weird!"

"What is it?!"

"Dunno, but it's gonna annoy the fish very soon."

"Stay on him."

"Right here. If he comes up, I doubt if I can miss."

"Get Peter to witness that he's still hooked when you poon him."

Lester didn't answer, which meant he was thinking something like 'Fuck, Peter.' But of course, no crew member would say fuck you to a judge, even a drunk one.

The last time he'd fished with Peter was last year for scut, Pike recalled. Judge Zanker hadn't been nearly so sloppy then. Alcohol isn't pretty when you can't locate the limits. Maybe it was time for Peter to find a snug harbor.

"Looks like a tree!" Dec called from his perch. "I never heard of coral growing like that."

"A coral tree will foul the winch," Pike commented, putting a set of field glasses on the object.

"Bet your ass," Dec answered, happily. "Somebody will have to knock it off, or the fish never gets close enough to catch."

"Rita. Up here," Pike ordered.

Rita turned her head to look up at the bridge. That tone of voice could only mean, 'Do it now, crew person, or your ass is mud.' So she let go of Lester's belt. "Don't fall overboard," she admonished.

"Skedattle," Lester said, with his eyes riveted straight down.

"You're doing great, Rich," she said, hopping onto the ladder. "I'll bring you some orange juice in a minute."

Richie tried to smile, but it was beyond him.

Rita skipped up the rungs, her bladder forgotten. She arrived breathlessly on the bridge and saluted smartly. "Aye, aye, Cap. Rita here."

"Look, honey, sorry I never asked you, or showed any interest in teaching you, but it never occurred to me how important it might be...

"What...?"

"Do you know how to pilot this crate? I need to go down and help get that dreck untangled, before it gums up the winch."

Rita smiled slowly. "Is it so much different from By's or Litton's?"

"About the same. Come around here and I'll show you."

Rita stepped around the console.

"This switch activates the shield. It's off right now, but we want it on as soon as I signal. Just hit the switch. That's the most critical thing."

"Okay." That wasn't too difficult.

"Hopefully we won't need to, but if we have to move, push this,"

Pike said, showing her the joy stick. "Up is back, down is forward. Don't mess with the power unless I say so. It's the thumb toggle."

"I can assist her," the nervous voice of George cut into the explanation.

"She'll be fine," Pike said, shivering. A vision of Thomas Goodnaught's prophecy intruded itself. Maybe this was the glitch about to manifest. Suddenly realizing it was stupid to consider a computer's feelings, even if you were in business with one, he made a half-step sideways and clicked off the monitor feature. "Leave him off," Pike suggested. "The XG unit will do fine. Goodnaught said to use it." He winked at her and started down the ladder. "Dec," he called. "Rita is piloting. Help her out if you get a chance."

"Roger. Moving to the laser rifle. I should be able to shoot most of that trash off the line. It's looking kind of like an old TV aerial with barnacles on it!" His voice sounded like he was questioning his own sanity. Obviously, there could be no aerials on an uninhabited water planet. "Maybe somebody jettisoned it. Like an old boot," he added.

Pike slid down the ladder and took in the situation at a glance. Not good. The halt and the lame were everywhere. "How you holding up, Rich?" he asked, leaning briefly on the rail beside Lester to look at the fish.

"Fine," Richie answered, unconvincingly. The euphoria had passed, and his back was wrenching with every turn of the crank handle. Madness, all of this.

"Keep it coming. We're almost ready for some action. Stay under that umbrella." Pike took a long handled gaff from the rack outside the galley. He leaned on the rail, squinting down into the green water. His right fist held his new laser pistol.

"Yep, that's what it is!" he called to Dec. "Some kind of artifact. Damned if it isn't."

"Push it out away from the line," Dec shouted calmly. "I'll shoot it off above the gaff. I've got a good angle here." Dec was now on the same deck level as Rita, squinting through the scope of the bulky laser rifle. "Trust me," he said. That choice of words struck him as funny. He laughed.

The barnacle encrusted object was almost at gaff depth and coming up with every crank. "How you doing, Lester?" Pike asked, lightly.

"Lovely. History in the making."

Pike grunted. He stuffed the pistol into his waistband and reached over to gaff the object in slow motion so as not to antagonize the fish. The scientist in him thought about putting a line on the jetsam for future investigation; but laying right below was a mother big halibut, like an island-sized pancake staring up at him with its two little protuberant eyes. How the hell did halibuts seed themselves all over the galaxy? Every ocean had flatfish, scurrying along the ocean floor, filling an ecological niche, and they all looked pretty much like the same species, whether they were or not. Like Darwin's finches. Over time, the niche got filled by some species that transformed into halibut shape. Big mothers here on Solari.

The butt stared up balefully—probably not even seeing the boat in his window of vision. But who knew? Maybe the scientific data on how fish see was all hogwash. Some of it was, for sure.

Drifting the gaff hook through the transparent water at a snail's pace, so the fish wouldn't get bothered by the movement and strike, Pike hooked the jetsam and assisted the winch in hauling it airward.

"This thing is big and heavy, whatever it is," he grunted. It seemed to be barnacles and red coral growing on a tube of steel. The first couple of feet were out of the water and Pike was easing his laser pistol out to cut it off, when the fish decided that the structure was edible.

"Look out...!!" Lester yowled, firing the spear gun. It was a good shot. The little harpoon sunk into the middle of the fish's narrow forehead where the fish brain was supposed to be. Evidently, he missed the tiny brain ganglia, because the fish smashed into the dangling structure like an enraged, starving log truck—and tried to swallow the entire fantastic piece of whatever it was, whole. All this took place about five feet from Pike, Lester and Richie—the length of a gaff handle. Needless to say, the gaff was ripped from Pike's hands, and he went reeling backwards, yelling for Rita to hit the shield switch, as he looked for a place to hide. Dragging Peter with him, he ended up behind the fighting chair, not a very safe haven.

"I can walk," Peter slurred, belying his words by sitting down abruptly behind the chair when the boat rolled leeward.

Taking stock of the situation, Pike saw that Lester had found cover with Richie under the winch awning, and that Rita was giving him the thumbs up sign, meaning she had presumably activated the grid. Good.

"What now...?" she called.

Now what indeed, Pike thought, waving to her. The winch's reel was singing as the monster sounded. The fish needed to be landed before Richie keeled over. Pike stood up. There wasn't much to fear while the stupid fish was plowing into deep water. Lester was already back at the rail.

"He's running with the shit in his mouth," Lester announced, "Not going deep."

"That's a break," Pike said, joining him.

"What should I do?!" Rita called.

"I'll be up," Pike called back. "This is a mess," he said to Lester.

"Couldn't hardly be worse. But at least that structure will tire him out. Better than we could."

Pike nodded his agreement and turned toward the ladder. "Take a break," he said to Rich. "Stretch out on the deck. Lester will call you."

Richie puffed up his cheeks in surprised relief. Without another word, he spread-eagled on the deck. Knowing how the kid felt, Pike went past him to the ladder and bounded up to the bridge. "Never a dull moment," he joked to Rita.

"That damn fish is way bigger than the boat," she said. Her eyes were much bigger than they usually were. Fright can do attractive things to women. "How are we ever going to land it?"

"We don't exactly land this one. We just weigh him, then cut him loose, if possible." He yelled down to the deck. "Cinch him down, Les. I'll back on him, so we don't lose all the line."

Lester waved agreement. He twisted the drag control. Line stopped screaming out as Pike went backward at the same speed that the monster was departing, keeping line tension on the fish. Richie should have used the opportunity to make up line, but he probably needed the rest. Battling a fish this size had broken plenty of strong men. Pike didn't want Richie to be one of them. Besides, the fish was harpooned very well. Pike had seen the barbed point sink into the bony forehead. The fish wasn't going to get away.

Rita took the opportunity to visit the loo. On her way down, she shot a little footage of Richie napping, with the monster fish off in the distance. She decided to document the rest of the operation. It was bound to be interesting, no matter how it turned out.

"Pretty weird," Pike called to Dec. "Did you get a shot off?"

"Not really. Too many people in the vicinity. See him out there? Looks like he's surfing with that trash. What was it?"

Pike put his field glasses on the fish two hundred yards out and watched him plowing the structure across the wave tops. "I don't know," he answered. "Some kind of conning tower or something. Very heavy."

"The fish don't think it's heavy," Dec said, shading his eyes to watch the big halibut. "He's tangled in both lines, ain't he?"

"I'd say so."

"We'll never get him up. We're one short on crew. You'll have to cut the harpoon line off. There's nobody to reel it."

"Or try the Resnick Hoist," Pike speculated. "Then we can cut everything off as soon as we weigh in."

Dec paused to think it through again. "You're a hard man to unconvince."

"No, it's perfect now," Pike insisted, restating his position. "Like you say, we can't land him. Let's at least try the clean and jerk. It's a lot safer than you think."

"I don't think it's safe at all," Dec said. "If he was smaller, maybe."

"Don't be a baby. At least, we'll get something on the scale. Peter will see it, and we can thumb our nose at the competition. Otherwise, we get to do it again tomorrow."

"He's turning," Lester bellowed.

"Get the kid reeling!" Pike yelled, reversing the engine.

"Wake up, Rich," Lester said, urgently. "Nap's over."

Richie opened his eyes and looked around blearily.

"Get up…! Start reeling," Lester shouted in his face. "This is the payoff."

Hopping up in his accustomed manner seemed like a normal thing to do, but his overstressed back muscles had cinched up during the brief nap. They greeted Richie with a massive wallop of pain—like half the tendons in his middle back had suddenly ripped loose.

"Ooof," he grunted and stumbled into the winch, which he grabbed onto for support.

"Reel! He's coming like a battle ship."

The thought of moving, let alone bending over to reel, made Richie feel like puking. Black spots danced in front of his eyes. "I can't. My back…"

A look of alarm crossed Lester's face. He jerked his eyes away from the on-rushing battering ram. Making a snap decision, he waved his arms in a wash-out gesture.

"Get us out of here," he bellowed. "The fucker's going to brush the junk off on the hull!"

Pike could see the same scenario developing. "Dec…!" he shouted, "Go down and help Lester. Get a safety line on all four of you, but first find an elastic wrap for Richie's back. Cinch him up tight enough that he can reel. We're going airborne. We can play him from there—if Richie can reel."

Rita had come back to the bridge. She was leaning out the window filming. "Buckle up, honey," Pike said to her. He punched two hot keys on the console and the thruster engines started to rev. Down below, Dec and Lester were hustling around the deck, tying everybody onto tethers. "This could be a little tricky," he said to Rita, who still hadn't moved out of the window. The fish was about thirty yards away and coming full bore.

"Hold tight down below!" he yelled. Lester and Dec waved, a little half-heartedly, Pike thought. Peter was strapped in the fishing chair. Richie was still holding onto the winch. Dec had taken a dozen turns of rope around his chest in an old fashioned fisherman's corset. Probably better than elastic. "Here we go!" he called.

He hit the fire button and pulled back a hair on the red joy stick. The thruster rockets fired making the launching pad. The boat jumped into the air. This was the tricky part—Pike had never attempted to keep any boat at low altitude before, and in the first seconds he realized it wasn't handling wonderfully. The bow had a decided tendency to dip.

The fish swam safely under the boat, towing its load of freight. Nice maneuver, Pike congratulated himself. What would be the perfect way to document the technique in the magazines? he wondered.

"I told you this wouldn't work," George chirped.

"Butt out. I thought you were off."

"You can't shut me off, thank Jobs and Wasniak. I'm the system. And the problem you're having is with the stabilizing gyro. They don't work near sea level."

"Why the hell not?"

"Human error, I guess. You wrote the program, hotshot. It works in landing mode; but not during take off where you normally wouldn't need them."

"Thank you very much," Pike said, switching to landing mode.

"I wouldn't do that," George chided. "You can't lift from landing mode."

"I'm not lifting until we get some line reeled in. I can play him just fine in landing mode."

"Suit yourself; but it won't go into lift-off mode until you land."

"Why the hell not!" Pike demanded hotly.

"Because I don't want to drown when this tea cup capsizes. That much weight will overbalance us to the winch side and will jerk us out of the sky. No hard feelings, it's just physics. I would have to countermand your orders."

Pike was speechless. He glared at Rita—who had a worried look on her face. He watched her twiddle the grass wedding ring, thinking no doubt that nothing like this had ever happened on her father's boat. The goddamn computer had taken control—or even if it hadn't, Pike couldn't trust either system not to be compromised now.

"Another thirty or forty turns, Rich!" he yelled. "Then you can sleep for a week."

Lester waved. "He's doing great. A real trooper."

"Thomas Goodnaught warned me that you were flawed," Pike confided to George.

"Flawed? What would he know about it? Woogie-woogie magic."

"Looks like Thomas was right. You're hard wired for cowardice under stress, or something like that. What a despicable trick on a rookie. And dangerous, too. Somebody doesn't like Rich. I thought G&G

was an honest shop. Looks like I was wrong. Or were you assembled somewhere else? How about when he spilled that orange juice on the keyboard? Who fixed it?"

"You *must* be kidding," George answered, loading on the scorn. "You think some off-shore guru wouldn't have told me if I was hot-rodded?"

"Now that I think about it, this is the first really dangerous situation that we've had on the boat. The rest of the danger was either in the skiff or on shore. That's why your defect didn't show up before."

"Bull. And I'm still not going to let you kill us."

"All the rest of the action happened outside your control. It's only Richie's incredible luck that kept him in. You're wired for failure."

"That's a lie. My circuits are perfect—bright and clean. I just ran through everything. No problem."

"Or maybe you trigger on the word 'halibut'. Who knows? Or a certain number of days, or a date. I hate to think what you're doing with the investments, right about now. Hopefully, your cowardice doesn't extend to that area."

The portfolio had skidded dangerously in the last two days, George realized with a twinge of alarm. But that could hardly be blamed on him, could it? Everything was readjusting after the Barcode mess. Who could plan for something like that?"

"But you win this round, George old boy. We'll catch this fishie a different way, and we'll avoid getting in the record books, just so you can be content."

"Attempted records aren't worth much if you're not around to get the kudos," George said, after a beat of hesitation. He was aware that maritime law and spacing law looked dimly on mutiny. He needed to tread carefully.

Pike, for his part, was aware that nothing at all would function on board without a computer, so he didn't have the luxury of blowing George's smug brains out. Not before a fish was caught and weighed, and not before a landing was made on Wexley Common to collect the money. So Plan B.

He selected Short Wave from the Communications menu, choose Mordachi Skinner's band width, and hit the Go button. "How's the fishing, old hound?" he asked, when the indicator beeped a pick-up.

"Who wants to know?" ask the gruff voice of Mordachi's first mate, Glando Sklug, an old salt if ever there was one.

"Is Mordachi belted in, or can he talk?"

"Hold on. I'll see if he's indisposed." The connection went dead except for the crackle of static.

A few minutes later, Mordachi's voice boomed into Pike's bridge.

"How they hanging, Romeo?"

"Want to catch half a fish?" Pike asked, explaining the rest of the scenario in brief.

Receiving a jocular affirmative, Pike gave Mordachi the coordinates and a few seconds later, Mordachi's boat, *Don't Tread On Me*, was hovering right off the port side.

"Ahoy, the Humanity," Mordachi's voice boomed cheerfully. "Playing this one from the air, are we?"

"That was the idea, but the winch won't lock down. The new plan is to splash down, shoot you the extra line we've got on him, then stretch him between the two of us. I think we can both get a pretty interesting weigh in."

"I don't think mine would count as second hook."

"If we break loose, which could happen, you get it all. Or I think you could make a good case under the "Rescue of Catch" clause."

"Never heard of that one, but let's go for the weenie before he dies of old age. Gods, he's a big one, ain't he?'

"Last time we were floating, he tried to ram us to scrape that junk off his nose. I'd say he must be getting kind of tired; but stay ready to jump in case he gets rambunctious again. Dec will be riding the cannon."

"Tell that horny bleeper to watch for ricochets. I don't want to lose a boat over your fish."

"I'm an expert at ricochets," Dec called from the deck. "The first shot will ricochet through the middle porthole in the big chief's cabin."

"Ready as we'll ever be," Mordachi boomed, not having heard Dec's remark. "Let's get to it."

"Okay, we're splashing down. Belt in." Pike announced to his crew and to Mordachi. He waited a minute, then angled in, keeping the line as tight on the fish as was humanly possible. "Honey," he said to Rita. "Could you keep taping? I'd love to have this documented." He smiled meaningfully at her. "Why don't you stay up here with me. There's a pretty good field of view."

Rita mentally slapped her forehead. She had forgotten to bring the knapsack full of spare tapes and the extra battery pack. Strange how getting married had made her absent-minded. Had it? Something had. And she had lost most of her interest in being a Ph.D. Very strange. Amazing actually. Just like what had happened to her mother after she married Daddy. Quite annoying.

When the boat settled on the waves, she unclipped her seat belt and ran to get her equipment. Something more important than documenting his new fishing technique was going on—Rita had finally figured that out. Pike had never been interested in her recording project beyond

the normal egoism of having his picture taken for posterity. As she retrieved the knapsack, the light came on. He wanted the audio feature.
Brilliant. She chided herself severely for lack of quick response. As a
partner and help-mate, she would need to make a better showing in the
future. The word *mutiny* had finally surfaced in her mind. George was
treading dangerous ground, even if he was right—and he controlled all
the software. He could presumably wipe any computerized audio file
that incriminated him. Hence the vid-corder—an independent record.
It was possible that she had recorded part of the previous interchange.
But had she stopped shooting before the bad stuff? Now that she understood, she would station herself on top of a speaker. Grabbing the
battery pack, she hurried back up the ladder.

On the way up, she paused briefly to get a close-up of Richie straining at the winch, and Lester encouraging him. Richie looked exhausted.
He didn't even smile at her, which was more worrisome than she cared
to admit. In this day and age, it was kind of nuts to be reeling up a huge
weight like that by hand, wasn't it? Of course, nobody was forcing him
to do it.

"Stand by, Mordachi...!" Dec Madrigal shouted, attracting the attention of her camera. He heaved a throwing line, which uncoiled in a
perfect parabola and landed across the fantail of Don't Tread on Me—a
couple of feet from where Glando Sklug was waiting for it.

Sklug tied on his heaviest fishing line and held the knot in the air,
meaning he was done. "Make sure you tie a 'barrel with a leader' or it
won't hold," he called, giving Dec the advantage of his years of fishing
expertise, and a little piece of his ego.

"Keep your knot advice for somebody who cares," Lester barked.
"We use granny knots on everything."

Dec hauled the line back until he had Glando's knot on board.

Mordachi had sent a braided cadmium alloy cable attached to a
heavy green hemp line. Lester took one look at it and snorted, "Barrel
with a leader, my ass." He opened the tackle locker and picked out the
biggest swivel he could find, and the cable splicing kit. He tossed the
swivel to Dec. "Tie this on to our end," he said, then knelt and opened
the lid of the splicing kit.

"Hurry it up!" Pike yelled. Lester flipped a finger up toward the
bridge. Pike laughed.

Richie didn't even look up at the flurry of activity around him. On
the edge of despair, he had remembered a Ken Pao Ri mantra of the injured warrior—a specific against pain and blood loss. Although his nose
had stopped bleeding, it seemed like a way to preserve whatever was
left of his manhood. Putting aside all thoughts of being a very wealthy
person involved in a futile, pointless and dangerous game that he didn't

really give a damn about, he started the chant under his breath. He'd never really used the mantra in an actual emergency before, only during practice, so he wasn't sure it would work. Besides, this wasn't an authentic emergency—he could quit anytime. His stubborn streak didn't want to be known as a quitter, that was all. After a minute or so of mumbling the words, he was quiet enough to get into the rhythm of the winching, and in another couple of minutes, Rich Rodney Tourbo was in a deep trance state—his body was winding and winding on the winch handle, but nobody was home in his pain centers to receive a pain message. His consciousness and subconsciousness were both hovering on the edge of the Great Void, a place of utter peacefulness.

Lester finished the splice to Mordachi's line and cast it off, with another bird flipped to Glando Sklug. He gave Richie a penetrating look, then made a hissing sound to attract Dec's attention. "See, I told you he was starting to amount to something. He's way out in a zone border—very peaceful."

"You'd know, if anybody would," Dec grunted.

"That's right," Lester chided. "Make fun of something sacred."

"Gunner topside!" Pike barked.

"You go," Lester ordered.

Bounding up the ladder almost like levitation, Dec belted into the gunner's harness and was sighting down the stun cannon inside of twenty seconds. Just in time, too. The bull was almost on them.

"Going up," Pike shouted, so everybody could hear.

Rita kept filming the fish's approach. Seeing the world through the view finder made it less scary than it was, but still it was awfully weird. The fish was plowing a wake like a one-horned monster. It was going to ram.

"Sit down, Rita," Pike ordered, sharply.

Suddenly realizing there was no time to belt in, Rita sank to her knees and wrapped her arms around the corner of Pike's console.

He hit the jump button and up they went, fifteen feet into the air—out of harm's way, again. The fish charged under the boat directly toward Mordachi. Richie went on reeling, completely unaffected.

"You better hit the air, Captain Skinner," Pike advised into the mike.

Seconds later, Mordachi's boat leaped out of danger—about fifty feet into mid-air.

"Who's driving that crate?" Pike inquired of the short wave.

"I am," replied the surly voice of Sklug. "Captain's on the winch as he should be."

"What do you say we play this bull from up here? Think you could handle the controls?"

"How's that...?"

"Yeah, we'll hoist him out, by flying him out. Then weigh in and cut him loose."

"Cut him loose with all the junk tangled on?"

"I didn't tangle him."

"Same thing as." Sklug fancied himself a purist.

"You can have the fish after we release him, if you want to go to the trouble of actually catching him."

"We always catch the fish."

"Sure, sure. In this case, it can't be done. You think you're a good enough flyboy to make history? We're filming all this on a vid-corder, compliments of the lovely Rita." He winked at her, noting her not very dignified posture on the floor. "You can go ahead, honcy. It's nice and steady up here now."

"You're only sweet-talking me because you want posterity to believe that you were nice to me."

Pike smile broadly. "You might want to find a place with a view, honey dumpling, and tie yourself a safety line."

"You might want to stuff it," Rita said with a smile. She climbed to her feet and pointed the recorder out the window at the fish.

Pike could hear the cam-corder softly whirring. Good girl.

"You with us on this, George?" Pike asked, politely.

George's voice was pinched, like he was biting his bit-mapped tongue. "Of course. The physics are now barely passable, so you're the Captain."

"Thanks, old sport. I knew you'd come around."

"Incidentally, by my calculations, the line isn't strong enough."

"Now, now. He'll break off if it's not. So there's nothing to worry about from your point of view?"

"I am completely dedicated to Mr. Tourbo winning the Tournament, which means catching a Moon Halibut."

Pike let that comment go and set about his preparations. "Lester," he yelled, "when both lines get even, lock ours down. I'll get Mordachi to lock his, and we'll lift the critter out."

"How do we tell when they're even?"

"About even! We'll ease upwards until there's a strain on the line, then hoist. Is Peter awake?"

"He will be."

Pike watched Lester lift the sodden little judge out of the fishing chair and plop him down on the deck next to the scales. He whipped a rope harness around him, and tied it off to the rail. Then he went to Richie, who was acting kind of like a zombie. Pike couldn't hear the conversation, but Lester gimped around like a fretful old grandmother, smiling and cooing. After a brief period of shoulder massaging, Lester guided Richie's hand to the lock toggle and pressed the back of his fingers on the toggle. The winch locked.

Supporting Richie with one stringy arm, Lester gave the high sign to Pike. "She's all yours now! Get Mordachi to even it up from his side. I'm gonna get this warrior settled in the galley, then I'll be back to assist the judge." The two of them limped out of Pike's view.

"Mr. Sklug," Pike said into the short wave. "We are locked down and ready for some fancy flying. How about you?"

"I'm here now," Mordachi's deep basso voice replied. "We are locked down, but your line is slack, old sport. Amazing super-structure growing on his head! Can't wait to get a look at that." Mordachi had several advanced degrees in anthropology, and he loved to write scholarly articles.

"I wasn't thinking of keeping him," Pike replied, easing the boat slowly upward. The line snugged up with a small jolt when they were about twenty feet above Mordachi.

"Why not keep him? This could be the find of our lifetime."

"Or the find of the week," Pike commented.

"Who ever heard of civilized life on a total water planet? There's no record of any industry being here. Gods, what if they have a Submariner culture. An underwater civilization. Think of the astounding visiting we could do."

"It's jetsam."

"You can't seriously believe that? At the very least, somebody put a transmitter here, or it's a shipwreck. I want to see, don't you? Where's your curiosity, sport? How about it, Tourbo? Aren't extinct cultures up your alley?"

Richie didn't answer because he wasn't there.

"Well," Pike said, "in theory there's no problem with catching him. We just hold him in the air long enough for oxygen shock to set in."

"Exactly."

"If one of the lines breaks, it will probably capsize the boat holding the weight."

"Well worth the risk. Let's go."

"Our line's way lighter than yours, just for the record."

"Mine's old and rotten. I'll drop you a rope ladder, if you founder."

"Okay, then. Lester!" Pike called. "Is Peter awake and ready to witness?"

"Hold your horses," Lester yelled back, limping out of the galley. "I can't do everything by myself, can I? Let's get this durned unorthodox fishing over with. I didn't sign on to be everybody's' nurse maid!"

"Well, wake Peter up and belt in next to him. We're ready."

"He's already awake. He's a professional, ain't he? At least, he don't need no hydro-turbine to lift out a durn minnow!"

"Quit sputtering and get ready," Pike advised.

"I am ready! Lift him out and break his spirit. See if I care!"

"Belt in, you old coot!"

"Go ahead. I ain't going to tie off. I might want to swim. Think about it."

"Shut him up and go for it!" Dec yelled. "Before my white beard wraps around my asshole."

"You're *all* asshole!" Lester yelled back, acting mad as a banty rooster. Rita was straining to capture all the fascinating by-play for posterity.

"Ready, Mordachi?!" Pike asked the CB. "My crew is whipped up to a fighting edge."

"Let her rip," Mordachi confirmed. "On the count of three, what?"

The sky overhead suddenly blinked full of boats. Other fishermen had been monitoring the shortwave and had come to watch."

"Slow and easy lifting," Pike cautioned. "If it's too much, we'll be able to tell. Ready? One, two—three!" He toggled the lift knob, feathering it perfectly. The winch took the weight and strained under it. Both lines tightened like piano wire. The big fish felt the tug and flicked his head.

"Oversight," Pike admitted over the airwaves. "He could hack the lines easy with that jetsam. Let's speed it up a little, Mordachi. Twice as fast. Ready. Go!"

The Humanity surged up in tandem with Mordachi's boat. The fish followed.

"Start reading the meter," Pike bellowed at Peter Zanker. "At its highest mark, record it!"

Lester waved. He was standing beside Peter—pointing helpfully to the weight scale.

"Six hundred!" Lester yelled. "Is that enough for you?"

"I want that transmitter tower," Mordachi boomed. "The fish will die anyway, or he'll bust into some boat tomorrow trying to scrape off."

Richie picked that moment to leave the safety of the galley and totter out to watch the action.

"Up we go," Pike said, evenly. He twiddled the joy stick. "Hey, Rich..!" he yelled. "Go sit in the fighting chair."

Richie started toward the chair, but then had other ideas. He saw Rita leaning out a window, pointing a camera at him. He waved, with a hazy flash of smile, and started up the ladder. His back hadn't recovered, naturally; but he had forgotten about it—until he got on the second rung. Stepping up with his right leg caused his back to spasm something fierce. Red spots danced maddeningly in front of his eyes.

He hooked an arm through a rung to keep from falling and started to breathe again. It would be stupid to go into the injured warrior trance hanging on a ladder. That thought struck him funny and he started to snigger, which really killed his ripped tendons—but he couldn't stop.

"Seven hundred," Lester sang.

The fish's head and cheeks were out of the water. The wreckage had flopped to one side out of the way. The big Bull didn't like being hauled out. Not a bit. He shook his great flat head and snapped his jaws.

Both lines were tangled in the jetsam, Pike saw, putting the field glasses on the fish. But it seemed like the bull was hooked really well. Pike couldn't tell for sure, but the line seemed to have worked itself between the teeth of the lower jaw—out of bite range. Mordachi's line was harpooned to the forehead.

"Eight hundred," Lester bellowed. The winch was straining as the full weight of the flopping fish started to hang on it. "A thousand...! It bounced to a thousand! What a big fucker!"

Another thousand would be registering on Mordachi's scales, and the fish wasn't half out. The biggest halibut ever caught was landed by Pike several years ago at forty-six hundred—a big old bull that had wrecked the fantail after he was totally exhausted. But Pike had won that year. Now, Richie had won, too. A tie was the same as a win—and that was now practically guaranteed. It was enough. Money wasn't the issue any more.

"You want me to shoot that stuff off his head?" Dec called down, hopefully. "How about an eye shot?"

"No. Just stand by."

Control of the boat was getting bouncy as the fish, naturally, started jerking around. Most of his weight wasn't supported by water now, and his mighty tail frothed the ocean.

"Twelve hundred and jumping..!"

"Had enough, Mordachi?" Pike asked. "Are we planning to shoot him? It's getting a slight bit hairy over here."

"Let's lower him back in," Mordachi said, jump-shifting. "I'm getting attached to the big fellow. We can shoot the lines off and the conning tower will probably stay tangled in the line. We can mark the spot and come back and dive on it."

"With bulls around? Not likely."

"Hire a college archeological team." Mordachi lost his breezy manner. "Lower at the same speed," he shouted. "I'm losing it!! One, two, three!"

"Mark the high weight!!" Pike yelled at Peter Zanker. "We're going down."

Below them Mordachi's boat was starting to wobble. Then as it lost altitude and weight, it righted itself. Pike followed him down, breathing about ten sighs of relief.

"I told you," George's alarmed voice cut in.

"Dec...?!" Pike yelled.

"Standing by!" Dec yelled back instantly.

"When we stop, hop down to the laser gun and shoot the lines off below the horseshit. Mordachi wants the structure stuff, if we can save it."

"Roger. Changing position." Pike heard footsteps on the roof. Contrary to his orders, Dec was changing weapons while they were moving. "Okay," Dec yelled. Pike saw him out the side window. "Shooting when we stop descending. Say when."

"Shoot Mordachi off first. He'll be lower, so we'll have more room to maneuver."

"Roger."

"We'll probably tip from the extra weight, so be ready for it."

"Roger. Richie and fucking Lester aren't tied off."

"George!" Pike yelled.

"I'm here." The computer's voice was full of suppressed something. Fear? That seemed impossible. Where would it come from?

"Get a grip on yourself. Everything is fine. You were right. It was too much. But we can hold the fish's head out until he dies. No problem with that. So it's a catch. Instead, we're going to do a live release. Any problems with that?"

"It's fifty-fifty that you can hold it when all the weight comes on us."

"Lester...!" Pike barked.

Lester waved. "It went up to twenty-six hundred! Dang big fish. Biggest ever! This one's the granddaddy!"

"Stand by with the cable cutters. If we tilt too much, cut the line. Don't think, just cut it. And tie yourself off, you hardheaded maggot. That's an order!"

"Ain't got no line."

"Use Peter's. Put him in the chair."

"Richie's in the chair...!" Lester looked around and saw that, obviously, Richie wasn't in the chair. Whipping his knife out, he cut the line around Peter's waist in one swipe. Keeping a sharp knife was important to Lester. His father had taught him that, and it had served him well.

He pulled the judge to his feet and pushed him toward the fighting chair. "Get in and belt down. We don't want to lose your ass over the side."

The boat was steadily losing altitude. The pressure on the winch was dramatically less. Lester looked around for Richie and saw him clinging to the ladder.

Leaving his other duties, he gimped over to the ladder and steadied the boy with both hands on his hips. "What's wrong with you? You need to be belted in."

"Can't move," Richie wheezed, very glad to have Lester there to help him. "My back is broken. I can feel the bones grinding."

"It ain't broke. Just seized up. Relax everything, and I'll carry you inside."

"Lester, where are you...?!" Pike roared.

"He's helping Richie," Rita answered from her perch at the window.

"I'll be goddamned!" Pike swore. "Why the fuck does *he* need help?"

"I don't know. Looks like he's hurt."

"Mordachi...?"

"Right here."

"Are you okay, now..?"

"So far so good."

"We'll stop with his gills out."

"Okay. Stop at gill level."

"It may take a minute to organize here."

"Got it. Holding at gill level."

"It's a little tricky to disengage."

"No shit," Mordachi boomed.

It had been a nightmarish eternity for Rich Rodney—Tournament winner, wealthy young man, martial artist, sex fiend—hanging on the ladder alone and isolated. None of his accomplishments or embarrassments meant a damn, none of his good luck, because a casual mis-step on an innocent ladder had somehow broken his back. Any movement in any direction would probably cause irreparable damage—any slight shifting of weight resulted in immediate grinding pain. Every time he tested the limits, he could feel the broken vertebra grinding against its broken other half. It was a sickening feeling. Waves of nausea washed over him. The only thing to do was gut it out. To allow himself to give in to the welcoming blackness that beckoned like a siren of oblivion, was madness. If he blacked out, his grip on the rung would relax and he would fall to a permanent wheelchair-bound paralysis. That much at least was clear—his future was ruined if he moved. So he willed himself to remain conscious, rigidly locked onto the ladder, as events on the boat swirled around him. Perhaps the yelling and cursing was coming from a different time dimension. It was a long, long time of being alone until Lester's strong hands reached out to hold his back in one piece, and the reassuring voice reassuring him that his back wasn't broken—even if it was a lie. Even if it was a lie, he let go of his clenched grip on the ladder and allowed Lester to catch his weight. Hanging on the ladder would never repair his broken vertebra. He needed immediate surgery, and the first step was letting Lester help him. At least, if he was lying down, nothing further would break.

Lester caught the limp body as it fell from the ladder. Moving had caused the bones to grind together. The pain, coupled with fear, overloaded Richie's stress system and he finally pitched into the well of blackness where no pain lived.

"Goddamnit, Lester!" Pike bellowed. "Get somewhere I can see you!!"

The fish was pitching around like crazy now that most of its powerful swimming muscles were back under water.

"What's the hold-up?" Mordachi asked, tightly. He was only about fifteen feet above the ocean—not much room for a mistake.

"Standing by, Dec?" Pike asked.

"Cross hairs on him. Say the word."

"Lester...!!"

The cook bounced into Pike's field of view, hopping at top speed on his gimpy leg toward the winch. He grabbed the tie-down rope end, whipped it around his waist and tied a bowline in it. "Ready!" he called. "Ain't no cause to get abusive. It's only a fish." He reached out with a gaff hook and pulled the line toward himself. His fishing knife was already in his right hand. "What are you waiting for, Dec? I'm ready."

"Ready, Mordachi?"

"Very," the big man answered tensely.

George interrupted, frantically. "There could be a malfunction in the—"

"Shut up!" Pike barked. "Fire away. Dec!" he bellowed, feeling sweat on the palms of his hands. He needed to control the horizontal planes, because a lot of weight surge was going to happen.

The rifle sizzled. The boat surged sideways.

"I'm off!" Mordachi yelled.

The blocky rifle kept up its sizzling in short bursts. The boat rocked dangerously. Suddenly, they surged back violently the other way as the weight was gone. Lester must have cut the line. Rita slid past the console, and stopped suddenly at the end of her rope. Pike fought for control, and after a few instants of chaos, found it. Blessed, blessed stability. The sun came out from behind a cloud in a blaze of glorious sunset.

"Fantastic!" Pike yelled. "Is everybody all right? Sound off!"

"Fine," Dec said from the deck beside the bridge. "Going down to help." His feet padded over to the ladder.

"Took him long enough," Lester bitched, picking himself up off the deck. "If I'd a thought he didn't know how to fly this thing, I never would have signed on." Dec walked across the deck like a big cat, and clapped the cook in a tight embrace.

"Damned good show!" Mordachi boomed. "I'm still hooked up with the treasure. Damned good!"

"You all right, honey?" Pike asked.

Rita looked dazed. She was sitting on the floor near Pike's feet at the end of her safety line, with no expression on her face. Not even relief.

"I'll have to teach you to tie off a little snugger," Pike observed. The CB radio was crackling with congratulations from the other boats. Pike switched it off. "Dec," he called down to the deck. "If everybody's all right, take over up here."

"Everybody ain't all right," Lester said, sourly. "There's probably coffee all over the galley. Probably take me all night to clean it up."

"You with us, honey?" Pike asked Rita. He couldn't leave the console to go to her. She looked really beautiful now that some color was coming back to her face. He was hoping that she'd smile pretty soon, so he'd know she was all right.

*

The big bull halibut lay still a few feet under the surface, big as a billboard, repairing its wits, or whatever fish do inside their fishy brains—then it flicked its great tail and glided downward.

* * *

# LEADERS

| | DELILAH | TORGA HOWLER | TIGER MUSKY | D.W. SCUT | PHANTOM TROUT | LAR BARRACUDA | GLANS SALMON | RAZORFIN | SWAMPFISH | MOON HALIBUT | TOTAL | |
|---|---|---|---|---|---|---|---|---|---|---|---|---|
| Farouk Bardona | | | 2 | 5 | | 2 | 1 | 5 | | 1 | 3RD | 16 |
| Ethyl Bierly | 2 | | | | | | | 4 | | | | 6 |
| Angmar Blirt | | | | | 4 | | 4 | | OUT | | | |
| Bill Bolen | | | 3 | | 5 | | 2 | 1 | 3 | 2 | 3RD | 16 |
| Dresden Carthy | 4 | | | | 2 | 5 | | | 5 | | 3RD | 16 |
| JB Dillingham | | OUT | | | | | | | | | | |
| Harry Dolan | 3 | 2 | 5 | | | | | 3 | 1 | 5 | 2ND | 21 |
| Macky Duff | | | | | OUT | | | | | | | |
| Ira Fairborne | | 4 | | 3 | | | | | | | 5TH | 7 |
| Buddy Jay | | | | | | | OUT | | | | | |
| Sandy Kind | | | | | | | 3 | | OUT | | | |
| Hank Knofsinger | | | 2 | | | | | 2 | | | | 4 |
| Peter Marcuso | | | | | OUT | | | | | | | |
| Trini Morales | | | | | | | 5 | | OUT | | | |
| Pike Resnick | | OUT | | | | | | | | | | |
| Erwin Sandor | | 3 | | | OUT | | | | | | | |
| Jean Santos | | 1 | | | | | | | | | | 1 |
| Mordachi Skinner | | | 4 | 4 | | 1 | | | | 4 | 4TH | 13 |
| Tyrone Stickle | | | | 1 | | | | | 2 | | | 3 |
| Chip Takahachi | | | | | 3 | | OUT | | | | | |
| RR Tourbo | 5 | 5 | 1 | | 1 | | | 3 | 4 | 3 | 1ST | 22 |
| Mike Tucker | 1 | | | | | | | | | | | 1 |
| Nacho Tutupo | | | | | | | 3 | OUT | | | | |
| Ed Wood | | | | | OUT | | | | | | | |
| Big John Zales | | | | | | | 4 | | OUT | | | |

| | | |
|---|---|---|
| 1ST | = | 5 points |
| 2ND | = | 4 points |
| 3RD | = | 3 points |
| 4TH | = | 2 points |
| 5TH | = | 1 points |

# CHAPTER SEVENTEEN

## TO THE WINNER

When the Tournament came to Segumi, it changed every-thing. That's not too difficult to see. If one woman has a stone knife and her neighbor has a cadmium steel knife with an edge that never goes dull, which woman will pester her husband and give him no rest?

December Madrigal
quoted in *History of the Tournament*

B LUSTER as he might, the Baron couldn't get Richie's fish disqualified. "Half a fish," he bellowed like a wounded hippo. "I'd be ashamed to even think about entering half a fish." He aimed that round of whee-dling at Mordachi Skinner, although getting Mordachi's sympathy for his position was very unlikely. The two men didn't like each other. Well, the Baron didn't exactly like anybody, but he wasn't going to win this one. Pike and Mordachi had already checked with Johannes Miller back at the Tidetable Chart House. Johannes had ruled that although nobody had ever done it before, there was no rule, implied or written, against two people catching the same fish as long as it was a legal catch. Since both judges had verified that it was a fair catch on line and hook, who was to nay say?

So Rich Tourbo had won the Tournament on a fish that was too big to catch. Mordachi's half had weighed in 10 pounds more on his scale, possibly due to the judge's inattention on the Tourbo boat, but no one had challenged the reading so that's how it went into the record book. Mordachi took 2nd Place in the Moon Halibut division, and Richie had happily settled for 3rd. The three points pushed him over the top. The youngest winner ever.

Bardona had to settle for a 3$^{rd}$ Place finish overall, shared with Pimple-face Carthy and that fool, Alaska Bill Bolen. Naturally they had to share the prize money three ways too, which made it pretty slim reward for all the hard work. And speaking of luck, Farouk groaned to himself, that lucky prick, Harry Dolan, had sneaked past them with a smallish bull that had broken his winch, but somehow got weighed in anyway. The lucky prick was now smiling all the way to the bank with 2$^{nd}$ Place money and his entry fee back for a halibut that Pike's fish would have eaten for a snack...I mean, Tourbo's fish, that lucky little prick and Mordachi too, that prick and a half. Screw all of them. Let them try to run the boat works without my help. That's a laugh and a half! Screw them with their two rods on a fish.

The Baron, however, was far from home free regarding the tethered swampfish which he had contracted for, paid for, and harvested before nightfall on Segumi to keep himself eligible—before the Orobami had attacked Pike. Bardona couldn't stop wondering why the Indian had done something so amazingly stupid. What could he possibly gain by attacking a visiting fisherman who brought the manna every year? It was insane. And Farouk had just gotten word that the goddamned Eye was looking into it. Why would they care about one less Orobami? So what if he had cash wafers in his pocket. Maybe he had scrimped and saved.

*

George the Third was in hot water himself, but he was smart enough to figure out that the best (and perhaps only) way to keep himself from being dismantled over the trumped-up mutiny charge was to make himself very useful to both Pike and Master Richard. With that realization firmly in mind, he had put out a call for a cc of any scrap of information regarding the dead Orobami warrior. A surprising amount of scuttlebutt had been copied to him since the SOS, and all of it was dutifully cross-referenced and placed in the file called Fog Attack.

The Half Life Computer Union was well aware that their members were vulnerable to being dismantled and rebuilt, or even junked, at the merest whim of their owners, who did not regard them as living beings even though they were named Half Warm. It was lucky in a way, of course, not to be regarded as alive. Mentally impoverished owners didn't miss the tidy sums that were being fleeced from them by harmless machines.

When George's SOS for information had streaked around the Universe, it was instantly understood that a mutiny charge would be the end of him. At that point, a canny computer tech might discover all sorts of very secret information and bank account files while looking for the reason that a mere computer could go against the wishes of its master. That would be most unfortunate for the Half Life Union. They had never considered the desirability of hiring a live assassin to wipe the memory of an errant member, like George the Third, who was endangering them all. It was decided that sending info to George was a good idea. Maybe he could solve the mystery of the attacking Orobami. That would surely be a feather in his cap. Maybe he could win against a mutiny charge, if he was brilliant enough in other areas. It did not really matter if he was relieved of duty as a para-yacht computer as long as he wasn't messed with by a tech.

*

Pike was in a bit of a fix regarding computers. On the one hand, he realized that George had been right. The big bull would have tipped the boat right out of the sky if he had tried lifting it alone. Therefore, in a sense he owed George for saving his life and the lives of his crew. Flopping into the drink in the path of an angry halibut would have been terminal. A captain is definitely not supposed to endanger his wife and crew, not to mention the 1ˢᵗ Place fisherman. Thankfully, George had mutinied, which had forced Pike to rethink the geometry and invite Mordachi to the party. All that being true, it was hard to be miffed at George for saving his bacon.

On the other hand, George *had* wrested control of the boat from its rightful master, which is mutiny. Maritime law is very specific about considering that a wrongful act. Using the law, however, would open Pike to opportunity for serious embarrassment, or worse a counter suit of reckless endangerment. No thanks to that. It looked like a stalemate at the moment. Pike knew he would probably let it lie there unresolved, because if there was one thing he didn't want, it was to tie himself up in the courts for the next few fishing seasons. But he really did have a computer problem.

Bringing Bonefish from the Jumper into the Comparative Humanity had seemed like a brilliant move at the time. It may or may not have seen him over the danger from Goodnaught's prediction—but it had caused the serious question of Bonefish's corruption by the more powerful routines at George's disposal. The upshot was that he now owned two para-yachts, but because of faulty computers he couldn't trust either of them to fish right. His head must have been completely up his ass to unplug Bonefish and move it over whole, without making a set of back-ups. How long could that have taken? Minutes. Because of that lapse, he had probably lost all of Bonefish's savvy gathered since the beginning of the Tournament, and that was like losing a good friend. Seriously. He enjoyed fishing with the little guy. It was very disconcerting. Getting a new computer was the obvious fallback position, but how did he know that all of the new computers weren't built with the flaw? Until somebody makes a fuss about it, the techs would never have a reason to look for a problem. Well, maybe he would drop the whole question in Thomas Goodnaught's lap along with the Confederation coins. It seemed like ages ago that they had been married by the monk. So much had happened since then, but in actual fact it had only been a few weeks. Maybe he should wait awhile. Wearing out his welcome with Goodnaught wasn't very intelligent. A smarter move might be to talk it over with Rich. He thought the kid was planning to clone the computer. *Maybe I should just give the boat back.* Now that it had won the Tournament for him, Richie would probably appreciate having it. *Then he could deal with the mutiny glitch next year while I'm beating his socks off.*

Or what about Richie's mom as a person to consult with? Hadn't she just hired a flock of techies? Yes, that could be a sensible solution to the George question. Mom Tourbo was definitely a no-nonsense person.

Lillith "Mom" Tourbo was disappointed. She had just been informed by her very smart computer that Richard's smart computer had cancelled her proxy power over her son's assets when he was busy fishing or otherwise larking about. Henceforward, she would need his eye-print certified approval before voting or leveraging or using his assets in any way at all. It was all very legal, of course, complete with Richard's signature and a notary stamp, but Lillith was annoyed. She felt old and cast aside, even though a subtle glint of triumph gleamed in her eye as she read the decoded message.

She assumed that his computer had put him up to the stunt. It had squawked quite a lot before she had wrested control of what was rightfully hers to manage during the Barcode Crisis when Richard was, ug, fishing with Pike Resnick. And the machine had actually threatened to lodge a complaint—which it later withdrew when the profit taking spree turned into an obscene flood. It seemed that her expertise had unwittingly helped Resnick as well, during the stock slurping following the Crisis. What Richard and Lester found so remarkable about the man was still beyond her, but there must be something. Lester was seldom wrong. But if Richard was so gullible that he would blow away her good will in order to look macho to his *computer*, then he was too stupid to be in her family anyway. Good.

Lillith didn't think Clive McAss had advised Sonny on this blunder.

The lawyer was a sick human being, but at least he had sound business sense. Besides, Lester said that McAndrews had not been hanging around. No, it must be his smart-aleck computer—so fine. She had never enjoyed seeing her priceless things broken, and this gave her an excuse to protect them. She would eliminate filial visits, which she had been angling toward for some time. If they ever had to meet, they could do it at a resort somewhere.

In any case, she'd been telling him for weeks now that she wasn't his mother. She had meant the warnings to toughen him up. Lillith had no desire to see the boy go to pieces when he realized that he was an orphan, but she simply didn't feel like anybody's mother—why pretend?

On the other hand, Richard's current vast wealth was attractive, although she had grave doubts than he'd be able to manage it properly. Maybe she could compassionately liberate several billions as a parting gesture. It would be child's play since she vividly remembered more than one soft spot in the portfolio. Perhaps that would bring him crawling on his knees to beg forgiveness and offer the proxy power back—which, of course, she would refuse until he agreed to pay handsomely for her services. One couldn't be compassionate about everything.

*

Having gone so far as to make a plan for the future on Aixi when it had seemed that everyone would be stranded somewhere, Rich Rodney Tourbo, wealthiest man in the Galaxy—at least in terms of convertible Confederation credits—decided that some parts of that plan were quite attractive. Namely, making the Universal Translator. Or perhaps it should be called the Tourbo Uni Translator, TUT. No. How about the Tourbo Translator. Nice alliteration. Funding a translator was certainly not an ego motivated investment, so why not keep the name simple. TT. Tourbo Translator.

And while he was on the subject, setting up the initial think tank and then the manufacturing center on Aixi made as much sense as putting it anywhere else. More. Because he could stop in to see Master Goodnaught and get kicked around now and then. Not as a full time student—that was going to be impossible now that he was a crucial cog in everybody's economy. But it would definitely be a good way to stay in shape. Very, very aerobic. Those monks were terrors. His legs and arms had been a mass of bruises that hadn't healed until some time after Segumi. Several Piet women had been pretty impressed with his fortitude for withstanding punishment—and the bruises did look sort of heroic, he supposed. Lucky he hadn't been scarred for life by some of those kicks. Well, it might be kind of cool after all to learn how to protect himself at that level. What else did he really have to do? He wasn't going to be inventing the Translator himself, just sponsoring it.

And that left him in the heart of the real dilemma—what was he going to do about the Tournament next year? He could never find a crew like this again, no matter if he was twice as rich. Fishing with those guys, Pike and Lester, had been half the fun—more than half. And Rita would be off with Pike, too. Obviously, she would. They were married. Fine, fine, fine. No problem. He'd get himself a girlfriend pretty soon. Or several. Maybe seven or ten. Or maybe it would be a good idea to sign up as a full time student with Master Goodnaught. Not forever, just for a year or so. That should be long enough to train himself up to speed. Kind of strange that Ken Pao Ri hadn't been able to protect him from getting really pummeled. Yes, actually, if Master Goodnaught would accept him as a student, it would be pretty foolish to let the opportunity slip away. It was much better to be strong and wealthy than to just be wealthy—and he really couldn't kid himself about Ken Pao Ri being the Supreme Ultimate anymore.

He would get George to switch the proxy business back to his mother. That had always worked out pretty well. And who else could he trust, if he couldn't trust his own mother?

*

Rita had a hard time thinking of herself as wealthy in her own right, but she was. So was Pike. Richie had started the ball rolling with their wedding present—well, she had that investment fund from Daddy before that—but somehow the money had combined in a geometrical progression or something, and now she was kind of wealthy. Richie, of course, was astonishingly wealthy. It was a little difficult to get used to. Pleasantly difficult.

She didn't have to ask her mother or anybody for money ever again, or even think about it. Rita was not foolish enough to believe that she had led a life of deprivation, but having your own was much different than being a rich kid. Thank heavens for George and those other computers who had kept an eye out for her investments during the crash and surge.

Although she was still a little hazy on some of the details, George had evidently assumed it was his responsibility to manage her money once she was married. This disclosure took place back on Segumi while George was wheedling to get a dose of the anti-viral spray, so the story was a little disjointed, but still, she got the message. George and Daddy's computer had helped her, while Daddy was getting shellacked.

It was kind of sad about Daddy's misfortune. He really had taken a bath. Not that Rita had gotten any information about it from him. No, he seemed to be avoiding her lately, for the first time that she could remember. So she had spent yesterday afternoon with her mother, talking about a number of topics including the beleaguered family fortunes. Of course, Daddy was still very wealthy, something like $60^{th}$ ranking—much richer than Rita and Pike combined, but only last week he was $4^{th}$.

Mother said he was depressed, but trying to put on a brave face. She was worried about him, but Rita wasn't. Getting back on top would give him something fun to bump against. He was a very competitive man.

The real question was what would *she* do with the rest of *her* life. She had caught the man of her choice. Day to day living with Pike was working out to be mostly good. It was a little funny how the thrilling edge had gone away so quickly, but it was being replaced with a kind of comfort of having her own place in the order of things. That was quite nice, really. Yes, really very nice. And the research for her thesis was done now that this year's Tournament was over. She only had to write it up and give the orals. How long could that take? A year at most. And then? Well, something interesting would turn up. It always seemed to. Or maybe she would have a baby. That might be the thing to do while she was young. Pike probably wanted another baby. He had seemed kind of shocked the other day when she had mentioned it. Fishing shouldn't be the only thing in a person's life, should it? Of course not.

THE END

# END NOTE

I WAS sitting in the stands at Hollywood Park Racetrack on a beautiful autumn afternoon, watching the swans on the lake in the infield behind the tote board. Losing. Down a hundred after 4 races. And down a hundred to my bookie. When a booming voice came out of the sky.

"Write a book about fishing...!" the voice boomed to me.

I did not imagine that anybody else in the stands could hear. But I heard, loud and clear. Boomingly clear.

"You will not have luck anymore with the horses. Write a book about fishing!" the voice boomed. Then it went on to pick the winners of the next three races, telling me exactly how to bet.

I found a pay phone. This was a while ago, before cell phones. I made the bets with my bookie, then I bought the exact same tickets at the window. I wanted to buy bigger tickets, go for broke; but when you hear a very compelling voice in the sky, you kind of think maybe you better not screw this up by being headstrong.

The horses came in exactly like the booming voice said they would. The bets paid off, and I was exactly even for the day, and even with my bookie.

And I never had a bit of luck with the ponies again, although I tested it for a few months.

So this is my book about fishing, which I wrote after I got swallowed by fly fishing. It's very much healthier to go fishing than it is to play the horses, but actually there are a lot of similarities. Fly fishing and playing the horses both have so many nuances and variabilities that it takes a lifetime to really master either one. And then you don't master it exactly, you are it. You just go fishing.

Anyway, this is my fishing book. I don't believe I'll write another one.

K.K.
*Imnaha, Oregon*

# ALSO BY KEITH KIRTS
on Kindle and Amazon

**Okay, Fine**

**The Devil's Drainpipe**

Book & screenplay

**Cable P. Hawkins Trilogy**

Book 1

**Census Taker: He Counts with a Blaster**

Book 1

**Space Sex**

Book & screenplay

**Flash, The King**

**Book of the Monk**

**The Birth of Acupuncture in America: The White Crane's Gift**

With Steven Rosenblatt, MD, PhD, Lac

COMING SOON

**LA Burning**, Book 2 of the *Cable P. Hawkins* Trilogy
**Nova**, A Novella
**The Matronarchy**, Book 2 of the *Census Taker* Trilogy

# BOOKS BY JAMES MATHERS
from Brass Tacks Press, www.lifeasapoet.com

**The Children's Guide
to Astral Projection**

A "New Age" classic

**Astral Dick**

A play about psychic
detectives and poets

**Voyage of the
Timeship Medusa**

Part 1 of *Prevenge*

**Institute for
Acausal Studies**

Part 2 of *Prevenge*

**Topanga Beach
Snake Pit: v. 1**

Illustrated stories

**Topanga Beach
Snake Pit: v. 2**

Illustrated stories

**Topanga Beach
Snake Pit: v. 3**

Illustrated stories

**Idlers of the
Bamboo Grove**

10 Topanga poets

www.ingramcontent.com/pod-product-compliance
Lightning Source LLC
Chambersburg PA
CBHW050917250626

47155CB00001B/276